The Six Cities

The Six Cities

CYRUS BALES

This is a work of fiction. Names, characters, places, and incidents either are the product of the author's imagination or are used fictitiously. Any resemblance to actual persons, living or dead, events, or locales is entirely coincidental.

Copyright © 2021 by Cyrus Bales

All rights reserved. No part of this book may be reproduced or used in any manner without written permission of the copyright owner except for the use of quotations in a book review.

First paperback edition April 2021

Cover design by Gary Trow @GTartwork
www.garytrow.crevado.com

ISBN 978-1-8384488-0-6 (paperback)
ISBN 978-1-8384488-1-3 (ebook)

Acknowledgements

Writing a novel is a very personal journey, however the contributions and help from others were essential to making this book a reality.

My friend and editor Tess deserves great thanks for not only sharpening my words but being an ear for endless updates on my progress.

Feedback is a fundamental tool for any author and I am grateful to my dear friends Dave and Paul for their efforts in this regard.

The world of The Six Cities would not be as it is without Kerri, not just inspiration but applying a rigorous scientific mind to quality-control my fabrications.

Lastly: my father, whose contributions to my life are impossible to fully recount.

Thank you.

PROLOGUE

Grief does strange things to people. It transforms a person in unpredictable ways: destroying passions, inflaming hatred and clouding minds. One such mind found itself challenging the very seat of power in Omdurtur. Such a challenge to the city's ghost protector was beyond living memory; this was no ordinary challenge of conquest. Far from a courageous warrior or warlord, this was a grieving father who held the limp form of what was once his child. A child whose light was suffocated out of him by the incessant choking soot from the stacks. Soot which gently fell as occasional flecks of grey snow around the rooftop courtyard, its dainty beauty at odds with the slow and ugly asphyxiation it had wrought upon the child. The man was unsure if he had even performed the rite properly; was it really as simple as speaking a set phrase before the thrumming pillar? As if in answer to his internal questioning, a milky-white light began to coalesce before him, bringing with it a sensation deep in the pit of his stomach. Running on pure emotions, he had neither time nor capacity to contemplate his actions nor fumble for regret. Within moments the vision of a muscular champion stood before him. Edges softly blurred and ethereal wisps of luminosity danced about his person in a blend of white, grey and malachite. Many wondered if the ghosts had been such impressive specimens in size and stature before their spirits were tethered or if the tethering itself had granted them such physical perfection. His name was Kadar. His face betrayed equal measures of surprise and displeasure to have been summoned for a challenge; no doubt the inconvenience of being drawn away from meetings irked him.

Pity was not within Kadar's range of emotions; long ago he had excelled as the city's undisputed champion, securing his right to be tethered as the ghost protector. A feat which pity would have only impeded.

"Really? This… failed attempt of a man is who summoned me for a challenge?" Whilst Kadar's words were full of contempt and power, his voice was soft and rich, defying the expectations his considerable presence portended.

"This city has taken my son from me. The stacks we slave away in did this. You and this whole system did this; now I'm here to end it." The trembling man surprised himself with his own clarity and projection of voice.

"Slave away? Do we not see that you have jobs to feed your family? These stacks you speak ill of provide you with the metalwork that fills every part of your life. Even standing here now I can see your shoe and belt buckles; not forgetting the sword at your side which I suspect you are going to attempt to use."

Kadar's words almost seemed reasonable, but the man had not come here for reason: he wanted vengeance. Vengeance and justice. Deep down he knew he would receive neither, but he had to do something; he couldn't stand another day being a disposable cog in the machine. Somewhere in his mind he clung to the faint hope of the prophecy. It was more than just a story of wishful thinking he told his children; it was real. He believed in it. He had to; the alternative was unthinkable. Maybe he really could be the one to bring down the ghosts and change everything. The prophecy existed for a reason, and he didn't see anyone else stepping forward.

He lightly kissed the cold dusty forehead of his son and, with a tenderness that would be forgotten in the brutality soon to pass, gently laid his body on the slick stone slabs of the courtyard that overlooked the city. Unsheathing his rather dull blade and readying himself, the father confronted this foe before him; a representation of all the excesses of the city and its rulers that had killed his son as surely as the soot itself. His poise reflected a sense of serene simplicity, of one entirely focused on a single task.

Kadar's patience had worn thin. This contest had been relegated to nothing more than an insignificant chore in his eyes.

"As you wish."

Kadar drew a sword from his side that shared his same ethereal nature, only with a greater shine. In a single swing the blade carved through the challenger's blade and torso as if gliding through the air itself. Each half of the man's body was cast in different directions from the force of the blow, a red smear joining the two pieces. Kadar sheathed his weapon and left the courtyard with a sneer of derision. Having completed this menial task, he had to return to more pressing matters.

Turning his head with the last vestiges of life he had left, the man looked to his son's lifeless body. In his final thoughts, the regret which was noticeably absent earlier had become all consuming.

Grief had condemned him.

ACT ONE

CHAPTER ONE

The city of Caspir was famed for its textiles, which was immediately apparent from walking down any street within its walls. The only things draped in greater finery than the nobles and upper classes were the buildings themselves, each one strewn with large intricate banners of shimmering thread. Along the central concourse, the display was at its most impressive: splashes of colour so vibrant they seemed unnatural. Even those who often walked this way found themselves stopping to gaze upwards at the brilliant cloths like they were seeing them for the first time; the predominant colour combination of this season was gold upon vivid blood red. One passer-by did not stop in awe; he didn't offer even a cursory glance. Despite his perfectly manicured beard and immaculate red and gold cape, Marin's thoughts were far from the splendour, for he had a job to do. The council meeting today was of the utmost importance. As the only member who wasn't noble born, Marin always considered himself an outsider, one who had to fight for his place in the chamber constantly.

    The council building itself put all others to shame; not only was it towering in stature, it was as if the seamstresses had invented entirely new shades of colour for its banners. It was a true sight to behold, but Marin's eyes were firmly fixed on the large oak door. Hurrying up the steps, he placed a hand on the grainy surface and paused to take a breath before pushing it open.

    Inside of this building, which could best be described as a monument, everything was pristine. The stone slabs of the street gave way to perfect ceramic tiles and walls layered in rich textured woods from trees that

CHAPTER ONE

were now extinct. The central corridor was long with numerous small apertures leading to offices, storerooms and other various components of council bureaucracy. There was no guesswork needed to see where the council chamber was located. An imposing door at the far end of the hallway glistened with the precious metals that adorned it; despite their age and the dim light produced from the lanterns, their shine remained eye catching. Marin produced a handful of papers from his leathery brown satchel, wanting quickly to refresh a few details in his mind before entering the chamber. Whilst others found the faint light of these passageways to be quaint and overflowing with traditional charm, Marin couldn't help but be irritated by their lack of functionality. He had worked hard to get here. "This place should be about practicality," he often thought; even more so now he was squinting in the flickering torchlight to check his figures. Cursing himself for his tiny handwriting, he arrived at the end of the passageway. Once again, he drew a lungful of air, puffing out his chest to assert himself in preparation, then shoved open the door to the council chamber.

The first thing one noticed about the chamber was its architectural modesty. There were no statues or carvings on the walls, just cold stonework and simple lines, echoing the functionality that Marin thought proper. The building was from a different time; a time of magic, long before the pressure to keep up to date with trends.

Predictably, this simplicity and practicality were masked by the expansive cloth banners draped on all four walls, the luminous threadwork attempting to cover the historic but unsightly execution of function over form. Marin approached the centre of the chamber, where the council convened around an immense timber table.

Most of the seats were filled but a few were still empty. He would never allow himself to be the last one to arrive. The impressive reds and golds of Marin's clothes seemed almost dull in comparison to most of the garments the other council members were clad in. The apparel of a successful textile merchant could never compete with that of the noblemen – a fact that he was frequently made aware of. The merchant took up his usual seat next to a man a good twenty years his senior with a welcoming face, although the softness of his features was lost in the painfully vivid hues of green that made up his attire.

"Morning! I see you've got your favourite red and gold number on again," the man joked from the corner of his wry smile.

"Oh, hello Edwin. I didn't see you there – perhaps try wearing something a little more noticeable next time?"

Giving as good as he got was something Marin had to excel at. Fully aware of the excessive brightness of his clothes, Edwin chuckled. The repartee between the pair reflected their deeper friendship, whilst the difference in status between a merchant and a member of a noble family still ran beneath.

"So, tell me Marin, have you got all the answers scribbled down amongst your notes? I'd take a look myself, but I wasn't taught that particular brand of chicken-scratch by my tutor."

"No need to make excuses Edwin, we both know you'd struggle with the numbers anyway."

Another victory in their verbal joust spread out a wide grin behind his beard. Their back and forth continued whilst the last few chairs found their occupants, all except for the most ornate one that sat at the head of the table. This one belonged to Chase, and had done for generations.

The customary mist of greys and malachite began to form at the head of the table, condensing until it found human shape: Chase had arrived. He was the ghost protector of the city, although few used the moniker of protector when describing him. The days of ghosts serving as the champions of cities had long since passed; he had instead been a ghost councillor for all of living memory and beyond. Each of the six cities had their own, selected for their prowess as duellists countless generations ago, now elevated to either permanent chairs of city governments; worshipped as a god, or feared as a brutal despot. All except the mad ghost of Latan.

Marin often pondered what right they had to govern indefinitely, but people were often quick to point out that the longevity of "indefinitely" was reason enough. Who else knew Caspir like Chase did? He had watched it grow and develop over a timescale that mortals could not fathom. He supposed

CHAPTER ONE

there was also merit in having a constant fixed point within a government; the chaos of regime change did not bear thinking about. Stability was not something to be taken for granted, although in light of the figures that had consumed his waking thoughts of late, was this supposed stability really anything of the sort?

Chase took his seat and looked across the chamber, confirming that all were present. Marin wondered if ghosts even needed to sit down; after all they didn't need to eat or require any visible sustenance whatsoever. "Probably just the result of learned behaviour from when they were alive," he concluded to himself.

"As you are all no doubt aware, we are here to discuss a quite pressing matter." Chase emphasized his words in a way that could only come from having led a council for numerous lifetimes. He continued, "Simply put, we are running out of money."

The noblemen seemed relatively relaxed about the situation; they had no reference points to draw from. Money had never been anything other than free-flowing for them, and whatever the affairs of the city their own pockets would remain well-lined. Marin knew differently; of course, he had never struggled or been poor, but frugality and learning the value of money was a necessity for expanding his father's textile business. He suspected that was why he was often tasked with the city's financial calculations, or rather he hoped his prowess with numbers was the reason, as opposed to the noblemen seeing both him and accounting as beneath them.

"Marin, explain to the council the situation we find ourselves in."

Marin was not what anyone would consider a powerful orator; his command of language was to the point and functional; witticisms were something he only felt comfortable with in personal exchanges.

"It is as councillor Chase said, the city's revenue will not cover our expenditure for the season. At some stage this month our coffers will run dry. In twenty-two days' time, by my estimations."

"Just raise taxes again!" piped up a voice that could have belonged to any one of the elderly noblemen, from both tone and content.

"It doesn't exactly work that way," sighed Marin. "We can't raise taxes any further without seriously harming our industries. The needlework guild won't stand for it, and without them our trade arrangements with the other cities fall apart."

Edwin raised his eyebrow in consideration as he prepared to voice his contribution.

"I also doubt that the needlework guild would take well to the loss of law enforcement or sanitation workers either. There won't be much call for their garments if their shops are filling with sewage now will there? Surely you have some solution scribbled away within those papers of yours?"

Marin did have a solution, of sorts, but he was certain the council would not like it.

"I've been going over the numbers. There *are* a couple of measures that, if taken together, can see us through the season. The first one is a levy on luxury goods. If we add a small charge to high-end products, we can fill in some of the spending gap and the guilds won't have to worry about their bottom lines."

"Sod the guilds, what about our bottom lines?" a rather distraught councillor bellowed.

"The people buying luxury items can easily afford it and it keeps things running," Marin countered. The councillor, who went by the name of Andros and could only be described as pomposity made flesh, was clearly flustered.

"Keep things running?! We noble families *are* the city. And you want to take the very food out of our mouths?"

"Come now Andros, I would have thought you could do with putting less food in your mouth," scoffed Edwin.

The councillor was speechless, whilst snickers fired off around the table. The head of the council raised his hand to quieten the room.

"I have seen traders come and go, taxes raised and cut, but two things have remained: myself, and the noble families that we depend on. Should we really be placing the burden on them?" Chase's words oozed with the classist underpinning that Marin had come to expect from the council.

"It really isn't much of a burden; a few coins here and there will barely be noticeable." Marin knew this was how they would react, and he knew what

CHAPTER ONE

Andros' next response would be before the words had even left his lips.

"This is *exactly* what I expected from a penny-pinching merchant. I told you all this would happen when he joined the council."

Aside from Edwin, Marin's eyeline was filled by those who supported this notion.

"I for one think Marin has added a great deal to this table of ours. Quite a few of these luxury goods in question wouldn't have even made it inside our walls if not for his business acumen." Edwin was a solitary voice of comfort, but an influential one.

"Marin, what was the other measure you spoke of?"

"The second thing we need to do is reduce the city's expenditure. We can quite easily reduce the number of city watch patrols, especially around the gilded quarter; after all, the crime rates there are so low anyway."

This only served to stoke the flames of outrage already consuming Andros.

"The gilded quarter?! First you want to take our money, now you want to take our safety too?"

"Well, if he's taxing all your money away, you won't need to worry about being robbed, at least." Edwin's rejoinder proved too droll for Andros; through his anger he could only respond with failed attempts at words.

Through all this, Chase's attention seemed to have been diverted elsewhere. Marin noted that his steely gaze hovered on the entrance; he'd picked up the sound of hurried footsteps in the hallway long before the mere mortals in the chamber had. Marin only noticed them as the doors to the chamber were flung open.

CHAPTER TWO

The vibrant metropolis found within the central concourse and gilded district of Caspir only painted part of the city's picture. A very different world was to be found within the city walls when one ventured outside these clusters of wealth. Generations of population growth all contained within the original walls meant that there were inevitable winners and losers. Many places saw the luminous colours of prosperity give way to dull greys and mottled browns. Whilst among high society these palettes would make one stick out like a sore thumb, in these districts they were a necessary camouflage. The more downtrodden and lacking in colour one appeared, the less attention one would attract, a disguise that Fredo hoped would work for his trip through the Brown Quarter.

Beneath a cloak of murkiest chestnut, Fredo concealed a perfectly stitched teal tunic. His weather-worn face and scrunched-up nose aided his charade. For all intents and purposes, he was best described as half spy, half diplomat.

Even though he was in his home city, the poorer districts felt more alien and hostile than any nobleman's ball he had attended in the other cities. Spying was not an endemic practice, but every city had its agents keeping tabs. Fredo thought this was a natural result of each ghost councillor being unable to venture beyond their own walls; subsequently each ghost seemed to know more about the intricacies of each other's council meetings than the goings-on in the slums that lay within their own domains. All of Fredo's thoughts on the matter now seemed almost irrelevant in the face of the news he carried; however, the life of anyone who dealt solely in information

CHAPTER TWO

would not be complete without these tangential musings.

The smells of the Brown Quarter were arguably worse than any potential assailant, thought Fredo as he passed by a dirty-faced woman of indeterminate age chowing down on something that was once fish. He hadn't eaten properly for two days, yet this assault on his senses removed even the most ravenous of hungers.

Every street was like an alleyway – dark, foreboding and unwelcoming. Regardless of the size of many alleys being quite ample, the claustrophobia of the impoverished tightened his chest as he felt like the very walls themselves were trying to grasp and cling to him. Fredo considered himself a practical man; nevertheless his desire to go out of his way to dodge the grey puddles betrayed his status and class. This was not *his* city; this was the unfortunate waste product of *his* city and its excesses. He knew full well that the heaving slums were part of a wider problem, although how to address it was beyond him. Fredo traded in information, not solutions.

The banners of thread that Caspir was famous for were not present here. Fredo noted the hooks that would have once housed the cloth, unable to even consider what these walkways would have looked like when Chase was still mortal. Every so often, one noble family or other braved a trip to these parts, hanging up banners in a shallow attempt to brighten up the place in the absence of providing any meaningful assistance. Fredo wondered how the great noble houses would feel, knowing that their immaculately crafted banners were torn up for use as loincloths or wash rags. In terms of shocking the nobles though, the news he carried was the motherlode; he could already imagine the panic and confusion it would bring. He himself struggled to come to grips with it, but "what next?" was the province of politicians; Fredo was only concerned with "what is".

"I wonder how these people down here will react?" he pondered. Would it change their lives? Would they care? Would they even know?

"The council hasn't cared about them before, so I doubt they'd start now," he concluded.

A small streak of colour above the dreariness caught Fredo's eye. The council building was coming into view, towering above other architecture.

An unmistakably elegant banner blowing in the breeze. The end of the Brown Quarter was in sight. Whilst there was no formal structure like a gate to signal its end, the visible change in colour was pronounced. Stonework slicked with dirt and filth halted abruptly; actual colours could be seen down the street.

Fredo was pleased he had avoided any altercations along his journey through the Brown Quarter; the information he held was stressful enough. As his lungs emptied out the odours of poverty, he swept off his cloak and rolled it up to reveal the splendour beneath. Nobody would mistake him for a nobleman, yet everyone could tell he belonged in such circles.

The number of guards in the area increased as he neared the respectable parts of the city and the seat of its government. Some offered casual nods; Fredo was well known and respected by the wardens – they called him and those who shared his profession "silver-tongues". It was a status symbol of sorts; stories of how a silver-tongue had seduced a nobleman's wife or successfully blagged their way into an exclusive merchant's guild were often exchanged between guards. Fredo enjoyed the glamour that came with his career and suspected that the embellished reputations of his profession actually made it easier, with some people seeming as if they *wanted* to be fooled by a silver-tongue as a badge of honour. The most important person to earn respect from, though, was Chase. On several occasions Chase had proclaimed Fredo to be his finest silver-tongue and that was all that mattered. Other councillors would come and go, but your ghost councillor would never leave. Or at least that was what everyone, including Fredo, had thought.

It had been many weeks since Fredo had been back to Caspir, let alone to a council meeting, and certainly not one to which he was not invited and would have to interrupt. Formalities seemed rather redundant given the situation. He never imagined that his appointment to the city of Illorne would have ended like this. Whilst Illorne's ghost councillor, Hectin, was always rather wary of outsiders and not the most welcoming, the city was generally considered unremarkable. It had its trade deals and was home to some fine carpenters indeed, but it never felt special, not like the bigger cities.

CHAPTER TWO

Who would have thought Illorne could have been the source of information so profound and terrible? Certainly not Fredo, who had been looking forward to what he had considered a straightforward and easy assignment.

Waving to the guards, he finally arrived at the council building. Knowing who he was and seeing the look on his face, the guards did not stand in his way and instead ushered him through. If a silver-tongue looked in that much of a hurry, they had something important to tell the council. A younger recruit briefly moved to inquire of Fredo as to his intentions, but was abruptly pulled back by another who knew better. Marching along the corridor, his wooden heels clicked against the ceramic tiles until he flung open the door to the council chamber, to be greeted by Chase's eyes already fixed on him, whilst others began to turn their heads.

"I assume you have good cause to interrupt our meeting." Chase sounded more curious than annoyed.

"I'm afraid I do," panted Fredo. "I bring grave news from Illorne. It's Hectin... He's been killed."

CHAPTER THREE

Beyond the packed streets of Caspir and past its monumental walls lies yet another world, a world of green. Boundless realms of farmlands and their communities encircle the city. Like all of the great cities, the perimeters of the walls stand unchanged since before the age of magic, with ever-more people populating the same space as time has marched on. The result of this is a constantly swelling arable domain stretching out from Caspir, only broken up by a few large slashes of dried-up ground for trade routes. More mouths to feed meant more crops needed to be grown and the threads for which the city is famed had to be produced out here in bulk. This industry had grown beyond imagining, with huge swathes of land dedicated to the thread ranchers. Forming the cornerstone of their trade with the other cities, thread had become more profitable than food for the ranchers, which had led to a dependency on trading it to secure the food requirements of Caspir – the food requirements of those who didn't live in the Brown Quarter, at least.

The thread ranches were awash with activity, everyone performing their functions with the precision that only comes from repetition. Everyone, that was, aside from Shiara.

Whilst the clothes of the ranchers were less extravagant than those of the city dwellers, they had a certain luminosity to them. This made Shiara's rather drab brown and grey cloak reveal her as being from other parts; however, she did not look out of place in this more rural of settings, her black hair having clearly been bleached a few shades lighter by the sun. Her

CHAPTER THREE

wiry frame was certainly not that of a well-fed noblewoman or merchant; coupled with her scuffed boots it signified that she was no stranger to life beyond city walls.

Beneath those worn boots, the damp ground synonymous with the thread ranches was soft underfoot. She had often heard stories about the life of thread ranchers from her father, yet seeing it for herself was something else. Countless pens housed the thick grubs that were the source of all those brilliant colours.

"How could such an unpleasant looking bug produce such wondrous threads?" she thought to herself, completely oblivious to her entomological misclassification. All their energies to produce something of beauty must have been used up on the strands, leaving nothing for themselves, she concluded. These squishy creatures were about the size of a new-born baby and slowly wiggled through the wet plants that filled their artificial habitats. Their natural aversion to dryness meant they were content in their pens and wouldn't venture beyond these moist surroundings. Shiara had seen them in the wild but they barely looked like the same species. Generations of selective breeding had removed their need for camouflage, replacing it with a tendency to grow fatter, a trait that saw their production rates increase vastly compared their undomesticated counterparts. They may as well have been a different creature entirely.

"These ones wouldn't last five minutes outside of their enclosures without their ranchers," she mused. Although she had to admit that they certainly looked a lot more satisfying to eat than the ones she had scavenged for herself in the wild. Shiara likened them to the noble families of the great cities. Just like them, these insects sat around gorging themselves all day and growing fat whilst everybody else ran about looking after them. Her thoughts grew a little less whimsical as she pondered how the noble families themselves were also unnatural, bred over generations to become ignorant of the lives of ordinary people, fed on a diet of privilege and apathy. Soon she would change all of that.

Approaching the perimeter of one of the fences, she saw the ranchers collecting up some of the threadwurms to prepare them for production. The insects had no qualms about being handled by people, their instincts of fight or flight having disappeared hundreds of years ago. A woman in a sleeveless black garment embroidered with pink and green stitching was placing them into a woven basket. Her skin appeared leathery, the result of a lifetime of working in the sun; she hummed an upbeat tune as she worked. A life outdoors was clearly not the anathema that many city dwellers would have you believe. Shiara watched as the woman took her filled basket over to a wooden rack, placing a fleshy creature into each of the sections. She then sprinkled a handful of powder across them, eliciting a reaction that started their process of cocooning.

Shiara had seen the threading process in nature before. She fondly recalled a dreary evening spent fascinated by one of these caterpillars spinning itself into a web-like cocoon, sheltering itself ready for transformation. Shelter that she was envious of at the time. Those threads were much duller than the impressive hues now emanating from the larvae she was watching. The rack was linked to a spindle on a handle that slowly wrapped up the strands as they were produced, never allowing a cocoon to be constructed.

Having noticed how engrossed by the process Shiara was, the woman gestured for her to come over.

"Would you like to try a spin?"

Taken aback by the request, Shiara found herself walking over before she had a chance to consciously make up her mind.

"Just grab hold of this handle and gently turn; let the threadwurms do the work," she instructed whilst guiding Shiara's hands.

"There you go, make sure you give them a little bit of slack, you don't want to be pulling on the threads." It was clear that this woman was not only adept at her work; she was proud of her place in the world. Shiara knew she herself had a fierce journey ahead of her before she could ever feel such contentment.

Spinning the handle, she was mesmerized by the shimmering fibres made somehow more impressive when juxtaposed with their unseemly creators, the slight wetness they secreted adding another layer of shine to the vibrant gossamer. It was delicate work, yet she found it strangely

CHAPTER THREE

cathartic, especially considering the far less elegant task she had trained her hands for, although the precision and grace required was certainly not alien to her.

"When do I stop?" she inquired.

"Eventually they'll run out of energy and stop making thread," came the reply.

"What happens to them if they don't have a cocoon?" The realization of how much this process interfered with their natural cycles had begun to dawn on her.

"Oh, don't worry about that; they still pupate just fine. We cover the racks over to keep them safe and let them do their thing."

She was somewhat relieved by the woman's response. For a moment she thought that the process would inevitably lead to the little creature's demise. Perhaps her bleak assumptions were due to her childhood growing up near the stacks of Omdurtur, where deaths were just part of the cost of production. It was easy to forget that life was more cherished by those outside the city walls, although one wouldn't expect it given the disdain urbanites showed for them. It wasn't all their fault, she thought; they really didn't know any better.

The strands were coming to an end now, the threadwurms having given up their lustrous bounty.

"Now just cut the ends of the threads off, as they are a duller colour, and we are all done with these reels," instructed the weather-worn rancher.

Shiara reached under her cloak to reveal a curved scabbard, from which she produced a gleaming cutlass. The blade was unlike anything the rancher had seen before. Swords were not that common outside of fashion accessories, but there was something about this one in particular that was different. Mesmerizing. A thin veil of incandescent colour shimmering along its edge like that of a rainbow reflected in oil. In all her years pulling thread, she had never seen something quite so remarkable yet somehow simultaneously subtle. With expert precision and speed the cutlass parted the strings in the perfect places before returning once more to its sheath. Shiara became aware of the rancher's mouth being slightly ajar in wonderment at her blade.

She did not want to dwell on it and decided to move things along.

"Where do you put them once they're out of thread?"

Placing a wooden cover over the top of the rack, the woman explained the process of storing them in the larger barns where it was cooler and the creatures wouldn't be disturbed. She elaborated on how they took about two weeks to transform into their adult forms and that they placed those expected to emerge each day into the largest barn in preparation. She gestured towards an impressively long building a few hundred yards closer to the city, then bid her helpful and inquisitive stranger goodbye.

The building was not audacious or gaudy like those within the city; nevertheless it was impressive in its own right – a well-crafted wooden barn of seamlessly joined panels as opposed to the immovable and robust medium of urban design, something that Shiara had never been a fan of. Her time spent in the wilderness probably explained her penchant for simple wooden designs. She half expected the door to loudly creak open as she pushed it, like every wooden door in the stories her father told her; it did not.

Inside the barn was a revelation. Every surface the eye could see was covered in hordes of moths. Their delicate wings unable to give flight to their chunky bodies. Each one glimmered with the colours of the strands they had produced back in their larval stages. All colours conceivable were represented in the most brilliant of hues. Whilst other textile industries relied on dying their threads, those surrounding Caspir had spent generations perfecting the diets and breeding of their caterpillars to produce the most astonishing of strands without losing any of their shimmer through the dying processes. All of this meant that the adult insects were especially beautiful, unlike the drab grey and off-white ones found elsewhere. Shiara surveyed these quivering walls of colour in awe. A living rainbow. Those in the city may obsess over the spectacle of their garments and banners but none of them could comprehend the magnificence of what she was seeing. She could spend hours here, and decided she would do exactly that.

CHAPTER FOUR

"Killed?! How could somebody possibly kill a ghost? Is that even feasible?" Andros seemed to effortlessly roll his indignation over from Marin's financial proposals to Fredo's troubling news, clearly finding it hard to believe, as did they all.

"Hectin was bested in combat by someone who issued him a duel." Fredo replied, still not really believing it himself.

"Preposterous! Who in their right mind would challenge a ghost councillor, let alone be able to win? Why would you make up such a ridiculous story?" Andros's surprise had turned into denial and anger.

"I promise you this is the truth. It was all over so quick, by the time we heard about the challenge Hectin was already dead. We don't even know who it was."

"So you're telling me that there is some mystery person out there who's able to defeat a ghost?"

Whilst Andros was livid at the prospect of the individual involved, Marin's concerns were elsewhere.

"Who's running the council? If somebody has slain Hectin why aren't they claiming their rightful dominion over Illorne? What's happening to their government and people?"

"Who gives a damn about the people?" Andros spat, "Hectin is dead!"

This attitude summed up the council in Marin's eyes. People were a necessary inconvenience for the noble families; their interests were irrelevant. The nobles were simply more important, especially the ghost councillors. Though there was no denying that the ghost councillors were certainly not the same as any other citizen, and Marin had to admit to himself that the news of Hectin's death was far more significant than the death of an ordinary mortal. Nevertheless, the elitist attitude of Andros stuck in Marin's throat; even in the face of astounding news he couldn't put his perceived superiority to one side.

"Marin makes a good point," Edwin chimed in; "if this person didn't kill Hectin in order to take control of Illorne, what was the purpose?"

"Control is certainly not a word I'd use to describe the aftermath. As the news came through, it was as if a powder keg had been lit. Looting, rioting, people taking the opportunity to go wild in a city without governance." Fredo seemed deeply shaken by recalling what he had seen: "I didn't even have time to arrange transport; I just had to leave on foot whilst I could."

"That's typical of the lower classes, always waiting for an opportunity to get one over on their betters; it demonstrates exactly why they aren't on the council." Andros's words were spite-filled, yet also laced with an element of fear at the prospect of what the impoverished subjects of Caspir would do to him given the chance.

"Have you ever even bothered to consider that maybe they are like that precisely because they aren't allowed representation?" Marin knew they saw him as only one small step above the "lowers".

Without giving Andros a chance to respond and instead leaving him open mouthed, Edwin pressed on with the matter at hand.

"Perhaps this is exactly what the mystery duellist wanted? To bring down the government and cause chaos?" He paused as the realization of what the alternative might be dawned on him. "Well. Either that, or their entire drive is the desire to kill ghosts."

The chamber fell silent at Edwin's words. Caspir was the next obvious target for a potential slayer of ghosts, since the only other city that could be considered nearby was Maluani. And very few ever got into Maluani, or out. Everyone had suddenly become aware that Chase had not spoken a word. He remained frozen in place, gripped by fear for the first time in forever. An emotion that nobody had even considered was possible for a

CHAPTER FOUR

ghost councillor to feel. The unending ghost councillor of Caspir had been abruptly confronted with the prospect of his own mortality. His end was not only possible, but potentially in sight from an unknown and secretive individual. Chase's terror distilled into paranoia and panic, whilst the crowded table sat in stillness, waiting to hear from their leader.

"This..."

The councillors seeing the most powerful being they knew lost for words was humbling and troubling in equal measure.

"This is worrying news. We... need to send word to the other cities."

As if possessed by some unholy force, an elderly councillor known as Kreg whipped out a pen and parchment and began to commit ink to scroll with almost inhuman haste. He was the councillor in charge of writing missives, but never had he composed something with such significance before. Trade proposals and notifications of noble weddings seemed entirely frivolous compared to the dismaying new paradigm they had unexpectedly found themselves thrust into.

There was a question on everyone's tongue that nobody dared to ask, but it was written all over their faces. What happens if this ghost killer comes to Caspir?

Chase didn't need the words to be spoken; every fibre of his being – not that his being was made up of fibres – was screaming out the question. But how to compose a response? He could not let on how petrified the situation had left him.

"There cannot be a repeat of these events in Caspir. We cannot let our city descend into chaos."

Marin saw through this facade of humanitarianism. Self-preservation could not be masked by this thin veil of benevolence, but almost by accident he did have a point. Marin may have been the only one in the room who genuinely didn't want the people to suffer.

"What can we do?" Andros asked.

Edwin did not relish saying it, but the law was clear. "The right of challenge is sacred and even older than our esteemed council leader. We can't prevent someone from entering the courtyard to invoke the right at the thrumming pillar." The wide-eyed stares from around the room prompted him to caveat his comments: "Regardless of how much we may want to."

He had carefully trodden a thin line; most importantly though, he was right.

"Are these old laws even relevant? It was a different time back then." Andros's conservatism and sense of tradition clearly played second fiddle to his fear of change to the status quo.

"You seemed quite fond of them twenty-odd years ago when you were cheering as councilman Chase dispatched the last challenger. I rather recall you revelling in it and being glad you "got to see it once in your lifetime." Edwin had a gift for highlighting hypocrisy, especially when it came to Andros.

Rather than see it as a verbal joust, Marin saw the similarities of Andros to the "lowers" who pitted animals against one another as a bloodsport. Despite Andros's oft-noted disdain of them, this was exactly the same thing, revelling in the extinguishing of a life. The discussion continued for a considerable length of time, various elderly voices speaking up about the sanctity of Caspir's laws. The truth was, people were scared to interfere with rules around the ghost councillors; outside of the ghosts, magic had long since left the cities. The occasional rumour or exaggerated story about goings-on in the countryside were all that remained; the educated types in the cities considered them nothing but entertaining fictions trying to recapture a lost age. The rules of the ghosts were laid down by great wizards of the past. Who were these ageing aristocrats to mess around in the affairs of wizards? Chase surveyed the conversation, himself just as ignorant as the others. Even though he had been around during the age of magic, Chase was nothing but a warrior. When he was still flesh and blood he had once met the Great Wizard Ezekiel, whose title was entirely colloquial yet perfectly captured his nature as the greatest of all wizards to have ever lived. Seeing the wonders of magic first-hand had not instilled within him any more knowledge of the subject than anyone else in the chamber. A being who only existed because of magic was a world away from understanding it. As far as he knew, tinkering with his thrumming pillar or attacking someone

CHAPTER FOUR

who spoke the words of challenge might just as easily end him as losing a challenge. So consumed by his own self-preservation, Chase didn't even hear Marin's next words at first.

"Surely we need a contingency plan? Just in case... the worst were to happen? We don't want to end up like Illorne."

This was enough to make even the refined quillmanship of Kreg scratch across his parchment, the writer open-jawed in surprise. The suggestion of a council without a ghost was unthinkable. Sacrilege almost. Yet there was truth in what he said. The council could not afford to lose their heads in the case of their leader losing his. That being said, thinking it and saying it aloud were two very different things.

"How...dare...you!?" Andros raged. "Concerning yourself with your own troubles, in the face of a threat to the head of our council?"

For once, Marin found the same verbal dexterity he had honed in his private exchanges with Edwin to convey his thoughts to the council.

"It is precisely because of the words of our esteemed leader that I am asking this. He put it better than I ever could: 'There cannot be a repeat of these events in Caspir. We cannot let our city descend into chaos.'" Andros was defeated more comprehensively than he had ever been before; the reward was reducing him to nothing but the silent nods of a man overcome.

"Of course, there's no reason to assume Chase would even be defeated in combat. He *is* an immortal ghost protector after all. Perhaps Hectin was nothing but a fluke?"

Edwin was not wrong; even if this somebody did challenge Chase, who's to say they could beat him? He was a more respected and proficient warrior than Hectin. How could anybody hope to match swords with this towering monolith of a being? This revelation sent a small wave of relief lapping over the councilmen. All of them, that is, except their ghostly leader. The expression of frustrated panic was immovable; however, he had formed a plan.

"The gates of the city must be closed. The challenger will never make it past the walls."

CHAPTER FIVE

Shiara hadn't long been in the city, but the commotion she was witnessing was clearly out of the ordinary. Dozens of city guards in their woven cloths and shimmering plates of armour were pulling people away from the gates, shoving back those who were trying to enter. Distraught and confused, each person was trying to clamour past the others to plead their case with the city protectors to be allowed in.

"No-one comes in. We're shutting the gates." The guards repeated these phrases to all who confronted them, with the occasional addition of a "sorry" in an attempt to calm the pulsating crowds.

Shiara watched on. She was not very accustomed to large crowds, having spent much of her life in the wilderness and rural communities, so the bustle held her attention. There were children tightly clinging onto their parents' hands so as to not get swept away by the tides of people. The colours of their brightly hued garments dazzled and glinted, adding an element of beauty to the somewhat panicked proceedings. These people were evidently not without coin, likely to be traders or even tourists who ventured between cities. From the way that many of them were reacting, one could be forgiven for thinking they were having their lives torn apart rather than just being inconvenienced.

All the while, this spectacle was also being observed by the less fortunate sat in alleys like the one Shiara had parked herself in. There were no vibrant threads to be found here; either their apparel began life as cheaper dull clothing, or it had been so worn down and dirtied over time that it matched

CHAPTER FIVE

the cold drab colours of the stonework upon which many of the wearers leaned. Those in among the ruckus were oblivious to the onlookers; this was how things always were. The poor of the cities never occupied the minds of those flush with wealth. Some of those with low incomes, however, were all too aware of those less fortunate and actively tried to put them out of mind. After all, it wouldn't take much bad fortune to end up just like them, which didn't bear thinking about. On the rare occasions that people did discuss the street dwellers in Caspir, they referred to them as "The Grey". Shiara often thought this description spoke volumes about the society she now found herself in. This was a name that not only reflected the Caspirian obsession with colour but that managed to relegate an entire group of people to the same status as something like a stone. It was the city that had failed these people. They didn't deserve this treatment; they were merely a by-product of a system that distributed resources unfairly. Shiara had lived with rural communities outside the walls of the cities where there were no Greys, where everyone had a place and was treated as a person, rather than a waste product of generating profit. "This all has to change," she thought. "And soon it will."

Taking her completely out of her trail of thought, Shiara was confronted by a small Grey child speeding round the corner and bumping right into her. "Sorry ma'am, I didn't mean to..." the young girl trailed off as she gathered herself and continued off down the alley. Straightening out her cloak after the exchange, Shiara noticed something was wrong. Something was missing. Her coin purse was not-so-mysteriously absent. She spun on the spot and slid into the darkened passageway in pursuit.

Shiara flushed with embarrassment. She prided herself on keeping her wits about her, an essential survival tool in the wilderness, yet had been undone by a child. The world within the walls was not the same place as the wild. Fortunately, her senses were sharp enough to pick up on the small footsteps that must have belonged to the slight thief. Darting around the corner, she caught the tail end of a dirtied dress float between the gap in some wooden boards at the back of a building. Her pace slowed as she stalked closer like the silent swoop of a Cara owl. She slipped into the gap and readied herself.

If her time living beyond walls had prepared her for anything, it was darkness. Her eyes adjusted almost immediately to the cramped space. A few paces in front there was a turning to the left, from which hushed voices could be heard and a flicker of what seemed like candlelight could be seen. Drawing in a breath she sidled round the corner.

Before her sat three figures. Two were small girls, one of them being the thief she had pursued and the other a very similar-looking child who Shiara suspected was the younger sister of the former. Between them sat a hunched man who was in the twilight of his years; regardless of what his exact age may have been, he did not look good for it. Wrinkles wove a tapestry across his face, accentuated by the candle's glow. Much of his hair had departed his head and seemingly taken residence around his chin in the form of a beard that it would be overly generous to describe as straggly. Sadly, what caught her attention most was the smell. Shiara suspected that this man had not left this hole in the wall for quite some time; the caked-on remnants of bowel movements adorned the tin pot secreted in the corner. The most oppressive scent was that of unwashed skin that had been stewing in its own sweat. Everybody crapped; even though the smell was potent, it was just crap; however, the unwashed odour that assaulted her nose could chiefly be described as desperation and defeat.

Fear crept into the faces of this thread-bare family. The hilt of Shiara's cutlass poked out from underneath her cloak and caught the light along with their attention.

"Please don't, ma'am!" cried out the young thief.

Shiara clocked that their eyes were fixated on her scabbard and instantly raised her hands in an attempt to gesture her harmless intentions.

"Forgive me. I'm not here to hurt anyone." Her words did little to alleviate the terror of the three.

"I know you took my coins, but I can clearly see why. I don't want to upset anyone or cause trouble, but I will need some of them back."

A shaking delicate hand produced a coin purse from underneath the girl's dress. Slowly she raised it towards Shiara, jingling the contents as the

CHAPTER FIVE

trembling increased.

"M... Ma'am. I'm sorry. Take it back, just don't kill us."

Shiara sighed. They clearly didn't believe her; could she really blame them? Their lives were unlikely to be filled with much in the way of kindness or compassion. Rather than taking the purse, she merely pushed open the cloth with her fingers and retrieved a small grip of coins, leaving the majority of the contents behind. Taking her other hand, she closed the child's fingers around the bag of money and gently pushed the dainty hand back.

"You can keep the rest. I just need enough to feed myself tonight; I've got a big day ahead of me tomorrow."

At least they didn't look scared anymore, Shiara thought; pure bewilderment and confusion had taken up residence on their faces instead. This didn't seem like an act of kindness; rather one of madness! The Grey family could eat for a couple of weeks on these coins and had probably never held this much money in their lives, let alone have someone give it to them.

"I... don't understand. Why are you helping us when we stole from you?" Inquisitiveness got the better of any fear that remained.

"That's what I'm here for, to help. Especially people like you." She could see that the concept was incredibly alien to them.

"But why give us all that money? You could take it back!"

Shiara smiled. "I don't think I'll need it. Certainly not as much as you."

The ramshackle man finally spoke up, his voice cracking from a dry mouth, but his curiosity was worth sating at the expense of a sore throat. "Why only take money for tonight's meal? What about tomorrow, or the day after?"

A knowing grin took flight across her cheeks. "Oh, don't worry about me. After tomorrow I won't need to pay for my meals in Caspir." This did nothing to dampen the puzzlement of the family; if anything it only raised more questions. Whilst the follow-up queries were still forming in their mouths, Shiara issued them a nod and left their makeshift home.

The three of them were left glancing between each other and the bag of coins, unable to find the words to assess this most peculiar of encounters.

CHAPTER SIX

The mood in the tavern was noticeably on edge. Closing the city walls had raised the anxiety of the citizens contained within. The Moth & Scale would normally be packed to its ceiling with laughter and joviality at this time of the evening, yet tonight everything was dampened down. By now the news of Hectin's death – if you could call the demise of a ghost "death" – had filtered down to most of Caspir's inhabitants. Of course, rumours were openly flying between tables. Everything from blaming the councils of other cities to outlandish theories of the Great Wizard Ezekiel having returned from the grave. The flickering of shadows from the candlelight gave each far-fetched tale a real sense of showmanship that elicited nods and raised eyebrows, as if to suggest "I think you are onto something there."

A pair of distinguished men sat on one table were not as interested in these fanciful speculations, for the reality of the situation applied enough weight to their shoulders without heaping on imaginary burdens. Marin slurped from his beaker of wine, wetting his throat with the ultimate in conversational lubricants.

"This talk of mysterious strangers is all very well, but when resources start wearing thin wide-eyed conjecture will be no replacement for a full belly."

Edwin ran his fingers along his perfect jawline whilst mulling over the situation.

"Honestly, I fear you may well be right. Caspir is far from self-sufficient; without trade coming in who knows how people will react. The idea of closing ourselves off just isn't workable for more than a few days. As it stands, we can't even bring in the food from our own farms or, more importantly, new thread. I may as well just cancel my appointment with my tailor next week and be done with it!"

"We both know that you could do with a new wardrobe."

The pair chuckled at Marin's jest, yet it was the half-hearted chuckle of men who were painted into a corner by events out of their control.

"What happens if this person *does* get to Chase and... you know." Marin didn't feel like fully articulating the thought, as if putting it into words somehow made it more real.

"One of us gets a promotion, I suppose?" Humour had always been their go-to in just about any situation, but it didn't sit well with either of them tonight.

"Seriously though," Edwin continued, "it isn't something we can prepare for. Illorne certainly didn't fare well. As I see it, we would be at the mercy of whomever this ghost slayer is. That *is* the law after all."

"The law?" Marin puffed. "Some archaic old nonsense written back in the days where magic was more than just stories? I mean, back then, the cities weren't full like they are now. It's obvious that the whole point of ghost protectors in the first place was to minimize casualties in conflicts when the walls didn't hold that many people."

"So, we should bring back war? Kill off a few people?"

"Obviously not, Edwin, but think about it. The world isn't the same place it was then. We surely don't need to be a slave to those same rules? Especially if that means ending up like Illorne."

Edwin couldn't fault Marin's logic here, but the topic wasn't about logic. It was about identity and tradition; their very way of life was tied to these "archaic rules".

"I'd hardly say we're slaves to the rules. Our traditions are what make us who we are."

"Tradition? Tradition is why you'll find hungry children a few hundred yards from that door," Marin spat. To him, tradition was an inhibitor of progress.

"If change is what you are after, maybe you should embrace the prospect of our esteemed councillor being slain. That would certainly shake things up."

Marin briefly choked on his wine at Edwin's words. It was both the brazen manner in which he had spoken, and the fact that he just might be right. Plainly it would certainly be easier to reason with a living, breathing human being than an immortal? This possibility offered Marin some comfort, yet he couldn't shift the thought of Illorne from his mind. He couldn't let that happen here but what could he do? He was just one man, and not even a noble one at that.

Swiping up the beakers, Marin stood to get a much-needed refill, registering a glance from Edwin that could only be summarized as "Make sure they fill it to the top."

Stepping past tables full of nervous citizens, the merchant councillor didn't recognize any of them; the usual warm faces of other regulars were absent this evening. Some paranoia was to be expected in these uncertain times, but the air was thicker with it than he expected. Marin knew he was just being daft thinking, "Who are these people?" After all, there were many who frequented this drinking establishment and he certainly never paid enough attention to most of them to conjure them from memory. Then it came to him. The reason why he was worried about who was there. What if *they* were already in Caspir? If Fredo had managed to get all the way from Illorne before the gates were closed, who's to say that Hectin's killer hadn't also made that same journey? Nobody knew who they were, so they could be any one of thousands of people. The cliff face of a man sat on his own in the corner perhaps? His enormous stature and craggy features certainly would fit the bill of someone capable in combat. Or how about one of the solitary drinkers or diners sat at the bar? They all wore swords; conceivably one of them could have been used to slay the Ghost of Illorne. The dapper gentleman sat between the scruffy drab woman and the rosy-faced fat man, for instance? Based purely on the impressively curled fine moustache of the man, Marin found himself imagining him as a poised duellist, taking apart his foes with exquisite motions like a painter putting brush to canvas. This was clearly ridiculous. Ornate swords were the fashion; even the scruffy lady had gone to the trouble of having a scabbard with some rustic charm to it. Marin sighed at the ridiculousness of these speculations, shook his head, then caught the attention of one of the barkeeps to refill their beakers.

Walking back to the table at a snail's pace, he skirted around other customers, making sure to not spill any of the ruby-red wine on his tailored garments. Sure, the city was on the verge of a crisis; nevertheless, he wasn't going to let that get in the way of looking good. "No point throwing all that hard work to waste," he said to himself as Edwin rolled his eyes at the slow and dainty steps that delayed his enjoyment of another drink.

"Take your time why don't you?" Edwin jeered. "Who cares if you spill it; you're wearing red anyway."

"*Some of us* care how we look," Marin smiled. "You should try it sometime." If he was keeping score, which he most assuredly was, he was winning their verbal jousts by a fair margin at this stage.

The pair raised their mugs to each other and quaffed a faceful of the crimson delight. It was a particularly good vintage that took full advantage of the perfectly hot days and cool nights of the year it was grown. A full body, rich, with smooth spiced notes and just a hint of plum. Edwin had often discussed his penchant for wine and whilst Marin agreed it was indeed tasty, the finer details escaped him. "Must be a nobleman thing," he would often muse, excusing his lack of interest regarding the subtleties of wine tasting by wearing his merchant class heritage as a badge of defiant honour.

It wasn't long before the discussion returned to its previous concerns.

"Do you think this could be the prophecy?" Marin didn't want to sound infantile by mentioning a story that was largely considered to be for children, yet he couldn't ignore it.

"The prophecy?!" exclaimed Edwin, his scepticism pouring out. "I highly doubt a fairy tale about someone slaying the ghosts to bring about a new age of prosperity, that was written who knows how many generations ago, is worth much thought in the real world."

"You must admit that what's happened to Hectin is far from ordinary."

"Look, Marin. It doesn't take a scholar to know that a ghost being killed would change things and if you write a prophecy about someone doing just that, each year that goes by the prophecy is either found to be true, or just hasn't happened yet. Eventually something will come along that seems close enough; that doesn't mean it's been predicted."

The bearded merchant was impressed by the logic of his elder's argument. It did sound ridiculous to believe that someone could predict events many years before they happened. Then again, the idea of magic being commonplace in the far distant past also seemed ridiculous by today's standards. If it wasn't for the ghosts, people probably wouldn't believe magic was anything more than folk stories either.

The way Marin had learnt about the prophecy as a child was that it offered something to those who weren't noble born; an inevitable change to the system. By becoming a council member that change had already happened for him, to an extent.

"The prophecy must be more than just some wild guesses about the future, or why else bother to write it?"

"Why does a musician play? Why does an artist paint?" Edwin punctuated his words with accentuated gestures in sarcastic grandiosity. "It's all about telling a story that people will remember, and we *are* still talking about it after all these years, so it's clearly worked."

Marin conceded the point with a shrug before replying, "But what about the promise of a better future and an offering of hope?"

"Well, you can't have a good story without a bit of hope!" The pair let off a light snort of laughter, before gulping down some wine in agreement.

CHAPTER SEVEN

Shiara had to hand it Caspir; the food was nothing short of sublime. Who would have thought a tavern called the Moth & Scale would offer up such a succulent and well-seasoned dish. Whilst she couldn't quite make out which leafy green vegetable it was that had been so excellently roasted, that didn't stop her shovelling it into her face. The addition of spices and use of a proper oven made all the difference to the basic meals she had become accustomed to cooking around campfires. Shiara wondered why they were so obsessed and proud of their clothing when the food was far more impressive. Scoffing was inevitable at this point, much to the chagrin of the rakish, moustached gentleman who sat next to her at the bar. A desire to sit anywhere else was written all over his face as he glanced around the bar with no success. Dining etiquette was an unnecessary frivolity in the scruffy woman's eyes. Shiara almost took pride in making the man squirm as she ravaged her meal, taking extra time to extract the best crunching sounds from the stalks, something that caused his eye to twitch with irritation. She could tell the man had never had to make his own fire to cook a self-caught lizard or fowl. Despite his flashy sword, his hands were that of a clerk or something equally dull, not fit for use outside of the walls. Tutting and sighs were all the trouble she could expect from him. There were far more interesting subjects around for people-watching.

    The art of listening in on the conversation of others was a tricky one. Certainly, Shiara could pick out specific dialogues and people quite easily; honing her listening skills for safety and survival was a given for her lifestyle.

No, the problem she struggled with was trying not to *look* like she was listening, or at the very least look natural whilst doing it in a public setting. That was especially difficult tonight since suspicion had been cranked up by recent events. Nevertheless, she gave in to the urge to snoop on what the people of Caspir were talking about. As expected, the crowded tables ebbed and flowed between talk of the "Ghost Slayer"; worries about being shut in the city, and of course the odd hair-brained speculative discussion about who could beat a Cara owl in a fight. After all, it was still a pub.

What did catch her attention was a more reserved pair of gentlemen, one of which was carefully navigating his way back to his elderly friend, desperately trying not to spill wine down his fancy red outfit. Shiara had heard snippets earlier regarding discussions of law and traditions: these were obviously not just regular citizens; they bore the unmistakable aura of politicians. Given her childhood living, if you could call it that, these were not her favourite people. Despite this, their discussion seemed far less arrogant than she had come to expect from such persons, which drew her attention all the more. Actual consideration for the supply of food for the people showed a surprising sense of philanthropy, which was at odds with her previous experiences of councillors in other cities. Maybe they were different in Caspir? Having seen the slums and meeting that impoverished family squirrelled away in a wall earlier, it was obvious to her that they weren't different enough.

Curious where their conversation would turn once the bearded man returned to the table, Shiara's eyes widened uncontrollably at the sound of the word "prophecy". The older man seemed rather dismissive, but the crimson-draped fellow spoke of it in a way that reminded Shiara of her father, definitely not the tone that one would associate with nobles contemplating the prophecy. A prophecy that gave hope to her and others who found themselves unfortunate enough to be born into poverty. This man was different. Or was he? Perhaps circumstances had changed enough to suppress the complete derision nobles usually afforded the topic? She could understand the scepticism; at her lowest points she too had her doubts. Could there really be some great magical sword imbued with power by the

CHAPTER SEVEN

great Ezekiel during the age of magic? Let alone someone able to wield it well enough to slay the ghosts and change everything? The age of magic was nothing more than a fiction for most, and who could blame them? The tales of what people could do in the past were so fantastical it was only natural to scoff at it. Furthermore, few had travelled much outside the big cities to visit the occasional rural village that had a healer or greenfinger who could go beyond what most people considered possible. Sealing a wound in minutes, ripening fruit in seconds, or clearing blight with mere touch – nothing that compared to the stories of the age magic but enough to let someone believe. And believe she did.

An abrupt guffawing from a nearby table shook Shiara from her thoughts. It emanated from what she supposed was a handsome figure of a man who seemed the centre of attention. Such a creature would have been out of place beyond the walls, with his soft hands and heavy perfume, and he appeared to be playing the crowd at his table as if they were instruments. He clearly knew exactly what to say and how to say it to generate the biggest laughs. These sorts of men seemed more like an amusement than a worthwhile person to Shiara, a caricature of the idea of a person and city life. Whilst in-depth knowledge of cities was not something she possessed, what little she did know was enough to persuade her this was no way to run a society; even she could guess who this person was, or rather what they were. A silver-tongue. She wrinkled her nose uncontrollably at the prospect of someone whose entire function was to indulge in the lavish excesses of wealth, purely as a means to pry titbits of information out of others to serve up to their ethereal masters. What could be a greater indictment of those ruling the cities than this? People were starving in these very walls, yet they cared more about who had slept with whose wife in a city several days' journey away. Silver-tongue. Even the name was ridiculous, Shiara judged. The idea that their tongues and ability to merely speak was somehow a great asset and worthy of praise. It was all gusto and bravado, the *way* someone says something shouldn't be prized more highly than the *content* of those words; however that is exactly how his ilk made their living. This wasn't so different from the councillors that occupied much of her loathing. It was all about finding the right way to say "Let's look out for my interests and sod everyone else" so it could somehow sound palatable to those in their districts. People sometimes spoke of the outlandish magic that once was; surely no magical spectacle would be as fantastical as some overweight nobleman convincing ordinary people that he would best represent their interests. "How could they not see what was going on?" she thought. It was plain for her to see; even as a child living in the stacks she could see it. Why couldn't they? Were people honestly that scared of change? Perhaps the very notion of things being different seemed so alien that it couldn't take hold. Finishing off the last drops of her wine she comforted herself thinking, "Well ready or not, these people will have to get used to change, and soon."

CHAPTER EIGHT

Today was the day.

Shiara stretched out her shoulders as she rose to her feet, producing a selection of popping and cracking noises. All things considered she had slept well. She'd spent many evenings curled up in the wilderness enveloped in her cloak for warmth, so the extra heat generated by a city full of people meant she was far from being cold by her standards. A brief forage beneath her cloak brought forth a hunk of bread and a steel flask that was disappointingly just filled with water. "Probably for the best," Shiara thought; it would help to remain as focused as possible this morning. A few chomps later and her slightly stale breakfast loaf was reduced to crumbs scattered on her clothes and the floor. Patting herself down to check for all of her modest belongings, she set out for her day.

She was still within the Brown Quarter and there was one more pressing matter that had to be attended to before the main task of the day could be attempted: the wine she had enjoyed the night previous was now asking to be released. Along a side street she tracked the guttering until it met with a drain. Her nose informed her that she was in the right place to relieve herself. Moments later she emerged back into the main street, nostrils flaring to dispel the lingering bouquet of bodily fluids. It was not the shortest walk to the centre and Shiara would have to take extra care not to attract any suspicion. Not the easiest thing to do when clad in brown in a world of shimmering colours.

Beyond the Brown Quarter, it seemed like Caspir consisted of ordered layers of society peeling back as one got closer to the middle. This was relatively common for the cities, as they were all built in the round and sat their governments in the centre. "It's like an onion," Shiara mused. Although sadly, just like an onion, the outer layer was always battered and discarded. She was now in a worker's district, populated by those who had jobs working for the better off. They were probably only a couple of weeks of bad circumstances from finding themselves in the Brown Quarter. She had seen it since she was a child, workers doing all the actual labour whilst the more privileged reaped the benefits. This reminded Shiara of her father. She tried not to think of him. It wasn't just that she missed him, she also felt anger about what he did. Burying thoughts of her dad was something she had become accustomed to doing, made all the easier today by the smell of a nearby bakery. Whilst not as fancy as the patisseries serving indescribable treats to the nobles, the smell of freshly baked bread was unparalleled. A comforting warmth filled her lungs, pushing thoughts of her past away. Each layer of Caspir had its own shops to accommodate the occupants; this way the various classes of the society would keep interaction to a minimum. Maybe it was intentional, to stop unrest from those less fortunate by making sure they didn't know what they were missing? Nothing was actually stopping them from venturing further towards the wealthy centre though. Perchance it was just too much for them to see what they couldn't have, so remaining within one's community was less painful?

The occasional building among the others was noticeably out of place – too grandiose and impressive for a mere worker's house. These were the homes of merchants who liked to live nearer the edge of the city for ease of transport. They appeared as monuments to inequality that loomed over those struggling to get by, a permanent reminder that the lower classes should always remember their place in the world.

Venturing closer to the hub of Caspir, bright hues gave way to truly splendid colours. The banners on buildings gleamed with the morning light, almost ethereal in their magnificence. Merchants and guild workers were not shy about their displays; the only things here more dazzling than

CHAPTER EIGHT

the banners were some of the outfits of their owners. A portly man in a shade of blue that Shiara had never seen before filled a doorway as he stared out into the street. A woman dressed in an identical shade of blue trotted towards him, her arms laden with freshly made goods. Even the buckle on her jet-black shoes somehow seemed more vibrant than metal had any right to be. These people seemed content in their lives, ostensibly unfazed by the destitution of the Brown Quarter that existed relatively nearby. Conceivably they could think it a price worth paying for their own quality of lives. "A very easy price to consider when you aren't the one paying it!" Shiara grumbled under her breath. In many ways these people frustrated Shiara almost as much as the nobles. At least the nobles had the excuse of being far removed and being indoctrinated into the system from birth. The moment she caught herself trying to excuse the nobles she uncontrollably wrinkled her face, disgusted at her own internal musings.

If the previous district was spectacular, the noble district was nothing short of a work of art. Houses were spaced far more generously, with grassy areas lining their perimeters. Shiara considered it perverse to have glimpses of nature as a status symbol when much of the world beyond the walls was carpeted in green. Sure, there were plenty of patches of grass or trees littered throughout the rest of the city, but they were not of this manicured level. It was as if the nobles wanted to not only demonstrate that they could possess a slice of nature but that they could also bend it to their will, to craft a lawn or trim a bush into a man-made spectacle. She suspected that not one of them would last a week surrounded by *actual* nature. Even the plump feathery Kerri birds found in the rest of Caspir were few and far between in this district. No doubt the unnatural obsession with keeping this area pristine meant fewer crumbs for the birds to scavenge. There was no place for the mottled browns and greys of the Kerri birds in the splendid world of colour the nobles inhabited. Shiara had become aware of glances shot at her by various people who were overly aware of her not fitting within these surroundings. If she wanted to get to the centre with as little hassle as possible, she would have to slip into the alleys and away from these immaculate displays of wealth.

There were always places to hide if one looked hard enough. She found herself in a narrow alleyway lined with drains; even the richest of people had to empty their bowels. In many ways this was the perfect path for Shiara to take, even if her olfactory system protested. The drains would run most of the way to the centre and the thought of a noble being remotely close to the sewer system was laughable. Guards were a possibility, but right now many of them were posted towards the outskirts of Caspir and only someone without a sense of smell would spend more than a few moments here. Unfortunately, Shiara's nose was working perfectly well. She noticed that these drains were far less pleasant than the ones further out, probably a result of the richness of the food that the nobles enjoyed. It amused her to think that not only were the nobles more full of more excrement than everyone else but it was far stinkier too!

The tricky part of getting there was still to come. The alleys did not run all the way into the centre; there was a square of space around the middle with a few buildings including the council chambers. She would have to circle around and approach the thrumming pillar from the opposite side to avoid going past the guards posted there. The guards were not to be feared – they were just an inconvenience. Fortuitously they were far from being effective at their roles. Peace had been relatively stable for generations so there was little skill required above breaking up a brawl or tracking down a lone criminal. It must have been a somewhat pleasant job, earning respect without having to do much of anything really. Peering around the corner of the alley, she spotted a handful of guards deep in conversation. From what she could make out, it was a discussion about a theatrical show; the important thing was that they were distracted. This made slipping into the alcove further along rather straightforward. From here, Shiara had merely to hug the contours of the archways and keep an ear out for footsteps.

Having shimmied her way around, she stood outside the courtyard that housed the thrumming pillar; however, unlike in Illorne the gate was chained shut. The smooth bars of the gate were difficult to climb silently, yet she still managed it. A swish of the cloak to avoid it getting caught on the pointed gold spikes at the top and she was over. She could feel the hum

CHAPTER EIGHT

of the stone's power as if the very air itself was dancing. Her hand drew her sword from its scabbard. A sword that buzzed with that same magical hum. Calming her nerves, her lungs filled and she began to speak the proclamation of challenge.

CHAPTER NINE

The council chamber teemed with a clawing panic that had been festering since the city closed itself off. It had been only a couple of days, yet the dynamic of the place had shifted immeasurably. Confusion and speculation had now given way to the stark realization that this could not go on indefinitely. Caspir could not survive this lockdown forever. In a matter of days the food reserves would dwindle to nothing and the traders outside the gates would be too great in number to avoid unrest. Marin knew this was what should be discussed this morning, but as of yet nobody seemed brave enough to raise the topic in the presence of Chase. A peculiar denial surrounded the meeting, and Marin could take no more of it.

"Excuse me, but what is the point of any of this?"

Unsurprisingly, Andros took it upon himself to oppose Marin's outburst.

"I think you will find that running this city is quite important; most of us take our duties rather seriously."

"That's the problem. We aren't doing our duty. How can you talk about trade figures and running the city whilst ignoring what's going on out there? We've closed the gates. Traders are camping outside the walls and we only have a finite supply of food to go around."

Everyone knew this was true, but dared not reply. The gravity of Chase's involvement in the situation was pulling the gaze of everyone around the table to him in the absence of any discussion. Yes, this was a council, but the fact that Chase was an immortal warrior of renowned skill who had suddenly been confronted with his own mortality was inescapable. How would he

CHAPTER NINE

react? There was nothing that any of these men could do to stop him if he snapped, and nobody wanted to end up like the city of Latan. The knowledge of what a "mad ghost" could inflict within the walls was a terrifying warning. Yet Marin could see that on their current course, the people of Caspir could themselves perform such an atrocity. Most people are only a few meals away from doing something dreadful in the name of survival, he thought.

Chase had been more distant than usual since the news of Hectin's death reached him, but the silence following Marin's interjection was something he couldn't fail to respond to.

"And what, exactly, would you suggest? Opening the city back up and risking my safety?"

Heads turned and eyes swivelled to Marin to see how he'd answer.

"By keeping the gates closed, we risk the safety of everyone in Caspir except..."

Regardless of how bold Marin felt, he cut off his sentence before reaching its almost treasonous conclusion.

"Except... for me? That's what you were going to say, wasn't it? After all, no food is required to sustain me."

The collective intake of breath was audible.

"That is the truth of the matter, councillor."

"So you would put me at risk? The very beating heart of Caspir that has seen countless generations come and go? The head of our esteemed council is something you wish to gamble with?"

Marin swallowed before attempting his reply.

"With all due respect, it won't be long before there isn't much of the city left to need a council. And what does a city without people look like? Latan?"

If Chase had still had blood, it would have boiled. The fury in his eyes was reflected back by the other councillors as fear in theirs. The city of Latan was not something to be invoked lightly. The implication that Chase's position was "mad" like that of the ghost protector of Latan was clear. Words were incapable of conveying his fury; a silent yet bubbling rage in the apparition's form expressed more than any language could. Despite this, the veracity of Marin's comments was ineludible.

"He is right, you know," piped up Edwin. "This situation *is* unsustainable."

A few of the councillors caught themselves nodding in agreement unconsciously and darted their vision away from Chase so as to avoid entangling themselves in tension-laden exchanges.

"However, it is also true that we shouldn't be putting the head of our council in unnecessary danger," Edwin continued. "A common ground between shutting everything off and leaving our gates open shouldn't be too difficult to find."

Compromises were something that the council and Chase had come to often, but the issue of his very existence was new territory. His somewhat indifferent approach to the lives of mortals had allowed flexibility in discussions on how to run the city; this situation could not be more different.

"You expect us to find a middle ground between me being attacked and being safe? Perhaps I'll just be slain a bit? There are no half measures when it comes to life and death. I should know, I've seen more lives begin and end than any of you could ever imagine."

"But surely you don't want to see a lot more lives ended unnecessarily? It seems reasonable that provisions could be made to keep you safe?" Edwin's attempts at diplomacy were valiant, if ineffective.

Andros decided it was his turn to interject.

"Frankly I think it's preposterous to suggest that this person could actually defeat you in combat. Everyone knows you are a finer duellist than Hectin ever was."

In Andros's mind he had offered words of reassurance that pandered to Chase's ego and would defuse the situation. In reality he had highlighted the ghost councillor's fear and fallibility. Andros's smug expression as he leaned back, considering the conundrum resolved, was nothing short of painfully awkward to the rest of the council, who could see the obvious. Chase had to select his words carefully so as to not openly acknowledge the existence of his dread and self-doubt.

"The point is, I shouldn't *have* to fight. We are a civilized city that shouldn't have to descend to this... barbarism!"

CHAPTER NINE

He was clutching at straws and everyone could see it. Everyone except Andros.

"I for one would love to see you give some upstart his comeuppance. Give them a little payback for Hectin."

Eyebrows were collectively raised to the highest point possible. No-one was foolish enough to put themselves in the middle of this exchange, so instead each councillor was now pondering whether new limits of awkwardness could be reached upon hearing Andros's next blundering comment.

"In fact, I hope they *do* challenge you, just so you can show them what for!"

Mouths fell open. Andros was redefining the word "misjudged".

"Let's throw open the gates and invite them in!"

Andros was looking around the table for support for his rallying cry. The horrified faces began to clue him in, and then the penny, just like the councillor's jaw, finally dropped. Within moments his features reflected back the rest of the council's: "Oh."

A grimace made its way across the ghost councillor's face; his fist balled up with a steadily building anger that looked like it was soon to explode. Fury was not something the councillors associated with their ghost protector; rather it was a constant nagging in the backs of their minds. Each of them readied themselves for what they were sure would be a vicious outburst. It didn't arrive. Something else had pulled the council leader's focus.

Chase's eyes widened abruptly as the situation changed beyond measure. All his fears and the discussions about his safety suddenly felt like a distant notion. Those who noticed his change in expression were the first to realize that his form was ebbing away, pulled elsewhere involuntarily, which could only mean one thing. Someone had made it to the thrumming pillar and had issued a challenge. Unsurprisingly, Andros was the last to identify what was happening, almost falling off his chair when Chase's tortured expression finally faded away. Disbelieving intakes of breath and panicked glances replaced words. No further communication was required. Springing to their feet, multiple chairs were cast to the ground as the councillors all bolted for the door. The enormity of the situation had placed the infirmities of age to one side as each member rushed out the chamber. The decorum of the nobles had descended into a furore, once-sedate people charging down the hallway and spilling out onto the street. Guards looking on in bemusement were unable to fathom quite what was transpiring until they noticed the train of councillors were scurrying towards the central courtyard. The caravan found new members as the wardens abandoned their posts to make a beeline for the action. Encircling the locked gates to the courtyard, the onlookers were confronted by a rather curious sight. For it wasn't a muscle-bound hulk of a man that stood before the coalescing presence of their ghost protector, but a wiry female draped in dull brown attire.

One thought unified the crowd: "Could this really be the challenger who slayed Hectin?"

CHAPTER TEN

The imposing ethereal figure of Chase towered over the scruffy woman. His pristine appearance had been preserved through the ages with magic, whilst several different shades of mud had coloured the challenger's boots. Despite the mismatch, there was no tremble or quiver from the woman, just resolute stoicism. It was clear she was either mad or knowingly confident; both at once was not out of the question either. The ghost was uncertain how this would play out; he moved his hand towards his scabbard and produced the spectral blade that was forever bonded with him. Billows of faint smoke cascaded as the air blew over its edge. The unkempt vagabond likewise reached for her weapon; none of the onlookers expected what she produced. Her cutlass subtly shimmered with colours, nothing garish but enough to signify something was out of the ordinary here. The appearance was its least impressive trait – there was a perceptible quality that it radiated; nobody could pinpoint what this was, but everyone felt it. Something mysterious. Something unknowable. Something arcane. And what's more, Chase felt it too.

Stepping forward, the drab contender didn't break her gaze with the protector and kept her sword arm perfectly trained with the tip of her blade perpetually pointed at her foe's eyes. This was not only for intimidation purposes; it helped obscure the length of her weapon from the councillor, as even a slight miscalculation on his part would provide an additional edge. As soon as she stepped within the arc of his arm, Chase unleashed one almighty swing, cleaving the air itself and casting a stream of smoke in its wake. The woman remained unharmed. Her limber frame had shifted so the blade sailed past without incident. Expelling a grunt, the apparition reversed, bringing the edge hurtling back towards his target; this time she did not dodge. A flick of her wrist placed her weapon in the way; another flick upon contact parried the blow off course, forcing the ghost into taking a wide step to avoid stumbling.

His next strike was executed with a shout of anger and frustration; again it was parried just the same. Another slash narrowly avoided by the small combatant followed; this one was answered with a cut of her own, slicing into Chase's upper thigh. To the astonishment of all present he let out a shrill cry, albeit brief. Blackened smoke ebbed from the wound, which itself was the colour of midnight – a stark contrast to the pale greys, whites and jades of his unblemished form. Any remaining doubts about whether or not a ghost councillor could be killed evaporated.

Whilst clearly calm and focused, the challenger did show signs of exertion. Sweat sparkled on her brow and her chest heaved with the effort she was expending, yet somehow the protector, who could neither breathe nor sweat, looked far more fatigued.

It was time for the woman to change tactics. She went on the offensive, carving upwards with her blade. Chase was knocked back a step as he blocked the attack; she had planned for just such a defence. Pivoting on one foot, she redirected the momentum into a low sweep, chopping out a wedge of blackness just below his knee. The response was a flail of his sword arm that forced her to step back, merely delaying what now seemed to be an inevitable killing blow.

Cracks and chips were beginning to form across the thrumming pillar that sat in the courtyard, the tether that bound the ghost to the city. An immovable and indestructible monument that hadn't even seen a scratch in its history, it now appeared that it would soon be reduced to rubble. It didn't feel like history was being made, but more like it was being destroyed.

A frustrated lunge accompanied by a roar saw Chase's weapon come as close to wounding the challenger as he had managed so far. Like a battering ram, the trunk of his arm applied an inhuman force to his blow. His wiry foe

CHAPTER TEN

was taken aback by its ferocity, only just managing to deflect it at the last moment. For her troubles she was flung back several feet by the momentum and grazed her knee as she fell onto it. The councillors looking on were instilled with a trace of hope that had been previously absent.

A wrist draped in brown fabric wiped off her brow as she rose to her feet. A look of disappointment in the complacency she had shown spread around her face. Still there was no fear to be seen, though perhaps a nagging doubt might have crept in. Puffing her chest steadied her nerves as she readied for what must surely be the conclusion to this bout. The city's protector wasted no time; empowered by the apparent success of his previous strike he bounded forward, gripping his hilt with both hands to imbue his attack with all the might he could summon. This was the opening Shiara was looking for. With all that force concentrated in one place he was unable to reposition once his swing had begun; sliding to the floor to avoid his arc, her blade cut through one of his arms just below the shoulder. As the limb fell it billowed into blackness, evaporating in steam as it hit the ground.

The next few seconds stretched to an eternity for Chase. His eyes widened as his executioner pirouetted whilst he tried to regain balance from his last assault. He was powerless to stop the edge that hurtled towards his neck, merely a spectator to his demise, perceived in the slow motion that was reserved for those about to meet their end. His mind raced, considering all that had come before. He pondered the thought that he was one of the few beings who still remembered the age of magic. The legacy and history dying with him. There would be one less bit of magic in the world without him. Yet that sword... There was a hint of something familiar about it... wait... surely it couldn't be?

Blackness.

Like the opening of a furnace in the stacks, an acrid black fog hung in the air where the ghost councillor had once been. As it began to clear, the crumbled remains of the thrumming pillar littered the courtyard. Amid the debris stood the victor. Her cutlass seemed to gleam a little more brightly as she sheathed it, probably due to the contrast of its immaculate steel against the dark haze. Caspir would be forever changed. The age of Chase was over. Perhaps the age of all ghosts was coming to an end. This inauspicious creature clad in threads befitting a beggar had done what time could not – end the life of a protector. But who was she? The bringer of chaos? The herald of Caspir's demise? Whatever she may bring, one thing was certain, she was the slayer of ghosts.

CHAPTER ELEVEN

After what had seemed to be an elegantly fought duel, Marin was now watching this untidy woman scramble over the gate surrounding the courtyard. The end of her cloak fraying a little more as it caught the tips of the spikes, she was clearly in a bit too much of a hurry to concern herself with such things. All around Marin his peers stood in shock; the blood having drained from their faces they themselves almost resembled ghosts. He was not exempt from such feelings either. Nevertheless, this merchant councillor always prided himself on his pragmatism and there was nothing pragmatic about gawping in such a manner.

The crowd began to part to let the stranger through; like a sandback parting the undergrowth she paced away from the scene of the challenge. The onlookers did not utter a sound or modify their expressions; it was a reflexive action to step back and allow her room. Marin didn't share such a reflex. Her footsteps ceased as her eyes came to rest on the immaculate beard of the councillor who had stepped into her path.

Marin felt her gaze as their eyes met; she then appraised him calmly. Presumably she was wondering what sort of a specimen would stand in her way after seeing what she had just accomplished. He didn't see her as threatening, more like a perplexing puzzle that didn't quite make sense. Cutting him down would be academic – he knew this; somehow he couldn't envision her as the sort of person who would.

"Excu..." His dry throat cracked as he attempted to speak, forcing him to clear his throat before trying again.

"Excuse me." He'd found his voice but wasn't entirely sure what to say with it.

"My... My name is Marin, my colleagues here and I are the councillors of Caspir. What should... how should we address you? Ma'am?"

Finally, the expressions of the congregation changed – to even more abject terror. Marin wasn't sure why at first, his brain took a moment to piece it together. This person had just killed one councillor, and here he was pointing out where she could find the rest of them. Regardless, he was sure that it was just the ghost she wanted to slay. Perhaps *sure* was a little too strong a word, on reflection.

"Ma'am? You can call me Shiara."

Her confidence with a blade far surpassed her oratory prowess. Marin was not alone in noticing it. The councillors surrounding them had spent their lives jousting with words and crafting their speeches with precise intonations, so the wobble within her voice spoke volumes. This was not the articulation of a noble or statesperson, nor even a salesperson; it was more like a farmhand.

"As per our ancient law, you are now this city's ruler."

The last few days had been non-stop talk of how to avoid chaos, so Marin was eager to see where things lay.

"Ruler?" Shiara puffed. "I don't want to rule you. Do you think I went to the trouble of killing your ghost just to take his place?"

Clarity, it seemed, was not something the councillors would be permitted just yet. Why would anyone go through that without wanting the rewards it brought? Unless... Marin cottoned on more quickly than the others, probably a result of not being born into nobility. The prophecy. This wasn't about changing the leaders but changing the system.

"Why not? That's what the law says!" Unsurprisingly, Andros was not quite on the same page.

"And what good are your laws?" Her fire smoothed over the cracks in her oration skills. "Your laws see slums swell within your walls whilst fat men grow fatter. Your laws see you wearing different cloth each day whilst others have but rags. Your laws..." The vocabulary to express her volcanic

CHAPTER ELEVEN

passion escaped her. Andros cowered.

Edwin chimed in, "That's all well and good young lady, but what happens now?" Cutting to the point as per usual.

"People no longer live under you like animals. That's what happens."

"I'm sure those words mean a lot to you, but that doesn't really answer my question. What do we actually *do*?"

Irritation smeared itself all over Shiara's face. Obviously she was not cut out to be a silver-tongue. Having remembered what she had just done to Chase, the mob took a step back as her expression soured.

"I think what my friend Edwin is asking you, is how? After all, we don't want to end up in chaos like Illorne."

Marin's words changed her demeanour from frustration to concern.

"I... liberated Illorne."

"Liberation? Panic on the streets with people fighting over food is not what I call liberation." Andros was obnoxious and pompous, but he was still right.

"I... didn't know that happened." Shiara seemed pained by the thought, which brought Marin some comfort with an inkling of hope; Andros just saw it as another opening to throw his weight around.

"That's what happens when you tear down a perfectly good system and leave without saying so much as a word!"

"Perfectly good?" Shiara's glare was as dangerous as any swing of a sword. The venom in her eyes made Andros shrink back into the crowd.

"Please ignore Andros; even the change of the seasons is too progressive for him. Caspir is far from perfect; I've been trying my best to do something about it." Marin was telling the truth, although he would admit that there was some embellishing upon his part.

He continued, "I understand what you are trying to do. As someone who wasn't born into nobility, I know how the system is unfair, but that doesn't mean we should throw the good away with the bad."

This wiry woman who commanded such fear from the crowd revealed an expression they had not yet seen, one of confusion and curiosity. Marin correctly suspected that she was positive about his comments but also wary that it might be nothing more than deception.

"Tell me, what are these *good* things that shouldn't be thrown away?" she inquired.

"We secure a system of importing and exporting goods, allowing people to have livelihoods with stability in getting their food and work." He could see the question on her lips before she asked it, so was ready to answer: "Granted the distribution of said goods is far from ideal, but the *process* works and can be fixed. It's certainly a damn sight better than the lawlessness left in Illorne where the strong prey on the weak."

Marin could sense the headway he was making, alongside the nagging disapproval from some of the nobles who felt like they were being sold out. Surely even they would see reforms were better than chaos? Wouldn't they?

"Your council leader is gone; this is your chance to fix everything that is broken."

The merchant councillor had long thought about what his ideal governance for Caspir looked like, yet never dreamed it would ever be in touching distance. He saw a council made up not of noblemen and himself, but of people representing every walk of life. A noble sat between a merchant and a seamstress, or a rancher, or a guardsman. But how? Was this dream even possible? He had learnt that the bureaucracy required to achieve even the most well-meaning of ideals could distort it beyond recognition. Getting a bunch of nobles to agree on something was challenging enough, never mind a council made up of people from all sorts of backgrounds. Supreme authority, that was the key.

"We will need you to make that happen," Marin concluded.

"Me? I have done my work. I am no ruler," she protested.

"That may be so, but you *are* the rightful head of Caspir. We need that symbol of authority to navigate change."

Shiara could see the logic of his position; it was undeniable, even though she didn't want to trouble herself with the affairs of bureaucrats.

"An authority is the last thing I want to be. However, I will do as you ask and remain in Caspir for a few days."

"A few days might not be enough," Marin warned.

CHAPTER ELEVEN

"That is all the time I can spare. You will have to make it enough time." Her voice gave away the tell-tale signs of irritation at getting sucked into something she wanted no part of. "I aim to be on my way to Fimego by next week," she continued.

Edwin rejoined the conversation. "So you are planning to slay another ghost?"

Shiara's eyes narrowed with a resolve that could not be bested.

"No. I am planning on slaying them all."

ACT TWO

CHAPTER TWELVE

Shiara travelled light, gripping only a couple of satchels as she made her way out of Caspir and towards the city's herpiary. Her journey from Illorne to Caspir had been achievable by foot, but she'd need transportation to travel to Fimego. Especially if she wanted to avoid the roads. Alongside her strode a man she had come to respect over the last week – the merchant-turned-councillor with exquisite facial hair. Beside him sauntered another man, one whose innumerate laughter lines and slight paunch gave away his life of luxury. Shiara was not fond of Fredo. She saw him as a jovial creature, part clown, part deceiver. A man who would swagger even when walking along a dirt track, he and his flowing garments seemed full of bluster and an unnatural air that she could only describe as smugness. It had taken Marin some time to convince Shiara that she could benefit from taking him along on the trip. Eventually she had conceded to his logic, albeit under protest. After all, he was right: she knew very little of the intricacies of city life, so having a renowned silver-tongue to help her navigate them would be of great benefit. Walking into Caspir was easy enough, but she suspected that ease would be a thing of the past with talk of her exploits spreading further. No doubt some would try to stop her entering Fimego, just as Chase had attempted in Caspir. Fredo's profession had taught him all the secret ways in and out of places and there was no point in denying that; her personal preference had no place in matters this important. Nevertheless, using the tool of a ghost that she had worked so hard to slay didn't sit well with her. Shiara hoped that once her ambitions were realized, there would no longer be any need for Fredo's line of work.

"Have you ridden much before?" Fredo inquired as they arrived at the herpiary. Shiara had not, yet she wasn't going to admit it to him, instead opting for a polite grunt. The herpiary was a large enclosure, somewhat reminiscent of the threadwurm ranches, although far less moist and with much more robust fences. They were designed to keep things in, rather than out. Within its boundaries sat a multitude of large reptilian beasts, about three times as long as she was tall. Shiara had not seen this many in one place before and was not ashamed to admit to herself that the spectacle was beautiful, even if it was unnatural to cage so many animals. She consoled herself by remembering the threadwurms, and how their captive versions no longer resembled their wild cousins. It was probably a similar thing, where they'd come to depend on people in the same way. The lizards were commonly known as "sandbacks", because of the colour of the scales on their backs as well as their texture. The rest of their scales were a darker mottled brown, the colour of churned-up riverbanks. Their dewlaps glinted with a silvery sheen as they hung down from the creatures' necks; Shiara had seen other animals in the wild use similar flaps of skin for mating displays. These creatures seemed much more streamlined and elegant than the ones she was familiar with, which the farmers used for ploughing. It was equal parts amazing and troubling to Shiara that people had bent the very nature of animals to their will, breeding them stocky and tough for fieldwork, whilst simultaneously rearing others differently, for transportation. Apparently in Fimego they had taken this one step further and raced the animals for sport. She could understand them being bred for necessity far more than for pleasure; that was to be expected given that much of her life had been about necessity. A part of her was excited at the prospect of watching these magnificent reptiles thundering around a track in all their glory, but her pride and dogmatism made sure to keep these thoughts pushed to one side.

As the trio approached the sandbacks and touched the rough scales of the animals, Shiara felt a twinge of nerves. She had slain two immortal guardians yet the notion of mounting one of these lizards made her wince with anxiety. In the wild, one steered clear of large animals like this and one

CHAPTER TWELVE

certainly didn't contemplate perching atop it. As was her way, necessity often meant confronting things she might rather not, and getting to Fimego as quickly as possible was essential. The longer it took, the more resistance she could reasonably expect to find.

"I'm just coming," called out a gruff voice from behind them; a voice that sounded like it was more proficient at shouting than most men were at talking. Turning round, they were greeted by the hurrying figure of a stubby little man with skin the colour of walnut. Whilst his stature was not impressive, his bulk suggested that solid sinew and muscle was all one would find under his shirt. Splashed across his chin was a wiry hedge-like mess of hair that somehow didn't seem to fit the definition of being a beard, especially in the presence of Marin's cultivated bristles. Gripped in his almost paw-like hands was a saddle, bridle and reins.

"Let me just get this one fixed up for you, then I'll do the other one," he assured them whilst gesturing to two of the fantastic sandback specimens before them. "It's a pleasure to serve you, ma'am."

Marin quickly responded, "Thank you. And a word to the wise, I don't think she appreciates being called ma'am."

"Beg yer pardon... miss?" The herpiary hand apologized.

Shiara exchanged glances with the merchant councillor, who gave off an air of being pleased with his correction of the man. Sadly he had missed the point – it wasn't about the "ma'am"; it was about the idea of him having to treat her any differently to someone else. She sighed and let it go. There was little point addressing it now but at least the man she had picked to chair the council was trying. Shiara couldn't expect everyone to change right away; it would take time. Marin had taught her a thing or two himself; whilst a ghost can be slain in a day, building something worthwhile in his place would take longer.

The saddle being affixed to the first sandback was interwoven with fine glimmering threads of stunning yellow and turquoise. Garish and lavish, she knew who it belonged to.

"Have you missed me, old girl?" Fredo purred as he caressed the now saddled lizard. It seemed responsive, perhaps his silver-tongue charms extended beyond his own species? The genuine affection shown by this "spy" for a simple creature surprised Shiara, who had expected Fredo to be the sort of man who did not care for others beyond what he could use them for. What was even more remarkable was the manner in which the creature's eyes seemed to echo the sentiments, its shutter-like eyelids fluttering over its bulbous pupils like a young girl snatching glimpses of her sweetheart.

Shiara turned her head to look at the beast that she would soon mount; the same rapport was not there. In fact, not much of anything was there; it could not be more uninterested as it tucked into the dried-out husks of moths in its trough. Its eyes swivelled and gave her a brief examination, then rolled back to focus on its meal. Clearly it was more concerned with eating its fill before having to travel than with who it might be taking along for the ride. Extending her fingers, Shiara caressed the sandback's scales, attempting to mirror what her travelling companion had just done. A snort was all the acknowledgement given, and she half suspected the act was more about discharging a piece of carapace from its nostrils than anything else. Nature was something to be respected and cautious of. She was well versed in surviving in the wilderness and how to interact with wild animals – as little as possible; much like with people, the concept of befriending or building a relationship with one was alien to her.

The stubby man now emerged with another saddle and began fastening it to Shiara's uninterested mount. Brown and grey, the saddle mirrored her own attire, which despite being offered the finest silks in Caspir, remained her threads of choice. Rumour had it that some people in the city had begun to adopt similar colours. Was it a sign of solidarity with her cause? Or had she accidentally become chic? The attendant stretched out his palm to help Shiara climb up; she considered ignoring the help but frankly she needed it. Once seated on the two steeds, the ropes keeping them tethered were untied and they both pivoted on the spot, eager for the journey. One more so than the other. If it was not for her strong will and even stronger thighs, she would have been cast to the ground.

"Have you ridden much before?" Fredo repeated with a smirk. He could see she was having difficulties. His perception was second to none.

CHAPTER TWELVE

"I'll be fine," she grunted, trying to maintain the illusion of control. Surely it couldn't be too hard to get the hang of this?

Marin looked up at them both with trepidation at this new world that was being shaped, saying, "Be careful out there." It was not sort of the incisive remark that he had come to expect from himself; it was fair to say his mind was racing with a million other things so could be excused.

"Marin, we'll be fine." Fredo pronounced.

"Make sure you are, and look after..." he paused, realizing that Shiara would probably be doing the majority of the looking after, at least until they got to Fimego, "...each other."

Shiara was finding herself confronted with emotions she didn't expect. Part of her would miss Marin's company, although she convinced herself that was just in comparison to her silver-tongued associate.

"You take care of yourself too, and more importantly, the people."

They trotted off out of the herpiary, with Marin and Fredo exchanging some parting remarks. The sandbacks moved with undulating grace, their bodies constantly snaking along in continuous motion. Their speed took Shiara aback; she knew it would be a quicker way to travel, but it didn't look quite this fast when she saw others riding. The walls of the city began to shrink behind them as the track opened out, and farmland filled the view. It would take half an hour to get beyond their limits and to the main trade route, but this would not be the path they'd take. It was more sensible to head east to trek through the rural communities and the untamed wilderness. Her lizard tossed her about in the saddle, much to the amusement of Fredo. Shiara thought Fredo would soon be the one to look silly once they were far from the comforts and lifestyle to which he was so accustomed. It would be a long week of travelling for them both.

CHAPTER THIRTEEN

The two riders dipped below the horizon, leaving Marin alone with his thoughts and his responsibilities. They'd accomplished much in the last week, yet that was only the beginning. A new council had been formed with representatives from all walks of life; now he had to try and get them to agree on things. This was to be done without the authority of Shiara standing next to him. Would they listen to him? Surely they could see what was at stake if they didn't? Today was to be the first full meeting with him as the council's chair, a position he relished when given but already suspected would become a burden. Marin's hand had strayed to twirling his beard whilst he contemplated his new reality, dislodging his otherwise pristine facial hair for a few seconds before catching himself and smoothing it back to its normal impressiveness.

    His boots were loud on the dirt track as he made his way back to the walls, and not even the sound of stones grinding beneath his feet could distract him from his pontifications. The first thing on the agenda was to provide shelter for the Greys. Shiara had suggested throwing out the noblemen and allowing their properties to be used, but Marin advised that this would just fuel the division they wanted to eliminate. You could take from people to help others, but everyone had limits. Marin had discovered the inflexibility of the nobles in regard to limits before; his new-found power did not make the prospect of confronting them any more appealing. The threat of being turfed out, or even executed as Shiara had once suggested – jokingly, he hoped – would presumably free up some room for him to manoeuvre?

CHAPTER THIRTEEN

The dirt cushioning his steps turned to stone as he made his way inside Caspir. There was a renewed hope within the people that he passed in the outer districts. For them, hope had always been something within the domain of fanciful stories and prophecies, not real life. The effect was that this reluctant positivity was very much tempered by cynicism and fear. Change often brought about horrible consequences for some, Illorne being a prime example. The older citizens were no stranger to popular figures boasting about how things were going to be different, only for them to carry on just as before. A saviour was a ridiculous concept, and even if it wasn't, Marin was conclusively not one. Shiara was the one to slay Chase. She was the person that some held their faith in, even to the extent of worship in some places. Rumour had it that groups of individuals were coming together to form a new church, one coalescing around "The Slayer of Ghosts". Religion in Caspir was something that just bubbled along – nothing extreme or overly devout like in Fimego, where deviation was not tolerated – but just a simple solace for people who could find the comfort of community together. Marin wasn't a believer; well, not really. He couldn't fathom how the world came to be, although was quick to acknowledge that there were many things in life that escaped his understanding. After all, magic used to be commonplace, which seemed quite preposterous by today's standards, aside from the ghosts of course. Religion had not been the cause of any strife in the city as far as he was aware; nevertheless, a new cult springing up during a time of radical change would no doubt bring challenges. The fervour of faith had done remarkably unpleasant things in Fimego, where their ghost Mara had styled herself into a sacred queen at the head of her own religion. There were cruel punishments for those who challenged her divinity, or so the stories went. People tended to just disappear, so information on their fates was patchy and assuming the worst seemed a safe bet. Marin dreaded to think how she would react to Shiara's presence, especially given her prowess in combat. She regularly held tourneys to keep herself sharp, either that or she took joy in slaughtering the challengers. People in Caspir and elsewhere often discussed Mara's rule and why Fimego had become a city of fanatics and cultists. Marin suspected it had something to do with being the closest city to Latan. The bloodshed at the hands of the mad ghost in the vicinity would certainly prompt respect and terror in equal measure. Perhaps deification was the people's way of trying to avoid a similar massacre? No wonder his mind was somewhat unsettled at the thought of a new cult of personality growing within his city's walls.

As Marin worked his way from one district to another, the demeanour of people changed. Whilst those with nothing hoped for any change, those with something to lose grew more suspicious and protective. By the time he had tracked his way to the council building, the expressions of people were distrustful at best. Many remained indoors much of the day, scared that if they left, they may not have a house to return to. The parade of "commoners" making their way to the council chambers did not reassure these nobles. Rarely would you expect to see their ilk among the fine tapestries at the centre, yet here they were. And what's more, most of the nobles had lost their seats on the council to these very people they deemed unsavoury.

The guards had been more vigilant than usual since Chase's death. Marin imagined that it was not only due to Caspir's new paradigm, but because it had been their job to keep Shiara out of the courtyard and they wanted to overwrite their previous failure. The merchant council leader had gained greater esteem in the last week, so that where a brief vocal greeting had once sufficed, the guards now dipped their heads in deference as he entered the building.

The council chamber was unlike it had been at any time before. Noisy. Crowded. Raucous. Today saw all the newly appointed councillors together in one place, and many of them weren't happy. Especially one familiar face, who had clung onto his last vestige of power: Andros. He sat next to Edwin and another one of the nobles whose name escaped Marin; he was sure it was something dull. Whilst he couldn't hear the conversation, he noticed every so often the glint in Andros's eye was snuffed out by an undoubtedly sensible retort from Edwin. It felt like a lifetime ago that he himself was part of those verbal jousts. He had accomplished more in the last week than he had during the rest of his tenure on the council. And he certainly felt

CHAPTER THIRTEEN

it; sleep was far more elusive than he would have liked and his hand ached from all the writing and rewriting he had been forced to do.

Marin came to the large chair where Chase had once sat. A feeling of awe, trepidation and bemusement flooded his body. He heard himself breathing and it took him a few moments to realize it was because the chamber had come to a halt, not because his lungs were working hard – even though they were. The cold stone was far less comfortable on his posterior than he would have liked. A cushion for future meetings was definitely in order. Perhaps a plush red one with gold trim.

"All right everyone. We've got a lot to get through today." That was an understatement of magnificent proportions.

Marin listed off the basic procedural structure of how the meeting would go and within minutes it was obvious that many had neither the stomach nor patience for such things. Say what you like about the nobles, they were nothing if not comfortable with bureaucracy. Murmurings grew as the members were eager to get to the first point of order.

"Settle down. The first point of order for this meeting is to work out how we house the people in the brown quarter."

An explosion of noise followed and a mixture of suggestions and snide remarks ranging from "Send them to work on the farms" to "Take the houses of the nobles for those who need them", tussled with one another in the air.

"Quiet down!" Marin bellowed, surprised by the force and gusto at which the words left his lips. "As difficult as it may sound, we need to find a way to do this that everyone here can agree upon."

Rather than shouting, the chamber erupted into laughter. After the sniggering subsided, a respected and intelligent voice posited a suggestion: "Now, of course we aren't going to take people out of their homes; making other people homeless doesn't achieve anything. What we need to do is use the space we *do* have more efficiently. I for one don't need all the rooms in my house, and I'm sure the other nobles are the same." Edwin's words struck a chord for many; glancing towards Andros, it seemed to have struck a bell within him instead. An alarm bell.

"Preposterous! I won't have my house sullied with the presence of filthy strangers!" Andros's outbursts were well known to those who had been on the council before, but for those who came from different walks of life it was the boot-heel of classism trying to stamp them out. The cacophony of noise began anew, this time with greater vigour. It took longer for Marin to regain order than before; his bawling could no longer compete with the rabble. Eventually he wrestled back control and tried to suggest a new path forward. As a start he offered the plan of consulting the nobles about how much space they could spare and surveying their properties. Obvious objections were raised by the nobles; those of less standing also felt aggrieved. They felt that the poorest being given luxury accommodation of the finest degree was an affront to those who worked hard and got nothing. Fortunately, Marin had an answer to these complaints.

"If you think groups of people sharing a room, even a luxury room, is better than having your own lodgings, then by all means we can arrange for you to change places with them."

It pole-axed some of the dissenters – there was a lot to be said for privacy and freedom, which was too often taken for granted. Several asked how long these measures were for, because if they weren't to be permanent arrangements, surely something else would have to be done?

"These measures will be taken to remove people from living in the streets, until we can get them back on their feet and earning a wage to support themselves."

This comment seemed to deflect scrutiny from others, even though Marin his own reservations. How were they going to just magic up some new jobs? What if they did create new jobs that ended up being better than the ones others had? Would that spark a new wave of complaints? It was obvious that pleasing everyone was impossible, but what he really worried about was whether it was possible to keep the powder dry in this keg of a city.

CHAPTER FOURTEEN

The wood crackled as reds, oranges and yellows danced atop it. Fredo rubbed his hands and held them towards the fire for warmth. Sleeping outside was something he had only done on rare occasions, usually with the aid of copious amounts of alcohol. Shiara was unfazed. It had become her natural habitat over the years, and nobody could deny the beauty of a campfire in the dark wilderness. They had made good progress on their journey but far less with each other. Essential communication was about all that they had managed, which was exactly how Shiara wanted it. Fredo was of a different mind altogether.

"It's amazing how loud the empty wilderness can be." A rather uninspiring opener, Fredo didn't want to rock the boat too much.

"That's because it isn't empty. All those clicks, hisses and hoots are living creatures. Just because somewhere isn't thick with people, doesn't mean there's nothing there."

He had struck a chord; a shame it was very much the wrong one.

"Of course, but you don't think of animals being as raucous and ready to spew noise everywhere as you do with people." Her distaste for people, especially larger groups, was not difficult to discern. Being the silver-tongue that he was, Fredo used that in an attempt to build a rapport.

"I can't disagree with you on that; however, I wouldn't call this noise," Shiara replied.

A spark lit up behind Fredo's eyes as some headway was finally being made.

"Absolutely, it's far closer to a musical composition. The percussion of insects and melodies of birds, bats and other miscellaneous flying things."

Shiara's body relaxed and turned towards him a little more.

"When I was younger, I used to lie back in the middle of nowhere and just listen. I always thought it was as if nature were playing its own song. Once we get closer to the river and add in the sounds of running water, you'll really like it." She felt a twinge of unease as her words opened up more than she would have liked.

"So you spent a lot of time alone out here whilst growing up?" Fredo probed.

"Yes."

"That must have been hard?"

"No. Not really."

Fredo had learnt that most people want nothing more than to talk about themselves; all they needed was an opportunity to do so. It was the secret trick that actually made the job of a silver-tongue far easier than one would first assume. The slayer of ghosts was apparently an exception to the rule.

"Not even when you started out?"

"Well obviously yes... but it doesn't take too long to get used to it out here. Not like living in the city with its unconquerable challenges."

The plan of asking a stupid-sounding question to put her in a position of superiority and thus encourage her open up more was a successful one.

"And which city was that?"

"Omdurtur".

Fredo knew she was opening up more than she wanted, so reassuring her was essential to keep the conversation flowing.

"I don't blame you for leaving. Especially if you lived near the stacks. No place for a child." It seemed to him a safe bet that her scorn mapped directly onto industrialization and the workers' struggle; the smokestacks in Omdurtur were the perfect representation of that. Rather than replying though, she looked sullen and lost to her memories, undoubtedly ones that were less than enjoyable.

"So tell me Shiara, how old were you when you left?"

CHAPTER FOURTEEN

She snapped back from her drifting trail of thought, becoming thoroughly disgruntled by this particular line of questioning.

"Old enough."

The abruptness punctuated the conversation with a considerable full stop. After a few moments where looks were exchanged rather than words, she decided it was her turn to go on the offensive.

"You know nothing about what my life has been like," she growled.

"Well I *am* trying to find out." His remark clearly had her flustered.

"How could some silver-tongue, whose entire purpose is to dine in the lap of luxury, possibly understand poverty or desperation?"

"More than you would suspect. I wasn't born into this life, I earned it."

"And how exactly did you earn a life of spying and deceit?" she spat.

"Through necessity." He paused for dramatic effect. "I started out on the streets as a nobody."

Shiara didn't believe him at first but there was something about the tone of his voice that gave his words sincerity.

"As a kid, me and a few others had to steal to keep ourselves fed, taking the occasional beating for our trouble." Her sneer morphed into puzzlement.

"Then how did you end up as a silver-tongue? I can't imagine the nobles were fond of thieves?"

"After one too many kickings from getting caught, I thought there had to be a better way. Rather than stealing from them, perhaps I could get them to give me what I wanted instead."

"Begging?" she queried.

"Scamming," he replied. "If you could trick someone into giving you their money, they'd be far less likely to resort to violence and definitely wouldn't report you. Who'd want to admit that they were conned?"

For all his tricks and silver-tongued charms, it was his honesty that was now beginning to break down the walls between them.

"How?"

Fredo grinned, clearly proud of his past accomplishments and relishing having someone to boast about them to.

"It's all about identifying what people want. For example, if someone believes they can save money by cutting corners on ingredients or materials, all you have to do is let them. They know they're getting something substandard, that's the point. Of course, they don't know quite how substandard it is until I've walked off with their money."

She didn't seem impressed.

"Even better is selling services that they don't need, or ones that don't even exist. If you can convince someone they *need* something to protect their home, business or possessions, you'll find them queuing up to give you coin."

Shiara was unsure whether such activities were admirable or deplorable. Despite the methods, getting one over on the nobles was certainly a cause she could get behind.

"So let me get this straight, you'd just make stuff up and they'd believe it?"

"You make it sound so simple. It's an art form. You need to learn about what makes them tick, then sell it in just the right way."

"And they made you a silver-tongue for doing that?"

"Once you've conned just about everyone worth conning, you get a reputation. They figured if I could trick them for myself, I could do the same in other cities on Chase's behalf and they wouldn't have to worry about me anymore."

She shook her head in amusement.

"Well, I say *they* figured, but I'm pretty sure I talked them into it."

Shiara snorted and let out a giggle.

It was a welcome relief from her intensity to see her laugh, for both of them. There hadn't been much for her to laugh about for quite some time. She didn't regret the focus that had consumed her life taking up the time for the things many considered normal; nevertheless it was good to find joy in something simple again.

From there the conversation began to flow more naturally; whilst Shiara didn't open up more about her childhood, she explained what it was like to live out in the wilderness.

"Out here there's no people to steal food from; you've got to forage or

CHAPTER FOURTEEN

hunt it yourself. And there's very little room for failure."

She described the different berries and plants that one could eat and how she discovered the ones you couldn't eat the hard way. Stomach cramps and sickness were all part of the trial and error required to survive out here, but the wrong trial could wind up in a fatal error.

There were plenty of questions that Fredo wanted to ask, but now was certainly not the right time. The groundwork was set for them to actually forge more than just an acquaintance of convenience, and instead build on some common ground to form a proper connection. Trying to sleep out here was not as easy for Fredo as it was for Shiara, snuggling up to a sandback was a poor substitute for threadwurm sheets in a heated mansion. It wasn't the surroundings that were the biggest factor denying him sleep, but his curiosity. And one question in particular that he looked forward to having answered.

"Where *did* Shiara get that magic sword of hers from?"

CHAPTER FIFTEEN

"All right, everybody line up" bawled the guard. The new arrivals to Caspir shuffled to form what could loosely be described as a queue. Their clothes were rather tattered and dirty; the looks in their eyes far worse. This wasn't the first batch of desperate newcomers they had received from Illorne, but it was certainly the largest. Those who had got out first told stories of lawless bandits stringing up the wealthy and installing themselves as supreme leaders in various districts of the city. Houses burned, people fought and lost to protect their belongings, and the entire city was shattered into warring factions vying for control via any means possible. Marin looked upon these crowds from behind the guards. It was heart-breaking to see. He himself had heard of one woman who was chained up for continual abuse by one gang; too weak to escape when she had her chance, she chose to take her own life. Another had told him that the dead lay in the streets untended and that some had taken to eating them because of the lack of food. These were only the stories he had heard; he couldn't imagine the horrors that these new arrivals, who'd been in among the chaos for longer, had seen.

Unfortunately, Marin had no time to wear his emotional hat; now was the time for practicality and solutions. These refugees had nowhere to go. Caspir was the closest city to Illorne, the next being Maluani, and they would be the last place to accept outsiders. Safety was paramount but Caspir was already dealing with its own people. How would it be able to manage a whole additional district's-worth of people? The redistribution of resources from the nobles was very slow going; in order to cope it would have to be sped

CHAPTER FIFTEEN

up, which undoubtedly would ruffle more than a few feathers. As for the citizens of Caspir, how would they feel about sharing their crowded city with more people? Marin was fully aware that the overcrowding was more a result of unequal distribution of land, but would the citizens see it that way? And who knew anything about these people they were letting in? What if some of the gangs who couldn't make it in Illorne were trying their hand here? What if this precipitated a similar uprising in Caspir?

These were questions that Marin needed to contend with – just not right now. Even in only pragmatic terms this was suffering that needed alleviating. They were all just people like himself, victims of circumstance. "A circumstance called Shiara," he thought to himself. She had meant well but he couldn't claim she had fully considered the effects of her actions. If it wasn't for his appeals to her judgment the same would have followed in his city too. Upheaval and change were not to be trifled with.

Thinking of "what could have been" was of no use now; leave that to the philosophers, he mused; what *was* happening was of infinitely more importance to Marin. He would need to make arrangements and make them fast. Where could he house this many people at such short notice? He'd need council approval to redistribute space from those well off and that would take too long. Everywhere with space inside the walls was already taken up with people. Or was it? Marin's days as a merchant were apparently behind him, yet he still had his warehouse. It wasn't much and still had some bits and pieces inside, but they could be sold off or used to help the refugees. He now lived in the council building so the room was going to waste. Marin was annoyed he hadn't thought of this sooner.

"Could you lot come with me? The rest of you, keep things calm, I've had an idea."

The head of the council peeled off a group of guards to help him prepare his warehouse down the street. It wasn't that far away; it made sense for merchants to keep their stock close enough to the walls for transportation purposes. The building was vast and ugly, blighted by the dirt and filth that was more abundant in this part of the city. It had very clearly seen a lot of use and was more about function than form, the opposite of most buildings in

Caspir. There were other storehouses that were similar in this area; perhaps maximizing space in them could free up another warehouse for habitation? He'd certainly have to look into that in the days to come.

Marin unlocked the substantive metal doors, and they juddered open to reveal what was once a treasure trove of goods. Marin and his clerk had already offloaded many of the goods, although he suspected that the clerk had probably skimmed a lot of the value himself. Boxes of fine cloth were still piled high in the middle and a few other textile products such as curtains and bedding still remained. They had proven difficult to shift due to being a couple of seasons out of date, yet not so out of date as to have come back around again. Now they'd come in handy to make the place a little more hospitable for its new tenants.

"So, the plan is to house as many of the Illorne refugees as possible here. I know it's not ideal, but there's plenty of cloth here to set up partitions and bedding."

The guards seemed perplexed. They had been tasked to do all sorts of additional duties in the last week that would have seemed alien before, but being home-makers was certainly the furthest departure from their skill sets.

"That's all well and good but we haven't got the faintest idea where to start," complained one of them, whose plain appearance was right from the pages of a children's book. "Average" was an insufficient word to describe how average he was.

"I can show you, and there are a couple of seamstresses I'll get to help you too."

The guards looked unimpressed by Marin's plan, but he was the boss. Somehow this immaculately bearded merchant was now in charge. Not just of them, but of the whole of Caspir. Marin would be the first to point out *he* was the one serving *them*; nevertheless, it certainly didn't feel like that for many.

Having set them to task, Marin returned to the rest of the guards and refugees to let them know of his ingenious solution. Almost skipping with pride, he was beginning to think he was getting rather good at this council

CHAPTER FIFTEEN

leader thing. This joviality soon found its perfect foil. He returned to the square where he had left the refugees and guards: now there were more people. A lot more people. Surrounding the lot of them was a ring of individuals clad in dull brown, each holding a candle. The "Church of Shiara" appeared to be far more organized and of greater number than previously expected.

Marin slowly approached the guards. They were on edge. Nobody knew what they wanted. The refugees were bristling with anxiety; some froze in fear; all looked up at the candle-lit faces encircling them.

"What do they want?" whispered Marin to one of the guards.

"How should I know? They just showed up," he shrugged in response.

The air became thick and cloying with apprehension. The councillor considered scenes like these were more akin to something found in Fimego.

One of the figures stepped in front of the rest and puffed their chest out to make their proclamation.

"Hear me children of Illorne. The old ways have died. The false gods we once called protectors have been banished into nothingness, yet we remain. We follow that which was prophesied and has come to pass. We follow the true religion and the prophet Shiara."

The brown-clad disciples parroted back the figure's last two words in an eerie low-note hum.

"You can surrender your heathen lifestyles and join us in worship of the one true faith. Lay down your sorrow at the passing of Hectin and be welcomed into our church. Those who come with us will be given shelter and food. The one true faith looks after its own. Give up being children of Illorne and join us as children of Shiara."

Again, the devotees chanted the last few words, "Children of Shiara".

Pushing back the hood of their cloak, the spokesperson revealed her face. A warm face. Gentle and compassionate, yet resolute. Her hair was lighter than most people's, almost touching on blonde and, like her clothing, it seemed unnaturally dull. Her skin was a light fawn colour; a comparatively pale tone for the six cities. She spread a smile across her face as people behind her parted to form a corridor. Holding out a hand to one of the refugee families she coaxed them in and hugged each one of them before directing them towards her fellow worshippers. The tension in the square dissipated more with each refugee that was embraced. "Where are they going to house them?" wondered Marin. He had underestimated their resources, it would seem. The majority of the crowd siphoned off towards her, leaving a smaller portion for Marin to rehouse. Once all had chosen their place, the candle-holding patrons turned and marched away behind them.

The guards looked none the wiser than when he had first returned, and for good reason. What did this mean for Caspir? The cautious part of Marin couldn't shake the feeling that this was something he would inevitably have to deal with at some point, for better or worse. At least on the positive side, housing those who had fled Illorne would be a much easier task now. With the numbers that remained, his warehouse scheme would easily satisfy demand and keep them in relatively decent conditions. This number of people could live quite comfortably for some time under his storehouse roof, alleviating the immediacy of finding a permanent solution. Perhaps the Church of Shiara had done them all a favour and made his job a little more likely to succeed. Despite this beneficial arrangement at present, an insistent feeling of worry continued to gnaw at the back of his mind. What was Caspir going to become? He hoped it would be a new beacon of freedom, prosperity and equality, but what if that wasn't the case? What if this was the beginning of a slide into becoming like Fimego? Or worse still... Maluani?

CHAPTER SIXTEEN

The walls of Maluani towered above the ground unlike any other city, for it was the only city to have built upon the original walls, extending them upwards like colossal monsters of steel and stone. In addition, an exterior wall outside of the farms had also been constructed on the tenuous premise of keeping people out, when in reality it was to keep people in. Atop these fortifications patrolled armour-clad guards, the most fearsome and potent of all the cities. Gripped in their powerful hands were ebony black crossbows capable of turning a man into a lifeless rag-doll in mere moments. Tellingly, these foreboding watchmen were not looking out beyond the limits of the walls, but within them – surveying those toiling in the fields, waiting for the slightest mistake upon which they could pounce. The farms were expansive and filled with activity. Unlike Caspir, the field-hands lived within the city rather than on the land, routinely corralled by their supervisors to work the soil each day during the light. Light which did not last as long because of the towering walls. Ferried between their meagre accommodations of night and their backbreaking labour of the day, little time or energy was left for much else. Especially not for questioning their circumstances. Questions were almost forbidden within Maluani, unless they related to accomplishing tasks for the glory of Takis, the ever-living ruler of the city.

There was no council here. No dialogue between the people and their ghost protector, just the dictates of an iron-willed despot. From this there was no respite, the slow death in the fields or the quick end of a crossbow bolt. Koralia would often weigh the benefits of rushing the guards and being put down quickly against the fear of survival and the unending torture that would follow. Her hands, rough and dirtied from a hard morning's planting, swept back a thick black curl of hair as she mopped her sodden brow. Delicate was not a word that was applicable to Koralia, but she was elegant in her own stocky way. She was sculpted into the muscular epitome of efficiency by years on the farm. Koralia still retained some of the exuberance of youth, more than one would expect from a woman in her twenty-fourth year. This meant she spent some of her limited "free time" pursuing goals other than eating and resting. The callouses on her palms were not just from digging, planting and harvesting, but also climbing. During the midnight hours, she and a few others would scramble up towers and even the wall in a bid to feel... something. To get above it all and taste freedom, however fleeting it may be. Up above it all, one didn't have to fear spies listening in and she could see anyone coming from a long way off. Tonight she had some news to share with her closest friend and climbing partner that daren't fall on the wrong ears.

As a general rule, the guards in the fields weren't too bothered about the labourers conversing, provided the topics avoided politics or change. Not all of Takis's agents were this accommodating. One in particular they had nicknamed The Owl, due to his heartless nature, beady-eyed observational skills and penchant for slashing people up. When he was on watch, field-hands would be wary. They were nothing but a commodity to him, just more animals in service of the ever-living Takis, and he was happy to cull any stragglers without hesitation. At least the other guards still saw them as people, albeit inferior ones.

Koralia had been working close to Minos for most of the day, yet was unable to arrange their plans for later because of the watchful eye of The Owl. Minos worked hard yet always carried himself with a sense of humour, which many thought baffling given the circumstances. The onyx curls of his hair wound tightly to his scalp giving the impression of short hair, despite the strands being a good few inches long when pulled straight. A powerful-looking nose and jawline gave him an authoritative look, one which was undermined instantly when he opened his mouth. Minos was not a serious

CHAPTER SIXTEEN

man, nor a contemplative one; he was best described as a clown. Koralia supposed it was just his way of dealing with life in Maluani. Some tried to rationalize their lot in life; others like herself burned with a passion of defiance; Minos preferred to see the world as a joke. She couldn't argue with that; she just didn't like being the punchline. The most the pair managed to exchange were nods of recognition and gestures to express they'd get together later. Koralia felt the day roll by quickly as her mind mulled over what she had to say and its implications for their future.

As the light faded beneath the lip of the wall, wardens herded them back into the stone domain of the city itself. Citizens were not permitted on the farms after dark, possibly for fear they would steal some of the harvest. Koralia reasoned it was down to Takis's domain extending only to the original wall. Whatever magic bound him to this world kept him trapped within Maluani's inner boundaries and it must be that his subjects remain contained by those same restrictions. The workers broke off into their various groups to sate their hunger. Minos's and Koralia's family lived in the same building and had done so since they were children. This is where their friendship had begun, preparing food with the elderly for the returning workers. Whilst people still had a use, the guards didn't bother them; it was only those deemed a burden on society that Takis ordered to be put down. In their building there were an awful lot of children; women would often choose to churn out offspring rather than work in the fields, mills or workshops. The arduous world of domesticity was more tempting than toiling in the dirt to many young women, and Maluani was always eager for new generations of labourers. "But how could any mother choose to bring a child into this life?" Koralia thought.

Despite the simplicity and blandness of the food, Koralia's hunger rendered its aroma almost divine. Basic starchy grains cooked until stodgy then wrapped in miscellaneous green leaves had never been so desirable. Perhaps her pondering all day had used up more energy than normal, for she was ravenous. Minos was his usual sarcastic self.

"Dolmas again? How will I ever contain my excitement?"

Considering his propensity for devouring inhuman amounts of dolma whenever possible, his disappointment didn't ring true. Koralia suspected that given a platter of the finest meats and fruits, Minos would still find something to complain about.

The building their families shared with a few others was far from impressive. Each group had one large room for several generations to share, divided up with string and fabrics to create some personal spaces. In the middle of the structure was its heart – the kitchen. Here all the families would come together to cook, eat and share in each other's company. If there was one good thing that had come out of their situation it was the binding sense of community that had blossomed. Nobody had the energy to be angry with one another, so everybody just simply got along. It was a small slice of utopia in the otherwise bleak world they had found themselves in.

Parking themselves wherever they could find room, the returning fieldhands were comforted by the respite. The older generation filled up bowls and plates for the children to hand around to the exhausted workers. The eating and conversing could then begin. Before the first bit of food could cross Koralia's lips, her greying aunt revisited her favourite topic.

"So Koralia, when are you and that handsome Minos going to get together?"

It frustrated her for several reasons; chief among them was that relationships didn't interest her, especially not one involving Minos. Aside from this, the notion that pumping out babies was all that she could aspire to was somewhat insulting – she had far bigger plans. Children were one of the few joys some of her family could find, even though she couldn't see it herself. She wasn't annoyed with them, but with the situation in general.

"Minos? Who'd ever want his babies? With a nose like his, they'd be sure to get stuck coming out."

Koralia wasn't adept at making jokes, aside from those that came at Minos's expense. It was truly miraculous quite how much material she could get from his slightly larger than average nose. Ordinarily she would have taken more time with her food, but her eagerness to share the news

CHAPTER SIXTEEN

with Minos in private was burning. She almost finished her meal before he did. Putting their plates in a pile, the pair left their home and headed out into the night.

"What's this big news then?" Minos queried.

"Not now, wait until we're up higher."

Minos rolled his eyes.

"You're always so paranoid; why would anyone care about what we've got to say?"

Koralia stopped, turned to him and placed an arm on his shoulder.

"This isn't joking around. This is serious."

His face was wiped free of smirks. He had only seen her like this a few times before, usually in the aftermath of Takis's or The Owl's brutality. Yet this time it was more intense. More resolute.

She led them to a large building that sat next to the city wall. They had been here before; it was unused and in poor repair, providing plenty of jutting stones to grip and climb up. In silence they mounted the edifice and crawled their way upwards. The surface was cool to the touch, a pleasant sensation on their heavily worked hands in the warm night. Weather had smoothed away some of the rougher edges over the generations, reducing the discomfort of jagged edges or coarse textures. Years of agricultural work had made their hands rugged, providing far better grip than those not subjected to similar struggles. The ground beneath them melted away into the darkness as they ascended; the shadow of the wall cast blackness throughout much of the city. As they reached the top, more moonlight fell onto their faces and the structure to which they clung. The air seemed lighter and more refreshing; they had escaped their lives – for a while. Perching on a ledge at the top, Minos and Koralia surveyed the city beneath them. Stone structures stretched out to the horizon, empty streets dimly lit by flickering lanterns in the homes lining them. In the distance, Takis's domed palace towered above it all, a looming reminder that they were beneath him. The odd silhouette of a guard atop the wall could be made out, far less fearsome as a black speck far away than as an armour-clad oppressor stood in front of you. It was easy to forget one's troubles here; not for Koralia though –

that was why she was here.

"Now you've got me up here, what's the big news?"

She sighed. Her whole life had led up to this, but that didn't mean she wasn't scared.

"Minos. The rumour about Hectin being slain. It's true."

"Nobody can slay a ghost; they're already dead for a start!" His disbelief was partly rooted in fear.

"I'm serious. The prophecy is coming true. The age of ghosts is coming to an end, and that includes Takis."

"Are you sure?"

Koralia didn't need to say it, her face was perfectly clear.

"So what does this mean?" Minos asked.

"It means that Takis is vulnerable. He's no longer an immortal but fallible like the rest of us. As more people learn about Hectin, his grip on power will weaken."

"But won't that just spur him to tighten his control and make things worse?" Minos's words were true; things would undoubtedly worsen before they showed any sign of getting better.

"Yes. Life is going to get harder. However, this will light the fire in the people that we need. This will be the moment when enough becomes enough. The people of Maluani will stand up to Takis. And we will win."

The enormity of the situation and what she was proposing was hard to process. A man largely regarded as a clown was hardly a revolutionary, yet there was no denying his way with people. Koralia had often expressed the desire to overthrow Takis and how such a feat might be achieved, but Minos had never thought it would actually come to pass. He had never seen her filled with such vigour and determination before. Not only was this actually happening but he couldn't stop himself from hoping that with her conviction, it might just be possible.

"Minos. We can do this. The revolution is coming."

CHAPTER SEVENTEEN

Fredo had never been this deep into the wilderness before. He was used to the large open spaces of agricultural land and highways, or the densely packed corridors of the cities; the overgrown thickets of trees were alien to him. It wasn't as if he had to fight through the foliage, but having endless trees boxing you in on all sides would take some getting used to. The fading light of the day filtered through the canopy of leaves above, accompanied by rustling sounds as miscellaneous animals of varying sizes snuffled around unseen. The silver-tongue was very aware of the little creatures populating the woods despite rarely being able to spot any. Outside of pets and working animals he had little experience, so each glance of something small and furry delighted him more than he would like to admit to himself as an urbanite. Their sandbacks snaked through the undergrowth, making far less noise than one would imagine for such sizeable beasts. Nevertheless, the disturbances they made were enough to scare off the wildlife, much to Fredo's disappointment.

"It'll be getting dark soon," Shiara declared. "We should make camp before the light runs out."

Whilst progress in their communications had been made, she was still a bit too matter-of-fact in their conversations for his liking, especially when they were travelling.

"You can pick the spot; try to find somewhere nice and luxurious. A bed with silk sheets wouldn't go amiss." Fredo's humour was still not always welcomed by Shiara, although he'd happily take an eye-roll over no reaction at all.

"We need to make sure we find somewhere away from an owl roost," she said.

"I suppose we don't want them trying to snatch up our supplies."

"Supplies? That's the least of our worries with Cara owls." She warned.

"I'm no expert, but I don't think we have too much to worry about from them? They may be four foot high with razor-sharp talons but when I've seen them on the highways, they seem more scared of us than we are of them. As long as we don't bother them we should be fine, right?"

Shiara shot him a disappointed glare.

"You're right. You're not an expert. I've been attacked by them on more than a few occasions."

"If they are so dangerous, how did you survive living in places like this as a child?" Fredo queried.

"They didn't attack me back then."

"What's changed?" He was puzzled.

"Magic. They really don't like magic. Whether it's my sword or the ghosts, it sends them into a feeding frenzy. Before the age of ghosts, Cara owls used to be pets in the cities, and now..."

"And now they'll rip your face off if you go near their cages. I always thought they just disliked captivity." Fredo's words suggested he wasn't completely convinced of Shiara's understanding of the situation.

"Having seen them out here, I can tell you it's definitely the magic."

She seemed to punctuate her words as if this was the end of the conversation, but Fredo had other ideas.

"Hold on a minute. Before the ghosts, our cities had actual wizards. And they were the ones famous for having pet owls. Maybe it isn't the magic?"

Shiara let out an angry snort as she realized his reasoning was not entirely wrong.

"It doesn't matter. What matters now is that we steer clear of them."

Despite his scepticism of the causes of the Cara owl's noted aggression, he was not going to argue with her solution.

Twilight was very much upon them; they would have to stop soon

CHAPTER SEVENTEEN

regardless of where they were, as travelling by torchlight was far from ideal. The trees in front of them were beginning to open up into a more spacious grove. They both lit their torches after jumping down from their mounts to survey the area for its viability as a camp for the night.

"How do we know if we're near an owl roost or not?" queried the silver-tongue.

"Look up." She may not have been a master of conveying tone like Fredo, nevertheless she had a good grasp of condescension.

Fredo surveyed the canopy above, manoeuvring his head in an attempt to see as much as possible. It occurred to him that he hadn't any real grasp on what an owl nest actually looked like; he assumed he'd probably know it if he saw it.

Tying up the sandbacks, Shiara collected dry twigs and leafy debris, stacking it in a pile in preparation to make a fire. It was important to get it going before the darkness fully enveloped them. Fredo lent a hand, collecting up what he could. His travelling companion clearly had higher standards, discarding at least half of what he collected as unsatisfactory. He couldn't see much difference and suspected it was nothing more than a sly dig at him. Friendship, it would seem, was a long way off.

This time of the evening precipitated a change in their surroundings, the day shift of woodland critters giving way to those of the night. Different noises began to take over the soundscape. One of them in particular was of note. A hoot. It was distant, but was the unmistakable sound of an owl. Fredo glanced over at Shiara, who did not seem bothered.

"Was that... a Cara owl?" he asked.

She nodded. "Don't worry, it's a long way off."

Shiara went back to preparing the fire; the silver-tongue did not feel as reassured as he would have liked to have been. He wondered what was stopping it from coming closer. He suspected sleep would be difficult to come by this evening. The fire flickered into life and cast an orange glow around the grove. For now, there was just enough light filtering from above to see beyond the treeline; Fredo was not looking forward to that visibility waning. He cradled his torch near as he sat down against a trunk. He was determined to stave off his concerns via the only way he knew how – conversation.

"I've been meaning to ask you, how did you get so good with a sword?"

Sitting back from the fire that was now in full swing, she replied: "Practice."

It was going to be another one of those conversations.

"How exactly does one practice for fighting immortal ghosts?" inquired Fredo.

"A lot. You practise a lot."

"Against who? Who is good enough to train you for that? Or did you just fight owls?" He wanted something out of her. "I know the finest duellists in all the cities and none of them come close to being good enough."

"That's because they weren't in any of the cities."

"You're telling me that some nobody on a rural farm somewhere is a greater sword-master than all of the duellists I know combined?"

The evening grew quiet as the words hung in the air. Even the animals seemed to have gone silent at the disbelief on Fredo's lips. Shiara lifted her head up but did not reply.

"Well? I suppose it's not any stranger than finding a magic sword," said Fredo.

Still no reply from the slayer of ghosts, who now seemed preoccupied with something else, or was simply bored of Fredo prattling on.

"Speaking of swords, how *did* you come across it?"

"Shhhh" hissed Shiara, raising her finger towards him whilst looking elsewhere.

"I was just asking."

Her head spun and locked her widening eyes on Fredo, telling him to be quiet for more than just having irritated her.

"Do you hear that?" she whispered.

He shook his head, not wanting to risk being shushed again.

"Exactly. It's too quiet."

She rose to her feet slowly and carefully, peering into the darkening canopy above. The silence broke with a sound they had been hoping to avoid. A screech from the branches above heralded the presence of a Cara owl. A few mirrored sounds from other directions confirmed there were at least three of them in proximity. The size of the owls meant they didn't really fly, instead performing augmented jumps allowing them to pounce on prey. They often did so from the branch of a tree, using height to add extra force to their strike. When hunting they were usually silent, which made their screeches all the more concerning and added weight to the theory of an impending frenzy rather than a coordinated hunt.

A pair dropped down onto the forest floor in front of them, black eyes glistening in the torchlight, razor talons on the end of long and powerful legs. Shiara drew her blade, which seemed to make a satisfied sighing sound as it slid out of its sheath. The magical glimmer of its edge sent the birds into hysteria, screeching and stretching out their wings to appear larger and more fearsome. Talons flexing, they were ready to eviscerate. Perhaps Shiara *was* right about their hatred of magic.

The creatures' feathers ruffled then flattened, making them appear streamlined and even more sinister than before. One surged towards Shiara whilst Fredo was still fumbling for his sword. His weapon of choice had always been his wits; his comfort zone could not have been further away. Springing from the ground with talons aimed at Shiara's face, the owl began its attack. Shiara took it in her stride; after all she had killed two immortal beings already, what was some lowly woodland creature compared to that? Her blade darted in front of her to deflect the razored claw. A pivot then a kick into the bird's side produced a crunching sound as the beast collapsed in on itself. The hollow bones of owls could stand extremes of torsion, but blunt force exposed their brittle weakness. The tip of her blade followed up in its neck to finalize the owl's demise. Another mess of feathers fell from above. Rolling away from its grip, she only sustained scratches from the debris on the floor rather than being ripped by the fearsome talons. Vaulting to her feet with a spring-like motion, she readied her stance as its beak lunged for the exposed flesh of her face. Instead of dodging, Shiara leapt right at the owl and into its chest: knees first. If owls could have a surprised expression it would have been wearing one. Its bite was not calculated for its target approaching this rapidly, and it couldn't help but crumple as its ribs cracked. As the pair fell to the ground, her full weight fatally compressed the bird's body, the owl shrieking as, with a popping crunch, the air escaped its lungs.

    She dismounted the dishevelled pile of feathers to the noise of a hissing sandback. A Cara owl was ripping hunks of meat from its back whilst the lizard, tied up, could do nothing aside from writhe ineffectually. Too preoccupied with its meal to notice her approaching, the bird was easily undone by the edge of Shiara's blade. Slumping the ground, the owl continued trying to devour the flesh in its beak even as its life seeped out through its own wounds. The bleeding injuries of the sandback invited another attacker that swooped down from above; a powerful claw sank its way into the back of the lizard's head and neck, puncturing scales as if they were parchment. A red slick cascaded from the laceration. A vital artery had been opened up and was spilling its bounty in a torrent. There was no salvation for the animal at this point. Each strip the bird tore off and consumed only added to the reptile's suffering. Scaled eyelids began to sag as its pupils dilated and rolled around in their sockets. The squirming gave way to a resigned twitching and panting. The spectacular silvery skin from its neck and the fine threads adorning it drowned under a tide of blood. A majestic creature was reduced to a quivering whimper. Shiara knew this was the way of nature, but that didn't stop her from taking some delight in separating the offending owl's head from its body. In a swift motion her cutlass slipped through the air and passed through the fragile interior of the bird with such might that the two separate chunks of owl careened off in opposite directions. She offered a slight shake of her head in deference to the dying lizard, then remembered she wasn't alone in this fight.

    Spinning on the spot her eyes widened as she saw two figures – one owl, one man – joined together. On closer inspection things were not much better. Fredo lay on his back with the bird fixed squarely on top. The animal was all but dead having impaled itself on Fredo's outstretched blade. Sadly, this was not before its talons had found the soft belly of the silver-tongue and torn it open like wrapping paper. "At least his insides are still... inside,"

CHAPTER SEVENTEEN

Shiara thought to herself; however, being able to see them at all was cause for concern.

"Fredo, are you all right?" It was a stupid question as he was clearly not, but she couldn't think of anything better to say.

"I've been better," came a whimper.

Looking upwards to check for more attackers – there were none – she hurried over to his side. Taking the weight of the animal, she cast it to the ground, the sword still rammed through it. Brushing away a few feathers she took a careful look to assess the damage. It was not good. There was no way she could even attempt to patch him up for anything other than a stopgap measure. She'd need to find someone who could. Running over to a pack and producing a length of cloth, Shiara shredded it to form a makeshift bandage to at least hold his guts in.

"Not my violet tunic... why did it have to be my violet tunic?" Fredo's humour at such a time gifted him new respect in her eyes, although for a moment she did wonder if he really was joking or not.

"This is going to hurt. A lot."

With that, she sat him up and began tightly winding the bandage around his torso, firmly pushing his stomach in to keep him all together. Banging his clenched fist on the ground in pain, he let out a string of obscenities, some of which were so colourful and unique Shiara wondered if they were his own creations. Tying off the ends of the extravagant dressing, it was time to help him to his feet and over to the remaining sandback. The lizard was still clearly terrified from what had just happened, so it was more than ready to get them out of there. Shiara managed to position Fredo in the saddle in such a way as to minimize discomfort. Gripping one of the torches, she threw herself up on top of the beast as well. It would have to carry them both; as long as it was getting away from these owls, she was sure it wouldn't mind too much. Unknotting the fastening on its harness, the sandback was free from the trunk and instantly on the move. Reigns in hand, Shiara gained control and they headed off through the woods by torchlight. She had been here before and knew there was a rural farmstead on the other side of the forest. There she could get Fredo the help he needed. As long as he could hold on.

CHAPTER EIGHTEEN

Marin thumbed the golden tassels of his cloak in his clammy hands. He was nervous. This way of feeling was not something his busy schedule had given him time for, until now. For the first time he was visiting what had become a city within the city; many referred to it as the Church Quarter. People from all walks of life had assembled under one banner, the Church of Shiara. They had taken in refugees and the poor; even a few of the nobles had given up their standing to join them, which went some way to explaining their ample resources. It was clear they were a substantial force in Caspir, but a force for what? That was what Marin was hoping to learn this afternoon. He had arranged a meeting with the straw-haired woman from a few days earlier in the square. He knew nothing about her, not even her name; this rendezvous was coordinated solely through messengers. The thought crossed his mind that maybe she didn't even know, and this was some kind of trap set by someone else? He dismissed these notions as best he could; after all, what reason did he have to fear them? Sure, they had different beliefs, yet so far their actions had been aligned. The Church was giving a home to the homeless along with trying to provide some stability and comfort to the people. There were no credible rumours of anything other than these people being compassionate and caring. Then why was Marin so on edge? He wasn't a ghost protector and was making a concerted effort to not follow in Chase's footsteps. Nevertheless, he couldn't help but suspect there was some animosity towards him and his position.

Walking through the streets of the Church Quarter, he stuck out like a sore thumb. The shimmering grandeur of his threads illuminated those he passed by clad in browns, greys and blacks. He had contemplated wearing something more sombre and outside of his usual comfort zone, then figured that being honest and open about himself would be the better choice. A sizeable part of him regretted that decision as every pair of eyes tracked him as he made his way down the avenues. There was nothing threatening about the glances he was given; it just made him feel self-conscious and out of place – not an unfamiliar feeling given his prior status as the only councilman not of noble blood. This was different though. Marin had often considered himself the plucky underdog, even if that was only relative to the likes of Andros, yet here he was: the symbol of authority and control.

"Blessings of the Slayer unto you," left the lips of many he walked close to as they put their hands together and gave a little bow. In some ways he was jealous of their shared sense of community and how previous differences appeared to have been put aside in favour of a common ideal. Marin wished he could do the same with the government he was just about managing to keep together. If nothing else, perhaps this mysterious leader of theirs could give him some pointers.

The scent of freshly cooked meals hung in the air; little assemblies of people gathered together on porches sharing their lunches in the sunshine. It was touching to see Caspir like this, how he always imagined it could be. Despite this, he was still gripped by an unshakeable sense of unease. Something wasn't quite right; he just wasn't able to put his finger on it. Some feeling of implied distrust and hostility he couldn't shake.

They had arranged to meet in a large warehouse that had been converted into their place of worship. It made sense for this to become their physical church, because as a general rule, buildings not involved in commerce were small in Caspir. Marin was familiar with this warehouse in particular; during his childhood it had been a food store that he and his father used to frequent. He wondered if they'd managed to get the smell of leafy greens out. Ambling up to the front door, it still looked largely the same as he remembered it. If he didn't know better, he'd have no idea it was a church.

Upon entering, the place was heaving with people adopting various posi-

CHAPTER EIGHTEEN

tions of prayer. Rows of wooden benches were symmetrically lined up to face a raised platform at the back. Atop this platform was a lectern, and behind that a freshly carved statue. Whichever member of the congregation had crafted this monument to Shiara was incredibly talented. The proportions and detailed features were impressive indeed, although the likeness was not. Marin had spent more time with the slayer of ghosts than anyone else in Caspir, and for all this statue's quality, it was far from accurate. This didn't really come as a surprise considering few people had seen her for any length of time, let alone spent enough time in her company to render her likeness. He couldn't help sniggering to himself – what they were worshipping amounted to nothing more than an effigy of some random person. When he thought about it more, it wasn't as if any religion *really* knew what their prophets or gods looked like, aside from those in Fimego who saw Mara as their god.

The sideways glances from people continued as they had done in the streets, although many were too wrapped up in their prayers to pay him much attention. Off to the side of the pulpit was a door that led to an office. Marin made his way through the crowd, trying his best not to disturb any of the churchgoers; he was here for a dialogue, not to barge through them and make demands. The head of the council was expected, so the door was already ajar for him. He had been instructed to go right in by a couple of robust-looking fellows waiting outside the room.

From his youth, he remembered the room being filled with trinkets, papers and all sorts of mess covering every inch of space. Times had changed. The room was virtually bare, save for a simple wooden desk and chairs. Resting neatly upon that desk were a few piles of perfectly stacked papers, an inkwell, and a couple of books. Settled just as neatly on one of the chairs was the woman he had come to see, her hair made still paler by the angle of the sun piercing through the window. The tips of her fingertips pressed against one another as if she were cradling an imaginary ball. Blotches of blue and black ink ran across what was presumably her writing hand. She broke her pose to gesture to an empty chair, beckoning her guest to be seated.

"Thank you for coming to see me, councillor." Her voice was as resolute as before, powerful yet not intimidating.

"Please, call me Marin," he said, taking his seat, "and tell me, how should I address you?"

"Well, Marin, some call me the First Child of Shiara; or Firstchild for short; but I think we can both agree that Alyssa is probably a bit better." Her jovial response certainly alleviated some of the tension; he wasn't expecting this new religious leader to be so... normal? Nevertheless, it was a welcome development.

"The reason I asked to meet with you is because your little congregation isn't so little anymore. So I feel that I have to ask what your intentions are? Sorry to cut straight to business; time is a resource I'm always finding in short supply these days."

Alyssa's expression didn't change; it remained welcoming. The question was so obvious that it would have been a surprise if she had been fazed by it.

"We want the same things as everybody else. Peace and prosperity." Her words were clear, yet platitudes like this meant nothing without details.

"That is all well and good, but I'm trying to keep this city together. That means I need to know specifics. Are you planning to convert everyone? Or march against the council to have *your* version of 'prosperity' enacted?" Marin was unsure if he was being too paranoid, or not paranoid enough.

"Have the Children of Shiara given you any reason to believe we mean harm to anyone?"

"No..." He drew a breath before continuing, "Or rather, not yet. But what is stopping your ever-growing church from posing a problem to Caspir and its government in the future?"

The Firstchild's cheeks raised to form a tight smile across her face.

"Why, I should think the fair and just governing of this city should suffice."

That clawing feeling in the back of his mind presented itself once more.

"As impressive as sound-bites may seem, what matters is policy. Do you have any problems with what I'm trying to do that I should know about?" It was Marin's turn to be stern.

CHAPTER EIGHTEEN

"Well, tell me councillor, what is it that you are trying to accomplish?"

"At the moment, just holding things together is an achievement enough. What I'm *trying* to do is make sure that everybody has somewhere decent to live and enough to eat."

She nodded in agreement. After all, who would disagree with such basic decency? Aside from Andros maybe.

"What about the bigger picture?"

"The bigger picture?" He scoffed. "I'll settle for making sure everybody has a future before I start planning what to do with it!"

"If you spend all your time looking down to save yourself from tripping, you might find yourself walking on the wrong path." Her words suggested she had something in mind, some greater plan, but Marin had no way of unpacking what that might be. She had given him a perfect opening to ask her what he had really come here to ask.

"I was rather hoping we could all avoid tripping over by looking out for each other. The Church of Shiara is undoubtedly becoming a big part of Caspir, so before I go, I'd like to offer you a seat on the council." He extended a welcoming hand. This idea had been perfectly calculated; she and her congregation would become part of the formal structure of Caspir, everyone would work together and the notion of any uprising could be discarded in favour of legal and practical solutions. An unlosable proposition. Or so he had thought.

"I'm afraid I will have to politely decline." Marin's hand was left hanging in the air. "My place is with my fellow Children of Shiara, not sitting in a council chamber pontificating."

The feeling of dread now spread from the back of his mind all the way through to his gut. He had lost with his unlosable proposition.

"I'm sorry you feel that way." The councillor was resigned to his diplomatic defeat; he headed towards the door before turning back for one last concession. "Thank you for your time. It would've been a great benefit to have the Children of Shiara around the table with us all. Good day."

As he turned his back to her and made to exit through the doorway, Alyssa had one final remark to feed to that awful feeling of his.

"Dear Marin, how can you be sure that some of us aren't *already* sat around your table? Blessings of the Slayer unto you."

CHAPTER NINETEEN

It was the day of rest in Maluani. All but a few were spared the toils of the day and could instead spend time with their friends and families away from the fields. Whilst Takis was undoubtedly a ruthless ruler who cared not for the suffering of his subjects, he was not stupid. He had been around long enough to know that if you worked people too hard, they would break. Or worse still, try to break the system. The day of rest brought the community together and strengthened their bonds. For Takis, this provided a way to enforce the notion that the people had something to lose, as well as refreshing them for another week's hard labour. Koralia, however, had other plans.

Today was the day she shared her plot with her closest friends and family. It wasn't just the workers who were at rest; the guards were fewer with more distance between them, presenting the ideal opportunity to discuss more treasonous matters. She had assembled a room of those who could be trusted; Minos was the only one she had already told of her scheme so far. Koralia wasn't sure if everyone here would be on board, but she knew that even if they weren't, they'd at least keep quiet about it.

It was only small group of eight including Koralia and Minos, but it was a good start. Her cousin Castor had been the first to arrive, a shaven-headed man sculpted from muscle who was intent on excelling at whatever he turned his hand to, even if that happened to be slaving away in the fields, which explained his physique. Whilst they had exchanged pleasantries earlier – asking after one another's family as was polite – Castor was perceptive enough to realize something big was happening. This was not a regular get together.

Next to arrive had been Lumis and his daughter Neela. Lumis was the oldest of those invited and wore the sort of beard that would make even the most lupine of men jealous. Thick and curly, it obscured his neck, and was matched by equally dense hair atop his head. He was in his late forties and worked in the metal shop, crafting farming tools as well as bits of armour and weapons for the guards. Lumis was not necessarily muscular or toned; nevertheless, one would definitely describe him as solid. Short-tempered yet practical, he and Koralia had always got along well. His daughter Neela was also fiery in her own way, but rather than being practical, she was explosive. She didn't just wear her heart on her sleeve, she held it in her hands to shove in people's faces. Despite her volatility, she was intelligent beyond her years. A sharp mind for reasoning and logistics, her hands were spared much of the physical toil as her talents for planning were put to good use calculating the best agricultural layouts and timings. It wasn't just her hands that were spared the hard labour – her whole demeanour was less weary and strained than most. Perhaps this was why she had so much energy for animated arguments. Her hair was a very dark red, close to black; in the sunshine its burgundy hues could be seen more clearly. Maybe it just had less dirt in it than everyone else's? Nobody begrudged Neela her less strenuous occupation; after all, her understanding and planning made their work a little easier, and it was hard to be annoyed at someone who had far more spirit than you for confrontation. Neela lived alone in a room with Lumis; her mother had taken her own life when her daughter was only ten years old. She had been unable to cope with living in Maluani, so just as assuredly as if he had killed her himself, Takis was responsible. This kept the fires stoked within the pair and Koralia knew they would jump at a chance to even the score.

The last three arrived together – Nasos, Stefania and Orestis. They all bore a very striking family resemblance, the striking part being that they weren't a family, although they all shared the powerful cheekbones and jawline of Orestis's father, whose famous charisma with the ladies might explain their similarities. Nevertheless, gossiping was too much hassle for

CHAPTER NINETEEN

the citizens of Maluani, so nobody asked too many questions, especially not the fathers of Stefania and Nasos. The trio were generally inseparable and did just about everything together; Koralia was hoping that extended to revolution as well.

Stefania and her male cohorts would be the hardest to persuade, in Koralia's opinion. They always managed to be upbeat and appeared less downtrodden by the circumstances than the others, yet it would only take one of them to get on board with the plan to convince the other two. They all had a view that they could accomplish anything given the chance; Koralia hoped that the challenge itself would be enough to tempt them.

All in place, it was time to reveal her seditious purpose. Customary greetings and thanks done with, she drew in a breath and began.

"I know some of you have heard the rumour about Hectin; well, it's true."

A few mumbles were exchanged, especially between the trio.

"How can you be sure?" inquired Lumis.

"Believe it or not," Koralia said, "there are a handful of guards who aren't happy with the way Maluani is run. They heard it from traders and confirmed it to me; some of the wardens seem like they could be sympathetic to our cause."

"Our cause?" sputtered Castor.

"Yes. Not a single one of you can tell me you're happy with the way things are."

Nasos wrinkled his bulbous nose. "Not being happy is one thing, but when you start throwing around words like 'cause', it sounds like you're about to suggest something insane."

Koralia was resolute, this was the start of everything she had been waiting for.

"Insane? Insanity is accepting all this around us without fighting for what's right."

"Fighting? In case you hadn't realized, we're ruled by an immortal tyrannical ghost! There's no fighting against that." Nasos wasn't helping her plan, but he made a valid point that she'd considered at length before calling this assembly.

"Not immortal. If Hectin has fallen, so can Takis."

"None of us are warriors. How could you possibly think we could offer up a challenge? And despite the guards who you think might be sympathetic, most would cut us down long before we even got close enough to issue one." Nasos was right; that would never work. But that was not Koralia's plan.

"Which is precisely why we aren't going to do that. We can't fight Takis. But we can fight his system."

Nasos was somewhat confused by the statement; his bemusement allowed others to speak up and be heard.

"What... does that mean?" asked Castor.

"I'm glad you asked," said Koralia. "You see, when Hectin died, his thrumming pillar crumbled. It therefore follows that if you destroy a thrumming pillar, its ghost will go with it."

Stefania cleared her throat loudly to gather the room's attention. "The way I see it, there are three things that confound me. One, that is quite a large piece of speculation. Two, that still doesn't address how we actually get past the guards. Three, what does any of this have to do with fighting 'his system'?" Stefania had an air of grace and class to her language, although nobody could figure out where that came from.

"Stefania, I won't lie to you. We don't know if it will work, but what we do know is that doing nothing will kill us just as surely as any sword. As for your other two points, that is where my plan comes in. We aren't going to do this on our own; we are going to inspire the city as a whole. Rather than attacking Takis, we undermine the institutes of Maluani. *We* are what makes this city tick. Us workers can disrupt everything, make life troublesome for his sympathizers who live off of our labour. We outnumber the guards at least a hundred to one! It'll inevitably give us the opening needed to get to his thrumming pillar and smash it."

Silence fell upon them all. Just being part of this conversation would be grounds for execution, let alone doing the things Koralia was suggesting. Nobody dared make eye contact. It was a moment for private reflection and contemplation of the treason they had just been invited to partake in. Several minutes passed without comment before Neela plucked up the courage to

CHAPTER NINETEEN

break the stillness.

"Let's do it. I'll burn it all to the ground if I have to."

Even for Neela this came across as wild, although nobody doubted the conviction in her voice.

"What do you want us to do?" came the voice of her father Lumis.

Minos had already agreed beforehand; now seemed like the time to pipe up and add to the momentum. "Count me in."

"And me," said Castor.

All eyes turned to the inseparable group of three. Orestis, who had been quiet up to now, began to speak. "As far I can make out, this whole thing seems incredibly dangerous and near impossible to achieve."

Disappointment surged through Koralia's veins.

"This sort of foolhardy idea will likely see us all killed," Orestis continued. "However, it does sound like a rather thrilling challenge."

The tension wasn't just broken, it was smashed into pieces. A rippling of conviviality passed through the plotters; the first hurdle had been crossed. With all of them on board, the real planning could begin in earnest. Koralia had worked out what each person's role would be in the coming days. The foundations of revolution were laid, the line had been crossed, the only outcomes for their future being success or execution.

CHAPTER TWENTY

Trees and branches flew by; occasionally one would claw and scratch at Shiara's face. With one hand on the reins and the other holding up Fredo she had no means to protect herself from the twigs invading her space. Tilting her head was the best she could manage. Fredo was still conscious, although his attempts at words had given way to murmurings and groans; he would not last the night unaided. Literal and proverbial light came from up ahead – the edge of the wood was close. Exiting the treeline, the last vestiges of twilight still lit the open ground. In the middle distance sat a handful of buildings lit by torchlight; between them and this farmstead lay a field of miscellaneous leafy greens. Shiara knew the name of very few plants, though she could instantly recognize whether they were edible and what they tasted like. These were the "floral, bitter and chewy ones". Their sandback had stopped to take a moment's respite after its sprint through the forest, its maw wide open and tongue hanging out. Unlike people, these mighty creatures could not sweat to keep cool, and had to vigorously pant heat away instead. Shiara would give it a few minutes to recuperate. Yes, they were in a hurry but working this poor creature to death just to save a couple of minutes wouldn't achieve much. After all, Fredo had just started muttering again and even managed the odd word or two, something along the lines of "Not my violet one...".

The buildings were simple yet had more character than those in the cities. Their bricks were a much richer terracotta colour than the largely grey or sandy blocks of Caspir. Their rooves were flat and provided a communal

CHAPTER TWENTY

seating area, saving the space inside for cooking and sleeping. Lanterns clung to the corners of the structures, gently swaying in the evening air. A handful of people that were milling around outside had lined up to watch the pair approach, their expression of curiosity shifting to concern when Fredo's bloody makeshift bandages were spotted. A commotion led to one of the younger men running off towards another building whilst the others approached to lend a hand to the ailing silver-tongue.

"What happened?" asked a mature woman with wiry grey hair.

"Owls," replied Shiara.

"Owls?" the woman queried, clearly confused by the explanation. "How unusual."

"Not in my experience it isn't." This comment only made the woman and other onlookers more puzzled. "What matters is that my friend here gets some help." Shiara had not referred to Fredo as a friend before, and would only realize she had done so hours later.

"Yes, yes, yes. I sent Darius ahead to let Cafer know you are coming. This way, this way."

The woman and her band of villagers led them through what constituted the main thoroughfare of their tiny settlement, where a few nosy bystanders joined them. Shiara suspected this was more excitement than many of them were used to. Near the far end of the village – which wasn't very much of a "far" end – they came to a building that was just like all the others. Its door was open wide and a young man stood there, ushering them inside. Dismounting from their sandback and tying it off to a nearby post, Shiara carried Fredo in with the help of the youngster who, she was informed, went by the name of Darius. The door closed behind them to keep away the prying eyes of spectators.

Inside, innumerate trinkets, herbs, books and arcane instruments filled shelves and the surface of a rudimentary desk. A man introducing himself as Cafer greeted them and helped Fredo onto linens laid out on a charpai bed. He reached for a pair of small scissors to begin removing the stopgap bandages.

"Let me take a look at what we've got here. Did somebody mention something about owls?" Cafer asked with his smooth, deep voice. His lips were big and full as he bit them in trepidation of the wound he was about to be confronted with.

"He got a bellyful of Cara owl claws, but I don't think he's missing anything," Shiara replied.

"It certainly looks messy; it doesn't appear as if anything has been ruptured though. What did you two do to piss off owls this much?"

Shiara gestured to the hilt hanging off her belt. "Magic sword; you know what owls are like with magic."

Cafer sniggered and wiped a bead of sweat off of his dark brow with his forearm. "I don't know what sort of magic you're talking about, but they don't seem to mind *my* magic; they even come out to watch me use it on the crops. Sometimes they even let me pet them."

The slayer of ghosts was disgruntled by the information. Nobody liked having their understanding of the world shown to be inaccurate, especially if some silver-tongued city dweller had come to the same conclusion earlier that day. Importantly though, she had found someone with magic to help Fredo; small bits of magic weren't that uncommon out here away from the cities.

Cafer reached for a bottle of something with a tinge of green and began pouring it into Fredo's laceration.

"The key thing is to make sure we clean it out properly. The wound is relatively easy to fix; it's the grubby bits from the owl's claws you have to be careful of."

Cafer was very obviously a man who performed all sorts of tasks in his community, and he did seem to know what he was doing here as if he were an expert. He grabbed another bottle, this time containing a reddish liquid, and dumped its contents into the silver-tongue's open belly. It immediately hissed and fizzed, causing Fredo's body to tense and his mouth to unleash an unpleasant combination of swearing and grunting. A few moments later the fizzing stopped and he relaxed back as if he was finally going to bed after a long week of work. One last vial of liquid, this time just water, was used to wash away any of the remaining foaming liquids and give the wound one

CHAPTER TWENTY

last clean. Cafer retrieved a needle and thread from his desk drawer and began stitching.

"That should have done the trick and numbed him enough so he won't feel a thing while I put him back together. Once I've closed him up, I'll use a bit of magic to help him along."

Magic wasn't the panacea that those in the cities may have imagined it to be. The best it offered was speeding up a process, whether that be growing crops or healing a wound. It couldn't fix something that was broken, just accelerate the recovery afterwards. No wonder the owls weren't bothered by Cafer, Shiara thought; this sort of magic was nothing in comparison to her sword. A sword supposedly forged by the Great Wizard Ezekiel himself. A blade able to cut down immortal beings – surely that must be why the owls hated it just like they hated the ghosts? There was no likening it to a bit of tinkering in the fields; she had decided to herself that must be the reason why, even though she was hardly an expert to weigh in on such matters.

Tying off the thread, Cafer put away the tools, placed his hands over Fredo's injury and began to slowly undulate his fingers as if playing an imaginary musical instrument. A very dim glow flickered in between the stitches as Cafer's expression became slightly pained; the sort of expression one has when trying to remember something that one can't quite recall. After a few minutes he stopped, looking a little perplexed.

"I'm not sure why, but I'm finding this a bit difficult. It's very... unusual." His tone echoed the sentiments. Then something caught his eye and he began again, with his eyes fixed on Shiara's waist.

"Interesting."

"What is?" she asked.

"Your sword. It seems to glow faintly when I try to use magic."

He was right; from where the hilt met the scabbard a small rainbow of glowing colours could just about be seen. It was becoming increasingly obvious to Shiara that her understanding of magic was sorely lacking.

"What does that mean?" she inquired.

"Well," Cafer said, "I have absolutely no idea. It's not often there is anything magical out here; maybe they are interfering with each other?"

It was as good a guess as any, and as was now firmly established in her mind, she was in no position to argue about the intricacies of magic.

"I suppose that would make sense," she said, trying her best to sound like she knew what she was talking about. "What do we do now?"

Cafer shrugged. "Let's try taking your sword further away and see if that helps?"

Shiara nodded. "I'll leave you to it; come and find me later to let me know how you got on."

They exchanged goodbyes and the slayer of ghosts left the building. Cafer returned to his task, hands poised over his patient. The dim glow began to shine a little brighter.

Upon leaving the house, Shiara was greeted by those whose curiosity had got the better of them and were waiting to see what was happening. Her sandback had become a plaything for a pair of local children in her absence; not that the creature minded having its belly rubbed. It certainly was a pleasant change from being in the middle of an attack by owls. After explaining what had happened to a few more people, to the predictable replies of "Owls?", she walked over to her sandback and untied it.

"Can you boys show me where I can hitch up my sandback for the night?" Shiara asked.

"Oh. Yes Ma'am. He can keep Tito company!" The young children seemed thrilled at the chance to do something useful, especially as this stranger had asked them and not an adult.

If her estimations of what this sort of magic could do were right – which given recent form might not be the case – Fredo would only need to be here for one night, maybe two. The boys led her away from the main buildings and towards a wooden structure apart from the main thoroughfare of the settlement. Within this open wooden structure was Tito, an enormous hulking sandback. Generations of breeding had produced something that bore little resemblance to the creature she had ridden. The scales on its back were larger and firmer, made coarse from pulling a plough mounted on its shoulders. Its head and neck were far more squat and thick-set than those

CHAPTER TWENTY

of the sandbacks used for riding; the beast was a solid mass of muscle. A truly powerful creature, it was the best of friends with these young boys, who ran over and gave it a hug. The sandback looked pleased at the human company, but pulled a face at Shiara's sandback as if to say, "Now what is that supposed to be?" Of course, her sandback was far more accustomed to its larger cousins as they worked on the farmland that surrounded Caspir. Without hesitation it sidled over and found a comfortable spot to sprawl in. The children kept pestering Shiara as to what her sandback's name was, to which she had no reply. After rigorous debate between them, the children settled on Scaley. She thought it was a silly name, yet she couldn't be bothered to offer an alternative. She plonked herself down next to her lizard and dismissed the children after a few minutes. Shiara would get some rest and hope that Cafer could work his magic. "Good night, Scaley," she said. Her eyes rolled – it was at that moment she realized she was actually calling her sandback "Scaley" and her travelling companion "Friend".

CHAPTER TWENTY-ONE

"And another thing, why should we have to keep paying import fees this high when we're bringing in less stuff?"

Marin had put up with hours of this, much of it spent with his head resting in his hand as he perched his elbow on the table. It wasn't that the concerns weren't important, it was just that they were dull and progress on them had been negligible from the outset. He wasn't opposed to explaining the situation and working towards a better solution, but having the exact same conversations every day grew tiresome; did they somehow forget all of the previous day's discussion? Or maybe they subscribed to the theory that the weight of the argument was less important than the number of times it was argued? Success via tedium, whereby everyone would give way just to be done hearing about it, perhaps? Such a tactic was certainly less effective when every single council member seemed to be employing it on a daily basis. There was one other consideration, the one that gnawed away at Marin: the Children of Shiara. Alyssa had hinted that she had some kind of power within the council, which was a worry the council leader could not shake. How could his mind be fully on task with this soaking up his attention? Moreover, if they *did* have members on the council, what was their purpose? He had offered her a seat at the table – what could the Church possibly gain from covert members rather than taking a seat? Every possibility he contemplated was a bad one. The thought had occurred to him that the continual impasses of the council could be related. What better way to undermine the government than making it ineffectual? It was safe to

CHAPTER TWENTY-ONE

say that paranoia was becoming the staple food of Marin's consciousness. But it was time to put an end to this particular debate, as it was becoming almost like a daily ritual.

"Look, as you're all aware, our trading with other cities has taken a bit of a hit lately. Illorne's collapse has dealt a major blow and in turn has prompted greater caution among the other cities. So yes, there will be reductions in trade for a while, and no, there isn't really anything we can do about it right now." It had come to the point where Marin was repeating these exact sentences to the council word for word each day.

"What if it gets worse?" Andros had generally been quiet on this issue before, thankfully, but was now weighing in, which was the last thing anyone wanted.

"We have no reason to believe it will get worse," Marin said. "If anything, it could get easier as Shiara eliminates the other ghost councillors and things open up."

"If..." Andros spat. "Who's to say she even will?"

The bearded merchant-turned-councillor was stunned. Not so much by the very relevant point that was being made, but by who was making it. Edwin butted in to offer his usual reasoned response.

"Well, my dear Andros, if she does fail, the other cities will have no reason for caution and thus will resume normal trading patterns."

Edwin was right; however, the notion of her dying didn't sit well with Marin.

"If that is the case, then surely her success bodes the greatest threat? For in such success we risk our trading partners being reduced to chaos like Illorne."

A lump formed in the council leader's throat and from the expression on his good friend Edwin's face, he had one too. Incisive arguments about the wider picture were not supposed to come from the pompous and self-interested Andros, yet here they were. Nobody could deny the tragedy of Illorne; they had all seen the refugees and heard the stories – what was there to stop it happening again? Arrogance aside, the other cities were a very different place to Caspir and perhaps they wouldn't have someone like Marin to step into the breach? Omdurtur was a hub of industry, so it wasn't too difficult to imagine it continuing in the same fashion without Kadar, but what about the others? Fimego revolved around Mara; she was the living deity that produced fanatical devotion in her citizens. Losing a council leader was a struggle for many, so imagine what losing one's god would do? As for Maluani, who knows? It was rare for outsiders to even enter, and what little trade they did do was carried out only within their outer walls. It was impossible for anyone to say much about the city itself. It seemed as if Takis ran the place more like a prison than anything else. Would Shiara even be able to get in? What kind of powder keg would it unleash if she did? Addressing the stunned council members, Andros had an uncharacteristically significant sound-bite to follow up with.

"It seems to me that we've spent all this time assuming she would kill the ghosts and given little time to consider whether or not she should..."

The supposed end of the meeting had already come and gone and with these thoughts in their minds, most people didn't feel like continuing. Marin adjourned the session and the councillors filed out, feeling rather sheepish and somewhat disturbed. Andros carried himself in a decidedly smug fashion; whilst his ability to reason had inexplicably been taken up a few notches, his pomposity remained unchanged. Left in the chamber were just Marin and his good friend Edwin, still exchanging bemused and concerned expressions until Edwin broke the silence.

"My friend, it seems to me that we could both use a drink."

Marin wasn't the sort to drown his worries with a cup of wine, although he was fond of the odd beverage. Amid all the chaos of recent weeks he had almost forgotten it was the time of year for his favourite wine. Whilst wines were generally fermented over a long period of time, most cities produced their own short-fermented wine to be drunk within a year of being harvested. The benefits of light maceration and fermentation were a lighter body and fruitier note. He wasn't a connoisseur like some, but he usually made time for a night of drinking this annual treat. When Edwin placed the beaker into

CHAPTER TWENTY-ONE

his hands and the smell hit him, it all came flooding back. If it wasn't for his friend, he would have missed out this year. It was truly comforting, and in this case delicious, to have a friend like Edwin.

"Now this is what makes all of this civilization worth it," Marin chuckled.

"It's a decidedly sweet batch this year. That extra week on the vine from those disputes the growers had really brought it together," Edwin said with a grin on his face. "Maybe we should have contractual problems every year!"

The pair laughed. "Well," declared Marin, "the way things are going now, it'd surprise me if we didn't get a much longer delay for the next batch."

Quaffing the rest of his cup, the immaculately bearded man grabbed the bottle and topped himself up.

"I joke, but I have to be honest with you, I don't know how things will turn out. And what worries me most isn't the squabbling or the disputes."

"It's the Church, isn't it?" deduced Edwin.

Marin nodded.

"I thought going down there would help me work out what they want but it only confused things more. On top of that, there's the petitions they keep sending us. If they want changes why don't they take up the representation I offered them? It doesn't make any sense."

The pair shrugged to each other. In the past they had mainly dealt with selfish motives based on ambition or wealth; in this case nobody was really sure what the Church's motives were. They had steadily expanded their territory as their congregation swelled, so it was only natural they'd need more space and want to be together. Something just didn't sit right.

"Just yesterday I received a handful of scrolls full of signatures demanding we do something about a whole street of residents and businesses who were making them feel unsafe. At the end of the day, we can't ignore that many people signing something, yet we can't go around evicting people either."

"It's a tough spot for sure," comforted Edwin. "A piece of paper is one thing..."

"Many pieces of paper," interrupted Marin.

"True, well pieces of paper are one thing; it's how they congregate in public areas that worries me. We can't even call it protesting because they aren't doing or saying anything; just standing there for hours."

It had become a common yet troubling sight in Caspir. Every day, the Children of Shiara would amass in spaces across the city, not preaching or trying to convert new followers, just standing there. Silent. At first it was a weird sort of attraction for some, but quickly it became something else. As if they were constantly watching the citizens of Caspir with some kind of self-claimed holy authority. Marin knew their "deity" Shiara was just a person, an incredibly remarkable one, but still just a person. That was what made this entire Church of Shiara situation so perplexing. Shiara herself had told him that her plan was to free the people of their ghost leader and hand their destiny back to them, not for them to find a new being to immortalize.

"You're right Edwin, it creeps me out. I can't tell if it's a display of power, frustration or some kind of religious thing. The only plus side is that with them standing around I don't have to do anything, unlike when I get a load of signatures on a piece of paper."

"Many pieces of paper," corrected Edwin.

The council leader and his companion knocked their cups together in a toast then chugged back their contents.

CHAPTER TWENTY-TWO

This was it. The night of the resistance's first act of defiance. Despite the enormity of the situation, Koralia was not nervous. Excitement and pride filled her veins at the prospect of starting what she had dreamed of for so long. "The tyranny of an immortal ghost is nothing compared to the resolution of an oppressed people," she told herself. And for now, she believed it.

Night had fallen; the cover of darkness was their great ally that made the plan possible. Lumis had managed to supply them with the tools they needed, carefully crafted and pilfered from the metalwork shop without the guards being alerted. They would have to work quickly if they wanted to avoid night patrols, although where they were going the guards rarely patrolled, as there wasn't anything of much value there. Or so they thought.

Maluani looked far more oppressive during the night, the moonlight amplifying the stark brutalist lines of the buildings. Long clawing shadows from the towering walls spread blackness in an unnatural fashion as if intentionally designed to cause unease, which, all things considered, was probably the case. Koralia, Minos, Castor and the trio of Stefania, Nasos and Orestis were approaching their target. Neela and Lumis had done enough in supplying the equipment, and the fewer the people, the less likely they were to get caught. They found themselves in the large open square that overlooked one of the poorer districts that they called home. At its centre towered a stone monument to their oppressor, Takis. A relatively good likeness, but it had worn down over the generations so edges and features were dulled. It acted as a reminder of who was in charge, as well as how long this had been the case. His presence had been an eternal fixture for the inhabitants of Maluani, so much so that he was thought of as unmovable and unending. Immortality was the perfect tool for shaping a populace to one's will. At least it had been up until now.

The trio took up places around the edge of the square to keep an eye out for approaching guards whilst Castor used his sinewy arms to hurl the ropes over the statue. Minos and Koralia scampered up the ropes once given the all-clear, tools strapped across their back. Ascending the effigy, they were now right in the face of their tyrant, albeit a facsimile. Neither of them had been this close to the real Takis and hoped that would remain the case. Having perched themselves at the top, they began to tie the ropes around the statue's head to keep it secure. They would have to lower the head down after removing it to keep the noise to a minimum; this would be the most difficult aspect of their night's vandalism. Castor tied off the ropes below and took a firm grip on them with Nasos giving him a hand. The destruction could now begin.

Koralia and Minos lined up their tools to begin the job. The tools' edges had been finished to a fine point that was reinforced by some precious mineral to make sure it was harder than anything it would be chiselling. Lumis had done an excellent job on them; his crafting skills would be invaluable in the coming weeks. The pair had to be cautious when hammering their chisels, making the most progress with each hit to keep the number of impacts, and thus the noise, to a bare minimum. Chipping away in the right spot meant that the weight of the head would do much of the work for them. Once through enough of the stone, they'd need to scurry down and help the others lower the head as they'd be unable to take the strain for long, even with it tied off around the base. The work was tense and gruelling; hammering away at stone was a very different prospect from working in the soil.

Almost an hour passed and the chiselling was complete. A definite crack across the neck of the monument was visible. The crew gathered around to ease the heavy stone head to the ground. Despite their best efforts they

CHAPTER TWENTY-TWO

could not avoid what was a sizeable thud as it hit the ground. A thud that reverberated through the empty streets and must have undoubtedly been heard by some of the wardens.

Hopefully they were not close enough to catch the group out.

With great haste they wound up the ropes and made sure the tools were securely strapped to their backs. They could not leave behind any evidence that might incriminate anyone; if they saw the tools, they'd know for sure that Lumis was involved and the entire plan would come crashing down in a bloody reprisal. The cohort slunk off into the night and down the side streets, each of them carrying different tools and treading carefully. In the distance they could hear footsteps heading towards the square; thankfully they were far enough off to not cause immediate concern. They would be back in their homes soon and live to see another day of freedom, as much as one could call life in Maluani free. Koralia led the way with her ears and eyes peeled. They were close now, but rounding a corner she was confronted with a solid wall. Not one made of stone, but one of flesh and armour. Before her stood a guard. He wore an expression of surprise that matched Koralia's; this soon shifted to anger. The leader of the plotters was frozen to the spot. She knew that confrontation with wardens would come eventually, but she had not expected it to be this soon on their treasonous journey. Terror grasped her, locking her muscles in place: only her jaw moved as it fell open in dread. The guard's hand began to slide towards the sword at his waist whilst his eyes remained fixed on Koralia's. The hiss of the metal blade sliding out of its scabbard was deafening to her. Redness splashed in her face. In her tunnelled vision it took a moment to work out where it had come from. Panicked breaths filled her lungs as she saw a chisel retracted from the guard's neck and thrust back in a few more times. His sword never fully unsheathed, he stood there twitching. Stefania buried the point in his throat and the side of his face a couple more times for good measure. The armour did not cover this part of the guards' bodies in order to give them flexibility in the neck, so they could look around more easily. Stefania retrieved the tool from the gaping wound as he slumped to the floor. She had acted swiftly and without hesitation. Death had already reared its ugly head in their struggle before it had really begun, and Stefania had delivered it effortlessly. It was always going to come to this at some point, yet the manner in which she dispatched such violence against another human was shocking. Hands locked around Koralia's arms and pulled her along. Her stiffness slowly dissipated as survival instincts kicked back in. Their tiptoeing around had given way to jogging along as quietly as they could manage; speed was now of more concern. If they were found splattered with the blood of a guard, they'd never see daylight again. The pain of a twisted ankle was irrelevant as adrenaline flooded her system. She could no longer listen out for the footfall of guards, or even hear her own steps – the pounding of her heart was all consuming. The rest of the dash home was a blur to her; she only regained awareness of her surroundings as Minos shuffled her through the door of her home. Her rational brain whirred into action as she could feel the splatters of blood on her face and smell its metallic odour. She needed to wash it off, not just to hide evidence but for the sake of her own nerves, which were shot. If she could clean herself up and hide that it had happened, maybe she'd feel normal again. After the night's events, she would soon learn that she'd never feel normal again. The water was cold, but this didn't bother her as her skin was flushed from exertion and emotion. Minos helped her rinse the remaining traces off and pointed to her clothes, which were peppered with burgundy droplets. She pulled off the top layer and flung it into the bowl of water; her friend rubbed the wet fabric, diluting the evidence of their deeds into nothingness. Koralia finally felt like she was getting a grip of herself once more and sat on the floor with crossed legs.

"Minos," she panted, still not quite having her breath back, "I froze... I just stood there."

"Of course you did, who wouldn't?"

"I'm supposed to be leading this whole thing... but when I'm confronted with a guard for the first time, I can't move. It's not good enough."

Minos shook his head and tried to comfort her. "You were caught by surprise; it's an understandable reaction."

"Understandable maybe... but not acceptable. It cannot happen again. I won't need Stefania to jump in next time, I'll do it myself."

CHAPTER TWENTY-TWO

"Well let's not get ahead of ourselves just yet," he replied.

"No, this is important. With what we are doing, people will be trying to kill us and we will have to kill other people. We have to accept that and be ready for it. The struggle against oppression cannot be bloodless; we've already lost our own in the fields. Taking the lives of oppressors is a price we have to pay. When this is all finished, we'll all be killers."

That realization, and the determined way in which Koralia said it, brought a lump to Minos's throat. He was always seen as the jovial clown, but she was right. They would all take the lives of others, and they had to prepare for that, or face losing their own.

CHAPTER TWENTY-THREE

Cafer had stopped by earlier to let Shiara know that Fredo was doing all right. His magic had done what time alone would have taken weeks to achieve. Fredo was going to be a bit fragile for a while but could travel. If all went to plan it was only his brain that was required and not his physical prowess, if one could even call it prowess. Shiara had taken to making herself useful whilst she waited for the afternoon in order to resume travelling; her blade made much lighter work of slicing through wood than any axe. Shiara took pleasure in saving them the trouble given all they'd done for Fredo, not to mention the free meal the kids had brought her in the morning. At first the children had stood and watched her effortless chopping by the woodshed as if it were some incredible spectacle, but even a magical sword loses its fascination after the sixtieth time it cuts through a log. For the past hour she'd been left without an audience to stack up the village's woodshed so they could later heat their homes and cook their meals. In some ways she was glad of the practice; whilst it wasn't life or death combat, honing her precision with every strike was certainly not a poor use of time. The shimmering, dancing colours of blade also provided a sort of therapeutic beauty that kept her enthralled far more than it did the children. It was a relic of the old world yet looked as if it were forged yesterday. Perfect lines and not a single dent or scrape to be found. The light reflected from its surface was like that of sunshine through raindrops: a clean and vibrant cascade of every hue. This weapon had been at her side for many seasons, yet somehow today it shone a little brighter than it had ever done before. It glimmered

CHAPTER TWENTY-THREE

with iridescence as if it were alive somehow. She had often attributed a character to the cutlass, talking to it on occasion as if it were a person; after all, one had to find ways to keep oneself entertained whilst spending most of one's time alone. It was only natural she needed to talk to something – better her sword than rambling to herself. The weirdest thing was that sometimes she couldn't shake the feeling that it was somehow listening in on what she was telling it. Shiara even thought the blade sounded like it gave off a sigh every so often, and on rare occasions like today, she swore she heard a faint whisper coming from it as it split the air with a strike. Was this really that weird? Ultimately it was a magic sword crafted by the Great Wizard Ezekiel, so the idea that it may be alive in some fashion was hardly that bizarre. It had helped a poor homeless woman slay two immortal ghosts; it offering up the odd whisper was hardly a far-fetched proposition. As she brought it down through log after log Shiara could almost pick out the odd word from the whispers. She hadn't told anyone about this before, not so much out of fear of being mocked, but just because she'd never been close enough to anyone to *want* to tell them about it.

"How would Fredo react if I told him?" she wondered. Perhaps she'd bring it up later, get him to try to listen for it as well. Maybe then she'd know if it really was whispering or if the great ghost slayer was a few grapes short of a wine bottle. With that in mind, was she even that interested in finding out one way or the other?

Stacking the last pieces of wood away, Shiara mopped her brow with a sleeve and took a look at her handiwork. All neatly arranged and piled together, every bit of wood had its place. If only the rest of the world was this easy to sort out. The thought of the chaos she had brought to Illorne weighed heavy on her mind. It was supposed to be simple: slay the ghosts, fulfil the prophecy and make the world a better place. The reality was quite different; if it wasn't for Marin then Caspir could have met the same fate. Nevertheless, she was confident she was doing the right thing. The reign of ghosts was over. Let the living run their own lives; change was bound to have its problems. Perhaps once all of the ghosts fell there would be peace and something new and wonderful could blossom, free from the shackles of immortal overlords. What came next wasn't really her domain; she wasn't a great thinker or politician. Killing the ghosts and ending the old order was all she need concern herself with; those who came after would shape things anew, and it would be better. It had to be.

Shiara had not been at the settlement for more than a day, yet everyone knew her. It wasn't every day a stranger with a magical sword rode into town after battling with crazed owls. As she strode towards Cafer's place she nodded and greeted those who passed by; most were in the fields harvesting but a few were ambling along the thoroughfare. She knocked at Cafer's door and let herself in, welcomed by the sight of Fredo slurping down a bowl of soup. Years of tuning his fine-dining skills meant nothing in a rural village like this; etiquette took a back seat when ravenous hunger came to town. Cafer's magic sped up the healing process but it also accelerated his body's other functions, resulting in an overwhelming need to consume vast quantities of food. Licking a drop of green soup from the corner of his mouth, Fredo greeted his travelling companion.

"Thanks for bringing me here. The food is great!" he joked.

"Glad to see you've been stuffing your face whilst I've been chopping wood all morning."

"Morning? Does that mean dinner is still to come?"

Unfortunately his sense of humour had clearly not been damaged by his ordeal, she thought.

"Cafer, thank you for your help; is he well enough to travel?" Shiara asked.

"Yes," Cafer nodded, "I should think so."

It was Shiara's turn to smirk. "Looks like you won't be eating dinner here after all, Fredo."

Cafer explained the extent of Fredo's recovery and that whilst he could ride, he should still take it easy. The wound was not going to reopen, but the muscles in his abdomen would take many weeks to recover fully. If he overdid things, he could risk tearing them internally, but Cafer assured them both that he would still be able to sit on a sandback and make wisecracks. The pair thanked him for his help and offered some coin, which he refused to take. At first, they thought he was just being polite; later they concluded

CHAPTER TWENTY-THREE

that coins were of little use to a small farming community like this. The older lady who had welcomed them the night before was certainly less picky about accepting money for the food she had prepared for the pair to take with them. They supposed she had been around long enough to know that having a bit of money set aside wasn't a bad thing, even for a self-sufficient farmstead like this.

Goodbyes exchanged, the children bid farewell to their new lizard friend. "Goodbye Scaley!"

"Scaley?" said Fredo, with a puzzled look on his face.

Shiara grinned at him. "But of course! Would you have preferred 'Furry'?"

Fredo rolled his eyes and dared not ask any further, instead gingerly climbing atop Scaley, trying to move his stomach as little as possible. Shiara sat behind to give him support so his muscles had as little work to do as possible.

"Where are you going?" inquired the mature woman.

"Heading to Fimego," Shiara answered.

"In that case," she said, pointing into the distance, "You're best off heading that way and following the river. It's quicker and you won't run into any owls."

The lady chuckled, still clearly amused by the notion of being attacked by owls.

"And be careful in Fimego, it's a weird place," the villager warned. "Well, goodbye...?" She didn't know Shiara's name and was prompting her for the information.

"Shiara. My name is Shiara. And this is Fredo."

"Goodbye then, and make sure you take care of him... Shiara, right? That is an unusual name." The older woman was clearly fishing for a further conversation that the two travellers were not interested in. As they began to move out, Shiara turned for a parting remark: "If you think that name is unusual, you should hear what *some* people call me."

They cantered away, with the villager's curiosity piqued: "What do they call you?"

When they were far enough away to avoid further entanglement in dialogue with her, Shiara turned her head and shouted back, "The Slayer of Ghosts!"

The woman looked fit to explode with the untapped potential of this gossip, as the pair rode off into the distance.

CHAPTER TWENTY-FOUR

It was the earliest in the morning that the council had ever sat. The sun was barely up and the councillors barely awake. This was supposed to be a concession to the farmers, who didn't want to waste valuable daylight on meetings if they could avoid it. It was a trial run, and the initial signs were not good. Nobody felt much like discussing the issues of the day, even though there was one significant problem at the top of the agenda. Caspir had never had much of a problem with violence, just the occasional scuffle due to alcohol or fighting out of desperation among the Greys. What they were seeing now was a lot more vicious: people beaten and left with broken limbs, not because they had had an argument or had wanted something – this was violence born of hatred and fear. Caspir was changing rapidly and that didn't sit well with some people. These citizens took it upon themselves to vent their frustration with kicks and punches. Refugees were often targets; they were newcomers who didn't have a place of their own yet, symbolizing the changing times that many were scared of. What really pissed off Marin the most was that the same people who were taking their rage out on refugees tended to be the ones who'd later blame those fleeing Illorne for the increase in violence. It was no fun being at the bottom of the pile, even though the council was trying to lift up the living standards of those worst off. The Church of Shiara was also intimidating to a lot of the residents of Caspir, and Marin could empathize. For him they were a cause for concern, a group mustering power for reasons unknown, whereas for most, the Church was yet another example of life becoming different.

Unsurprisingly, that meant some of their brown-clad worshippers were also the target of attacks and the refugees who'd joined the Children of Shiara got it doubly bad. This was what they had come to discuss. They had been inundated with correspondence from the Church, especially from Alyssa, demanding action be taken. Whilst they were obviously exaggerating the problem to push it up the agenda, Marin couldn't deny they had a point. It was the government's job to keep its citizens safe. Making sure everyone had a roof over their head and food in their belly had been challenging, yet it was purely logistical in nature, the perfect problem for his business mind to tackle. Combatting fear and violence was a different prospect entirely. He'd hoped that securing the essentials for people would avoid violence and promote contentment: he had been wrong. It seemed that regardless of how positive a change may be, there would always be those who despised it just because it was different.

"I know it's early, but can we please try to focus. We're looking for any ideas to curb the rise in violence we've been seeing."

One of the younger councillors put his hand up as if he was still a pupil. "Why... why don't we just set up more guard patrols? Keep an eye on things?"

The council let out a laugh in unison, which only served to paint confusion all over the youngster's face. He thought it was an obvious solution and couldn't understand why it received such ridicule.

"There are two problems with that idea," Marin started. "Firstly, we can't just turn Caspir into some military state where we watch everyone; it's just not how we should run the city."

"And the second problem?" the sheepish councillor inquired.

"We can't bloody afford it!" bellowed a particularly rosy-cheeked fellow to an outpouring of guffaws. The sheepishness of the young man intensified. To stymie the laugher and explain, Marin gestured to the room. His position was always that telling someone they were wrong was useless without explaining why.

"There just isn't the money. Having lost trade with Illorne, business isn't exactly booming with other cities right now. We can hardly tax people more; if anything that would further fuel the dissatisfaction."

CHAPTER TWENTY-FOUR

Despite the deep hue of embarrassment colouring his face, the immature councillor understood and had learnt something. Not only about the financial situation, but also how a considered response was better conduct than derision.

A familiar adversary reared his pompous head. "It's all very well saying what we *can't* do; however, nobody is saying what there is that we *can* do."

On yet another occasion Andros was making a salient point. It was becoming the norm over the last week, and of all the worrying developments of late, Marin found this one to be the most troubling. Could it be possible that the upheaval of losing Chase had inspired him to be better? More analytical and incisive? Considering the years he had known Andros, that didn't seem likely. The obvious fear was that Alyssa was pulling his strings from the shadows, which tallied with the comment she had made to him. Even if that *was* the case, the continuous question of "Why?" continually plagued him. And truth be told, however irritating his picking apart of things was, the points he made were relevant ones. Marin sometimes suspected his paranoia over Andros was more about projecting concerns over his own failure.

"That's what we are here to discuss. I'm open to ideas."

The members fell into silence as they looked back and forth at one another in search of someone with something to offer. A shrug was the closest they came to an idea. It was up to Marin to propose a course of action, as per usual.

"I suggest we focus on the rule of law. We don't need to monitor the people more thoroughly, just make sure that those breaking the law are caught and brought to justice. There needs to be consequences for their actions."

"Hang them!" screamed an almost bird-faced elderly man whose eyebrow hairs had come to resemble long whiskers. Several people cheered; others jeered. If there was one thing Marin was sure of in regard to how a civilized Caspir would be run, it was that those in charge should never have the power to take the lives of citizens. Capital punishment was not on his agenda.

"If people don't think they'll be caught, it doesn't matter what the punishment is, they'll still think it's worth the risk." The merchant councillor's beard vibrated with the forcefulness of his words.

"What we need to do is make sure that we catch the people committing these crimes. The best way I see of doing this is with the help of the people."

"I thought you said we couldn't afford to hire more of them as guards?" sniped Andros. Marin wasn't talking about hiring guards.

"We don't need to hire people; we need to build trust between the people and those enforcing the law. If we show everyone that their interests are important, they're far more likely to come forward and help us investigate any..."

The council door burst open, interrupting the council leader's sentence and everyone else's train of thought.

A heavily panting guard mopped the sweat pouring down his face as he hunched over, trying to gain breath to speak. "It's bad.... You've got... got to come... murder."

A sharp intake of air into everyone's lungs showed that their fears had been realized: violence had escalated to killing. Marin stomped over and placed an arm around the guard, who was doubled over from exhaustion. "Show me," he said. The man looked up, nodded, then continued panting.

The guard had led them through the city to the crime scene. It was the last place Marin wanted to find a body, right on an intersection of three districts: the ever-growing Church district, the district where many refugees were housed, and an old working-class district of Caspir. It was the ideal place to light the powder keg that the city was becoming. Crowds of people peppered the street; there was no sweeping this under the rug. Before they could see the body, they could smell it: the foetid reek of insides laid bare. The scent attacked the nose, conjuring up brutal images of the macabre. Marin's expectations were repulsive, yet the scene itself was even more grisly. From where once a shimmering banner of splendour had hung, a corpse was now installed. High up and visible for everyone to see and be horrified by, this wasn't about killing someone; this was about sending a message. The unmistakable brown threads of the Church of Shiara adorned the body; any

CHAPTER TWENTY-FOUR

other clothes had been torn through along with the flesh beneath. Entrails dangled from the savage wounds like glistening red and pink cords. Smears of brown and black from the mangled bowels and clotted blood covered their lower half of the body. The face was relatively intact, albeit decorated with splatter. It was the face of a young man in his early twenties that had been contorted by the agony of his final moments. Whilst this entire spectacle had been constructed to send a message, there was the horrible thought that this gruesome artist had done their sculpting when their "canvas" was still alive. Marin covered his mouth and nose to fight back against this assault on his senses. He noticed another key feature of the victim that added further complexity – his hair was tied in an unmistakable knot as was the style in Illorne. Was this an attack on the Church or on refugees? Perhaps both?

As expected, a large cohort of Children of Shiara were present on the scene waiting for an authority to voice their concerns to. Alyssa herself stepped from the throng of people and made a beeline towards Marin. People parted before her like grasses in the wind. She had not given anyone a reason to fear her; she just commanded such authority and presence in Caspir that people dared not get in her way. Her gaze firmly fixed on the council leader, unblinking, she paced towards him until she was right in his face. She didn't need to use words to convey her meaning. In reality, words were unable to truly describe the seething emotions everyone was feeling, let alone what was going on inside the head of the First Child. She wore a stern, resolute look of anger and determination. For a minute that seemed to stretch out like an hour, the pair just stared at one another. Marin's brain desperately searched for the right thing to say, but in a situation this inherently wrong, he had nothing. It was the first time Marin had seen emotion painted so clearly on Alyssa's face. Up until now she had been an irksome mystery to him, yet laid bare on her features was now the unmistakable look of abhorrence. He became increasingly aware of the sound of his own breathing and the undulations of his chest. At least, he thought, they were squarely on the same side here. Such an atrocity must be punished; his main concern was making sure it was the rule of law that did the punishing, rather than the Church taking it into their own hands.

"I..." Marin thought he was ready to say something, but fell woefully short.

"Don't." Alyssa was firm, with more composure than seemed humanly possible given the situation. "We warned you. *We* told you we were at risk and you did nothing."

The onlookers were already watching with bated breath; upon hearing her words they slowly edged back.

"Alyssa, I am deeply sorry for your loss. This will not stand."

"Your words are meaningless. What we need is action. And justice."

It was now the time for Marin to put everything he had been working for on the line. What good was a government that couldn't keep people safe?

"I promise you... I will... personally do everything in my power to see whoever is responsible brought to justice and face the full force of the law."

The corner of Alyssa's lip curled upwards and one of her eyes narrowed in a way which unnerved Marin.

"I expect nothing less. And if you fail, I'm sure we can *all* agree that neither your power, nor your law, is fit for purpose."

There it was.

He had been unwittingly playing a real-life game of Bahlea and had just moved his pieces right into her trap. The only way out was right through and doubling down.

"You... have my word. I will see that justice is done."

His entire battle to reform Caspir was now reduced to a gambit of solving a murder. He felt as though he had nearly lost the war before knowing it had even started.

CHAPTER TWENTY-FIVE

Even though the blood had long since been washed off Koralia could still feel its presence. The previous night had been far more eventful than any of them had bargained for. Sleep had eluded her for most of the night, a mix of adrenaline and fear of what the dawn might bring. There would no doubt be consequences; given Takis's record, they would be severe. Koralia splashed her face with water yet another time, worried that the guards might be able to see a drop of blood that nobody else could. Paranoia was often a necessary precaution in Maluani. Day had broken some time ago and people were in the process of leaving their homes and heading to the fields. The fact that people hadn't been dragged out during the night and that even this far into the morning there was no sign of retaliation for their sedition was concerning. Why not? Her mind raced with possibilities. Perhaps it was a cover-up? Maybe they were so concerned about wider civil unrest that they wanted to bury the evidence of their midnight dissent? "That can't be it," she thought; there was no way they could hide what had been done to the statue. Somebody would see it. So then why hadn't they made a move? Then it occurred to her: the guards were just as scared of Takis as everyone else was. Who would want to be the one to tell him what had happened? Especially disturbing him at night – despite Takis not requiring sleep, he retired to his solitude every evening. His palace contained a library of an incomprehensible number of books and he spent his nights turning through endless pages by candlelight. Waiting until morning to tell him might well have been the guards' best choice for self-preservation. Not wanting to dwell much more on the subject, she threw her belt around herself and swept back her hair to leave for the fields.

Immediately upon exiting she was confronted by a handful of guards directing the workers not towards the fields, but towards the scene of last night's treason. One saw her emerge from the doorway and angrily gestured for her to follow the others. Confusion peppered people's faces, whilst others seemed so resigned to doing what they were told that they thought very little of it. Koralia's eyes scanned the other workers, checking to see if any of her comrades were around. Had any of them been caught? Was this an execution they were walking into?

The square was packed, quite the contrast to the last time she was here. Guards lined the perimeter, containing the crowds within. At the centre of the square stood the vandalized monument, given a fair amount of space out of deference. A couple of guards, including the Owl, were in the middle, surveying the masses as they shuffled in. A ripple of glee flowed across the face of the Owl. A ripple that many had come to recognize and dread. It was the look that came before an act of abject brutality, from whipping the life out of a field hand to arresting someone whom he would then torture. As the last few workers huddled in and saw the decapitated effigy, they let out gasps that echoed around the silent crowd. They all knew the wrong word or move was all the excuse required to put them on the receiving end of something terrible.

Koralia spotted a few of her crew among the masses. The briefest meeting of eyes between them was enough to convey all that was needed: a shot of relief that they hadn't been caught. She picked out Stefania on the other side of the courtyard. Surely if *she* had not been apprehended, none of them had.

Quiet fell on the entire square. No footsteps. No talking. Even people's breaths were shallow and muted. The situation spoke for itself. Like a child being forced to view the mess they had made, they all fixed their gazes on the statue's severed head. A couple of minutes passed like this, dragging for an eternity. The waiting for what came next was virtually intolerable, but everyone knew what was about to follow would be worse.

CHAPTER TWENTY-FIVE

Another minute, maybe three, passed without note. Then it began.

A tiny point of smoke popped into existence from nowhere. It billowed and quivered as it grew to form the outline of a towering man. Coalescing and shaping to the features of their ruler, the formidable image of Takis manifested before their eyes. His deep brown eyes maintained much more colour than the rest of his form, which appeared somewhat washed out due to its ethereal nature. His garb, that must have once been a vibrant orange, was now pale. A perfectly wrapped turban of the same colour concealed his hair aside from a few strands that seemed to float in a breeze that wasn't there. He bore an impeccably shaped moustache, preserved in all its exquisite glory for all of time, never growing or changing in the slightest. In another world this would have been the appearance of a great scholar or learned man, but this was not a man. No ruler or dictator could compare to this ever-living force of nature standing before them. In that moment Koralia's heart sank. It was rare they ever saw their overlord up this close. Takis being such an imposing figure, she couldn't help but feel that any opposition was pointless. No-one could stand up to this. And if Koralia thought that, she could only imagine what was going through the minds of the others. "I can't think like this," she admonished herself. Yes, it was true that standing up to Takis was an unimaginable prospect, but that was not their plan. Head-on conflict with an immortal ghost was the exact thing they wanted to avoid. No, the plan would still work. It had to.

Takis stood resolutely, slowly looking over the crowd, then glancing back at the statue's head, then to the crowd again. It was obvious what his message was. Very, very slowly, his hand slid over to his waist and carefully wrapped his fingers around the hilt of his weapon. He stood frozen in this pose for several nerve-jangling moments that saw the throng of people inhale in unison and hold it.

Without consciously seeing him move, he was now up close to the front row of people, his blade raised in the air as if at the end of an arc of his swing.

Redness showered those in the square.

Chunks of flesh and bone followed.

Where before stood three fellow workers, there were now only legs with the remnants of what were once torsos. The upper halves of all three of them had exploded into pieces from the force of the blow. Indistinguishable fragments of former people littered the square. On people's clothes. In their hair. Painted across the walls and pavement. The amount of fluid contained within the human body was disturbingly more than one imagined. It took several moments for the realization of what had occurred to be processed.

Nothing moved that fast.

At least no living thing did. A fraction of a moment was all that it took for Takis to extinguish their lives. The smell was what first hit Koralia, then the taste. Her mouth had been open; as had that of many others; there was no time to blink let alone close one's lips. The guard's blood from the night before had a distinct metallic note that surprised her, but this carnage was something else. It wasn't just blood. Organs and bone pulverized in such a way produced a very different odour. Not just metallic but meaty and acidic too. Like the offcuts from an animal that one would only eat begrudgingly. Several people suppressed screams; not drawing attention to oneself was a hardwired defence mechanism. Stomach convulsions were harder to control. The noise of vomiting punctuated the crowd, adding bile to the already repulsive scent in the air. After a minute of letting this spectacle hang in the air, Takis stood upright and took several slow and deliberate steps back as he sheathed the hulking blade of his phantasmal scimitar. He then revisited his previous actions of surveying the crowd, then the statue, then the crowd again. His eyes narrowed at the onlookers, then he faded into the aether from whence he came.

Even the guards looked disgusted at the grisly spectacle; all except the Owl. It was all he could do not to let out a sadistic laugh. Now their tyrant had left, some citizens felt confident enough to break into tears. Family members cradled each other and tried to quieten those crying. The guards were a far less horrific prospect, yet they were no strangers to inflicting cruelties either. The wardens began gesturing for people to move out towards the fields. Everyone was glad to get away from the scene of this atrocity. A couple of the guards stopped some people from leaving and ordered them to clean up the mess. A truly unenviable job Koralia was glad to have avoided,

CHAPTER TWENTY-FIVE

even though she couldn't help feel that this mess was in some way her fault. Because of *her* actions, those people were killed. Casualties were always going to happen, although she couldn't have foreseen it in such a fashion. What really concerned her was whether this reprisal would bolster or diminish their cause. Such a display would indeed instil fear into the people, but perhaps it would also reinforce how much this unjust system needed to be brought to an end. As much as it sickened Koralia, she could see the opportunity this morning had provided.

She could use this.

Those people would not die for nothing. Today she would capitalize on the tragedy to drum up sympathy for the cause, a sly shake of the head here and a few words there. The hatred for Takis ran through the blood and bones of everyone in Maluani; it was just a case of fanning those flames. There was another interesting development that she had noted. Takis's "justice" was all about the statue. The murder of a guard didn't even figure in his thinking. The wardens must have all felt less than worthless in the face of an inanimate monument being more important than their lives. This was something else she could use and before this was all done, they would need to get some of the guards on their side.

En route to the fields, a scream could be heard from the square. Takis may not have cared, but the Owl was claiming his pound of flesh.

CHAPTER TWENTY-SIX

The river had provided a rather picturesque companion for Fredo and Shiara's journey. Cutting its way through the terrain, it wove essential water through the landscape, all the way from Omdurtur to Fimego and beyond. These cities were originally built along this life-giving thread of blue so it could irrigate crops and provide drinking water; however, at some point, the cities had drawn the water into their industrial processes. Whilst Fimego created run-offs from the body of the river to supply their forges, Omdurtur was on a whole other scale. Its towering smokestacks and metal shops required the full flow of the water to cope with an unending demand. In general, the cities shared a lot of characteristics, yet Omdurtur was unique with its soot-stained atmosphere and spires of industry. Shiara detested the place, but much like the river; her path was eventually taking her there. That was a concern for the future; right now she had to focus on Fimego. As with other cities, the first thing one noticed on approach was the surrounding farmland needed to support the population, followed by the outer wall looming beyond them. She had listened to countless anecdotes from Fredo in the time taken for them to reach this point; now Fimego had finally come into view. After his ordeal, Shiara hadn't the heart to tell him to be quiet, so merely nodded along when boredom struck, and it struck often. She couldn't be certain, but she was sure even Scaley turned around to give him the occasional look as if to say, "Shut up, already!"

 Fredo didn't even notice the city appearing on the horizon at first; he was too busy watching the birds on the water. Considering his previous

CHAPTER TWENTY-SIX

encounter with the owls, it was surprising that he seemed so taken with these other feathered creatures; then again, these were far less threatening. There were quite a few different birds; the most common ones were black with short orange bills and a tuft of feathers on the backs of their heads like the hairstyle of an eccentric noblewoman. They seemed to float around carelessly, every so often diving under the surface of the water then popping up a few moments later with something green in their bills. On the far bank in the shallower part of the river stood some peculiar birds, the likes of which Fredo hadn't seen before. They had exceedingly long legs with beaks to match; it was as if somebody had stretched a bird out to make this gangly curiosity. Their feathers were a dark blue that got lighter towards the tips of the wings, with striking white lines along their backs. Iridescent orange feathers lined the side of their heads and necks. The ends of their black beaks looked like sharpened spears as they stalked up and down the bank, eyeing up the fish that swam by. Other birds flew and floated by, variations on either of these themes but with their own colours and unique honking or chirping noises. In among the thicker undergrowth and bushes that punctuated the riverbanks flitted smaller birds. Most of them were small perfectly grey balls of fluff with tails. They were too small and timid for him to get a good look at beyond identifying the different colours and sizes as they darted by. It wasn't just the birdlife that fascinated Fredo; he'd never seen so many flying insects before either, not even in the gardens of the richest nobles. Chunky black buzzing insects flew between the delicate purple and yellow flowers that sat atop thick and robust stems. It was quite the realization that life as people knew it in the cities was a far cry from "normal". Animals were seen as food or trivial pets, not even a part of day-to-day life, aside from the mottled Kerri birds that fluttered around the streets looking for crumbs. City dwellers unfairly referred to them as winged rodents and saw them as pests, which summed up attitudes towards the natural world quite succinctly. Nature was something that got in the way of people, or was there to be used and exploited. Most people had never left the cities and certainly had not ventured beyond the farmlands. Even though Fredo had travelled more than most, he had stuck to trade routes, which wildlife tended to avoid. Travelling with Shiara had already changed his perspective of the world. Within these landscapes, the idea of governments, ghosts and silver-tongues meant nothing. If it wasn't for the odd bug biting him or flying into his face, he'd go as far as describing it as idyllic.

"We're nearly there now."

Shiara's words snapped Fredo out of his nature-watch and back to reality. It wouldn't be long before they'd be surrounded by bricks and stone, the chirps of birds a distant memory. It was time for him to earn his spot as Shiara's companion and navigate the intricacies of city life for her, and intricate was an understatement when talking about Fimego. The people were unlike those in any other city; they worshipped at the feet of Mara and treated her like a deity. Rather than running the place, she was just a figurehead that people willingly served. The menial operations of a city were seen as beneath her immortal holiness. They lifted her up as a living god, administering to her every whim and keeping things running in service to her. Fredo wondered if she had sculpted Fimego to be like this over generations, or if the people had gladly given themselves to worship? The speculation was moot as there was nobody living who could remember a time where she wasn't treated as divine. He'd met her on numerous occasions and, to be honest, he quite liked her. She was sharp, witty and enjoyed a good laugh, which was Fredo's speciality. There was a streak of arrogance about her, but could one really describe it as arrogance when she was in fact an immortal warrior of renowned prowess? Mara held regular contests to keep her skills honed, although Fredo also suspected there was an element of showing off her power too. After all, what competition could she really expect from mere mortals? The government seemed very keen on keeping these competitions going, allowing citizens to best each other in combat before earning the right to face Mara. In some small part Fredo mourned the prospect of Mara meeting the same fate as Hectin and Chase, but he would not miss those who ran the city. The so-called government was what creeped him out about Fimego. He had explained to Shiara earlier that they weren't so much a government, but a force for controlling every aspect of the people's lives. Adoration of Mara was an essential part of every citizen's

CHAPTER TWENTY-SIX

life and those who didn't were disappeared. It made his time in the city very stressful. He could laugh and joke with Mara, but with any of the officials he had to watch every word. Fredo doubted they'd do anything without him saying something truly horrible, but you couldn't be too careful with religious fanatics.

The plus side of having a city filled with government spies and shadowy operators was that secret ways in and out of Fimego were plentiful. Fredo had used several of them over the years and such knowledge would surely come in useful today. It was unlikely anyone would recognize Shiara, but as Caspir's famous silver-tongue he was bound to draw unwanted attention. From the angle that they were approaching the city, Fredo had already mapped out their entry point. There was a storehouse that for all appearances was just an ordinary functional building, but concealed within it was a passageway that led under the wall and came out near one of the racetracks. One of the friendlier government clerks had shown him this route during a drinking session; it was the quickest way to get to one farmer's stock of particularly potent spirits. What exactly said spirit was made of was never made clear, but it tasted like perfume and most definitely did the job.

On reaching the outskirts of the farmland, they dismounted and led Scaley to a decidedly run-down-looking livery. They were some distance off the main trade route so there wasn't too much demand for stabling sandbacks in the area. Exchanging a few coins, the pair left their trusty transport in the capable hands of a welcoming fellow with hands like sandpaper. His disposition changed to that of suppressing a snigger when Shiara used Scaley's name to bid him farewell. From here they were better off walking – far less conspicuous.

The area of farmland they were crossing was more of an orchard. Rows of trees were evenly spaced and well cultivated so as to produce as many fruiting bodies as possible. Shiara was unfamiliar with what the crop was, which was unusual considering her time spent outside the walls.

"What are these?" she asked, picking off one of the pale pink fruits to try.

Her silver-tongued companion eagerly watched in silence as she popped it in her mouth. Within seconds she was spitting it out and screwing up her face with the intense bitterness overwhelming her palate.

"Ugh... How do people eat these?" she spat.

Fredo was happy to elaborate from behind the smirk on his face.

"Oh, we don't eat them. Well not like that at least."

"Why didn't you tell me?" Shiara barked.

Fredo's smirk had spread to a full grin.

"I can't see why they're growing rows and rows of these awful things." She may have slain two ghosts, but this taste had her beaten.

"They're pressed for oil. See those large drums over there with the crank handles and mechanisms? They fill them up and push the handles round which drives a heavy stone wheel inside, crushing out the juice, which forms an oil."

Her nose wrinkled at the prospect.

"And... people drink that?"

Fredo let out a laugh that was met with a scowl.

"No, of course not. It's aged a little then used for cooking and flavouring things. It's actually quite delicious... when used properly."

Somehow, she managed to maintain her scowl whilst drinking from her pouch and washing the flavour out of her mouth. Fredo carried on about the various styles of pressing and ageing; Shiara resigned herself to silence.

After what felt like an endless lecture on pressings, they had come to the storehouse. Inside it was stacked with various containers filled with oil, from wooden barrels to stone vases, as well as cases of bottles containing the perfumed spirit. If one could smell bitter, this would have to be close, thought Shiara. Fredo led them towards a back corner of the building and opened a hatch that could only be described at the least-concealed secret passageway conceivable. Clearly the government clerk wasn't the only one with a penchant for this spirit; there was even a self-service box for people to pay into underneath the shelves of alcohol.

The tunnel was dark. A brazier lit the entrance and a selection of torches stood next to it ready to be used to light the way. Fredo dunked a torch into the coals and they were on their way. The passageway was more or less straight, so even in the dark it would have been possible to navigate with one hand along the wall. In the far distance the glow of another brazier flickered, marking the other end of the tunnel. The sound of their footsteps carried through the underpass as they made their way to the end. Chucking the torch into the brazier they pushed through the hatch at the end, finding themselves in a small room littered with a couple of empty bottles. They had made it into Fimego without any commotion. Fredo pushed open the door into the street. Their eyes took a second to adjust to the brightness of day, but they soon realized their entry was not as stealthy as they had wished. Before them stood a handful of government officials with guards at their side. It appeared that government spies were indeed everywhere, and someone must have spotted them at the other end. They all stood staring at each other, unmoving. What were they waiting for? The familiar coalescing of smoke answered that question. The city officials bowed their heads in respect as the shape formed. Mara had arrived. A powerful bone structure and a chiselled physique were topped with flowing black ringlets of hair, which despite her ethereal form maintained their pitch-black darkness whilst the rest of her had the washed-out colours common to all ghosts. As with the other ghosts, she was a perfect specimen eternally preserved by magic long forgotten. Despite the dirty looks on the faces of those around her, she seemed receptive and amiable.

"Good to see you again, Fredo," Mara's voice was authoritative yet unabrasive. "And you must be Shiara. It's a pleasure to meet you. I understand you are here to challenge me?"

This was not what Shiara expected at all; she didn't speak, only nodded.

"Excellent! I look forward to facing you. I have a contest put aside for us in two days' time. Until then, I invite you to join me and enjoy all the hospitality Fimego has to offer as our most honoured guest."

ACT THREE

CHAPTER TWENTY-SEVEN

The body was stretched out on a raised slab. Set in a basement level, the room was cool and prevented the remains from festering. Marin was no expert. He didn't even know what he was looking for but knew that he had to find *something*. His own fate and that of Caspir's now depended on solving just one single murder; this was far from the logistical challenges he had expected to be their downfall. The fuse on the city's powder keg had been lit and it was his job to blow out. Sadly, he was fully aware that if he managed to steer Caspir through this crisis it would only be a matter of time before another touch paper was lit for a different catastrophe, but that was a problem for later. He wanted his government to be about improving lives; in reality it was a continual scurrying to put out fires getting in the way of building much of anything. Because of all this, he found himself staring into the guts of some poor soul whose insides had become a buffet for the flies and Kerri birds. It was difficult to work out what was damage caused by a weapon, and what had been pecked and pulled at by the city's avian inhabitants. A merchant turned politician was not the ideal skill-set for such criminal investigations. Usually when somebody got murdered in Caspir it was pretty obvious who had done it and there were always plenty of witnesses. Failing that, the victim generally wasn't that important, so the guards never felt much impetus to investigate the whos or whys, an approach Marin had been displeased at in the past. Now that he was the one trying to solve a case, he began to understand why they were content to abandon such investigations: at least in other crimes you had a victim to talk to. The deceased wasn't going to be talking but maybe he could offer some sort of clue? For that he was hoping Bemus would assist.

Bemus had served as a guard in Caspir for about three decades and was one of the few who volunteered for murder cases. Murders were very rare in the city and often the result of a small dispute, making them easy to solve. Perhaps their rarity was what attracted Bemus, a break from the more mundane tasks. His hair was thinning and seemed to be in two minds about turning grey; perfect white strands were peppered through a general backdrop of midnight-black hair. Stubble mimicked this trend on his slenderly pointed chin, whilst for some reason his eyebrows had chosen a middle ground and were uniformly grey. As one would expect from a man whose working life was spent wandering the streets, his skin was a weather-worn deep chestnut colour, which only drew attention to his ageing hair follicles. Regardless of his actual abilities, he certainly had an air of wisdom. He paced around the corpse looking at different angles, carefully studying various bits and pieces. Marin tried to examine the same parts in the same way; it was all just a mess to him.

"See d' edges of where 'is skin were cut open?" Bemus said in his gruff smoker's voice.

"Yes?" Marin replied tentatively.

"'s like animal's hide."

Marin stared at the guard prompting him for further explanation.

"Dat means 'e were sliced up *after* 'e were dead."

Nodding along in agreement, Marin wasn't sure what use this information provided other than a modicum of relief that the victim wasn't conscious for the disembowelling, as he had once feared.

Bemus started poking at the body with a pocketknife, lifting up the flaps of skin and peering inside, giving the organs a little jiggle as if this was as normal as stirring a cooking pot. The councillor's constitution was far weaker; he could feel his stomach turning over. This probing had the added side-effect of dispersing more foul odours into the air. The constant smell of the cadaver was bad enough, but these inspections had now released the foetid odour of the victim's bowels, which had been torn asunder. A

CHAPTER TWENTY-SEVEN

handkerchief raised to Marin's mouth and nose was pathetically inadequate for masking the scent that caught in his throat. The thing that really surprised him, though, wasn't the revolting smell – he had expected that – it was the pungent sweetness. It had never occurred to him that a body breaking down might have a sickly syrupy smell to it. His experience with bodies was restricted to those carefully prepared for funerals, not those who'd had their lives so violently ripped from them.

As a curious man, Marin was fascinated by the inner workings of a person, but sadly his stomach wasn't quite up to the task, so he often cut his observations short to look away and take a breath. Bemus continued his study of the gaping wound, speculating about how many times he was stabbed and what sort of angle the stabs came from. He even mused on the force required and what sort of a blade was used; however, for every possibility he constructed there was an equal and opposite scenario he also offered. It gave the council leader the impression that perhaps Bemus wasn't all that adept and was merely listing every possibility he could conjure up. Marin had already spent too long gazing into the wet innards of the victim, so focused his considerations on other parts of the man's body. They didn't even know who he was; they'd need to establish his identity to find out who they needed to question. The Church hadn't helped at all; he was just one of countless people draped in drab clothing that worshipped alongside them. Somebody would know him, even if Alyssa didn't. Unless of course she *did* know him but didn't want to say. Although her anger and distress came across as genuine, it hadn't taken her long to shape it into an angle to get at him, so who could be sure. All he knew was that she wasn't going to be of help in identifying the victim. Perhaps something on his person could help them learn about who this man was? The victim had some coins on him, so it ruled out that motive, if the display of the body hadn't already done so. Circling round the slab, he hoped that some magical angle of view would break the case wide open and give them a clue to pursue.

Nothing.

Bemus continued his disturbingly thorough commentary of the man's guts. Meanwhile, Marin couldn't see anything useful, no matter how many laps of the room he did. Eventually he resigned himself to sitting on the bench with his hands propping his chin up. Staring blankly forward as Bemus muttered away, the former merchant wondered how his life had come to a point where he was sitting in a cold room looking at the muddy shoes of a dead body. Where did he go wrong? He'd made a good name for himself as a trader, with the decent money that brought with it. Why on earth did he get stuck into politics? Describing it as a thankless task was an understatement. He spent all his time getting his hands dirty in other people's problems, and for what?

A thought began to form.

"Dirty..." Marin unknowingly said out loud.

"Course 'e's dirty. You would be too if someone split yer open like dis," Bemus replied.

Snapping out of his thoughts, Marin was revived. "No, not the body. His boots."

"'is boots?" asked Bemus.

Jumping to his feet and gesticulating wildly at the corpse's feet as if he was some kind of mathematician solving a theorem, Marin exclaimed: "There's fresh mud pressed into the bottom of his boots!"

Bemus wasn't quite on the same page and waved his hands in a motion that said, "Go on then".

"There's no way his boots would get like this inside the city walls, or even travelling from Caspir to Illorne along the main route."

"So dat means..." said Bemus, before being cut off mid-sentence.

"He must have worked on a farm or a ranch!" proclaimed Marin.

Excited by his deductions, he shot around the slab to examine the man's hands and frantically pointed to the body's left palm.

"See? I knew it! Look at this!" shouted Marin. "See how rough his hands are? There are plenty of people from Illorne who sought work outside the walls of Caspir after Hectin fell; he must have been one of them."

"Could be. Migh' be bit of a stre'ch," Bemus noted, clearly a little put out by having missed this whilst being focused on the more gruesome features of the corpse.

CHAPTER TWENTY-SEVEN

Marin began lifting up the clothes of the deceased man and turning out his pockets like a grave robber possessed. Then his hectic hunt came to an abrupt stop as a smile spread across his face – a very smug smile, although one he had certainly earned. Raising his hand, he had something grasped between his forefinger and thumb. A single shimmering strand of unwoven thread.

"Well, what do you say about that!? An unwoven thread that's far too colourful to be part of his wardrobe. I bet you a brand new golden-hemmed jacket that this man worked on a ranch. And what's more, with the proximity of the Church to the east gate of Caspir, I put it to you that I know exactly which ranch our victim worked at!" Marin couldn't help feeling self-satisfied; he was proud of his investigative work and it very much showed.

Bemus had to hand it to the councillor; he'd exceeded expectations. "So, wot next?"

"Now we know where he worked, we need to find out who he is. That's why I brought Kreg along with me to wait outside. Not only is he an excellent scribe; his artistic talents extend to both painting, and more importantly for us, drawing. He'll sketch the victim's face so that we can take it to the ranch and show people until someone recognizes him."

Marin's plan was a good one and it stoked Bemus's jealousy. He'd been doing this his whole adult life and never thought of it. That being said, there had never been any reason to bother identifying an unknown murder victim before, so upon further reflection he wasn't that perturbed. In his head he convinced himself that given time he would have come to the same conclusion, even if deep down he knew that was unlikely.

Marin popped his head out of the door and called in the city's scribe. With trepidation Kreg entered the room; even the wispy white hairs of his head and beard seemed to radiate nervousness. Approaching the corpse on the slab, his eyes widened and his colour drained. Darting to the corner of the room he evacuated his stomach and kept his head turned away. Taking a minute or two to himself before wiping up the droplets of vomit that hadn't soaked into his beard, he weakly asked his council leader, "Would you mind covering his body up? Unless for some reason you wish me to draw this poor fellow's insides?"

Marin flushed with embarrassment; he had shown off a grisly spectacle needlessly and caused undue stress. Sweeping a blanket over the victim Marin, ushered Kreg over to begin his sketching. Fascinated by his ability to render likenesses onto paper, he stood peering over Kreg's shoulder.

"Do you mind?" Kreg asked. "This will take me a while and I'd rather not have you hovering over me while I do it."

The council leader was apologetic and resumed his position on the bench against the wall. A plan of action was now fully formed; he'd take the drawing to the ranch nearest the east gate and ask around. Someone would be bound to know him and start the ball rolling but he was concerned where the trail would lead. What wider conspiracy might he accidentally unearth? It was a sorry state that he was just hoping for a bit of blind ignorance and religious intolerance. At least that way he could send the Church a message that the government of Caspir was looking out for them and head off any potential unrest. Even if he did find out who this poor victim was, that didn't mean he'd be any closer to finding out who did this to him. That would be one of the many problems for another day.

CHAPTER TWENTY-EIGHT

Shiara and Fredo gazed out from their third-floor balcony over Fimego. The city was clean; remarkably so. From this vantage point they couldn't see a stray piece of litter or collection of rubbish anywhere. There were no homeless people living on the streets or huddled in alleyways. On the face of it, Fimego was a picturesque place of well-maintained buildings and statues with no visible signs of poverty. Yet there was *something* unsettling about it. A kind of eerie emptiness. Yes, there were people going about their daily business but there didn't seem to be many of them. The hustle and bustle of life felt absent. Even the Kerri birds that were such a common sight in other cities were few and far between, although given such a clean environment of brick and stone, there wasn't much in the way of scraps for them to feed upon.

"Fredo, there's something not quite right about this place."

The silver-tongue swallowed his sip of finely aged wine, "A four-poster bed each and all the wine we can drink seems quite all right to me."

She rolled her eyes. "You know what I mean. This city, it just feels... sort of... lifeless."

"It's all about routine and tradition in Fimego. Give it an hour or so and the streets will be filled with people going to afternoon prayer. Then, sure enough, half an hour later it'll be empty again. Everyone keeps their head down and does what's expected; a place for everyone and nothing out of place."

The slayer of ghosts took a slurp of wine and swished it around her mouth as she pondered a moment. The time she had spent in Caspir demonstrated how difficult the smooth running of a city was, even free from the grip of their ghost 'protector'; however, here in Fimego everything ran with precision: cold calculated precision. It was as if each person was an insignificant part of a greater whole, which was both a simultaneously comforting and terrifying thought. How much of their individual humanity had been surrendered to the collective, she wondered. Was this a price worth paying for stability and relative comfort? For being part of something?

"Do you think that they're happy?" she asked.

Fredo's lips flapped as he exhaled sharply at this query.

"It's a good question. I suppose you'd have to ask them. Then again, I wouldn't let anyone catch you asking too many questions in case they report it to the Shurta. Which in some ways, gives you your answer."

"Shurta? What is that?" Shiara inquired.

"They're the city's 'cultural enforcers'. Basically a bunch of zealots tasked with policing the allegiances of the people. I've been visiting Fimego for years and they are lurking just about everywhere; everyone is terrified of them. Even those in government."

"So the people," she said, "they aren't really free at all?"

A laugh erupted from her companion's belly with such force that it took him a few moments to regain his composure.

"If you wanted to be pedantic, you could ask 'is anyone free?' As soon as you start establishing governments and systems of money you're surrendering some of that freedom."

Shiara was stunned to hear someone so intrinsically connected to the government saying something like this. She had a moment where she almost thought she could hear someone sniggering beside her at this comment.

"Of course," he continued, "Fimego is a bit of a different prospect; it's all a case of perspective really. Every city has its rules; the ones here are just a little stricter, the upside being a greater sense of community and safety. You could argue that poverty takes away freedom more than strongly enforced conformity ever does; either way, you *definitely* shouldn't go around here asking people about freedom. That's a good way to get yourself

CHAPTER TWENTY-EIGHT

disappeared."

"Disappeared?" she said tentatively.

"That's what happens to people who question the status quo a little too much. I learnt that on my first day. The orientation they gave me was especially relevant, what with my penchant for smart remarks."

"Why does Mara permit them to do that?"

"Truth is, I don't think she knows. Even if she did, I doubt she'd care. She comes across as being quite pleasant, yet she doesn't really grasp what being a human is like anymore. She's spent so long revered as a god, that the day-to-day lives of people are rather insignificant to her."

Another swig of wine lubricated Shiara's musings. She hadn't spoken with Mara for long before her officials led them to this luxurious room in the most impressive of buildings; nevertheless, she was far from the tyrant that she had expected. In fact, she was rather friendly. And why wouldn't she be? An entire city was dedicated to worshipping her whilst she had none of the responsibilities. In that way, Mara mirrored the nobles with their decadence but instead of having disdain for those beneath her, she was simply oblivious to them. This was the crux of Shiara's plan; it wasn't *about* individuals being nice or not, it was about ending systems of oppression, which led her onto the next topic that was concerning her. Mara was not like Chase, nor Hectin either. She was a different prospect entirely.

"Have you seen Mara fight?" she queried.

Fredo nodded. "Many times. It's compulsory for us visiting silver-tongues to attend the arena. I can't tell you how many lives I've seen ended in that place. It never appealed to me, but the people seem to love it."

Shiara stroked her chin and paused before asking her next question – one that she already knew the answer to, but just hoped she was wrong about.

"And... is she good?"

"Good? She's an immortal ghost protector who actively seeks out the finest duellists in Fimego to fight, and she's never even come close to losing. I think good might be an understatement."

The blood drained from her face, lightening her complexion by a few shades. Fredo, having realized what he had said and the effects of it, was quick to backtrack.

"Saying that, everybody thought Chase and Hectin were unbeatable too and you very much showed them."

His attempts to alleviate her worry were too little, too late. The damage was already done. He often forgot about the deadly risk that was the central theme to her plan. Her having dispatched two ghosts wasn't reason enough to dismiss the mortal danger she took upon herself. His assessment of Mara's formidable prowess wasn't exactly an understatement either. Chase and Hectin, whilst being perfectly hewn physical specimens, spent their time as councillors. They didn't engage in the sport of combat whereas Mara lived for it, if you could call being a ghost living. Nothing gave her greater pleasure than demonstrating her power over life and death in the arena. Although she had been bested on occasion, it was only for brief moments. Challengers had managed to land blows on her in the past and present something that resembled a contest rather than an execution, but these moments were always fleeting. In reality she had never come close to losing a bout and Fredo had often speculated that perhaps she went easy at times in order to provide more of a show. Shiara would most certainly not be given any such courtesy.

"How does she fight?" Shiara asked, breaking the tension.

"Formidably?" Fredo had misunderstood the intention of her question.

"No, not how well does she fight, but *how* does she fight?"

"Oh..." his face reddened with mild embarrassment. "Honestly, I'm not remotely close to being an expert on such things, so I'm not sure what I can tell you."

Shiara sighed. "You're an observant man. I suspect you know more than you think you do. Does she like to keep distance from her opponent and control the space, or does she like to work close in?"

Fredo wondered what had happened in Shiara's life to turn her into this refined duellist and how she had learnt the art of combat in the first place. Regardless of that, her inkling that he knew more than he thought was spot on.

"Well, when you put it like that, I'd have to say she keeps people at arm's

CHAPTER TWENTY-EIGHT

length. She uses a glaive, which gives her a range advantage, especially given her towering size compared to most."

"Excellent," remarked the ghost slayer, clearly taking things on board in a way that escaped Fredo's understanding. "And how does she like to use her glaive? Does she prefer precise thrusts, or does she whirl her weapon around in slashing arcs?"

Yet again her knowledge of fighting surprised him. He hadn't much considered differing styles of using a weapon; he'd thought of it more as instinctual than something so practised and reasoned – a perspective that seemed infantile compared to Shiara's detailed understanding.

"Now you mention it, Mara does have a habit of spinning it around in quite an impressive display. Whatever that means to you."

The colour was returning to her cheeks. Fredo assumed that he must have said something right for a change.

"It means a great deal to me. So tell me, does she herself spin and pivot too?"

"She does indeed," answered the silver-tongue.

"Good. I can use this."

Fredo was out of his depth trying to grasp what she was deducing; he just knew it was important. It reflected back how he had learnt the power of a slight inflection or a pause in one's sentence could be a useful tool or a chink in someone's armour. The arena of negotiations and spying was different, yet the principles were not too dissimilar. Every little moment was important and could be capitalized on; the slightest slip up or over-forcing of one's hand could result in disaster. With that in mind though, he was certainly glad he'd chosen his intelligence and tongue as his weapons rather than squaring off with steel in hand. The death of a trade deal was bad enough; actual death was taking it a bit too far in his opinion.

"Without meaning to sound ignorant on the topic, may I ask *how* you can use this information?"

"It's simple. From what you've told me her fighting style favours power over precision. That extra force she uses in sweeping motions provides more openings for me."

"If that's the case," Fredo asked tentatively, "why would she opt for a tactic that leaves her more vulnerable?"

Shiara raised one eyebrow and her shoulders.

"Well, the trade-off is that it gives her opponent much less room for mistakes. The openings she leaves will be very small, and every blow from a whirling arc of her blade will be fatal."

He could not quite fathom why she came across as pleased with this situation.

"You are the expert, I suppose," Fredo said in a manner so as to lighten the situation.

Shiara snorted jokingly, "Small windows of opportunity being opened for you are better than having to construct them yourself. So that's something."

He shrugged in agreement but a niggling doubt entered his mind. She was relying on his account of Mara's duelling techniques. What if he had misremembered...?

CHAPTER TWENTY-NINE

The whole of Maluani now knew of Hectin's demise. What would have previously been seen as traitorous discussion of the ghosts' mortality was now common gossip. Takis's horrific spectacle prompted questions from people: Why had this happened? What had made people take a stand and vandalize his statue? These conversations always ended up at the same place – the realization that life didn't have to be the way it was. Takis, for all of his power and terror, was in fact mortal. There was no policing of these discussions because the guards were also having them. Individuals could be silenced; the entire community could not. Understanding this was the key to what Koralia had planned. No force could stand in the way of an uprising of the people, and now people were starting to believe in one.

Koralia stood in the square, the temperate evening breeze ruffling her hair. She was gazing up at something that had become a familiar sight in recent days – a piece of graffiti that was cropping up around the entire city. It was a rudimentary depiction of a headless statue. This one was slapped on the wall in red paint; she'd seen others in just about every colour imaginable. A few days earlier, after the gruesome spectacle in the square, Neela had the idea to create a symbol for the movement – something that immediately captured the nature of the struggle and its goals. There were several suggestions, Minos's idea of a city without walls being the worst. Sure, it was a nice idea, but in practice it would only be a handful of buildings that didn't mean anything to anyone. Neela herself suggested the statue. Aside from being iconic, it was also simple enough to be easily replicated by anyone, which was already happening now. Between them, they only painted it two or three times before it caught on around Maluani. Now there were dozens; several sprang up each night. They had captured the minds of the people; the next stage was to turn those thoughts into action.

There were obvious difficulties in leading an increasingly public movement whilst also avoiding it being so public that it landed them in the laps of the guards. Discussions had to be kept to trusted circles, but said circles were rapidly expanding. It made things riskier but that was a necessary danger if the movement was to become a full-scale uprising. Tonight was set to be the biggest meeting yet and she'd be exposed as the face of the resistance to many people this evening. It would only take one to betray them and the guards would bring the whole thing crashing down. Yes, it was growing at a phenomenal rate, but it was far from being the unstoppable mobilization it needed to become; a misstep at this stage would spell disaster.

Organizing this larger meeting had been surprisingly easy. The guards' response to the graffiti was to increase highly visible patrols as a means of deterrence. However, the more visible they were, the simpler avoiding them became.

Koralia ducked inside the building. This storehouse was unused and unguarded as the harvest that would fill it was still weeks away. A crowd had formed within it, awaiting the beginning of the meeting. Some of them knew what it was all about, others were just curious or seen as sympathetic enough to be invited to listen. Koralia was reluctant. She was no orator or great speaker, but it was her idea and as Stefania pointed out, she had the passion. Stefania probably would have made a better spokesperson, thought Koralia. She was charismatic, eloquent and quick thinking, although if someone was going to take responsibility for this and the peril it could bring, it had to be Koralia herself. The rest of the gang were all there for support, except Lumis, who had already done plenty and was exhausted from a day's work. Conversations between attendees were in hushed voices; nobody wanted to attract the attention of any guard that might be passing. As a result, Koralia didn't need to call for order to address the crowd – just standing up on a makeshift platform was enough to quell any rumblings of conversation.

CHAPTER TWENTY-NINE

"Thank you all for coming," she began. "Most of you know why we are here today; to those of you who don't, let me explain. This city has never truly been our *home*; it's been our *prison*. And Takis, he is our jailer."

The people seemed to respond well and were awaiting her next words attentively. Koralia was glad she had worked on some lines for the speech with Stefania.

"For longer than even the memories of our ancestors, nobody thought it could be any different. Flesh could not compete with the might of an immortal ghost. However, now we know differently. The ghost ruler Hectin has fallen at the hands of one of the living. And what's more, he isn't the only one. Today I learnt that Chase has also met the same fate."

She'd actually found out yesterday when the guards were overheard talking about it after having conversed with traders from Caspir. The demise of one ghost was a hopeful sign, but two was a definite trend.

"One woman, by the name of Shiara, has slain two ghosts. Imagine what an entire city of us can do if we work together."

The audience had mixed feelings. The idea of ending the barbaric rule of Takis was easy to get onboard with; being the one to do the overthrowing was another thing entirely.

"You've all seen the symbol of defiance: the headless statue. We needn't stop at his statue; we can end Takis himself and with it, our subjugation. We're not asking you to directly confront him; we have a plan for that, but we will need your help. And the help of as many people as you can persuade."

Koralia glanced over at her friends. Castor and Orestis both gave her reassuring looks whilst the others were busy surveying the audience to see how the speech was landing. So far so good. The obvious trepidation was there – that was to be expected – the promise of change was enough to inspire most of them.

"We need to find as many people who are sympathetic to our cause as possible. We've lost enough loved ones to the fields and the guards; soon we make our stand. What we need from you is a revolt against the guards when the time comes. They are few, we are many. No amount of armour can change that fact. When the moment is right, rise up and take the fight to them. Let the fires of freedom and justice flow through us all."

That line felt a little heavy handed to Koralia, but she was assured that powerful imagery like that would be a hit. She was far too pragmatic to find such things compelling, yet the crowd were clearly getting pumped up. The message was resonating.

"Whilst you end the tyranny of the guards, we," she said gesturing to her comrades, "we will end Takis."

The plan was an excellent one. It utilized all the strengths they had, most notably their numbers. If the guards could be defeated and suppressed, Takis would surely be forced to intervene himself, giving her the opportunity to destroy his thrumming pillar without encountering him. However, there was no way she could say that without the guards, Takis was just one individual who wouldn't be able to stand up to a whole city. Everybody knew the story of Latan and the mad ghost. She had to be clear that there was indeed a plan for dealing with their immortal overlord. Koralia wasn't going to tell the people that part of said scheme involved Takis being provoked by the rebellion into trying to put it down himself, no doubt with devastating brutality. Some people would die – that was the nature of rebellions. There was no other way she could see them doing it, and waiting to see if this Shiara would even come to Maluani was not worth the suffering in the meantime. The moment had to be seized. In Koralia's eyes, this had to be a revolt of the people, not an outsider. *They* had to be the ones to throw off their shackles of oppression.

"Together we will be free. Go and find as many people as you can to stand arm-in-arm with us and fight when the uprising is upon us. And please, be careful. We cannot allow the guards to discover our plan until it is in action. Thank you."

She climbed down off the stage, prompting widespread whispered discussion among the attendees. The bed was made; now she must lie in it. It would only take one of these people to end the whole movement; nevertheless, she trusted her friends and the message of hope and salvation even more.

Several people came to shake Koralia's hand and thank her. The speech had done its job for now. Realistically they'd need more than just a storehouse full of people to topple Takis; it was still a promising start though. A few days ago, it was just her and her crew; now each day would bring others to the cause.

Shaking one person's hand, she felt something odd. Looking down, she saw that a piece of parchment had been placed in her palm, whilst its owner slunk off into the crowd.

"Somebody just gave me this." she said to her companions.

"What is it?" asked Minos.

"It's quite obviously a note," quipped Stefania as Koralia unfolded it.

"What does it say?" pestered Minos.

"Give her a chance to read it first." Stefania snapped back again.

Koralia's eyes darted back and forth across the parchment, taking it all in. Her expression stoked the curiosity of her compatriots. Whatever it was, it seemed important.

"It's from a guard," Koralia answered.

The group reeled back and gasped.

"That's it then; if a guard knows, we're finished," Minos said in dramatic fashion.

"No," said Koralia, "he doesn't want to stop us; he wants to help us."

"I don't trust it," spat Castor. The guards were not people as far as he was concerned.

"Having a guard on our side would be a real help. Most of them fear and hate Takis as much as we do. There's bound to be a few willing to help us." Koralia spoke with a sense of hope that the others didn't share.

"We should also be worried they found out about this meeting. Someone's been talking to the guards." Castor was cynical but factually correct. One of the people invited to the meeting must have told a guard, but if the message was genuine then they had good reason to.

"If this guard does want to help, then we should be glad someone told them," reasoned Koralia.

"So how do they want to help?" inquired Minos.

"It only says that it's important and that they'll tell me in private. They want to meet me tomorrow night."

"Koralia," warned Castor, "this sounds like a trap."

"I agree," said Minos.

"If it is a trap, they already know enough to have us all executed. The way I see it, there's nothing to lose if I go and meet them, but plenty to gain."

Koralia wasn't as sure as she sounded, but these sorts of risks had to be taken at some point, so why not now? Anything to tip the balance in their favour would be of extreme importance, even if that meant risking exposure and death.

CHAPTER THIRTY

Shiara had been cooped up in the room for long enough. They had been told that when the time came, they would be escorted to join Mara for the afternoon's races; until then they were to wait in the hospitality of the rooms provided. Despite the luxurious nature of said rooms, the hospitality was obviously meant to keep them detained. Fredo had explained the way things worked in Fimego, but Shiara was having none of it.

"That's it. I'm going out."

This did not come as a surprise to the silver-tongue, who had been witness to her pacing and incessant sighing.

"They won't let you wander about the city unaccompanied," he warned.

"Really," she huffed, "I'd like to see them try and stop me. Anyway, I won't be on my own; you're coming with me. After all, the whole point of you coming with me was to help me navigate the cities."

Shiara headed for the door. Fredo felt obliged to follow, but he wasn't going to put down his goblet of wine. Pulling open the large solid wood door they were confronted with a man, who had presumably been stationed there for quite some time. A short man in middle age with an impressively long and thin moustache and a narrow beard to match. Dressed in fine green and gold threads that rivalled the nobles of Caspir, he was clearly part of the governing class.

"Can I help you?" he asked, hands clasped together in front of him with a disconcertingly pleasant smile decorating his face.

"I'm going to take a walk," snapped the slayer of ghosts.

Tilting his head to one side, he answered back, "I'm afraid I'm not sure I can let you do that."

Shiara was unsure whether to laugh at this or shout him down; somehow she split the difference and managed an angry grin laden with sarcasm.

"Well, I'm afraid that there isn't much *you* can do to stop us."

"Don't bring me into this!" joked Fredo in an unsuccessful attempt to lighten the mood. The man tried to keep the concern from his face; it shone through regardless. Torn between self-preservation and duty he had to make a decision, a particularly difficult one given that doing one's duty was also self-preservation in Fimego.

"I *was* tasked to administer to your every need; if feeling the streets beneath your feet is indeed a requirement of yours, it would be my duty and pleasure to assist you in such desires. An able guide like myself will improve the quality of your perambulations."

Shiara looked to her companion with an expression of befuddlement.

"He says he wants to escort us," explained Fredo.

"As the afternoon draws to its conclusion, my task is to convey you to the locale of planned festivities. That is, the racetrack." The man's continued laborious use of language prompted another look from Shiara to her silver-tongued friend.

"He'll take us to the sandback races when it's time."

Shiara huffed with indignation and gave a flourish with her hands to signal that she had gone beyond caring and just wanted to leave the room. Fredo noted that she had become far more expressive around him than she had been before the incident with the owls.

The trio headed down the hallway and descended the large stone staircase that opened out into the lobby of the building. It was obvious that this place wasn't for anyone to live in; it just temporarily housed high-profile visitors. Precious metals and fine silks framed the walls to add an extra air of luxury. She hadn't seen much of the city yet between arriving and being escorted to this lavish accommodation, but even within that space of time it was plain for her to see that this extravagant building was not representative of Fimego. Similar to Caspir, only the buildings nearer the centre bore

CHAPTER THIRTY

glimmering threaded banners and aesthetic adornments. A fellow perched at the front desk who bore more than a passing resemblance to their guide – presumably such facial hair was the style – narrowed his eyes at the trio with suspicion. Assumedly he was just as displeased with Shiara leaving the building as their guide was. He didn't offer more than a sneering look.

The street outside was remarkably clean and largely empty. Nothing coming close to a crowd could be seen, only occasional handfuls of people conversing as they passed by, clearly on their way somewhere else. Fimego did not seem like a city where loitering was tolerated.

"Allow myself to direct your venturing forth this way," said their guide.

Fredo gestured to let Shiara go first; he himself had been round Fimego a number of times and knew exactly where this tour would take them. He suspected Shiara would not be pleased by such a strict plan; he would immediately be proven right.

"Sorry, what was your name?" she asked the guide.

"Malrang," he answered.

"Well then Malrang, *we* are going in *this* direction."

Malrang was noticeably taken aback. She suspected he was not used to being treated like this and that encountering strong-willed individuals was uncommon to say the least. The slayer of ghosts couldn't help feeling bad for him when she thought about it. He was just doing his job; teasing him any further would be unkind.

"Come along, tell me all about... everything." She smiled to try to set him at ease as they headed down a thoroughfare. Her week with Marin in Caspir had done a lot to change her approach and perspective; rather than merely slaying ghosts and leaving, she was beginning to consider the consequences somewhat more.

Their guide scuttled alongside them, taking a multitude of tiny steps rather than normal-sized paces. His hands remained clasped together in front of his chest only parting briefly when he would point out something to talk about.

"Removed but fifteen paces from our current stead in a leftwards direction, one of our numerous 'chambers of prayer' stands. An honour and a privilege would it be to direct your footfalls thusly."

Shiara was beginning to learn how to decipher Malrang's exceedingly flowery use of language, and she had little interest in seeing a place dedicated to worshipping a system she intended to bring down. The real Fimego was what she was curious about. How did people actually live in this place that felt so alien to her?

"And what's down here?" she asked, gesturing down a side street that looked less glamorous than the main walkways they had been treading.

"Nothing. That is to say, an absence of anything that would provide your esteemed self with anything of value nor engagement." Malrang's tone seemed to suggest a reluctance to stray from their current path. The occasional darting of his eyes towards onlookers dressed in a similar manner to himself helped fill in the picture of what was going on. *He* was being monitored just as closely as Shiara and Fredo, and diverging from their route and the surveilling eyes could be seen as suspicious. Suspicion was a dangerous thing in Fimego. Despite this, she had made up her mind and diverted their tracks away from prying eyes, and more importantly, prying ears.

The further away from the main thoroughfare they ventured, the less refined everything seemed to be. No banners or gilding, just plain walls. It was still clean and empty but appeared sterilized, as if all the life and character had been removed. Even in the Brown Quarter of Caspir one couldn't deny that it had character... of sorts. These side streets were just cold, charmless places.

"Now it's just the three of us. Tell me, what's it like to live here?" Shiara asked their guide.

Before replying, Malrang nervously glanced all around then answered at an unnaturally loud volume, as if he wanted someone out of sight to hear him.

"Why, joy and contentedness be the bedfellows of any of those deemed fortunate enough to call Fimego their home."

Unsatisfied with what she had heard Shiara leaned in closer and whispered, "No. I want to know what it's *really* like. I've yet to see a smile that was

CHAPTER THIRTY

convincing from anyone."

Malrang rubbed his hands anxiously together at an accelerated rate; this was matched by his eyes, which were unable to stay still even for the briefest of moments.

"We are blessed to share our lives with Mara, regardless of any... indignities." His words were chosen carefully and he voiced them much more quietly than before.

"Would you not rather be spared these... indignities?" asked Shiara.

"Questioning is not a position in which we wish to find ourselves," replied Malrang.

"Why not?"

"Lest one invites the wrath of the Shurta... which I have no doubt is justly delivered unto those inviting disrepute."

Fredo had been quiet throughout and was ill at ease with this questioning. Putting this poor man through such an inquiry that played on his fears didn't seem fair to him. Why did she need to find out about the people and the city if she was planning on killing their deity and breaking the system anyway? Then he remembered what had happened to Illorne and how she had stayed in Caspir for a while to try to avoid a similar outcome. Fimego was not like Caspir. Mara wasn't their leader; she was literally their god. They worshipped her. It wasn't just a political system that Shiara was poised to disrupt, but a belief system too. Even if she got people like Malrang to talk candidly, it was a long way away from establishing a new order.

"Tell me, what happens to those who invite disrepute?"

The tension in the small man was manifest across his whole body.

"The Shurta... They keep the city safe." His voice trembled almost as much as his hands.

What Fredo had told her about Fimego was accurate, yet it did not convey the true level of fear that was bred into its citizens. Fredo moved his hand near Shiara as if to touch her arm but without making contact. He shook his head and mouthed "I think you should stop" at her. He had known of people who had been "vanished" for the smallest of infractions and felt she was pushing Malrang too hard. She nodded; the Shurta and their activities were not a topic safe to pursue.

"How do you feel about Mara?" From what she had learnt, there was a significant disconnect between Mara and the Shurta.

Malrang's disposition changed; rather than shaking with apprehension, he came across as being at peace and comforted by the mere thought of Fimego's ghost protector.

"Blessed it is to be in her orbit. The perfection of her divinity is the instrument which breathes life into our very being."

For the first time she could honestly say that she had seen a genuine smile on the face of a citizen of Fimego.

"Does everyone feel that way?" Shiara was grateful to see the little man's eyes light up with joy.

"As the sun rises and sets each day;" preached Malrang, "as mortals must grow old and die; as one jumping must see the ground return beneath one's feet. That is to say, none of these constants possess the same certainty as the love for Mara that features within each of us."

Malrang's passion spurred on his elaborate use of language to a point where Shiara couldn't keep up and needed to look to her silver-tongued companion.

"Yes," said Fredo, "They can't get enough of her."

With that out of the way, she continued her quizzing.

"In that case, how do you feel about *me* being here?"

His hands parted and raised up as his whole demeanour oozed delight.

"Elation! No! Ecstasy! No! Euphoria, for your very presence within our walls permeates down to my very organs."

Shiara was perplexed. Given what she had come here to do, his reactions made little sense.

"You *do* know why I've come to Fimego, don't you?"

Vigorous nodding, and a face that wore an enormous grin, came across as overly eager.

"Of course. You are within our fine city to challenge the holiness Mara."

"I've slain both Hectin and Chase, and it doesn't bother you that I will face her?" Shiara asked reservedly.

CHAPTER THIRTY

"Bothered? Honoured is the only word befitting such a situation as to find ourselves in. You, having slain the false idols which do reside beyond the horizon, such is thy respect and admiration for our supreme deity, thou do offer thy life unto her in tribute! No finer display could be imagined nor conjured by the most erudite and creative of minds."

Everything now slotted into place. The fervent manner in which they wrapped themselves in their faith meant they really did believe she was an immortal god; that somehow she was different from the other ghosts and could not be slain. The reason none of them saw Shiara as a threat was because they couldn't grasp the concept of their god being defeated. If Hectin's demise threw Illorne into chaos, what would happen to Fimego if Mara was removed? She had to think it would at least be a fresh start. Rather, that's what she hoped. If she could just show them that the underpinning of this constrictive system was untrue, they'd be free from the Shurta, who could no longer use Mara's name to exert their control. Surely it was the right thing to do. Even if it wasn't, the course was already set. There was no deviating from the prophecy now.

CHAPTER THIRTY-ONE

Since becoming council leader of Caspir, Marin had only left the walls once, and that was to see off Shiara and Fredo. As a merchant he'd spent a long time examining the threads at the ranches and travelling to other cities. That all felt well in the past; walking around one such ranch he couldn't stop himself from reminiscing over those easier times. He'd built up a reputation in other cities as a trader in fine silks and garments, supplying the nobles and officials in top positions. The jockeys of Fimego had once depended on him for their iconic jerseys. On many occasions he had been the first to view a new hue of thread that had been produced through the ranchers' almost magical methods of breeding and feeding. Today could not have been more different. He was not looking for thread, but information. Rather than a bag of coins and business ledger, a sketch of a dead man's face rested in his hands. A mutilated man whose murder threatened to herald far more chaos and destruction. Marin had asked a few ranchers if they recognized the drawing: no luck so far. The occasional individual draped in Church garb seemed to avoid him and walk in the opposite direction. A growing distrust between the government and the Church had been fostered by Alyssa and whilst he had hoped that they'd be more willing to cooperate given the circumstances, he didn't expect much. He had his suspicions that the ranch workers who belonged to the Church didn't integrate much with other members given their exclusion within the walls. This would also explain why he hadn't much success identifying the victim yet, but someone had to have given him a job; it was just finding the right ranch manager to

CHAPTER THIRTY-ONE

ask.

It always surprised Marin quite how green it was just beyond the walls. Many of the trade routes were browner and didn't benefit from the substantial irrigation systems of the ranches and farms. The city itself may have shimmered with threaded banners, but for the most part it was just stone. The farm and ranch land that rimmed each city was a sizeable reminder of what was required to keep a city like Caspir functioning. The government fiddling with money and services was all well and good yet it meant nothing without this agriculture. It really was the fuel for their entire way of life. Then it dawned on him. A horrible realization, one of many he'd had lately. Noticing that there were a fair few Church members here, the same would be the case on the farms too. Their biggest export industry, alongside their essential food production industry, were both being slowly infiltrated by the Church. Sure, it was paranoid, but Marin's job was to safeguard Caspir, which he was finding with alarming frequency involved heavy doses of paranoia. No wonder Alyssa wasn't interested in being in the government, she knew where the real power lay – the fields. All the taxes you could imagine meant nothing without food; trade likewise depended on the production of thread. What if this entire situation was conjured up by the Church as a pretext to lodge a grievance then begin to control the fields in an outraged response? It was all very clear and calculated in Marin's mind. The more he thought about it though, the less it seemed to add up. Yes, there were Church members here but hardly enough to stage some kind of revolution, let alone them being equipped to do so. Then there was the murder; was it really to push some kind of leverage over the fields? Considering nobody was really aware of this dubious leverage in the first place, how much power could it really wield? Whilst the death of one individual sent a message, Marin wasn't sure that message was one that could promote a revolt. Whilst Alyssa seemed manipulative, trying to relate this murder to her own actions did seem a little far-fetched – and even more problematic for this theory, not that effective. Yes, it would rile people up and stoke tensions but if she wanted a big display to inspire a full-blown coup or power grab she'd be far better off burning one of their buildings. An attack on their community as a whole would be a bigger statement than the murder of one seemingly unknown person. Marin could see her sacrificing one person for political capital; a grander scheme based on that was a little ridiculous though. If there was one thing he knew about her, it's that she was smart and calculated; his paranoid thinking here didn't pan out on further scrutiny. That being said, it was worth keeping a closer eye on who was working in these fields, just in case. It took him a while for his own cynicism to catch up with him and the result was to make him feel quite disgusted by himself. By all means he figured he should keep an open mind, yet his thoughts kept factoring in Alyssa as complicit in this whole affair, which on the face of it was quite unfair. It was one thing to consider her using opportunities presented by the murder for her own ends, but suspecting her involvement in the crime based on no substantive evidence made him question how he came to this state of mind. Was it the stress of running the council that caused him to doubt everyone and think the worst? Perhaps this was just what power did to people, made them suspicious and callous? He shook his head. These musings did nobody any good. If the facts presented themselves in such a way as to implicate the Church, then he'd follow that thread; right now he just had to identify the victim. One step at a time. No conspiracy theories or other nonsense, just trying to bring a little bit of justice to this poor individual and whatever family he may have.

If the victim did work on this ranch, there was one person who would be sure to know him: Nova. Ranchers didn't come much more experienced than her. She'd grown up doing it and it was all she had ever known. Marin had often shared a drink with her when coming here to secure new threads during his merchant days. She wasn't a businesswoman; there were others far more suited to the numbers – she just loved the ranching. Because she knew every in and out there was to know about raising threadwurms, part of her job was to assess new ranchers and teach them the skills required. If the victim was indeed from Illorne, as seemed likely, and if they worked on this ranch, Nova would know about it. Finding Nova was a little trickier; as an expert on all things ranch, she could be anywhere. Marin had already covered quite some ground and was now heading towards some of the

CHAPTER THIRTY-ONE

warehouses where they stored the threadwurms in their makeshift box-cocoons. As he approached the building an unmistakable figure came into view, ferrying wooden crates to and fro. It was Nova. She was one of the few women Marin knew of who kept her head shaved, which seemed odd considering the top of her head wasn't fully round but formed a small bump at the top. It was the sort of thing a balding noble would try to cover with a hat, but Nova wasn't bothered. She loved the wind on her head and frankly didn't give a damn what people thought of her – an attitude Marin envied at times. Upon seeing Marin making his way towards her, she placed her hands on her hips and adopted a pose as if to say, "Hurry up then!"

"To what do I owe the pleasure of your visit, your highness?" Nova's words came with a playful air of mischief.

"You know, I thought I'd check in on the little people."

The pair exchanged smiles. This was far from the council meetings of barbed words and constant bickering and it pleased Marin to see a friendly face with a sense of humour.

Nova curtseyed in a mocking fashion. "How should I address you these days, oh great leader?"

Marin chuckled. "Great leader does have a nice ring to it... perhaps supreme overlord?"

Her eyes rolled whilst a smile spread across her lips.

"Seriously though Marin, what brings you here? I thought you'd have had more important things to do?"

His body language morphed into one of far less exuberance and joy, hand running through his beard in an anxious fashion.

"Unfortunately, the reason I am here *is* for something important. I'm trying to solve a murder."

Nova's eyes widened. Her mind leapt to several questions: Whose murder? What did she have to do with it? And most perplexing, why was he the one investigating?

"Let me guess," she said, "it's a long story?"

The council leader nodded.

"In that case, you can help me with these crates while you fill me in."

Marin did as she suggested and began helping her move the crates like he had done on previous occasions. She was a busy woman, and if you wanted her time you had to earn it. He told her all about the tensions between the Church and others, the powder keg nature of Caspir and the delicate balance within the council. Nova seemed surprised by his concerns over the Church and noted that in her experience they were good workers who were friendly enough and gave nobody any trouble. If anything, she thought they were better than the usual seasonal workers they dealt with. Marin continued and laid out the grisly spectacle that brought him here, then showed her Kreg's sketch that he had with him.

"You were right to come here; I know exactly who this is. His name's Rhodes. A pretty likeable sort, a bit more outgoing than the rest of the Church lot, you could have a laugh and a drink with him. Rather easy on the eye as well. It's always the good ones, isn't it?"

Marin had himself a name. Rhodes. His deductions had been correct and the first stone on the path to solving this murder had been laid.

"Have you got any useful information on him I can have? Where he lived, that sort of thing?"

Heaving a crate onto a shelf, she turned back to him.

"I can definitely find out for you. We have records on everyone who works here; we wouldn't want to be making mistakes with paying our taxes to our glorious leader now, would we?"

He rubbed his hands together as if he could feel the progress he was making between them.

"Your glorious leader would very much like to see these records."

"I'll just walk over to the main building and grab them, but..." Nova raised her finger like a tutor addressing a child, "these crates still need someone to move them."

The implication was clear; yet again she'd found a way to put Marin to work for her doing something she'd rather not do herself. He was more than glad to oblige her. Without a word he resumed the task of ferrying the crates.

"Good to see that our supreme overlord is happy to work for the people,"

CHAPTER THIRTY-ONE

Nova joked as she started for the other buildings.

He continued to lug the boxes. "These little threadwurms have got it made," he thought. They sit around eating all day and get their own private little rooms once they've had their fill. He sometimes wished he could go back to the days of being a merchant with plenty of time for lying around and eating. Setting aside enough time to eat properly was challenging in his new position. Cities were complex places, not like this warehouse. This warehouse was simple, thousands of threadwurms all tucked up in their wooden boxes in lieu of a cocoon, reshaping themselves for rebirth as moths. It was a whole city of the little creatures, all orderly and neat. Perhaps the real problem was people; they complicated everything, not like nature. Nature just got on with things. The irony of thinking about nature whilst being in a room full of an entire species unnaturally bent to the will of people was not lost on him, yet the world outside the walls did seem a simpler place. Maybe somewhere along the line civilization had taken a wrong turn; he was beginning to see Shiara's perspective a little more clearly. Conceivably things were now heading in the right direction for Caspir. Freed of their ghost protector, things could be changing for the better; those mistakes could be corrected. However, none of that mattered for poor Rhodes, and if Marin didn't solve his murder, it wouldn't matter much for him either.

CHAPTER THIRTY-TWO

Malrang had spent the last couple of hours trying to answer Shiara's questions in the least heretical way possible. Even when no Shurta agents were in sight, he still maintained a heightened level of caution. It was the only way Shiara was going to learn about Fimego and his obvious concerns spoke volumes. It wasn't all business of course; having a brief tour of some of the city was surprisingly rewarding. Cities were not her sort of thing but Fimego was architecturally quite unique. Functionality was the general trend in such places, even in Caspir where threaded banners were used to brighten up the place. Yet here in Fimego the buildings themselves were peppered with intricate carved patterns and sculpted icons mounted on their corners and guttering. Most of them were likenesses of Mara, presumably part and parcel of the worryingly zealous devotion they all had, but that didn't mean they weren't impressive or beautiful. In their own way they showed the changing styles throughout history – the older statues, which focused on minute details, had become weather-worn over time, whilst the more contemporary ones were less about capturing details and more about accentuating broad lines and bold angles. Chiselled patterns cut into the stone led one's eyes up the face of the buildings and towards the expertly made effigies. It was as if the whole city was a piece of art paying tribute to their ghost. For all its elegance and poise, the city's lack of activity countered this glamour. What was the point in all this artistry if most people spent their time indoors? Aside from a rush of people to afternoon prayers, they had hardly seen anyone, and it wasn't just the people that were conspicuously

CHAPTER THIRTY-TWO

absent. Cities were the ideal environments for Kerri birds; they nested on cliff edges and natural rock formations to keep their offspring safe from predators, so a city offered a wide array of man-made cliffs for them. In the other cities she visited, Kerri birds were just as numerous as people, gathering in much greater numbers than they ever did in the wild. Whilst civilization had been a bane to some creatures, these birds thrived, not only because of the architecture but from the waste, the dropped food and stored produce that came with urban life. In Fimego, this just wasn't the case – nothing left unattended on the streets; no scraps for them to scavenge. Their definitive coos being noticeably missing changed the entire backdrop of the environment. Most people in Caspir wouldn't think much about their calls – they were just backdrop that scored everyday life, yet every time Fredo visited Fimego it unsettled him. It was eerie, daunting, and made him feel like he was under close watch, which of course he was. Every conversation was more likely to be overheard, meaning that people had fewer conversations in the first place, which again made listening in easier, causing a terrible cycle of quieting a whole population. Fortunately for the visitors, the ambient noise was taking a turn for the louder. They were approaching the racetrack. Rounding the corner of a street, they could see the crowds at the far end of the next street with the raised up oval of stands towering over them. For once, the people looked animated and engaged as opposed to just plodding through their daily activities. Shiara and Fredo were to be Mara's special guests for this afternoon's races and as such, Malrang led them around the throng of people towards a different entrance. If the architecture of the streets they'd seen was impressive, this venue was mesmeric. Depictions of sandbacks and their riders were etched into the face of the stone, busts of past winners were raised on plinths and some truly prodigious statues of sandbacks stood outside the entrances. Each and every scale had been perfectly hewn from the stone to give them lifelike appearances with unparalleled detail. These magnificent sculptures gave the creatures powerful expressions and poses, as if they were great scholars grasping a formerly unknown concept. Having spent most of her life outside of cities, Shiara's exposure to art was limited, especially pieces of this high quality. The shimmering weaves of Caspir's textile industry had failed to impress her; clothes were still just clothes. Threadwurms and their threads were indeed impressive, but the magic of that seemed to get lost along the way to them becoming garments. Sculptures, on the other hand, really grabbed her attention. Turning something so coarse and solid into a thing of artistic grace felt like a real accomplishment. When the starting thread of Caspir's textile industry was already so exquisite, it didn't seem to be that much of an achievement to make pretty clothes. In her mind, these sculptors had made beauty from something shapeless, honed a formless slab of nothingness into a precise masterpiece. It wasn't too dissimilar from her own life experiences in that regard. She had moulded herself into the slayer of ghosts from the starting point of a malnourished youngster, although she'd have to admit her magic blade played quite a significant role. Perhaps in another life she could have been a sculptor, she thought. She was good with her hands and preferred solitude, so could envision herself chiselling away in isolation on one thing or another. Maybe after she'd slain the ghosts she could ponder on this more.

A few burly Shurta agents covered the entrance they were heading towards and parted to allow the three of them through. Malrang bowed his whole body in an ostentatious display of fealty that was very in keeping with his mannerisms. The inside of the building was even more spectacular: countless little alcoves cut into the stone with special carvings housed inside each one; trophies made from precious metals; paintings of victorious riders with sublime details and colours. All this was perfectly lit with mirrored sconces to amplify the light and project it onto these artistic marvels. It surprised Shiara how few depictions of Mara were on display, especially considering how they adorned the rest of the city. She found it strange yet refreshing to see so much dedicated to others in a city that was so fixated on their ghostly deity. The corridor in front of them split off at various points; down one of the branches she caught a glimpse of a jockey clad in a colourful shirt that wouldn't have been out of place in Caspir's high society. Soon they came to a large, spiralled staircase, which they ascended. Malrang's small shuffling steps seemed almost comical as he climbed them.

CHAPTER THIRTY-TWO

"Escalating upwards we shall find ourselves installed within the box that yields the grandest of views for the impending events. Where thou shall be granted the highest of privileges to find oneself in the company of our most esteemed and cherished divinity."

Shiara began to tune out; she wasn't interested in Malrang's flowery outpourings of love for Mara, each more excessive than the last. The entire situation was bizarre. She was here to slay this ghost, and now she found herself spending an afternoon in her company watching sandback races. Was it a ploy to change her mind? Doubtful, Mara and the people of Fimego considered her an immortal god so fear was not a factor. What if she found herself enjoying Mara's company? Would it make it more difficult for her to do what had to be done? Probably not. This was a ghost, not a person; at least it hadn't been for a very long time. Shiara was here to kill the system, not the individual. It was bigger than any single personality. For all of her puzzling, she came to the conclusion that this afternoon wasn't about sending a message or playing games, it was about Mara having a good time and showcasing the highlights of Fimego. Fredo had been forthcoming about Mara's hedonistic streak, despite her perceived divinity. Daylight was streaming down from the top of the staircase as they neared its end, opening out into Mara's box in the stadium.

The entire sweep of the stadium could be seen from here yet the distance from the centre wasn't enough to obscure the track. As anticipated from the crowds outside, the stands were packed. The chatter of voices filled the air in a display of life that the rest of the city had been lacking, in Shiara's opinion. Each section of the stands had a different colour scheme woven into it, with a mixture of painted seats and rails, alongside banners that presumably related to specific competitors. Mara's private box was lavishly decorated with finely crafted metalwork of gold and silver lining the railings, chairs and tables. It was obviously a place used to entertain and could accommodate a party of moderate size.

"It's been a while since I've been up here," Fredo mentioned as they took in the sight. Earlier in the day he'd professed his appreciation for his experiences at this track in days gone by. He'd told Shiara that this was by far the most impressive of the racecourses in Fimego and she could see why. The tables in this box were laid out with bottles of wine, fruits and immaculately crafted pastries of numerous varieties. It made Shiara think back to something Malrang had said earlier; she was seen as a special guest, not a rival or threat, but someone who was coming to lay down her life in worship of Mara's divinity. They were wining and dining the slayer of ghosts as if it was her final few days of living. It unsettled her; nevertheless she had trained for a long time for this. Then again, Mara had been training for more lifetimes than one could imagine. Shiara had the prophecy and her magical blade on her side; that would be enough. She hoped.

Malrang began bowing and scraping again as a small group of people filtered into the stand from the stairs. From their demeanours and attire they appeared to be city officials flanked by a few Shurta agents; a whisper in Shiara's ear from Fredo confirmed as much. Sitting themselves down, they exchanged greetings with Fredo, keeping to slight nods with regard to Shiara. Despite the general feelings of the people towards her, those in government were more apprehensive of any possible upset to the status quo, even if they saw it as incredibly unlikely. With everyone seated there was only one individual missing. As if with superhuman timing, the familiar coalescing of smoke began in front of them. These officials must have seen this countless times, yet their expressions reflected that special childlike wonder only reserved for religious experiences and the adventures of youth. Within moments their ghost deity was formed, complete with a warm embracing smile and perfect cascading ringlets of midnight-black hair.

"Glad you could join me." Mara's words were aimed at Shiara and were velvety in quality whilst still being authoritative. Shiara had the distinct impression that she didn't have a choice in being here, which barbed Mara's comment with a point of dishonesty. She directed them to seats next to her and offered a passing introduction to the officials as a formality she clearly had little interest in.

"Tell me, what do you think of our city?"

Shiara shifted in her chair a bit. Mara was quite an imposing force, whereas Shiara was happier left alone in the wilderness; however, her use of the word

CHAPTER THIRTY-TWO

"our" instead of "my" painted her in a more relatable light.

"I... have enjoyed the architecture and sculptures." She was grasping for something to say, although the stonework was genuinely impressive to her. The city officials nodded and looked between each other in silent, yet vigorous, approval.

"It pleases me to hear you say that. Personally, I prefer the older works. All of these newer pieces with bold suggestive lines don't have the same allure of detail for me."

One of the officials scribbled down something furiously on parchment that then was dispatched down the stairs by the others. It was obvious that an offhand remark from Mara was enough to spur them into action and entirely change fundamental aspects of the city.

"I remember when the first of these sculptures of me were being chiselled," Mara continued. "The hours and passion put into every strike of their tools. Back then, I was just a warrior; I couldn't fully appreciate it. Even so I marvelled at their skill and precision."

Her words drifted off somewhat. No living being could grasp the passing of time in the same manner as one of the ghosts. Reminiscing over a time that barely even existed in folk tales was a lonely burden, since what good were recollections with nobody else having shared them? Shiara perceived a wistful nature about Mara. For all of her luxuries and being idolized by an entire city, something was missing. There was a pang of longing when she mentioned her previous life as a warrior, a time when the cities fought each other instead of trading. That was the whole purpose of the ghosts after all, having just one individual protector who could be challenged for control of the city rather than wasting an entire population in conflict. Whilst it did promote peace and establish trade, the populations of each city had ballooned within the walls. The scale of change Mara had seen was truly staggering. From war to peace; from conflict to trade; and most importantly for her, from warrior to divinity.

Mara relaxed back in her throne-like chair and shifted the conversation. "Have you attended a race before?"

Shiara shook her head and apologetically said she hadn't. Rather than disappointing Mara, it filled her with a renewed sense of purpose. Excitedly she began explaining the intricacies of sandback racing, paying special attention to detail. She began by noting how these special lizards had been bred for generations going back to when she was still human. Selectively choosing the sleeker and faster ones to breed with one another, they ended up with what they called "racing-backs". They looked nothing like their cousins who worked the fields or your average mount like Scaley. Their scales were smaller and coupled with their more powerful legs it allowed them flexibility and speed. Overall, they were far smaller but the muscle density of their legs was a sight to behold. It wasn't just their physical attributes that had been honed over time; their temperament had been too. She was convinced that they had an extra air of pomposity and stubbornness about them, as if they knew full well how important they were. The strict diets they were fed probably compounded this – the finest threadwurms, the most succulent of fruit and leafy veg were not for the people but for these magnificent creatures instead. Then there were the jockeys. Each one was a well-known personality in Fimego and treated like a hero by the people, clad in their own unique skin-tight uniform. Their fans emulated their colours and patterns, as could be clearly seen from the crowds below. Mara continued by talking about how it wasn't just a mad dash for the finishing line; pacing was important. Sandbacks had to pant with an open mouth to cool themselves because they didn't sweat, which meant working them too hard could take you out of a race early. As Mara covered every aspect of racing, Shiara didn't feel like she was conversing with an immortal ghost, just a passionate person deeply invested in their hobbies. It made sense; she couldn't leave the city so had endeavoured to make the most of it, growing the entire culture of Fimego around her own interests.

 Mara hadn't come close to finishing her talk on the virtues of racing when the jockeys and their sandbacks started lining up for the start of the race. The cheering and stomping feet reverberated around the whole stadium and up through the floor of the box. It was energizing. Each jockey did a little twirl for the fans in order, producing enormous cheers as they did so.

 Now they were all poised at the starting line, the starter held aloft a

CHAPTER THIRTY-TWO

small parcel containing blast powder and counted down from five before dropping it into the brazier at his side. An almighty crack sounded out as the powder ignited and the thunder of racing-backs began, their pounding feet hammering into the ground as they hurtled themselves forward. A green-jerseyed jockey propelled himself and his mount into the lead around the first bend and had extended it even further by the second. By the halfway mark he was beginning to flag and his lead weakened until eventually several others pushed past him. Mara jumped up and shouted, "I told you so! See what happens when you push too hard!"

The race continued with different riders pulling ahead; a couple toppled over and skidded to the ground and the green-jerseyed rider came to a stop as his sandback gave up. The man jumped off and paced around in a huff, hurling obscenities at his lizard, which didn't seem to care in the slightest. Within a few minutes the entire affair was over. A man garbed in a rather fetching purple jersey went on to do a victory lap on foot with his trophy. The people bubbled with jubilation as he neared them and clapped with unparalleled gusto. Mara recounted her favourite parts of the race to Shiara as if she hadn't been watching. It was an almost innocent, childlike fascination and joy she possessed.

"What happens now?" asked Shiara.

"There will be another four races presently, and all of the winners will join us for the banquet tomorrow. Are you looking forward to it?"

Shiara wasn't adept at etiquette; nevertheless she felt obliged to be polite to this person she planned on killing the day after next.

"Of course, if it's as... interesting as the racing, I look forward to it."

Mara smiled. In many ways she had found a friend, of sorts. Someone who had slain two ghosts was the closest she'd ever get to an equal and it raised her spirits. Her next words flowed naturally, but they demonstrated the different perspectives they both had.

"You shall sample the finest foods Fimego has to offer. It's the city's honour and pleasure to make your final feast a spectacular one."

CHAPTER THIRTY-THREE

Was Koralia walking into a trap? Only time would tell; the guard's offer of help was exactly what the movement needed. She felt good about the previous night's meeting and had already heard about more people organizing. Her crew shared her optimism, but that didn't extend to tonight's rendezvous, which they had tried to talk her out of. Castor had offered to come with her, but the note was clear: come alone. If this was a trap, it made no sense to bring anyone else as they'd surely be no match for a bunch of guards lying in wait. Better for it to just be her that got caught rather than the whole lot of them.

The night air was cooler than usual; the clear skies had let the heat of the day evaporate. It was by no means cold, yet she felt the need to wrap a shawl over her light tunic. The place where she was to meet this anonymous guard was quite far into the city. Close to the central hub and Takis's library, this was far from her comfort zone, if you could call anywhere in Maluani one's comfort zone. She was a long way from home, which forced her to be extra cautious in how she navigated the streets and alleyways. A wash-room was the specified location. Separate from the interior of the nearby properties, it would be empty at this time of night whilst also being accessible and allowing for some privacy. It also only had one entrance, so if it was a trap there was no escape.

The cold tiles in the wash-room made the entire room feel cooler than outside. It was dark and her eyes took a moment to adjust. Nothing. As far as she could see there was nobody there. Slowly making her way around

CHAPTER THIRTY-THREE

the interior and checking all the partitioned sections, there was still no sign of anyone. Then she heard footsteps on the hard floor tiles. Someone had entered the wash-room. Koralia's heart began to race; silently she peeled back around and peered towards the entrance. A solitary figure stood in the doorway. She waited a moment to see if they were alone or not. As far as she could tell, it seemed they were.

"Hello?" she asked from out of the blackness.

The figure didn't make a sound, but advanced towards the sound of her voice until they could see one another clearly. He was a young-looking man who hadn't fully grown into his face. Facial hair seemed hard to come by for him. He was an average height and build sort of fellow, much less imposing than most of the guards. The situation of being boxed into the wash-room made him far more intimidating.

"I'm glad you came; I was worried you wouldn't show." The softness of the stranger's voice, enhanced by the fact he was speaking in hushed tones, set Koralia somewhat at ease.

"Your note said you could help, and frankly, we need all the help we can get." She marshalled her strength to sound confident and in control.

"I appreciate you taking the risk and I think you'll find my help will be worth it. I know how to get to Takis."

What did he mean? Had he come to the same conclusion about the thrumming pillar, or was it something else? she wondered.

"Go on," she said, trying not to sound too eager.

"He doesn't care about people. Not the workers, not the guards, nobody."

"Tell me something I didn't know," interjected Koralia.

"And whilst he enjoys the power, he doesn't need to keep any of us alive; we are all in the service of one goal for him."

"What is that?" she asked.

"His library. All the food we export that isn't traded for things like ore to make weapons is used to procure books. He has agents that scour the other cities and rural villages to collect books on everything from history and literature, to poetry and magic. Within the walls of his library there is an unrivalled repository of knowledge. This is his great weakness."

How exactly was their dictator's love for reading supposed to help the cause to overthrow him? Distracting him with a particularly riveting story was unlikely to work.

"If that's his weakness, how can we possibly use it?" Koralia inquired.

The young man looked around nervously as if about to commit an even greater treason.

"We burn it down."

There was a lot to unpack here. If this was indeed the greatest collection of knowledge in the six cities, destroying it would be morally reprehensible, yet if it was as important to Takis as it seemed, it would provide the perfect distraction. There would be no danger of him confronting them at the thrumming pillar if he was preoccupied with saving his books. Was the destruction of these tomes a worthwhile price to pay for their freedom? Koralia convinced herself in mere moments. The art and knowledge in those pages would indeed be a great loss but real people were suffering here and now. Whatever the cost, an end to Takis's tyranny was all that mattered. She'd already come to terms with the fact that some people would die in the uprising; better to die fighting than worked to death in the fields.

"Can you get me inside?" asked Koralia, with the determination that had become her signature.

The guard nodded. "Most of us dislike hanging around the library; there are rumours that Takis once killed a guard for getting too close. He's incredibly protective of it. That being said, I've found a back way in and have even read some of his books."

Koralia was surprised; a dangerous interest in reading books was not something she could easily associate with a guard. How could someone compassionate who wanted to help to overthrow the system even end up in such a job, she wondered.

"I have to ask, why are you helping us?"

The man ran his hand across his chin as he formed his answer.

"I see what happens. The way people are treated in Maluani, it's not right."

"But... you're a guard?" queried Koralia.

CHAPTER THIRTY-THREE

"That doesn't mean I don't care."

She was annoyed by this response. "You lot aren't the ones suffering – you are often the ones causing it! How can you say you care?"

He gave a guilty shrug.

"It's true that us wardens have a lot to answer for, but given the opportunity of a better life as a guard you can't blame anyone for taking it."

This thought had not occurred to her before. The guards were the enemy; even though some of them were better than others, they were all on the wrong side. Whatever she thought, they *were* people, just like everyone else, looking out for their own personal interests. If they couldn't see a way of opposing the system, it did make sense for them to do what was in their own best interests. Her mind flashed back to the night Stefania killed a guard. The man's body splashed with blood as the life drained out of him. Under different circumstances he might have been a painter or a baker. They knew nothing about him; did he have a family or friends who missed him? There was no shortage of bastards among the wardens, yet Koralia was beginning to see that they weren't all necessarily evil. She had wanted to get some of them on side and the truth was that some of them already were, just tempered by personal fear. It was this city that forced people to become monsters. No. It wasn't the city. It was Takis.

"I want to make things better," he continued. "Just because I'm taking part in the system, doesn't mean I don't want it to change. And I'm not the only one."

This was welcome news. What was once merely an idea or a hope was becoming a fully fledged resistance.

"Are they also willing to help us when the time comes?" asked Koralia.

"I know some who definitely will; others may take more convincing but I think we can get through to them. What's the plan?"

The man's question suddenly gave her a gnawing feeling in her gut. What was easier than interrogating a determined revolutionary for information? Getting them to freely admit it to a supposed co-conspirator. She became increasingly aware that he stood between her and the only way out of the wash-room. He seemed like he was alone, yet how did she know there weren't others just outside, ready to pounce? If she tried to run she wouldn't get far. It was better to be smart.

"When the time comes, we'll set fire to the library, and the people will rise up. As for the guards who want to help, all they have to do is not get in their way."

"And what about Takis?" inquired the man, whom she was becoming increasingly wary of.

"Let us worry about him."

She'd given him enough information so that he could help if he was genuine, but not enough to disrupt the plans to take down Takis.

"All right, you can count on me." He sounded sincere. Koralia was caught up in a mire of caution, optimism and paranoia so couldn't be sure of anything. She walked past him to poke her head outside. He didn't try to stop her in any way. Peering out to survey the street she saw nobody. His hand on her arm stopped her tracks. She turned to see the guard's fingers grasped around her bicep. Not in a malicious or forceful way, but it startled her nonetheless.

"By the way, my name is Harun." He smiled. "We shouldn't meet again until it's time. For both of our safety." He let her go.

She nodded.

"How should I get in touch with you on the night we burn the library?" she asked.

Harun paused in thought, then his face lit up with an idea as he produced something from a pocket.

"I'll leave this piece of charcoal on top of this door frame where nobody can see it. All you have to do is come here and use that charcoal to draw a cross on the wall by the door. I'll check this wash-room every morning and if I see it, then we'll meet back here that night. Sound good?"

It was a pretty risk-free way of signalling and quite ingenious; sure, she'd have to sneak around outside of curfew but she did that all the time anyway.

"And what if somebody finds the charcoal and takes it?" she said, trying to smooth out any potential problems.

Harun dived into his pocket and retrieved another piece of charcoal then

CHAPTER THIRTY-THREE

handed it to Koralia.

"I guess I'll be seeing you soon. Take care," he said.

"You too, Harun."

The pair traded nods and slipped out into the night. Koralia stopped and turned back for one last exchange: "And thank you." He didn't reply, just raised his hand to acknowledge her comment. They disappeared out of each other's sight. For all the fear and pessimism surrounding this rendezvous it had yielded a very useful ally. More important than that, a better plan. The burning library would be the perfect signal to start the revolt. And even more significant was the news that more of the guards were sympathetic to the cause. The age of ghosts was truly coming to an end. Even in Maluani.

CHAPTER THIRTY-FOUR

Tomorrow Shiara would face Mara in combat and decide the fate of Fimego. Tonight she'd have to face her around the banquet table. Yesterday's time spent at the races was a real eye opener; the city had more to offer than Shiara had first thought – there was passion and culture within these people. They weren't just the shy cogs in the machine that she first suspected. Was it right to so dramatically change their way of life by slaying their god? That was provided she could even win such a contest. The Shurta acted as a constant reminder that what she was doing was indeed in the best interests of the city; everywhere she went they were always a stone's throw away. If Shiara was unsettled by their presence, she could only imagine how it felt for the ordinary people who could be disappeared much more easily than a high-profile visitor. She felt like it was out of her hands at this stage; it was the work of prophecy rather than people. Countless generations had lived under the ghost protectors and this was now coming to an end, just as the prophecy stated. It was easier to consider herself a tool of a great destiny than think about what she was doing, reducing the emphasis on her own personal responsibility. Nobody else had slain a ghost before so she must be the one the prophecy spoke of. Once all the ghosts were dealt with, things would improve, even if right now they seemed turbulent or downright catastrophic in the case of Illorne. The prophecy promised that much; salvation and a better future for all once the cities were rid of the ghost protectors. That was what she had been fighting for and would continue to do so; obviously she didn't fully understand the finer details of the situation,

CHAPTER THIRTY-FOUR

but this was an ancient prophecy written in the times of magic, so who was she to question or judge it? Tomorrow she'd slay Mara and that would be it. On to the next challenge.

As for right now, she and Fredo had been told to wait for Malrang to bring them their outfits for the evening. Mara had been adamant that they should wear the finest of garments made in Fimego for what she worryingly called Shiara's "last meal". She'd been happy to play along with Mara's wishes so far; after all, the duel was already scheduled so her own plan was still on track. A few days of being treated like special guests and learning about how the people lived was a welcome break from travelling around on Scaley. Fredo was his usual relaxed self; dinner functions were his bread and butter, often literally. Nothing made him more at ease than telling anecdotes to a bunch of people sitting around swilling wine and eating copious amounts of food. Shiara was the opposite. The previous day at the races had been difficult enough; Mara had continuously elaborated on the nature of the races and had kept asking her for her opinions on something of which she had no knowledge. How was a commoner who had spent most of her life living in the wilderness supposed to speculate on which bend was best for overtaking? Or what diet prompted the best results? If it wasn't for the distraction of the race itself, Shiara suspected that Mara would have grown tired of her company rather quickly. At a dinner table there would be no distractions; making conversation in such a setting would be difficult, even more so considering she would be facing her host in mortal combat tomorrow.

The knock on the door they had been waiting for finally arrived. To her surprise, it wasn't Malrang who stood there but another man of similar stature and facial hair but with a distinctly different nose and brow. The man was bearing bags of clothes in his arms.

"Oh, where's Malrang? I thought he was supposed to bring them?" asked Shiara.

A slight cautious shift flickered across the man's eyes before he raised his shoulders in a faux expression of confusion.

"I'm sorry ma'am. I don't know of any... Malrang, was it?" His words sounded very reluctant.

"You must know Malrang. He's the one who escorted us around the city yesterday and took us to the races. Dresses like you and bows a lot; surely you know who I'm talking about?" Shiara pursued.

"Apologies ma'am; you are mistaken. It was I who took you around our streets and to the racetrack yesterday. You must be confused." He sounded as if he was trying to convince himself as much as anyone else.

"Nonsense. Fredo, tell him."

Fredo understood the situation far better than she did, having seen it all before. He got up from his chair and walked over to Shiara.

"Yesterday was a busy day Shiara; perhaps you aren't remembering fully."

Fredo's words triggered a pang of anger in Shiara. She knew her mind and wouldn't be told otherwise. Fredo leaned closer and whispered to her, "I'll explain in a minute, just go with it." This sent a flurry of questions scurrying through her head, but she trusted him enough to give him the benefit of the doubt.

"I see..." Shiara contemplated how to finish her sentence; the wide-eyed fear on this substitute's face had started to shine a light on the situation. "It was a very hectic afternoon. My mistake. Remind me again of your name?"

The fear subsided, covered by a wave of relief that was perceptible to all.

"It's Mamon."

"You must have misheard, it does sound a bit like Malrang," Fredo interjected. "An easy error to make."

Mamon nodded vigorously.

"I'm sorry, Mamon," said Shiara as she took the bags of clothes from him.

"Not at all, the clarity of my own speech is most likely the culprit."

Nervous smiles were exchanged all around. Mamon backed out of the room and said he'd return to escort them to the banquet later that evening. Closing the door, Shiara turned to Fredo.

"What exactly was that about? And where is Malrang?" she asked.

He shook his head.

"Gone."

CHAPTER THIRTY-FOUR

"Gone where?" she pressed.

"Well, that is the golden question. Who knows where the Shurta disappear people to?"

She had suspected something like this given the terror in Mamon's face, but having it confirmed by Fredo was a whole other thing.

"Why?"

"I suppose they didn't like him taking us around the city," he replied.

"But it wasn't his fault! It was my idea; he could hardly have stopped me."

"Sadly," Fredo sighed, "that's just how they operate. They can't punish us, so they punished him."

Shiara's mouth was open in disgust and frustration. This was exactly the sort of thing that she was here to put a stop to. This was the system that needed breaking. Even though it was the system that did this to Malrang, it didn't prevent her from feeling guilt.

"And what about Mamon and the whole pretending Malrang never even existed?"

"Whoever controls the narrative about what's happened in the past can control what's happening now. Everyone will just accept what the Shurta presents as reality because questioning them isn't an option. If they act as if someone never existed, it makes their disappearance irrelevant. Entire families will play along and even convince themselves their loved one never existed."

It was all very matter-of-fact the way Fredo recounted it, which in many ways made it all the worse.

Stunned for a few moments at the enormity of the situation, Shiara finally drew breath and proclaimed resolutely, "At least I will end all this tomorrow."

Over the last few days Fredo hadn't thought of her as the slayer of ghosts or a peerless warrior; the way she spoke these words certainly caused him to do so again.

"Let's try not to think about it and get through this evening," he said, trying to change the subject. "Why not have a look at what she's sent us over to wear?"

Her eyes said, "Fine, whatever," as she opened up one of the bags. Taking a step back, she placed her hands on her hips with an exasperated look. "She wants me to wear THIS?!"

All eyes in the room focused on the slayer of ghosts as she entered the banquet hall. Not just because of who she was, but because of what she was wearing. Her usual dull, pragmatic clothes had been replaced by a billowing dress of orange and black encrusted with shimmering jewels and lined with silver threads. Several cascading layers of fabric created a flowing effect that undulated as she moved. It commanded a lot of space as wispy gossamer-thin sections floated off the dress that extended outwards at the bottom. Having seen herself in a mirror earlier she noted that it looked as if she had no legs, since her shape from the waist down was obscured by a seemingly infinite amount of material that somehow managed to feel almost weightless. It had taken her some time to work out quite how to put the thing on; without Fredo's help she probably would never have worked it out. The constant fear of knocking things over in this flouncy outfit preyed upon her mind. Fredo was decked out in similar colours of black and orange in the form of a slim-fitting tunic and sash. She had offered him a swap of clothing earlier, which he had declined, much to her chagrin.

The banquet hall itself was almost as glamorous; jewelled sconces kept the room well-lit and reflected the light in a way that made everything brighter. The stonework and sculptures that featured so prominently around the city were also to be found here. At one end sat a long table that overlooked the rest, which were laid out perpendicular to it. Most of the evening's guests were already there, since Shiara had lost quite some time finding her way into her dress. They were all decked out in shimmering robes and extravagant accessories studded with precious metals and jewels. Every single hair in the men's beards was carefully combed into place with a sort of precision that put even Marin's impressive facial grooming to shame. Fredo remarked to her that this was exceedingly fancy, even for Fimego; her presence was the most special of occasions. The unmistakable scent of copious amounts of fine wine filled the room alongside a low rumble of

CHAPTER THIRTY-FOUR

conversation. Mamon escorted them towards a couple of open seats on the top table. In the middle of this table sat a large throne-like chair clearly left open for Mara. Shiara and Fredo sat to one side of it whilst the other side was occupied by one of the jockeys from yesterday and a public official she recognized from the previous day's races. As per usual, Mara was the last to arrive. She was never made to wait for others. Lined up along each wall were a selection of men and women dressed in black and silver dinner suits who were obviously the waiting staff. Some had jugs of wine whilst others prepared to shuttle to and from the kitchen once the banquet had begun. Between them every so often was a Shurta agent, keeping an ever-vigilant watch over the festivities. Such an obvious stamp of authoritarianism, even at an event like this, was quite disconcerting to Shiara, although the rest of the attendees didn't seem to care much. She supposed they were used to it.

All of a sudden everyone rose to their feet. Glancing to her left to see the smoke coalescing Shiara understood why and got to her feet too. Within moments Mara stood there in all the glory of an immortal ghost worshipped as a deity. She raised her arms and addressed the room.

"Thank you all for joining me on this very special evening. Tonight we celebrate the presence of our most special of guests, Shiara, the slayer of ghosts. Both Chase and Hectin have fallen to her blade, now she has come to our great city to partake in her last meal before offering herself to me in the arena tomorrow."

The room cheered. Shiara and Fredo managed an apprehensive clap. She found the situation staggering. Not because the people thought Mara would win the contest, but that she herself was not a challenger but a sacrifice. Faith had the power to convince people of just about anything.

"Perhaps she may finally offer me the worthy challenge I've been looking for," Mara continued. "Please, raise your goblets to toast her, and let the banquet begin."

As instructed, the crowd chanted Shiara's name in unison, then a flurry of activity and conversation broke out. The waiters flitted in and out of the room depositing trays of food across each of the tables, starting with Shiara's. The first dish was dough rolled into fine grains seasoned with something sweet and woody, topped with vegetables in a thick reddish-brown sauce. The aroma was beyond words. Her mouth welled with saliva and she suddenly became aware of a ravenous hunger within. Then came a tray bearing a large red and black fish that had been grilled. Its scales and features remained intact, aside from its eyes. A slit ran down its length, revealing the succulent pink flesh within. She'd never seen one of these fish this big, let alone this delicious-looking. Another, then another, then three more dishes all came out. Diced-up green vegetables, cured sandback meat, metal bowls of bean soup, savoury pastries topped with dried fruit. The barrage of appetizing marvels continued to come. Exquisite odours she didn't know existed now filled her nostrils. The waiters served portion after portion onto her plate until it represented a breathtaking canvass of mouthwatering food. Mara instructed her to go on, commenting that everyone was waiting for her to start before they also tucked into their own. Something to do with etiquette.

The first piece that entered her mouth was some kind of vegetable tuber glistening with oil that had been perfectly fried to create crispy edges. The taste was overwhelming. A perfectly balanced saltiness and slight bitterness combined with something she did not have the vocabulary for. Living out in the wilderness was not conducive to a wide lexicon for flavour.

"This is incredible," she proclaimed as she stuffed another one in.

"I'm pleased," smiled Mara, who could not partake of the feast herself.

Fredo leaned over and slyly said to her, "You'll never guess what makes it so delicious."

She made a noise whilst she chewed that could easily be interpreted as "What?"

"Remember that horrible bitter pink thing you spat out before we got inside Fimego? This was cooked in the oil made from those."

Of all the revelations in recent weeks this widened her eyes more than any other. How could such a miserable, disgusting little thing produce flavours this spectacular?

"And dry try dipping the bread in that pot of oil too." Fredo had barely finished making his suggestion before the food was crammed into Shiara's

CHAPTER THIRTY-FOUR

mouth. A loud "Mmmmmmm" noise accompanied vigorous nodding and a delighted face. She continued to indulge in sampling the various treats in front of her, managing to find a slower and more etiquette-friendly pace at which to do so.

Once the shovelling of edible delights had slowed somewhat, Mara sparked up a conversation with her.

"I take it the food is to your liking?"

Gulping down a mouthful that she probably could have done with chewing a little more, Shiara gleefully answered, "Liking doesn't cover it. I had no idea food could even taste this good."

Mara grinned. The races hadn't been great for getting to know Shiara; a plateful of food instantly opened her up and made her feel more at ease.

"I trust Fredo didn't undersell our culinary excellence. Caspir may have us beaten with textiles but they can't hold a candle to our cuisine. Which reminds me, do you like your dress?"

Her face felt hot. Was she... blushing? It was probably just the spices, yet she was embarrassed about how out of character the garment she was wearing was.

"I only ask, because you seem to be decorating it yourself."

Shiara looked down to see splodges of sauce, oil and even fragments of vegetables and fish covering the fine fabrics she wore. If she wasn't blushing before, she definitely was now.

"Oh, I'm terribly sorry." She apologized.

"Don't worry, it's your dress, you can do what you like with it. Although I do think it looks better without the food," Mara smirked.

"It's just that... I'm not used to things like this. I feel more comfortable in trousers and a tunic... Not that this isn't lovely..."

The ghost didn't seem to mind, and actually thought it quite amusing. Fredo had said that she was rather fun, for an immortal deity. Mara was happy to move the conversation on and asked her to try and describe the food she was eating. It had been forever since she had tasted anything and relished the opportunity to do so vicariously through Shiara. Unfortunately, the slayer of ghosts was not well equipped to characterize the complex and nuanced flavours she was experiencing. She fared a little better with mouthfeel because even the less elaborate food in the wilderness had a multitude of textures. "Squishy" seemed to be her favourite descriptor – which Fredo tried to correct her with "doughy" or "soft and cohesive" as proper terms – but she wasn't to be told and didn't budge from "squishy". "Crunchy" proved less divisive, along with her assessment of the roast Kerri bird as being "succulent and tender". Quite where the bird had been procured from made her wonder seeing as Fimego was weirdly absent of them. Perhaps they were bred in captivity for food, which would add yet another reason for them to steer clear of the city. As the courses continued, she developed her vocabulary and palate. Mara was curious about every bite she took, especially when it came to the sweet pastries filled with nuts and dried fruits that she made special mention of adoring before she became a ghost. The other guests at the table were continually snubbed; Mara had dined with countless officials and jockeys so they held little excitement when juxtaposed with the slayer of ghosts. The jockey next to her had no doubt spent his entire career trying to secure such a seat for a banquet, only to become an irrelevance when he got there.

Mara asked her about how she had fought Chase and Hectin and seemed to want details out of genuine interest and curiosity, rather than trying to glean an advantage for tomorrow. The conversation then turned more personal.

"Why didn't you challenge the rest of the ghosts first, before offering yourself up to me?" asked the immortal host.

Shiara had become friendly and comfortable in talking to her, so without thinking of the context and consequences, answered truthfully. "It was just convenient. This was the next stop on the way before I went to the others and I didn't want to travel back on myself needlessly."

Mara finally grasped Shiara's perspective. She wasn't offering herself up as some sacrifice; she not only intended to win but had planned around it being a certainty. For the first time Mara could remember, the concept of her own mortality entered her mind.

CHAPTER THIRTY-FIVE

Rhodes had lived in a pretty unremarkable second-storey little place near the outskirts of Caspir. It consisted of two-and-a-half cramped rooms, in which Marin and Bemus now stood. They'd asked the woman who ran the building about Rhodes but hadn't got anything of much use. Just like Nova had said, he was inoffensive and likeable.

The rooms were barely separated; thin hanging pieces of fabric served as dividers. This wasn't that uncommon, particularly in the poorer parts of Caspir. A charpai bed took up most of one of the rooms; a few of its braids were broken and the wooden frame had several gouges and knocks from years of use. The other room was cluttered, filled with everything from clothes to food. It wasn't notably dirty; lived-in was the better description. At the far end of this room a small alcove-like half-room housed pots for his daily ablutions. The scent of stale water and urine from one of them reminded Marin of seeing Rhodes's body on the slab. The smell of human waste was bad enough, without bringing up memories of a grisly corpse. He wondered if that odour would ever stop reminding him of slashed up human entrails; it seemed unlikely given that one didn't forget such things in a hurry.

So far, they'd identified the victim yet were no closer to solving his murder. The councillor wasn't sure what he was expecting to find in Rhodes's home that would magically break open the case but it was all he had. He needed a lead. Something to point him in a direction. Any direction really. As of yet, nothing jumped out.

"Least dis tells us sumfink," chimed Bemus.

"And what exactly is that?" asked the former merchant, whose deductions from the room formed the sum total of nothing.

"Look 'round. Whadya see?"

"Nothing. Nothing out of the ordinary whatsoever," Marin answered.

"Exac'ly!"

Bemus was beginning to irritate him.

"How does nothing tell us something?" Marin made sure to enunciate the word "something" as a snide way to voice his frustration.

"I fort you were s'posed to be smart," Bemus remarked offhandedly. "If nuffink is outta place, it tells us dat 'e weren't killed 'ere."

It was a simple observation; Marin couldn't fault it. It made perfect sense. No signs of struggle, no blood, no ransacking. This all ruled out these rooms as crime scenes, but whilst being progress of a sort it didn't get them any closer to solving the case.

"That's a very good point Bemus... Although I was hoping this place would give us a bit more than that."

Bemus shrugged.

"I was hoping to find something that could lead us in the direction of the killer's identity," Marin sighed.

The guard gestured over to a small dresser by the charpai, topped with piles of paper, whilst he himself rifled through the discarded food and bowls in the kitchen area. Marin was not sure what sort of clue he expected to locate among the leaves of green vegetables or unwashed pots, but Bemus seemed to know what he was doing. He hoped.

Scribbled-down notes were the much better bet in the councillor's mind and he eagerly examined them. Having read through several of them, a pattern was emerging. Rhodes was most definitely popular with the ladies. And from the content of some of these love letters, he was also popular with quite a few of the men too. Whilst most of the notes were full of affection and longing, some of them bordered on explicit filth. Marin was not an inexperienced man, yet he found himself amazed by what he was reading. It'd been a while since he'd had the time or inclination to explore his more

CHAPTER THIRTY-FIVE

carnal desires but he could feel his blood starting to pump as a result of what he was reading. There were a few pieces of parchment that weren't of this ilk. Notes regarding Church activities and meetings, as well as the odd bill of goods or receipt for his wages having been paid. Nothing that seemed relevant, at least. Opening up the small drawer in the dresser, the immaculately bearded man found what appeared to be a journal nestled among quills and ink pots. If Rhodes knew someone was out to get him it had to be written in here. Unless, of course, his murder was nothing personal and just an act of aggression against the Church rather than Rhodes. If that was the case, finding the perpetrator would prove nearly impossible without a witness coming forward, which didn't seem likely. Marin's thoughts were interrupted by a loud crunching noise. He turned to see Bemus chomping away on a pale-looking root vegetable he had found.

"Wot?" Bemus countered with a mouthful of food. "'e were 'ardly gonna eat it now."

Marin had barely touched his wine. He was more concerned with thumbing through Rhodes's journal, much to the consternation of Edwin who was trying to play a game of Bahlea with him. Edwin moved a piece across the board and went back to waiting. The really annoying thing was that Marin's head wasn't really in the game, so he offered up even less of a challenge than usual.

"It's your turn," Edwin said in a tone that reinforced his boredom.

"Let me just finish reading this entry," Marin replied, oblivious of Edwin's apparent discontent. When he finally got round to moving one of his pieces there was no deliberation or plan. The intricate multi-step strategy Edwin had constructed was lost on his opponent, whose current level of distraction could have seen a child defeat him with ease.

"All right Marin, this is pointless. You're not even trying and I have you beaten in seven moves anyway."

"You do?" asked Marin, whilst he surveyed the board as if it was new to him.

"I've spent the last half hour gazing around the Moth & Scale whilst waiting for you to make your moves, which have frankly been laughable."

"I'm sorry," apologized the council leader. "I'm just really caught up trying to find something useful in this journal."

"Any luck so far?" asked Edwin in a more kindly timbre.

Marin scrunched up his face. "I don't think so..."

Moving the Bahlea board to one side, Edwin gestured encouragingly. "Rather than playing Bahlea with me – if you can call that playing – why not tell me about what you've read and maybe together we can see if there's anything there?"

Marin nodded.

"There's a few mentions of people he's working with, fellow Church goers, even a couple of entries about Alyssa. But most of it is just... well... carnal."

Edwin chuckled. "You mean to tell me you've been sitting there this whole time reading erotica and didn't think to share?"

The pair of them laughed together, more loudly than some of the establishment's other patrons would have liked.

"I'll be honest, some of the things he's written about doing sound *exhausting*," Marin joked. "It seems like every few days he's onto, or rather into, a different person!"

"Oh, to be young again," Edwin mused.

"I doubt you were ever *that* young."

Edwin laughed at Marin's comment and found himself from nodding along in agreement.

"I'm not sure what this tells us though. Aside from the fact that he was a man with incredible stamina," concluded Marin.

"Actually," Edwin said, "it does tell us a few things. He was a strong and fit man, so it seems unlikely that one person could have done this unless they knew him and he let his guard down. And secondly, if he's as successful a lover as his journal seems to make out, he's going to have pissed off a few people off along the way."

He was right, thought Marin. Those conclusions all made sense; he should have seen them himself. If missing simple deductions like this was the level he was at, how could he possibly hope to solve the case? Self-doubt had

CHAPTER THIRTY-FIVE

been an ever-increasing feeling in recent days.

"So, a spurned lover? That could make sense, but why string him up like that?" Marin questioned doubtfully.

"What's the best way to cover up a murder of passion? Make it look like something else. And for all we know, someone else put him up there."

It was certainly a workable theory and the journal would offer up suspects to pursue. Marin didn't completely put it past Alyssa and the Church to have done this in the first place, so the notion of them stringing Rhodes up after having found him dead was definitely a possibility.

"In that case, I need to get this journal of his read as soon as I can," said the council leader.

"Just make sure you don't get too excited while doing it, eh?" quipped his older friend.

Edwin placed the Bahlea board back in the middle of the table and began resetting the pieces to their starting positions. He instructed Marin that this time he should pay more attention and provide an actual contest for a change. Topping up their beakers of wine from the bottle, they were ready to go again, but a noise from outside distracted them.

The sound of a rabble of people with angry voices, punctuated by the odd anguished shout, portended something troubling. The uproar tracked around the outside of the Moth & Scale then stopped at the door to the establishment. Whatever it was, was coming inside.

Doors burst open revealing a crew of people clad in the unmistakable robes of the Church of Shiara. Alyssa stood at their head and led them into the tavern; behind her was a small man that had been beaten and bound, held in place by a pair of stocky churchgoers. He was the undoubted source of the anguished cries. Wounds on his face and arms appeared in varying degrees of freshness; clearly he had been subjected to ill treatment for quite some time as the full rainbow of bruises was on display.

Marin rose to his feet ready to ask what was going on, but was cut off by Alyssa before he could form the words.

"*This* is your murderer. *We've* done what you couldn't and found the perpetrator. Where Caspir failed, the Church of Shiara has succeeded."

She was grandstanding; this was a display meant to intimidate and to construct a narrative. One which could be devastating for the stability of the city.

"It's not the role of citizens to capture suspects and do... whatever it is you've done to this man." The immaculately bearded man was puffing out his chest as he said this, trying his hardest to exert some authority in a situation where he seemed to have very little.

"It's also not the role of citizens to be murdered, but here we are." Alyssa was quick witted and had the perfect response for everything. "Tell him!" she demanded of the battered man.

"I... killed that man. It... was me." He spluttered out the words, evidently struggling to speak with his swollen face.

"There you go. Whilst you were sitting around drinking wine and playing Bahlea, we were getting a murderer off the streets." Alyssa spoke these words as if they were a speech of an official running for office, gesturing assertively and scanning the room to engage with as many people as she could, meeting their eyes to hammer home her message.

"Now," she continued, "our work is done. It is now up to the council of Caspir and your legal system. We have done all we can and offer you a chance to demonstrate whether this city is indeed a place of law and order, or whether we need to look elsewhere to find the justice that is the right of every citizen."

The gauntlet had been thrown down. This man had obviously been tortured and no doubt would have confessed to anything. This wasn't justice. This was a power play. If they didn't arrest this man who had just confessed, albeit under duress, the legitimacy of the rule of law would be strained in the public's eye. If they did arrest this poor man, the actual integrity of the law would be at risk. He could only see one choice.

"Justice is indeed the right of every citizen." He paused briefly as a lump formed in his throat. "That right extends not only to victims, but also to the accused. We will arrest this man, then we will ascertain his guilt. Not with methods that leave him bloody and swollen, but with facts."

The hill upon which he, and indeed this new Caspir he was trying to build,

CHAPTER THIRTY-FIVE

was poised to die on had been constructed. There were only a handful of outcomes, most of them bad. Most worryingly, there was always the possibility that this man *had* killed Rhodes, in which case Alyssa could only win from the situation. If one thing was certain though, it was that Marin wasn't going to be getting any sleep that night.

CHAPTER THIRTY-SIX

The last few days of luxury were coming to an end for Shiara and Fredo. Today was the day that she was to face Mara. The fine evening dress of last night, complete with food stains, had been cast aside in favour of her familiarly dull and practical clothes. She hadn't slept well. With the previous two ghosts she had slain there wasn't any hanging about or days of spending time with them, it was just all business. This time had been different. Shiara had experienced the city and Mara's company. Having seen the staggering levels of devotion everyone in Fimego had towards their ghost deity it played on her mind. Killing a god was not the same as killing a politician. How would people react? Illorne fell into chaos and Mara was a far more integral part of people's lives than Hectin ever was. On the other hand, Caspir seemed fine, albeit needing a guiding hand and a lot of work. Perhaps freed from the shackles of their beliefs they'd finally rise up and overthrow the Shurta; put the people first. The prophecy was clear that only by removing the ghosts could people flourish. There was no reason for the prophecy to lie and it seemed to have foretold all her actions up until now. She was from a poor background and had suffered more than most from the world that the ghost councillors had shaped. The bereavement of her family also tied up with the prophecy. It was obvious that she fitted the description perfectly, especially since she had managed to slay two ghosts. Shiara had come this far; she would fully enact the prophecy and end the immortal tyranny of the ghosts. Even if she couldn't help feeling the word "tyranny" was perhaps a little strong in some cases. It seemed to her that Mara was more of a useful

CHAPTER THIRTY-SIX

figurehead for others rather than a tyrant, yet there was no denying that the authoritarian Shurta derived their power from her.

Whipping out her blade and examining it, she thought its glimmering sheen was slightly duller than usual, even if it still impressed Fredo. It had been a while since she'd unsheathed it though, and it was an exceptionally bright day with the sun streaming in through the balcony windows.

"Are you ready?" asked Fredo.

"To be honest with you, I've been ready for several days," she replied whilst re-sheathing her sword.

The knock on the door they had been waiting for finally came. Mamon entered the room and placed a finely woven wreath of red and white flowers around Shiara's neck. Behind him in the corridor was an entourage of identically dressed people carrying large bags that appeared to be light, judging by the way they were holding them.

"Ma'am. Allow me to escort you to our magnificent arena."

There was an almost fervent look in his eyes, like a ravenous sandback who hadn't eaten for weeks finally getting a meal. This level of contest was not something any of them had experienced before. For them it was the ultimate tribute to their divinity and a chance to see Mara in all of her glory. Those in the corridor slowly started moving forward whilst throwing handfuls of red and white petals from the sacks they carried, producing a light floral carpet that Mamon instructed her she must walk on. Shiara couldn't begin to fathom how many flowers must have been picked to fill these bags and regardless of how pretty they were, it was a shame they were being thrown to the floor and not left on the plants.

Mamon led the way, followed by Shiara and Fredo. Once down the stairs and out of the building, Shiara saw the street was packed with onlookers trying to get a peek. Fredo had never seen a crowd this silent before, just watching on in quiet curiosity. The slight breeze in the air carried the fragile petals somewhat, making the path far less tidy than when inside. The odd one blew into her hair or got caught on her clothes; at first she brushed them off, but the rate at which new ones accumulated made her give up. She'd wait until they arrived at the arena and get them all off in one go. Spectators closed ranks behind them and began to follow them towards the centre of the city, their silence replaced by incessant whispering to one another.

"Quite the turnout. You realize they're all wanting to see you killed?" Fredo's attempt at humour was clumsier than his usual efforts; he was obviously not without nervousness either.

"Well, a whole lot of people are in for a big surprise," she retorted. The closer it got to their duel, the fewer nerves she seemed to have. This wasn't a duel; this was destiny being exacted. No ghost had managed to stand in the way of prophecy so far.

The towering arena had been in view for some time; nevertheless, the true extent and scale of the building could only be appreciated when they neared it. Lengthy shadows cascaded outwards from this colossal and imposing structure. The racetrack had been impressive; this was far more magnificent. Like the racecourse, the building was covered in sculptures and etchings. Depictions of courageous warriors and fallen combatants spiralled endlessly around the monumental walls, although gigantic representations of Mara were the main features. Her likenesses showed her off in one victorious pose after another. She wasn't a contestant; she was the god of battle. The whispering of their cohort broke into loud chattering that added to the noise billowing out from the arena. The citizens dispersed and headed for other entrances whilst Mamon led Shiara and Fredo through a grand archway inlaid with gold and silver. The noise rose to a cacophony of such volume it was disorienting. They soon found themselves in what could only be described as a shallow holding pen that joined onto the venue's battleground. The ground was laid with light sandy coloured stones, a slight sprinkling of dust across its entirety. In the middle stood the thrumming pillar. In tribute to her love for combat, the entire coliseum had been constructed around Mara's pillar so that she was at the heart of every bout. A small quiver ran through Shiara's hand she had placed on her sheath. Around the arena floor was a very tall wall, above which the audience stands were built. Four tiers of seats overlooked them, every one packed beyond capacity. People were squashed in, unable to sit for lack of room. Their hysterical chatter made the entire place feel like it was shaking. This was a far cry from the courtyards

CHAPTER THIRTY-SIX

of Chase and Hectin, which had been rather understated affairs. Fighting Mara wouldn't just be a battle, it would be a spectacle.

From the other end of the arena, a couple of men wielding swords, with sparse plates of armour covering a couple of places on their bodies, walked into the centre. A booming voice from one of the high-up boxes drew everyone's attention as the crowd quietened down. Shiara didn't recognize this man, but Mara was alongside him in the box. The man stoked up the audience with all the vigour of a great thespian, producing cheers from the onlookers whenever he so commanded them.

"Our esteemed guest for the main event," he bellowed whilst directing his hand towards Shiara, eliciting roars from the spectators, "shall first see what the fighters of our great city have to offer!"

The announcer introduced the warriors below and declared this would be the first of three exhibition matches to warm the public up for her anticipated bout. Mamon directed Shiara and Fredo to petal-strewn seats to view the contests from. Mara herself gestured from above to begin to duel.

Clashing of steel and exaggerated dashes and rolls across the arena gave the whole affair a sort of artistic merit. The slayer of ghosts couldn't see the attraction of wanting to see one man kill another for sport, but the crowd seemed to disagree strongly as they bayed for blood. Despite the rippling muscles and displays of strength, she was not impressed by the fighters' prowess, once again finding herself at odds with the audience's very loud opinions. She'd noticed the otherwise introverted people of Fimego cutting loose at the races, but the intensity of their emotions now far surpassed that. One could sense the desire for carnage oozing from the stands. All that pent-up expression that was normally denied was finally given an outlet and it was a troubling one for an outsider to see. The whole purpose of the ghost protectors originally was to avoid the deaths of ordinary citizens in conflicts, yet now they were opting into it and cheering for gore. The contest lasted considerably longer than Shiara thought it ought to; numerous times she saw an opening that she herself would have used to end the fight. Eventually one of the men's shoulders was wounded in such a way as to make his defence virtually non-existent. One body blow later, he was on the ground meeting the tip of his opponent's blade with his internal organs. Red flowed out across the pale stones; she suspected the colour was intentionally chosen to make the blood stand out more to the viewers. Applause rang out for the victor. Servants scuttled over to the body to remove it. Before long, another pair were making their way into the middle to start up the violence all over again. The same underwhelming combat ensued, met with the same joyous reactions from the onlookers, the quality of the duel taking a back seat to the bloodlust. Mercifully this bout was quicker, but the final of the warm-up battles was not. Rather than a mortal battle of life and death, it came across like a protracted dance. If it wasn't for the impending loss of life, Shiara wouldn't have been able to stop herself sniggering at what passed for an entertaining clash.

The final body was removed and the arena cleared. The clapping and jeering dissipated into a reverent silence. Shiara had stood up to do a few stretches and felt the eyes of the whole place focused on her. Mamon instructed her that it was time. She paced out to the middle, stepping over a few spots of blood, both old and new. Standing near the thrumming pillar, she craned her neck upwards to the box only to see that Mara was now missing from it. Looking to her left, she saw the familiar materialization of a ghost protector.

"And now, the moment we have all been waiting for! Shiara, slayer of Hectin and Chase, will offer herself in combat to our immortal saviour." The orator's words echoed around the walls, the entire venue acting like a funnel for his voice.

Mara widened her stance as a ghostly weapon formed within her grip. The long handle of her glaive coalesced, and finally the glistening bladed tip was complete. Shiara drew her own cutlass with its unique rainbow shimmer that sent a few gasps through the stands.

Mara herself raised her hand; even as one of the fighters she still commanded the opening of proceedings. Unclenching her hand was the signal for combat to begin and for the crowd to build a raucous ecstasy and deafening noise. The loudness of the chants took a few moments for Shiara to get used to and briefly put her off balance; fortunately Mara was not quick

CHAPTER THIRTY-SIX

off the mark, choosing instead to survey her opponent and start the whirling arcs of her weapon. The ghost's blade was cutting curves through the air as the pair circled. This was Mara's domain; she was this city's god, so she made the first attack, sweeping across Shiara's face and spinning back to attack her legs, both blows narrowly missing. The slayer's agility and nimbleness offered quite a contrast to the previous combatants of the day – where their bulky raw strength would have been cut down, she instead ducked and weaved through each successive strike. The better part of a minute went by in this fashion. No rebuttals from Shiara, just a successful series of dodges threaded together. Mara's failure to connect glaive with flesh caused her to ramp up her aggressions and opt for larger sweeping arcs that invaded the brown-clad duellist's space even further. The edge nearly stroked her face each time, but no attack landed. Sensing a failure in approach, the deity flipped her stance and tried an angled lunge. This was the opportunity her opponent had been waiting for. Her sword turned the glaive aside then struck Mara's arm in one smooth motion. A small stream of black ascended from the wound like a river polluted with slag rising upwards. The pair jumped back from each other and the onlookers' chants slowed with a collective sharp intake of breath. The divinity glanced at her cut. This was new territory for her. She had not bled before, if one could call this bleeding. The curiosity and frustration in her face turned to anger and determination. She had wanted a real contest, now she had one.

Racing forward, she changed her approach. Smaller arcs of her weapon gave her more control, but Shiara remained unfazed. The slayer's plan was simple – keep herself alive and wait for something to take advantage of. As minutes went by in this battle of wits and weapons, the concentration and exertion began taking its toll. Shiara barely had enough time to catch her breath between assaults. Her skin became slick with sweat. Despite her accomplishments, Shiara was still human. Mara, on the other hand, would never tire. In a battle of attrition there would be no victory for the warrior made of flesh. There was no longer time to wait for opportunity; she had to make her own.

Beating back the ghost's weapon and swiping low, Shiara took Mara by surprise with her change of tactic. It forced the ghost to take steps backwards to avoid further injury, creating a greater distance between them.

This was it.

The pair both readied for another clash and stormed towards one another. Rather than keeping the fight at the same distance it had been so far, Shiara had other ideas. Instead of the parry that Mara expected, her foe rolled past her glaive and popped up within the sweep of her arms rather than her weapon. The slayer's cutlass came with her. A plume of black erupted from a gouge in the ghost's chest. Bobbing underneath her arms again, Shiara struck once more, separating a leg at the thigh. Before Mara's frame could topple to the ground, a final cleave from behind split her body diagonally. Onyx mist streaked across the arena, extending from the arc of Shiara's blade, followed by fragments of stone from the thrumming pillar as if it too had been struck. The immortal god of Fimego disintegrated into ethereal rubble, matched by the pillar that bound her essence. The rainbow glimmer of Shiara's blade shone brighter and she could hear a relieved hiss, almost like a "Yessssssss", come from its edge. Its magic had always produced an array of noises that one could ascribe character to, now more than ever. There was much she didn't understand about it.

It was only possible for her to hear this sound because of the deathly silence that filled the stadium. Fimego was stunned, unable to utter anything in that moment. The crowd was beyond horrified. How would they react?

Each face in the crowd contorted with bewildered horror. There wasn't panic; not yet at least, for the ability to grasp what they had just witnessed took considerable time to be found. Shiara slowly stepped away from the centre of the arena and looked to Fredo. His mind was already planning the quickest route out of Fimego if required. She looked to the stands above; even the Shurta were immoveable, lost in what they had just witnessed and the implications it would hold for them. Shiara made her way slowly to the arena-side holding pen and her companion; trying not to draw attention to herself seemed ridiculous given the circumstances but she tried, nonetheless. The stretched-out quiet grew increasingly troubling. She wished someone would make a noise and end it.

CHAPTER THIRTY-SIX

Then came the screaming.

CHAPTER THIRTY-SEVEN

The resistance was growing. It was no longer a secretive underground movement but one hiding in plain sight. Very few were sure who had started it, but there was a gesture people had taken to giving one another to identify their support for the cause. It was a simple salute where the hand meets the neck rather than the head; this was supposed to reference the beheading of the statue and the iconography that had sprung up around the city since. There was a sense of optimism about the place that Koralia had never seen before. People were brazenly greeting each other with the salute, even in front of guards. It had become so commonplace that there was no effective method of combatting it that the guards could take, and Takis – as per usual – had no interest in the affairs of mortals. There were even rumours of other groups organizing their own resistance movements, which filled Koralia with hope. If for some reason she was stopped before the plan came to fruition, others would take up the cause and she wouldn't be able to give up any information on them either. Operating as separate cells would give them all a bit more safety and protection from the wardens, who were becoming increasingly curious. Stopping a person was easier than stopping the people; she had never wanted to be a leader – she just wanted to make sure it happened. Having secured an ally in the form of Harun, the pieces were falling into place. The word was slowly going around that it would soon be time. A few trusted sources were told that the trigger for the uprising was Takis's library going up in flames. When the night of the revolt came, these sources would tell as many as they could so all of Maluani could rise up as one.

CHAPTER THIRTY-SEVEN

Lumis had surreptitiously fashioned quite the stash of weapons; they were no match for the fine work of the guards' weaponry, but they would suffice. Heavy, blunt instruments were harder to make with the limited resources they had available, so the stash comprised mainly blades of varying sizes and piercing tools like picks. Clubs and suchlike could easily be fashioned from household objects. Farming tools would be repurposed for killing and wounding; one of the first acts of the rebellion would be for some to break onto the farmland and retrieve those tools. Once equipped, the fight they would take to the guards who stood in the way would be much more even.

Working in the fields seemed easier over the last few days. The toil of backbreaking labour was lessened by the knowledge that it would soon end. There was a new lease of life in the people, who were now far more inclined to get together and enjoy one another's company rather than shuffling between eating, work and sleep. The movement hadn't just given them hope; it had given them a stronger sense of community. Commonly held desires for what life could be like forged new bonds. Koralia could see it writ large on the faces of her comrades working the soil; this building of social collectives was something she had always considered natural. Her own group of friends had been sharing meals and each other's company for years, and she suspected the virtues of youth were responsible for the energy required to do more than just rest in their free time. Now she saw that same spark reflected back throughout the city.

This evening's gathering of her friends and co-conspirators felt special; indeed each meeting of late had this same vibe. They were closing in on their goal and every night together had the possibility of being their last, for better or worse. As per usual the evening's conversation had worked its way towards speculations of what they'd do when this was all over.

"I think I'd make a great musician," declared Orestis in a whimsical manner.

"A musician?" scoffed Nasos. "Can you even play an instrument?"

"There's no reason I couldn't learn. And if my singing voice is anything to go by, I'm a natural," Orestis replied.

"A natural? There's nothing natural about the way you torture victims with this supposed singing of yours," retorted Nasos. It was easy to make Orestis the butt of the joke; he almost seemed to invite it upon himself.

"People always say I have a lovely voice!" said Orestis defensively.

"I didn't know you knew so many deaf people," Stefania mocked.

"All right, I'll prove it by singing the one about the woman who turns into a bird."

He puffed out his chest but before he could warble a single note, all present – Koralia, Minos, Nasos, Stefania and Lumis – let out a loud cry of "NO!" in unison.

"Your loss," countered Orestis.

"Better than our loss of hearing from that screeching you call singing." Stefania's impressive command of language also extended to insults.

"I've always fancied sculpting, and it would be nice to have statues other than Takis in various menacing poses," said Minos. The group nodded and seemed receptive to the suggestion, all except Orestis.

"Oh, I see, you all jump to mock me for wanting to be a musician, but sculptor boy here gets a free pass?" protested Orestis with a smirk.

"I think he'd be well suited to it, actually," said Koralia.

"And why's that then?" Orestis demanded to know.

"He can use that big ol' nose of his as a chisel," she quipped, to rapturous laughter from everyone, including Minos.

"What about you?" Lumis asked of Koralia. "This whole thing was your idea; you must have an idea of what you want to do when it's all over and done with?"

She opened her mouth to reply but the words weren't quite there. So much of her life had been spent wanting things to be different that she hadn't taken the time to imagine what that would be like for her personally. There was a bleak notion in her mind that she wouldn't live to see it. Bringing the rule of Takis to a close *was* her end goal; as lovely as it would be to have a life afterwards she was content to die so long as Takis was gone.

"I... guess I'd just like to walk outside the walls," she finally answered. It wasn't some future career or pastime, but it was honest – a simple expression of the freedom they'd all been denied since before they were

CHAPTER THIRTY-SEVEN

born. The others fell silent in reflection. It was a humble desire they could all immediately share in and it came across as far more profound than she had intended.

After a few moments of reflection, Lumis broke the silence.

"Personally, I'm just looking forward to sleeping in late for a change." The joviality had returned after only the briefest of pauses for profundity. The speculations about what their futures held continued, all the while ignoring the massive hill they had to climb in order to get there. It was a coping mechanism for them; there was no point in dwelling on what had to be done at a time like this. At one point it was suggested that Stefania should be a writer, to which she replied with a simple "I know". They valued their time together, even though two of their usual members had not yet arrived.

The door opened and in stepped a panicked-looking Neela and Castor, their chests heaving from the exertion that must have led to their sweaty demeanours. If it hadn't been for the horror in their eyes, Minos would have cracked a joke speculating about what the two had been up to.

"What is it?" asked a concerned Lumis of his daughter.

It took numerous pants before they could answer.

"We've heard... that one... of the res...istance... groups is... attacking... tonight!" Neela exclaimed.

Everyone looked at each other and knew what this meant. An uncoordinated attack at the wrong time could disrupt their plans significantly.

"What are they doing?" inquired Koralia.

"They're sneaking into a wardens' barracks... they plan to murder a roomful while they're asleep," replied Castor, his muscular chest quivering from both emotion and exercise.

"No..." let out Koralia with an air of defeat.

There were so many problems that this threw up. Antagonizing the guards before the time was right could result in horrific reprisals, and whilst that could add fuel to the cause, it could also put out the fires of rebellion entirely. Then another thought came to the forefront of her mind with alarming implications. "What about Harun?" Despite it being unlikely, what if these foolhardy rebels unwittingly happened to murder the movement's secret weapon? There was no chance of getting into the library and setting the fire to start off the whole thing without him. Even if this wasn't his barracks, who knows how he'd react to a direct attack on the guards, especially if he wasn't forewarned for his own personal safety? There was always a risk that individual cells of the resistance could act in such a way, but they honestly hadn't thought it likely. For generations, cowardice had been the survival instinct for the people of Maluani; Koralia had not realized how easily this could be squashed with the promise of change. She carried a faint hope that maybe this was just a rumour, but Castor and Neela put paid to that with the veracity of how they came to know of the plot. The morning would no doubt be full of terrors and offer a real test to the integrity of the resistance.

The black-clad figures slipped in undetected. The security provisions around the wardens' barracks were virtually non-existent. The general assumption was that nobody would be stupid enough to attack the guards, and up until today, that had been the case. Those on night shifts were out and about in the city; those left here were sleeping in preparation for their morning starts. Numerous rooms in the building housed about ten people a piece; in total thirty slept whilst the same number were out patrolling. The corridors were still and empty as the shadows snuck down them. Coming to the first room, the leader of the group gently pushed open the door. There were ten rebels: one for each guard in the room. This was less of an attack and more of a planned slaughter. Each of them readied themselves above their prone victims, gleaming blade in hand. All eyes turned towards the head of their group, waiting for the nod to commence the butchery in unison. Knives slid deeply into throats and ripped across their necks, producing jagged tears. Ten sets of eyes opened in unrivalled horror. Mouths opened to scream, but the only noises they could produce were low gargles as the wet death filled their lungs. Their lifeblood soaked their charpai beds and blankets then dripped to the floor to fill the cracks in the tiles. The room smelled of sweat and iron. The last few convulsions of struggle dissipated, leaving the room a silent tableau of carnage. Treading red footsteps out

CHAPTER THIRTY-SEVEN

and along the corridor, the butchers made their way to the next room to continue the bloodletting. Within the hour, all thirty wardens would be separated from their lives, the black garb of the assassins stained crimson.

These people did not just have a need for violence, but a lust for it too.

CHAPTER THIRTY-EIGHT

Deafening shrieks and howls filled the air. The stands convulsed with anguish. It had finally sunk in that the people of Fimego has seen their deity torn from them. Now they turned on themselves and each other: clawing at their own faces and their fellow citizens.

THUD.

A body dropped onto the arena floor.

THUD.

Then another. Then three more. Waves of people throwing themselves to their deaths rather than face the reality of what they had just witnessed. Some were thrown off by others; most launched themselves off rather than comprehend the destruction of their world view.

"Run!" a voice shouted to Shiara. She looked down at her brightly shimmering blade.

"RUN!" it instructed her once again.

Turning on the spot, she bolted, Fredo signalling the way. She dodged and weaved through writhing bodies as they fell from above. To say she was shaken was an understatement. Never had either witnessed such carnage and horror before, even in Illorne. They looked on in revulsion as ordinary people descended into an orgy of meaningless violence, disembowelling each other with their bare hands. Blood flowed and the terror-filled screams were not enough to drown out the atrocities. They could hear the tearing of flesh and cracking of bones above the rabble, a noise that nobody should ever hear. Tears welled in Shiara's eyes as she saw what was being wrought;

CHAPTER THIRTY-EIGHT

Fredo fared little better.

"We have to go!" bawled the silver-tongue. Shiara tore her view away from the mess behind them and followed him to escape the arena.

The cries from within were harder to escape. Blinking the tears out of their eyes, full function returned to their limbs.

"Fredo, I need you to listen to me. We have to get out of the city. And we have to do it now. You've got to get us out of here."

Shiara's sturdy grip shook enough sense into him to steady his fraying nerves. Fredo looked around to get his bearings. For now, the chaos was contained in the arena, but it wouldn't be long before it spilled out to the rest of the city.

"Hurry up!" shouted a disembodied voice.

The silver-tongue looked around, confused, before settling his eyes on Shiara's blade, then glanced at her with an expression that asked the obvious question.

She shrugged.

There was no time to unpack this. Fredo started them out on the escape plan he had worked out earlier. Gesturing to his companion, they took off in an understandably panicked fashion. As the pair left the amphitheatre behind, a final over-the-shoulder glance saw the first few bloody patrons staggering out of the building. A middle-aged man with shoulder length hair hobbled out, splashed with wet crimson; his expression went beyond anger or fear and instead seemed empty. His outstretched hand, held up in a claw-like position, dripped freshly drawn blood onto the street. A woman behind him in torn clothes was far more animated, tackling the older man to the ground. He barely put up a fight as she repeatedly slammed his head into the pavement whilst gnawing on his raised hand. Another man collapsed to the ground, running his hand through an open wound in his stomach like a bemused child at play, pulling at his own innards until he could hold them aloft. The throng of the broken expanded as more left the arena, some throwing themselves over the side of the stadium and landing with a crunch. The lucky ones died on impact; others writhed and twitched until the pack set upon them in a frenzy of teeth and nails. Mouths awash with red, fragments of people strewn across their clothes, these people were insurmountably broken, and they were shambling out across the rest of the city. As long as Shiara and Fredo didn't get lost, they'd be able to make it out before this chaos enveloped the entirety of Fimego.

Turning a corner, they left the carnage behind them, out of view. They passed a few citizens going about their business who clearly did not know what had happened. They knew that Shiara was meant to have faced Mara at about this time, yet here she was, alive. It wouldn't be long before they put the pieces together and joined in the mass calamity or the rabble caught up with them. Perhaps their first thoughts would be that Shiara had run from the battle rather than having slain their god, giving the pair a few more minutes to evacuate. Considering the unwavering devotion the people had for their former ghost protector, it seemed likely that this would be the first conclusion they drew. If their luck held, they'd make it to Scaley and away from Fimego in time.

Barrelling down the streets, the pair – especially Fredo, who was well beyond his comfort zone – were running on pure adrenaline. This was worse than what he'd seen in Illorne; that was merely people taking advantage of an opportunity, albeit with sickening levels of brutality. What they were seeing here was a city going collectively insane. There was no rhyme nor reason to the chaos, just an outpouring of indescribable emotions ranging from grief to anger. Fredo's level of fitness paled in comparison to Shiara's and the taut scar tissue from his recent injury pulled with each step he took. No doubt he'd pay for pushing his body like this later on, but at least he'd still be alive.

The outer wall came into sight. They couldn't tell if they'd been running for minutes or hours; perceptions of time had been blurred by survival instincts. Kicking open a door to a small building revealed nothing. Just an ordinary building. Then another door. And another. Fredo was positive one of these led to a tunnel, but for the life of him, perhaps literally, he couldn't specifically remember which one.

"Well, which one is it?" Shiara pressed him.

They were becoming increasingly aware of a growing sound in the distance.

CHAPTER THIRTY-EIGHT

The chaos was catching up with them. Finally, they kicked down the door of a conspicuously empty shack. As hoped, the faint outlines of a moveable panel were visible. Levering it up, they opened up the passageway beneath the wall. Hurriedly, they entered, closing the panel behind them. The darkness was slightly alleviated by the shine from Shiara's blade: its rainbow glimmer was entirely independent of sunlight. Up ahead, the flicker of torchlight cast long shadows. The brazier was almost burned out; clearly nobody had been this way recently. Fredo picked up an adjacent torch and lit it on the flames. It sputtered into life as it struggled with traces of damp. Down here, the chaos within the walls was beyond their hearing. They now began to pay for their physical exertions, especially Fredo, whose legs ached and lungs burned from the exercise. Still with high emotions, they reduced their pace to a steady walk, gulping in air to feed their overworked muscles. The silver-tongue wheezed, drenched in sweat and red in the face.

The march down the tunnel was sombre, neither finding words to express themselves, preferring to keep it bottled inside. This was beyond words. All they could do was put distance between themselves and the horror, hoping to leave it behind them, not just physically, but mentally. The latter would be far more challenging to achieve.

By the time they reached the end of the tunnel they had still not regained their breath fully. The racing of their hearts for emotional reasons was also not helping. Climbing out of the passageway into a small brick building, they had escaped unscathed: at least on the outside. Stepping out onto the farmland, they were greeted with the relative tranquillity of the ordinary. The pair looked out across the calming fields, a stark juxtaposition to what they had escaped. Their sweat mixed with tears across their faces; a part of them would be forever tied to this moment. Nightmares would be fuelled by this for as long as either dared to dream. Whatever salvation may lie at the completion of the prophecy, the human cost was undeniable. The beating of her heart pounded in her ears. Slumping onto her haunches, a sigh left her lips. She was drained emotionally, arms weighed down by forces more exhausting than any duel. The price of her victory was other people's lives, a realization that was as inescapable as it was grim. Shiara's silver-tongue companion knelt by her side and tried his best to console her. An arm on her shoulder was not going to relieve the burden; nevertheless, it was something. There was not enough time to grieve the loss of life or even process it; personal safety had to take priority. The proud woman Fredo had come to know had lost that spark of righteousness he had become accustomed to seeing in her; things would never be the same after today, and neither would she.

ACT FOUR

CHAPTER THIRTY-NINE

Dawn came to Maluani and with it, fury. The previous night's slaughter was discovered as morning broke; now the reprisals would begin. Koralia had only managed passing moments of sleep. Shouting in the distance was the first sign that terror was inbound. Dashing outside she found Minos, who was peering towards the far end of the street.

"What's the damage?" she asked him.

"Can't say just yet, but I bet it's not good." Minos replied.

The shouts turned to screams as wardens entered houses with weapons drawn. Only minutes later, some emerged from the buildings with vivid red splashes covering their blades, the rich crimson colour standing out even from the other end of the street. Out of one doorway sprang not a warden, but a half-dressed and bloody citizen, their face chiselled from pure fear. They sprinted towards Koralia and the few others gathered there, fuelled by pure adrenaline and panic. One of the guards raised a crossbow, drew back the string then loaded a bolt. Taking careful aim, he waited for the runner to get up close to the onlookers so they could watch the life snuffed out. The air hissed as the bolt flew, halted by a mighty thud as it met flesh. The force of the projectile left it protruding from the victim's chest and sent them careening forward with a spray of blood. Writhing turned to twitching, then to stillness. The wardens looked at Koralia and the others; would they now turn on them? In answer to this question, the guards entered the next building instead. They weren't looking for a chase or a fight, this was about butchery. Koralia knew that this same exact scene would be playing out

CHAPTER THIRTY-NINE

across several districts of Maluani – the retaliation for crimes committed was always far greater. Entire families would be executed before work in the fields began today. It was all about sending a message: the wardens' lives were worth more and the cost of dissidence was far too great. Koralia hoped that other messages would also be delivered from these events: that this was no way to live; that the city was a broken brutal mess of a place that needed to be stopped; but alongside this, she hoped other rebels would realize that they had to work together and wait for the right time. These events were the wardens' first real inkling that something was brewing among the people of Maluani. They could see it wasn't just a bit of disrespect or vandalism – it was something more powerful and worrying for them. This level of rebellion was unheard of, so they made sure nobody would forget the consequences. Although they questioned their victims briefly, in case they could find the culprits, they were far more concerned with restoring the terror that kept them safe. Terror, which they themselves were now more familiar with.

For the resistance, the element of surprise was well and truly blown. Sure, the guards wouldn't know where or when the revolt was coming, but they were now vigilant. Everything had been made more difficult and dangerous. On top of all that, they had to watch in horror as this waste of life unfolded in front of them, powerless to intervene. Everyone would know one of the victims of today's reprisals and that was the point. It was supposed to feel personal and painful to all, as well as putting people in that horrible frame of mind where they found themselves hoping someone else's family got the worst of it rather than their own.

"We should get out of here," said Minos desolately.

Koralia nodded. "We don't want to be standing here when they get up to this end of the street."

The pair walked off. Others followed, but a few couldn't tear themselves away from the abhorrence just yet, standing frozen in disgust and despair instead. For Minos and Koralia getting to the fields earlier was for once preferential. They could talk to others, allowing them to gauge people's reactions to the carnage and what impact that might have on their movement. It was grim to have to focus on how this would impact their plans rather than on the loss of life, but something bigger was at stake.

There was a sombre mood in the fields, a sense of everybody keeping their heads down even more than usual. They figured it wouldn't take much to aggravate a guard and mark yourself as a target. They'd lost a lot of their own and only required the flimsiest of excuses to exact revenge. Koralia herself felt some concern at their loss, mainly because she was worried that Harun might no longer be on board with the movement; or worse still, had he been one of the wardens that had been slaughtered?

Conversations were few and far between, yet there was a distinct undercurrent of anger bubbling away under the surface. The people had been conditioned for so long to just feel remorse, fear and hopelessness; now, thanks to the movement, there was something else. Rage that was once pointless had been given a useful outlet.

Minos sidled up to Koralia after having made his way around to chat with others in the course of his work.

"Everyone I've spoken to is angry and determined. If anything, this whole episode has grown support for the cause," he reported.

"I've found the same, although we won't really be sure until all the dead are known. It's one thing being outraged at what happened to others but when it's your own loss, that can be different."

Minos nodded in agreement. The pair continued turning over the soil between plants and removing weeds. In many ways, the boring menial labour was a welcome distraction from what had become their reality of late. They were young enough to not feel the physical strain from years working in the dirt, so the exertion was far less of a burden. Looking at the leafy greens sprouting around them, it wouldn't be long before it was time to harvest. It was essential that the revolution took place before the harvest; the last thing they needed was Takis trading away precious food reserves at a time of turmoil. Thinking of Takis, Koralia was surprised that he hadn't made his presence felt. She knew he cared little for any mortal, yet such a blatant display of defiance against the wardens felt like the sort of thing that should have caught his attention. Perhaps he was just as

CHAPTER THIRTY-NINE

preoccupied by the existence of this "Slayer of Ghosts" as everyone else was. She could envision him reading through countless tomes in that library of his, looking for anything to do with the prophecy in the hopes of preserving his own existence. Koralia despised Takis, not just for his malice, but for his indifference and the waste he made of his immortality. Being an immortal ruler should have given him the perspective to shape a harmonious society from the ground up. An everlasting leader who could, with benevolence, see past the petty struggles of mortals and establish a utopia. Instead, this gift was squandered by treating others like insects and accumulating books. However, even she had to admit that the stockpiling of texts was in some ways noble – the finest things created by people, committed to parchment for all eternity. She imagined the wonders held within the library walls, only for it to be soured by the selfishness of Takis, who kept them for himself. It was a shame about what she had to do in order to facilitate the rebellion, but this was not her fault. She had been driven to such actions by their callous oppressor. "Violence in defiance of tyranny is a necessity caused by the oppressor's action," she told herself. Dwelling much longer on this topic would only kindle her anger, so she decided to check on some other workers to see how the morning's events had affected their support.

A hard day's labour had been fruitful. After the morning's atrocities, resolve had hardened rather than dissipated. If the same thing was playing out across the city, then the revolution was very much still on. Leaving the fields behind them for the day, Minos and Koralia were walking the streets home when they noticed a smell. An odour of something foetid and disturbingly sweet. Accompanying this was the sound of birds cawing. It was coming from the nearby square and was getting more powerful as they approached. Turning the corner, they were confronted by a monumentally grim spectacle. The square was filled with a mound of bodies – the victims of the reprisals, piled on top of one another as if they were harvested crops. A monument to cruelty made of lifeless flesh. People were crowded around trying to see if they could recognize any of the dead. Wails and tears flowed freely. Koralia noticed Orestis and Stefania at the far corner consoling one another; she and Minos dashed over in dreadful anticipation.

"Who did they get?" she asked, but emotions were too high for them to respond with words; instead they merely pointed. Looking at the heap of corpses the familiarity of one of the faces stood out. The proud nose of Nasos jutted out like a signpost drawing their attention. One of his eyes was missing, the soft squishy bits were always the first to be fed upon by avian scavengers. Some people tried to shoo the Kerri birds away, but this only deterred them for the briefest of moments. They had no concept of mourning, dignity or appropriateness. To these birds it was just an easy meal. Koralia's heart plummeted into her stomach. Death was a natural part of living in Maluani, but not like this. And not for someone so young and closely connected to her. The inseparable trio of friends had been parted. What they all felt was replicated by countless others; all in Maluani shared the loss today. No doubt there would be other squares with similar scenes of misery and pain. Today framed the entire movement not just as something to save them all in the future, but as an immediate fight for survival here and now.

There was no acceptable way to comfort people in such times; as the head of the revolution she had to see this in terms of the wider cause. It was another reason, another motivation to overturn the way things were. It was fuel for the fires of justice and she would not see them doused. Vengeance was creeping in to bolster the cause as she offered words to her friends.

"We'll get them for this. For everything. And we'll do it soon."

CHAPTER FORTY

Fimego was no longer in view. They had left the city but what had happened there would never leave Shiara or Fredo. The silver-tongue had penned a message to Caspir about what had occurred and had one of the livery hands set off to deliver it; thankfully they had managed to get there and retrieve Scaley before the bedlam escaped the walls. Conversation had been non-existent, and now that their occasionally weary glances back could no longer take in the city, they began to regain their composure. The capacity of people to adjust to and accept even the most gruesome of realities was something that always troubled Shiara; nevertheless, she could finally feel her mind moving on to other things. To do so felt disrespectful, yet she pushed this feeling down inside her with considerations of the bigger task at hand and the prophecy she had to fulfil. There was something else that had been plaguing her mind that she only now had the resolve to ask her companion about.

"Fredo, can I ask you something... weird?"

He was startled that she had broken the silence to speak up, but glad to interrupt the terrible scenes continually replaying in his head.

"Yes. Go ahead."

"When we were in the arena, did you hear someone shouting at us to 'RUN'?"

Fredo nodded. "I thought that was you."

Shiara shook her head. "It wasn't. I figured I'd just imagined it in the heat of the moment, but I could swear it came from my sword."

Her companion looked understandably bemused.

"That's because it did," came that same disembodied voice from before. Both Shiara and Fredo visibly jumped at hearing it.

"You... can talk?" asked Fredo of the weapon, which seemed to him at the same time a rather silly thing to be doing.

"Why of course. I *am* a magic sword."

"I've been carrying you around for years and now all of a sudden you've decided to start speaking?" exclaimed Shiara.

"Perhaps it was just shy?" quipped Fredo, enjoying the welcome distraction this revelation provided.

"I was crafted by the Great Wizard himself; I do not suffer from shyness," the blade retorted with an air of prideful whimsy. "As for why I am only talking now, how much do you know about magic?"

"Not much really," replied Shiara.

"Shall I explain?"

"Sure, although I have another question first."

"Yes?"

There was something arrogant about the way this sword spoke that rubbed Fredo the wrong way.

"The prophecy about slaying the ghosts; what can you tell me about it?"

The blade was clearly more interested in the topic of magic and let out a huff as it began to outline the prophecy in more or less the exact terms that most people were familiar with. It seemed to offer nothing new, much to Shiara's disappointment. After her recent experiences in Fimego, she was becoming more sceptical of prophecy given the harm she'd seen it cause. The sword was very quick to shut down such doubts, adamant that it needed to be seen through until the end. She questioned the misery it had brought so far, but the weapon pointed out that the prophecy was still not yet completed and laid the blame for the horrors squarely at the door of the ghosts. Were it not for them, none of this would have happened, so in a way that made sense, but it still didn't make Shiara feel better.

"Shall I explain all about magic now?" piped up the blade.

The sword almost seemed offended, as it had been building itself up to

CHAPTER FORTY

explain all only to be distracted by this talk of prophecy.

"Oh, I'd forgotten about that," replied Shiara.

"Yes, I had noticed," commented the blade snootily.

"Sounds like you're dying to tell us," said Fredo as he rolled his eyes. Despite not having any breath, the sword let out another huff.

"I am a magic sword with knowledge about things you couldn't possibly comprehend; I'd have at least expected a bit more interest. Especially since I've been waiting to talk to someone for hundreds of years."

"All right then, why haven't you spoken for all these years?" asked Fredo begrudgingly. The magical blade was really beginning to get on his nerves.

"Since you've *finally* asked, allow me to explain. You see, there are two kinds of magic in the world. Normal magic, and soul bonding, which is the sort that created and sustains the ghosts."

"What's the difference?" interrupted Fredo to annoy the blade, knowing full well that it was about to tell them.

"Unsurprisingly, I was getting to that. You see, both use the same resource of magic, just differently."

"Ah, I see," chirped Fredo, trying to continue winding it up.

"Fredo, now you play nicely with each other," Shiara scolded jokingly.

"As I was saying. They both use the magical energy that naturally occurs in the world. Think of it like the water level under the ground. Normal use of magic is like digging a hole and allowing the water to gush out on the surface. A relatively small amount is used but plenty more flows out. Some animals can drink it up, plants absorb it and so on. It's a natural cycle sort of thing."

Shiara had never really considered *how* magic worked; she barely had any idea what it even was. It made sense that it would mirror other things in nature. She had to admit that for a sword, it was rather eloquent with its explanations, although she supposed she would be too if she had hundreds of years to think about things.

"But soul bonding is different. It uses the same... essence, yet instead of creating a cascade of magic, or rather water in our analogy, it creates a massive sinkhole sucking in all the magic, or water, from the surrounding areas.

This means there's none left to go around for anything else. Like hoarding all the water in one place to create an artificial drought. Animals that hunger for magic become ravenous. Plants that used to grow abundantly instead wither and disappear."

"Like the owls," surmised Shiara.

"Exactly. Once people kept them as pets; now they are seen as feral. This is why you see so few plants and animals in the cities. The vacuum created by the soul-bonded ghosts has made it inhospitable for them and this extends way beyond the city walls."

It was a lot to take in. The prophecy also made more sense too. Of course, it would require all of these "sinkholes" to be removed to return a natural balance to the world. She had herself witnessed "normal" magic heal Fredo and do pretty incredible things; opening up the world to more possibilities for magic would surely bring about greater prosperity moving forward. Imagine the food they could grow with magical assistance. Nobody would need to go hungry anymore. It all started slotting into place now. The sacrifice in Illorne, and even Fimego, would be worth it down the road.

"So, what was it like?" she asked. "You know, before the ghosts."

There was a brief pause for thought, then the blade spoke up.

"It was... different."

"We worked that much out already; *how* was it different?" said Fredo somewhat sarcastically. "Was it better?"

Again, there was a pause.

"Honestly, it was still bad, just in different ways."

Fredo huffed. "Not exactly the font of wisdom we were hoping for."

"As you may know, the original intent of the ghosts was to end the wasteful deaths of citizens in wars, instead offering a champion to challenge. Countless people were dying over the petty squabbles of those who ruled. It was the same disparity between those in power and those at the bottom as you see today."

"If they didn't care about the people, why did they bother with the ghosts?" interjected Shiara.

"It certainly wasn't for the good of the people. There were only so many

CHAPTER FORTY

casualties the cities could sustain before it started to impact on production and the day-to-day lives of those in charge. By creating ghost protectors who couldn't leave the city, no mortals were ever able to successfully challenge them, so peace came about naturally. Rather than warring with one another it was easier to put their populations to work for their own interests at home."

"You're saying the ghosts weren't implemented to save the people from the horrors of war, but to maintain the lifestyles of the powerful?" Shiara sounded surprised, but in reality, she wasn't at all.

"Exactly. Why waste the resources of human lives when they could instead be exploited?"

"What about those with magic? Didn't they stand up for the people?" she questioned.

"The wizards were part of the ruling classes. It was their suggestion in the first place. Little did they know at the time that it would see their magical resources dwindle and fade. Served them right."

"Even Ezekiel?" asked Shiara.

"No, not Ezekiel. *He* wasn't like other wizards. *He* advised them against it; of course *they* wouldn't listen."

"Why didn't he try and stop them?" said Shiara.

"Like I said, Ezekiel was different. He wanted as little as possible to do with the world of courts and rulers. I'm sure if he'd known how it would pan out, he would not have been so apathetic and would have crushed them where they stood."

"Crushed them? How powerful was he?" inquired a shocked-sounding Fredo.

"Being called the "Great Wizard" is probably a big enough clue, wouldn't you think?"

Shiara laughed at the sword's wit; she'd almost go as far as to describe it as being sassy.

"People these days can't really comprehend how it used to be," continued the blade. "Before the resources were all sunk into keeping the ghosts alive, the possibilities were incredible. Imagine constructing a palace without ever picking up a stone."

"Or 'crushing' one just as easily," chimed in Fredo.

"Precisely."

The pair reflected on what they were being told. This world of magic was something they knew nothing of, yet here they were, on the road to bringing that magic back into the world. They were well aware of the fact they had no idea what this could mean for people's way of life, but the rural communities with their little bit of magic seemed to get on all right. No fighting, just a simpler and friendlier way of life.

"There's something you said that's bothering me," Shiara declared.

"Go on," replied the shimmering weapon.

"You said that before the ghosts, things were different but not much better; how does ending the ghosts make any difference?"

"Well, I'm no expert on prophecy..."

Fredo interrupted the sword to make his own witty rejoinder: "No, you're just a magical talking sword that's hundreds of years old. I'd say that makes you the closest thing to being an expert we're going to get."

"Quite... As I was saying, I'm no expert on prophecy; nevertheless, it seems obvious to me that it isn't just the ghosts you are taking down, but the entire system of rule around them. Before the ghosts there were still oppressive rulers and that is the *real* problem."

"You make it sound like the ghosts aren't even that important," Fredo suggested.

"On the contrary, they represent an unbroken line of rule dating back hundreds of years. Never before in history has there been such a good opportunity to break a system by slaying only a handful of individuals. Of course, that is just my opinion."

At that moment the nagging realization of doubt crept into their minds. This magical talking sword clearly had a personality of its own, and with personality comes bias. What possible reason could it have to lie or steer them towards a certain way of thinking? They couldn't think of one, yet that didn't mean there wasn't one. Fredo was keen to find out more about this wondrous weapon.

CHAPTER FORTY

"When you say it's just your opinion, I can't help but ask, how does a simple blade like yourself become a living... thing, with opinions?"

"I assure you I am far from simple." The sword sounded offended by the remarks. "And like I mentioned earlier, the possibilities of magic are incredible. I wasn't just enchanted with information, I was brought to life by the Great Wizard and taught, just like any other person."

"You consider yourself a person?" Fredo quizzed.

"I have thoughts, do I not? And what description fits a person better than that of a thinking being?"

Fredo had to agree. It was an interesting philosophical question; there was no denying this sword communicated like a person, complete with hubris and self-entitlement. Although how could a wizard create a living person, of sorts, from nothing? And more importantly, *should* they have done so?

"So Ezekiel taught you everything you know?" asked Shiara.

"You could say that, although I've learnt a lot since I... parted company with him."

"Really?" asked Shiara. "What happened to him?"

"Honestly, nobody really knows. After the ghosts were created, he left the cities behind and tinkered with magic on his own. That's where he made me and taught me about the world."

"Does that mean your knowledge of the world before ghost protectors came second hand from Ezekiel?" she questioned.

"I... suppose you could say that."

"So perhaps it wasn't like how you described it?" she followed up.

"Hmmm, second-hand knowledge of history certainly seems a whole lot better than the 65th-hand knowledge or whatever it is you people have these days."

Again, the sense of superiority and a disdain for being challenged became apparent. Shiara figured that this was in some ways understandable, given however many hundreds of years the sword hadn't spoken to anyone.

"Anything else you'd like to ask me? I'm just a magical sword with hundreds of years of life experience as well as having been taught by the greatest wizard of all time. But by all means question my veracity some more." It mainly came across as jovial sarcasm, although there was still a detectable undercurrent of frustration.

"You never said what happened to him," Fredo pressed, noticing that he hadn't properly answered last time.

"I'm afraid it's a very uneventful story. One day he simply went out and left me behind, then never came back. Nobody found me until several years later and by then everyone had just assumed he'd died or disappeared off further into the wilderness, or north beyond the shore. As I said, nobody really knows."

Fredo formulated a cutting remark but thought better of saying it aloud – who could blame someone walking away from this "person"? A lot of questions remained, but they were mostly the kind that the sword couldn't answer. Things like "Why did Ezekiel make him in the first place?" Fredo was sure he'd think of more things to ask, but both he and Shiara had been given a lot to think about. The truth was that neither of them knew much about history and even less about magic. Their best guide to the past was a talking sword that was more than just a bit conceited; nevertheless, they weren't going to get a better source of information.

"Shiara, we'll have to start heading north soon to head to Omdurtur."

The slayer of ghosts turned her head towards the silver-tongue behind her.

"We're not going to Omdurtur yet," she replied.

"Aren't we? It makes more sense than going right out of our way to Maluani first and I have no idea how we'd even get within their inner wall at the moment."

"We aren't going to Maluani either," Shiara said.

At this point, Fredo was confused. There were five cities that people lived in. He'd visited them all for trade and relations, even Maluani a few times. Then it dawned on him. This wasn't just about cities full of people; this was about the ghosts. Which could only mean that...

"We're going to Latan," she declared.

CHAPTER FORTY-ONE

Questioning suspects in custody was not something the guards of Caspir were used to, especially not one that was likely to be innocent. Ordinarily he'd have been locked in a cell and spoken to through the bars if necessary; however, these were not ordinary circumstances. Instead, Marin and Bemus had the accused – still bruised and bloody from his run in with Alyssa and her congregation – sat in an office. It was not the most spacious of rooms, crammed with a couple of desks covered in parchments, empty food bowls and cups that had no doubt been filled with wine in the past. If justice was going to be a priority moving forward, Marin would have to change this entire setup. Rooms dedicated to interrogation, with no windows or clutter to distract the person and to keep the passing of time from them; tidied desks that reflected the seriousness and professionalism required to execute the law. Perhaps changing the entire way individuals were determined guilty too; there was no doubt in his mind that innocent people had probably been seen as an easy resolution to a crime and treated as guilty from time to time. These were all ideas for later. For now, they had a suspect who had said very little to them aside from his name.

"Look Farid, I think we both know you didn't do it, so why stick to your confession? It's obviously been coerced from you via a beating," asked Marin for what felt like the hundredth time.

"It was me all right. I killed him. Can we just stop this?" replied the suspect feebly.

"Oh, glad you've decided to join in with the conversation. Now tell me, if you're so sure you killed him, can you tell me his name?" said Marin.

Farid squirmed in his chair and his frown ruffled a swollen eyebrow that looked more like an engorged threadwurm.

"See you can't, can you? Because you didn't do it," Marin accused.

"I... didn't know what his name was. I just attacked him," came the reply.

The council leader placed his boot on a chair and rested his arms on his risen knee.

"You're telling us that you brutally murdered a man you didn't even know, then carved up his body and displayed it for all to see? Tell me Bemus, when was the last time you saw a murderer who didn't know his victim that wasn't a mugging that got out of hand?"

"Never. Not even once," confirmed the gruff guard.

Marin widened his eyes and gazed into the purplish-blue face of Farid, right between the swelling and bruises and into his nervous eyes. The former merchant's expression clearly demanded an answer.

"That's it. It was a mugging; I took his money and he fought back." The inner workings of his mind were trying but they had fallen into the trap laid for him.

"Why then did you string him up afterwards and mutilate his body?" asked Marin.

Obviously there was no good answer for this, yet a part of Marin was curious what Farid would make up.

"I don't know... I just did." Farid's reply was devastatingly underwhelming. If Alyssa was going to scapegoat someone, she could have at least found someone with a bit more imagination.

"Let me get this straight. You took Rhodes – that was his name by the way, Rhodes – so you took his money by force, then when things got rough you killed him and cut open his body to hang up? Are you *sure* that's your story?"

Farid agreed and nodded profusely under the false assumption that Marin had given him a story that would work and that would be the end of it.

"Bemus, was there any indication that Rhodes had been robbed?" asked Marin slyly, about to expose the Farid's lies.

CHAPTER FORTY-ONE

"Nah. 'E were found wiv a bag o' coins. No way a mugger could 'ave missed 'em."

And with those words from the veteran law enforcer any illusions that Farid could have sold this lie fell apart, and his face showed it. He began running his hands through the tight curls of his hair crusted with spots of dried blood, making a slight crispy sound. Desperation was ratcheted up to new levels.

"You can't let me go. You don't know what they'll do to me if you let me go!" he pleaded.

Marin looked his battered body up and down; he was pretty sure he could make more than an educated guess as to what would happen, which was why he wasn't going to release him just yet.

"Do you know anything about who *did* kill Rhodes?" Marin inquired.

Farid shook his head, tears streaming from his least inflamed eye.

"That's all we needed to know," said Marin. "If you'd have said so earlier we wouldn't have wasted so much time and could have been out looking for the real killer."

The bruised man was clearly just as broken on the inside too.

"You have to keep me here. Please," he begged.

Marin nodded. "You'll be safe for as long as we can keep you here."

The council leader shouted to a guard outside the room, who came in and was instructed to put Farid on his own in a cell and keep an eye on him. They left the makeshift interrogation room, leaving Bemus and Marin to ponder over the case they had made little progress on.

"I know the answer is in here," said Marin, tapping Rhodes's journal. "There's no shortage of jilted lovers, jealous rivals and people cheating on their partners. The most recent entry mentions somebody that could be our guy, but he's only referred to by a nickname, as is the woman involved."

Bemus scratched his bristly stubble. "Yer really reckon dis whole fing is all over a lover?"

The council leader shrugged; it was his best guess and the only avenue that had something to follow.

"Yer know wot, I fink yer might be right. In all da years I been doin' dis, der is one fing yer can be certain of. People do crazy fings for love. 'Specially wen someone gets in between 'em."

Bemus's language may have been fractured but his reasoning wasn't. Nobody in Caspir had the knowledge of crime that he possessed and here Bemus was, adding weight to Marin's suspicions. To begin with, this man of stubble and greying hair had not been particularly receptive to what the council leader had been doing; professional jealousy had made him somewhat standoffish. However, having worked together with the former merchant for a short while, a mutual respect had built and Marin's forensic approach had rekindled something within Bemus that hadn't been nurtured for quite some time: a passion for solving crime. The only guard who actively wanted to handle murder cases, he'd been merely going through the motions, but the urgency of this current case, alongside Marin's eagerness, gave him a new lease of life. The pair discussed some of Bemus's previous cases. Husbands murdering wives and lovers out of rage, doing horrific things when they generally seemed like completely normal people. In fact, Bemus said that a lot of crime fitted into this category: impulsive and unplanned reactions. It was generally that, or theft that got out of hand, that resulted in serious crimes. There was one particularly concerning story of a man who had murdered his wife's lover, but to avoid anyone discovering the body had sawed it into pieces and buried it in the garden of their home. After a few weeks, his wife discovered it and told the guards. Many people came forward to say how out of character it was for him, how much of a lovely person he was, yet there was no denial from him. A rush of blood over a loved one had turned a mild-mannered individual into someone stashing body parts in the ground. The whole idea that some people were just evil or opportunists didn't really make sense in the real world. Understanding this complexity behind crime was probably the best way of tackling it. The council leader stroked his impressive black facial hair and thought about the future; what could they do when this crisis was over? Caspir was hardly some kind of nightmarish cityscape where crime was out of control, but things were changing, and change usually meant danger. Especially with refugees coming from Illorne, and other cities if Shiara were successful,

CHAPTER FORTY-ONE

this would create a breeding ground for conflict between the newcomers and those who hated change. There was also the need to prepare for the possible conflicts with those who'd taken control of Illorne through fear and violence. The current system of law and order in Caspir was dated and insufficient for modern needs; for starters a council member shouldn't have been leading a murder investigation. When this was all over Marin would formulate these ideas into something workable. Marin admitted to himself that he had been wrong about Bemus and that the pursuit of justice in Caspir could probably learn a lot from him. The conversation rolled back around to the case at hand.

"I'm hoping that if I can finish reading it all, there will be some clues to who these people are; he quite often wrote the real names of people before he nicknamed them so there must be something we can go on in here."

His veteran guard laughed. "Den why is yer wastin' time talkin' to me wen yer should be readin'?"

CHAPTER FORTY-TWO

This week's day of rest was anything but restful. The bodies of those killed in the reprisals had lain untouched in their heaped piles for a few days; the wardens would not allow the people of Maluani a break from work in order to deal with them. Now, on their day of peace, they finally had the opportunity to lay them to rest. Long lines of grieving family and friends carried the remains of their loved ones out of the city gate and beyond the exterior wall. This was the only time citizens were permitted to go beyond the perimeter wall. Burning bodies on farmland or within the city was not an option. The entire district's contingent of guards also attended. Not out of deference or respect; rather to ensure anyone trying to flee the city met with their end. Crossbows in hand, wardens lined the wall, just itching to add to the body count. The morning had been spent felling trees and splitting lumber to build the pyres upon which to burn the dead. Dozens of wooden structures were now topped with corpses, corpses that had dried out in the heat of the last few days. They no longer looked like people; instead they were repulsive caricatures of what they once were, a final insult. It didn't help that their eyes had long been taken by the birds, although one couldn't blame them – a soft, squishy and nutritious meal was something not easily passed up.

The people stood around the pyres, taking one final look at the emaciated sacks of skin and bone that were once key parts of their lives. The first of the pyres was lit; the rest soon followed. Having been more or less desiccated, the bodies went up quickly. Grieving onlookers saluted to their necks in solidarity, the symbol of defiance that had become a powerful message in

CHAPTER FORTY-TWO

recent weeks.

Considering the sheer number of the dead, it surprised Koralia how little smell they produced. The resiny odour from the wood was the far more potent aroma. The sounds of the flames seemed like moaning and roaring at the injustice; however, a much more unpleasant sound drowned out the crackling of timber: laughter. Bellowing, cruel laughter from atop the wall. It was The Owl. A menacing cackle left his lungs that permeated the very minds of all those in attendance. Some looked up in disgust, and this was the exact reaction he was hoping for. He fed off the misery of others and it only produced more laughter from him. Many broke into tears – it was indeed a wretched day; others refused to give him the satisfaction and stood resolutely. Stefania stood by Koralia's side, her expression better described as a sneer than mourning. Her tears had all been used up, leaving only anger in its place.

"When we kill them," she whispered, "there won't be any funeral pyres, just throwing them in the dirt where they belong."

Stefania had always been clinical and abrupt with her opinions, but Koralia had never seen her like this. Physically twisting with undercurrents of rage and spitting venom, her pragmatism was giving way to vengeance. Who could blame her? Watching the barely recognizable body of your closest friend being burned was a far cry from pleasant. Orestis seemed to be taking it better; as the third of their trio he was generally considered the jovial one. He was not in good spirits, but nevertheless he had found positives to cling to.

"We'll have no trouble rallying these people when the time comes. Those who are gone won't have died for nothing; this will be the final push that encourages people to join us," he said.

The others just nodded. This was neither the time nor the place for a multitude of words; now was a time to reflect on what had been lost and galvanize their resolve for what must come.

Personal mourning was interrupted as one of the people by the outer row of pyres made a break for it – a panicked dash to flee the horrors of Maluani. The person in question was an athletic-looking woman, long wavy dark hair billowing around her as she ran. Her destination was a line of trees; if she could make it that far she'd no longer have to fear crossbow bolts and the armoured guards wouldn't be able to keep up. What exactly she'd do in the world outside the city, not knowing anyone or having anything with her, was anybody's guess, but for her it was just a case of being anywhere other than Maluani. The gap was closing and she was near to freedom; then it struck her. A bolt tore through her leg and sent her tumbling to the ground. Her run had been reduced to slowly pulling herself along; a pair of wardens closed in on her at walking speed. Her fingertips just about touched the first tree when the pair of guards picked her up by the arms. Any wriggling she tried to shake them off with was put down swiftly by gut punches. Having carried her back to the pyres they looked up at The Owl atop the wall as if to ask, "What now?" The Owl had already decided upon her fate.

"Throw her on the pyre," he shouted gleefully, intoxicated by the idea of someone being burned alive. She struggled but it was no good. Her writhing body was thrown onto the flames, and even the wardens seemed to wince as the heat engulfed her. Her hair was the first to disappear into the inferno. Skin blistered and popped. Her flesh and fluids sizzled in the incandescence, sticking her to the ignited wood. Screams were muted as her throat burned, becoming useless. It was grotesquely impressive how long she convulsed for, trying to find a way out of the flames even though her eyes had liquefied, clawing out in the dark with arms that resembled charred tree branches rather than part of a human being. Inevitably the fight left her, leaving behind another lifeless form dispatched by the fire, the only difference being the smell. The melting fat and roasting flesh was a disturbingly pleasant odour for the citizens of Maluani, for whom meat was a luxury. A wave of revulsion crept through the crowd as they came to this realization, some appalled by their own uncontrollable salivation, others vomiting from the recognition of what was filling their noses. Koralia had to cover her mouth; Stefania was steadfast – nothing seemed to faze her anymore. Ever since she murdered the guard to protect Koralia, her pragmatism had taken on a ruthless bent. Where she had once only killed because she needed to, now there was a desire for it, so a lungful of cooked

CHAPTER FORTY-TWO

human was not going to unsettle her. Koralia always thought Stefania would make a far superior leader than herself, yet this cold-blooded streak gave her pause.

Many of the pyres were collapsing in on themselves now, and nothing recognizable as a person remained. Most people were retreating into the city, sombre expressions on downcast faces. This was the low point; soon they would no longer be victims and instead fight for themselves. Koralia noticed how dejected some of them were and pondered how they would fare in combat versus the armed guards of Maluani. They weren't warriors, at least not yet. Stefania remained to watch the piles slowly shrivel up as the flames ran their course. Nasos was gone, forever. The things he worked on would still come to pass. Eventually she and Koralia left, the last of their friendship group to go back inside the walls.

"You know what really vexes me about today?" Stefania asked her companion.

"Go on," Koralia replied.

"It's that, however horrible and abysmal this was, it's not the worst thing we've been through. Remember when we were kids?"

Koralia nodded.

"I can't seem to shift a certain image from my mind. When the guards would round up those who couldn't work and just slaughter them. I still recall seeing an elderly man, no idea who he was, but his face. That tortured look. He'd just been left in the street to bleed out. All alone. Whatever terrors I see it just brings me back to the look he wore: sheer hopelessness distilled into flesh. I'll never forget it."

Koralia was unsure how to respond to such a personal recounting of Stefania's childhood memory. It was clear she wasn't after comfort, just a desire to share.

"For me it's the face of that guard I can't shift. The one you stopped from killing me," said Koralia. "It's just a stark reminder of how fragile we are. I've seen dead people before but never watched someone die up close like that. The thought keeps occurring to me that he was just another part of the system, just like us."

"No," interrupted Stefania, "not like us. Never like us."

CHAPTER FORTY-THREE

Marin had missed the previous council meeting, which had certainly irked a number of councillors – most notably Andros – but he was here now and chairing such a meeting had never been more difficult. His previous absence had made him look weak and had sparked the idea that he didn't much care for his duties, something which certain dissenters were quick to point out. The reality was that he was busy keeping tensions in Caspir from exploding, yet his inability to juggle everything at once had a heavy cost.

The needlework guild was particularly concerned today, as were the merchant representatives. The loss of trade due to the fall of Illorne was starting to be felt deeply. Their levels of production were outstripping demand and their revenues had fallen. This was only compounded by the swelling ranks of the Church of Shiara, whose drab attire ruled them out as customers for Caspir's famous luminous threads. The combined effect of these things meant they were earning a lot less money – not just those in the guild but all those connected to them. The merchant representatives were incredibly vocal; as people who spent their lives trying to sell and barter, this came as no surprise. With one of their main trade routes now cut off, there wasn't enough business to go around.

"You can't expect dozens of us to travel up to Omdurtur to sell the same things. Lots of people I know are going out of business because of all this. What are you going to do about it?" cried one merchant.

It was a good question; what *was* Marin going to do about it? Indeed, what *could* he do about it? He needed to think quickly to control the situation;

thankfully his time with Bemus hadn't dulled his verbal dexterity.

"It's not a case of what *I* am going to do about it; it's what *we* are going to do about it. The point of this council is that we are all equally invested in this city and want to work together for its betterment."

"Equal? It's easy to say that when *you're* the council leader. When you turn up, that is." Andros's uncharacteristic incisiveness was now the new normal. Marin was certain that somebody was coaching him and was more certain than ever that somebody was Alyssa.

"I have one vote, just like the rest of you," Marin pointed out, fully aware that he was losing the crowd, "and I only missed a single meeting. In case you were unaware, Andros, we've been trying to catch a murderer."

The chamber instinctively turned back to Andros, waiting for his cutting response. He did not disappoint.

"Whilst you've been running around playing detective, we've been doing the real work of keeping this city running. Anyway, I thought you'd already arrested someone?"

The council leader's suspicions about who was the brains behind Andros were all but confirmed in his mind. He was laying a trap, one that Marin had no choice but to walk into and hope his principled stance carried him through.

"The investigation is still ongoing," he said.

"Ongoing? I heard he confessed!" retorted Andros.

The amount of times Marin had felt the need to run his hand through his once immaculate beard had ruffled it into appearing almost scruffy. He envied Chase's time as leader, since he had never had to deal with this sort of concerted attack.

"A confession under duress is not acceptable. What's more, the evidence doesn't even fit with his confession."

A smug grin spread itself across the elderly councillor's face.

"So the murderer can't get his story straight. Surely that's merely a sign of his guilt, or his mental state, which must be appalling to force him to commit murder. Just have him charged and be done with it."

Even Edwin couldn't offer Marin much of a comforting look. In the past

CHAPTER FORTY-THREE

he'd relied on his friend to have his back in council meetings; as leader he had never felt more alienated.

"I take justice very seriously. We have evidence that points to a different suspect and want to investigate all possible leads. We need certainty. The last thing we want is for an innocent man to suffer." Marin's heartfelt plea landed well across the room and evoked several nods. There was no way this would put the issue to bed, but it would offer respite and hopefully stall such inquiries until the next meeting. Andros had other ideas and saw it as a new line of attack being offered up.

"That's very principled of you. However, your claims about wanting to avoid suffering of the innocent fall a little flat given the situation in your slums."

Slums?! The council leader's heart leapt into his mouth.

"Excuse me?" he spluttered.

"Oh, have you not been down there recently? It certainly shows. All those poor people crammed into your warehouse. That's what I call suffering, not the charging of someone who confessed to murder."

The chamber fell silent. It was a damning accusation voiced with flawless precision from Andros. It felt less like Alyssa had coached him and more like she'd re-sculpted him into a new person altogether. There was only one option for Marin.

"Andros... Thank you for bringing this to my attention. I will take your advice and go down there to see what can be done to improve things. I trust you will help with necessary measures?"

In terms of the verbal joust, it came across as a fatally wounded man getting in one final swing. He had been defeated in this instance by Andros but if what he said was true, he was right to have been pulled up on it. With the investigation of Rhodes's murder, he hadn't found time to see how the refugees were living and this was his mistake. Not because the situation gave Andros ammunition, but because he genuinely cared and wanted the best for these people. This did him no favours in terms of how the rest of the council viewed him. He needed a win, but it was proving difficult to get one, especially without having much time to finish reading Rhodes's journal. For a man who spent so much of his life making love, he most definitely found the time to write about it extensively. If he couldn't get a victory right now, he'd settle for a distraction; fortunately just such a distraction entered the council chamber. It was a young messenger boy draped in shaggy clothes with dirt beneath his fingernails and a face that needed a wash. He was flanked by a guard who had clearly permitted his entrance to see the council. His eyes widened with a touch of awe at being in the most esteemed company the city had to offer. This was the heart of government for Caspir, and clearly a long way from his usual experiences.

"This is for Marin," he said in a soft and cautious voice whilst producing a letter from his holdall. Marin signalled for the boy to bring the letter over to him; slowly he obliged, still taking in his surroundings.

The councillors were mildly curious as Marin opened the seal and unfurled the parchment, but were more interested in the affairs they had just been discussing. That was until they began to see the nature of the document play out on Marin's face. A tangible sense of grief and horror swept across his expressions. Something big had happened and it was assuredly something terrible. By the time he had finished reading, all eyes were fixed on him. He looked up from the page and saw everyone around the table eagerly awaiting the news.

"It's Fimego. It's fallen," he finally said.

"Fimego?" asked his friend Edwin. "You mean Shiara has slain Mara?"

The council leader nodded but bit his lip slightly in an expression that said there was more to the story.

"The letter is from Fredo. He says that Shiara killed Mara, then the entire city went... berserk."

"Berserk?" questioned several council members.

"What exactly does that even mean?" queried Andros.

Marin was clearly disturbed by what he had read and took a few pained moments to compose himself and explain.

"According to this letter, as soon as Mara died, Fimego just... exploded with violence. People killing themselves and each other in something that Fredo describes as a 'blood-crazed frenzy'."

CHAPTER FORTY-THREE

What had been a quiet chamber burst into a cacophony of discussion. Each member turned to those beside them and speculated wildly. What did this mean for them? How extreme was the carnage? Is this what Shiara wanted? These were all topics being bandied around. In the flurry of debate, they failed to acknowledge one individual becoming increasingly unsettled and visibly panicked: the boy who had brought the message.

Almost like a sideways homage to the events in Fimego, this boy was about to snap. He let out a shrill cry and grasped his head in his hands. At first people took no notice, then he dropped to the floor and his groans became louder, his breathing rapid and uncontrolled. He drew a hand to his chest as if struggling for breath. "Do something!" shouted various people in the chamber. The guard who had shown him in dropped to his knee and tried to hold the young man down and calm him. It didn't work. His writhing became more vigorous and convulsive. This continued for a couple of minutes, each breath shallower and more rapid than the previous until he eventually lost consciousness and finally went limp; he'd worn himself out. The guard cradling him inspected the boy closely and nodded that everything was all right. Council members looked between themselves and then to Marin. Such a shocking display required a response from their leader. They needed someone to take charge and tell them what should happen next.

"Imagine this, but played out over the whole of Fimego. That's what we are talking about," he said calmly, as the situation required.

"But why?" asked Andros without even attempting to think for himself. Away from what were likely rehearsed discussions on the topics previous, he had reverted to his less than impressive levels of discourse.

"Isn't it obvious?" said Edwin.

"Well we didn't go crazy when Chase died, so why would they?" replied Andros.

"Fimego isn't like Caspir," Edwin explained whilst shaking his head. "For us, Chase was an immortal politician; for the people of Fimego, Mara was their god. Can you imagine what seeing your god killed before your very own eyes would do to someone?"

Andros made a brief attempt to think on this notion yet failed spectacularly, as was his way.

"I've always considered the people of Fimego to be hysterical. We shouldn't really be surprised."

A collective of eyebrows was raised around the room. The pomposity of Andros to say such a thing in the face of a tragedy did him no favours.

"Regardless of your opinions towards the people of Fimego, this *has* happened and we're going to have to deal with it," Marin proclaimed.

"What has it got to do with *us*?" asked Andros, not knowing when to give up.

"Since it seems to somehow have escaped you, I don't think we'll have much luck trading with Fimego like we used to, and if Illorne is anything to go by there'll be a lot of hungry and scared people knocking on our door very soon."

Considering they'd spent a great deal of time talking about the consequences of lost trade with Illorne, the realization that things were about to get worse crept through the chamber.

"More people to put in your slums then?" said Andros, after having misjudged the tone of the room yet again.

"You're right about it meaning more people, and like you, I agree they shouldn't be living in slums. I'm going to go down there and see what we can do. Since you are so interested in the living conditions of these people, I look forward to seeing the significant resources you are willing to donate to improve things for them."

Andros may not have been the quickest of thinkers but even he knew that he'd been bested. Somehow, after his earlier prowess, he'd snatched a defeat from the jaws of victory.

CHAPTER FORTY-FOUR

The route to Latan had not resembled a path. Due to the lack of travel it saw, plants had grown over anything that could be described as a track. A few stones as waypoints along the route were the only sign they were heading in the right direction, yet even these had succumbed to nature and had plants enveloping them. Latan was now on the horizon. The city stood as a monument to the dangers of ghost protectors and the folly of bestowing that much power upon someone. An entire society slaughtered by just one ghost. There were rumours of people sneaking in to retrieve books for Takis's famed library in Maluani, but as far as everyone was concerned, nobody had stepped foot inside Latan's walls for generations. Fredo and Shiara had needed to traverse wilderness to get this far, giving Scaley quite the workout to carry them both. Former trade routes had been buried under flora but as they neared their destination the wild plants became tamer and smaller. The walls of the city were themselves generally free of greenery, keeping the sun-washed stone colour that was shared by all the cities apart from Omdurtur, whose stonework was blackened by soot from the stacks.

"I wasn't expecting it to still look this pristine," commented Fredo.

"Like I said before, it's the magic that keeps the ghosts alive," replied Shiara's blade. "Most plants need magic to thrive."

"What about all the crops around the cities? They seem to do all right," Fredo probed, trying to find an inroad to "one-upping" the talking sword.

"Most plants need magic, not all. Crops have been carefully bred for thousands of years; they could not be further from wild plants if they tried.

If anything, the lack of magic keeps some of the weeds away from those farmlands, making it easier to cultivate said crops."

Unsurprisingly Fredo had no retort. Despite being a silver-tongue, he had been bested by a chatty weapon yet again. To be fair to himself, this sword had been around for hundreds of years so there shouldn't have been much shame in knowing less than it did, yet it still irked him somewhat.

"I wonder what it's like inside the city," asked Shiara rhetorically.

"I'd assume it's a mess. I doubt the mad ghost would have spruced up the place. Although with all that time to himself, who knows," Fredo mused.

"Wasif," said the sword.

Fredo required more context for this comment. "Sorry?"

"His name is Wasif, not 'the mad ghost'."

The silver-tongue furrowed his brow. "When you murder an entire city full of people, I think it's probably fair for people to call you 'the mad ghost'."

"I'm not sure what happened to him; he always seemed like the only ghost protector who actually got it. From what I was told."

"Got it? Got what? Blood on his hands?" Fredo had spent years around the ghosts and always lived with fear in the back of his mind, the fear of angering one of them enough to recreate an atrocity like Latan.

"Wasif was one of the few who saw that the real issue was with the ruling classes. He understood that what they were doing was swapping death on the battlefields for death in servitude. Ezekiel spoke very fondly of him."

Shiara wasn't sure what to make of this information. Ezekiel was more of a mythical figure than a real person; no-one really knew what he was like and there was just an assumption that he was some great wise figure. Now it was beginning to sound like he was as radical as everyone assumed he was wise. A recluse, who they were now finding out sympathized with the greatest mass murderer in history. She couldn't let this stand and asked for further clarification.

"Do you think Ezekiel would have sympathized with what Wasif did to Latan?"

"Ezekiel disappeared long before the troubles in Latan, so who could say?"

"Troubles?!" blurted out Fredo. "I'd say massacring a whole city is a bit

CHAPTER FORTY-FOUR

more than just troubles."

"Indeed. Ezekiel expressed to me that Wasif was opposed to the system of rule, so it comes as no surprise that he set about breaking it. The argument could certainly be made that the manner in which he chose to do so was... excessive."

There was a worrying ring of familiarity with this assessment. Breaking the system was the exact task Shiara had set out to do and the fallout from her actions so far was not too distant from the fate of Latan, albeit accidental on her part. Was this what she was being set up to accomplish? The magical blade upon which she depended had clearly been cast in the same radical mould as its creator. Suffering was an acceptable consequence of breaking the system, but the slayer of ghosts was beginning to realize that breaking the system was only part of it; replacing it with something better was necessary too. From her youth in the slums being choked by the stacks, she had always thought there must be a different way. A better way. She wasn't slaying the ghosts just to end the way things were but because she saw there was a fairer way. The details weren't something she was well equipped to handle, yet Marin had shown her that it was possible and there were those who were willing to work towards this goal. She was an agent of change without the tools to shape that change: a catalyst at best. Would she one day be considered in the same manner as Wasif? It was a troubling thought; then again, maybe the callous approach was somehow optimal? Significant turmoil in a short space of time might prove to be more humane in the long run. It had to be better than continuing as things were. A moment of introspection caught her sensibilities off guard; what was she willing to justify for her cause?

"Excessive?! You certainly have a unique turn of phrase when discussing genocide." Fredo was visibly annoyed; he'd failed to best the sword in intellectual jousts but he was damn sure going to take the high ground on morality.

"Need I remind you, I've not spoken to anyone for hundreds of years, so forgive me for my lack of appropriate vernacular."

"It's not just the words," said Fredo. "It's the message you're conveying.

We're talking about the ultimate stakes of life and death. Unimaginable horror and carnage, yet the way you describe it sounds like you're discussing a minor disruption in trade."

The blade had spent centuries only being able to think and not communicate, so it had no problem in taking a few moments to formulate what it wanted to say before replying.

"Having not experienced the events, the best and most accurate way in which I can discuss them is in the terms I've used."

This was not a good enough answer for the irate silver-tongue.

"There can be no discussion of an entire city being slaughtered without emotion. Where's your compassion? Where's your disgust? Where's your humanity?"

The retort came much quicker this time.

"Humanity? I'm sorry, you seem to have mistaken me for something other than an enchanted sword."

The silver-tongue had become a lead-tongue. There were no words or arguments he could reply with; his tongue sat in his open mouth, heavy and useless at having been verbally bested yet again. He had crossed wits and won against immortal ghosts and the finest of debaters; despite all that, a shimmering length of steel had rendered him speechless. However Ezekiel had made this thing, he sure did some job of it, Fredo thought to himself.

Shiara had largely ignored the last part of the conversation; deep in her own thoughts, she had no interest in verbal sparring. The city itself was approaching fast; Scaley was picking up the pace as the terrain evened out. This wide tract of land would have once been for farming. It still bore some of the scars of agriculture where wild plants had failed to heal them over. Many of the structures still stood, albeit weather-worn and in states of disrepair. In some ways it was surprising that this area of land had been abandoned. The ghosts were unable to leave the city walls, so there was no danger posed and the land was perfect for growing crops. The emotional distress of living in the shadow of Latan was probably too much to bear, and how were people to be sure of the limits of the ghost protectors? After all, they were meant to be protectors, yet Wasif had done the exact opposite.

CHAPTER FORTY-FOUR

There was no harm in being overly cautious.

Underfoot, the plants were sporadic and unimpressive. Cultivated crops were not well disposed to living without care and attention. The ones that had survived all these years were smaller and more hardy, barely reminiscent of their distant ancestors that once fed the city. They'd adapted to requiring far less water and looked tougher and far less fleshy than the plants encircling the other cities. If it wasn't for the magic sinkhole effect created by the ghosts, these plants would have been overrun by the wilderness, but as it stood, they were instead stalwart reminders of the past, rugged imitations of what once was.

Scaley slowed pace as they neared the gate. There was some apprehension from the lizard; not because of the magic sinkhole effect, since sandbacks had been bred around them for hundreds of years just like the crops, but because something was amiss. Just like Shiara and Fredo, Scaley had never seen a city devoid of activity like this; and his encounter with the Cara owls had taught him to treat the unusual with prudence.

The walls were still solid and offered no way in. The main gate on this side of the city was also fully intact. Were the doors locked? One would have imagined that the people fleeing the city would have left the doors open as they made their escape, so why were they now closed? Had Wasif barred the way to maximize the havoc? Or perhaps he closed it when the bloodshed was finished, sealing himself off from the rest of the world. Trying to guess what had happened hundreds of years ago was pointless, especially when the main figure involved was known as "the mad ghost".

"So, do we just... try to walk through the front door?" asked Fredo.

Shiara shrugged. "I guess so."

It was a surreal feeling to be stepping up to the site of the most famous atrocity in history and just casually pushing the door open to walk inside. Scaley was unused to being brought right up to the city gate and was looking around, examining the door surreptitiously. Shiara thought it best to bring him along inside the city. They may need to move fast and he offered the best chance of being able to do that. They dismounted and led him by walking with the reins in hand to give him some respite from carrying them; they had to make sure he had as much energy as possible if it needed to be called upon.

Shiara placed her hand on the door and began to push. At first, nothing. The door had been closed so long it was as if it had forgotten how to open. Fredo joined in and the pair managed to get some movement from it. It appeared that it was indeed unlocked. It took a few hefty heaves but eventually the door came free and was open enough for them to steal their way inside. There was no widening it any further; something felt as if it was blocking its path. They shuddered to think what it might be; however, once inside their expectations were completely overturned.

CHAPTER FORTY-FIVE

Marin didn't feel any pangs of guilt over neglecting a council meeting but the pit that formed in his stomach when learning about the refugees living in slum-like conditions was very real. He was supposed to be different from the others, a person who genuinely cared about the least fortunate rather than pontificating in a dusty old council chamber; yet here he was. Walking towards his former warehouse, he pondered that he had given it up to help the influx of refugees, only for it to become a slum. There was an important lesson in this for him. It wasn't just about doing the right thing; without constant care and attention the best of intentions could be subverted by the circumstances of life. Yes, somebody could have told him about this before Andros brought it up as a weapon to get at him, but then again, he could have asked. Or walked down to check it out. Instead, he was too caught up with the excitement of solving a murder. Even now he was still discussing the details of the case with Bemus as he accompanied him down to what was once the merchant district.

"I've just about finished reading the journal now, and I'm positive who we need to talk to is a woman he refers to as 'Starshine'."

"Starshine?" quizzed Bemus. "'ow we s'pose' to find 'er?"

A shrug of the council leader's shoulders and a grimace suggested that this would be quite the hurdle.

"We've got a rough area to start looking, as Rhodes's journal mentions specific parts of a district. But that's still a wide net to cast."

"Ya reckon dis is da one we's lookin' for? 'Ow come?"

Marin unconsciously resorted to the smug and prideful expression that had become commonplace when making deductions of late.

"Glad you asked. 'Starshine' was not only one of the last people that Rhodes had been intimate with, but she was also the only one he was meeting in secret."

"I get it. So der wer someone she were 'fraid of findin' out. An' ya fink dat is da person we is lookin' for? Sounds 'bout right. Guess we be knockin' on lotta doors soon den."

Precision in language was not Bemus's strong point; nevertheless, his mind was surprisingly perceptive.

They were now in sight of the warehouse. Around its perimeter were dishevelled looking people slumped against the walls; they looked hungry and weary. Many clung to a smattering of possessions, relics of their old lives in Illorne. The glint of jewellery stood out on a few of them, family heirlooms salvaged as they fled, giving them something to cling to and remember their past with. Marin wondered about what these people's lives might have been like before... Shiara. How could they have gone from comfort and safety to... this? In what must have seemed like only the briefest of moments. Change had come fast and hurt them in a big way. Daily struggles over which outfit to wear had been replaced by considerations of how to feed themselves. Do they sell the few remaining things they had - their legacy and history – just to put scraps of food in their bellies? Sure, food packages had been arranged for these people but obviously they were insufficient. Finding them work also proved challenging; the infrastructure and organization of the Church had seen its own people placed into working the fields and ranches so the poor people who didn't join them were left without prospects.

Bemus pointed out a few of the buildings nearby; they looked run down and seedy, a sad reflection of what went on inside them. The veteran guard explained that many of the female refugees has been recruited into prostitution just to feed themselves and what was left of their families. Before Shiara had changed things, similar practices had gone on around the Brown Quarter; it was the unpleasant way of things. Where some saw misery and desperation, others saw opportunity. The elderly men on the council

CHAPTER FORTY-FIVE

had continually blocked moves to stop such practices, presumably due to the allure of younger women that their money could buy time with. The more affluent places they considered when thinking about prostitution were not like this. This was flat-out exploitation and would need to be stopped. Edwin had pointed out in the past that simply making it illegal would only serve to make it more dangerous for those who were being exploited. Regulation would help, but the real solution was to tackle the root cause of the issue: poverty. So far Marin had failed to meet this challenge on a daunting scale.

Faces looked up at the pair of them as they walked by. Not only did Marin feel more out of place here; he also felt guilty. "Let's take a look inside," he said.

Sliding back the heavy door that was only open a couple of feet, they were immediately greeted by a foetid smell. An odour consisting of human waste and bodily scents of the unwashed. Their eyes took a minute to adjust to the dimly lit surroundings. Candles did most of the work yet left large pools of darkness. He couldn't blame them for not wanting to see much of what lay around them. People were stretched out on the floor, alive but devoid of vigour. It wasn't just that they were hungry; there was something else. He could see it in their eyes. Hope, or rather a lack of it. The confines of the building were designed to keep the heat out, but the same features did just as good a job of keeping the heat in; this meant dehydration was also a problem. Whilst they were free to come and go as they saw fit, they didn't really have anywhere to go; they knew no-one and nothing of Caspir. At least if they were here they would get occasional food rations. Marin could see they were trapped by circumstances. A trap that he had unintentionally laid for them via poorly thought-out good intentions. He expected them to view him with disgust, yet they didn't; apathy had taken over. They had gone beyond caring or blaming, almost as if they were resigned to their fate. The councillor could not let this folly of his stand. He wanted to know what these people were feeling and how they wanted him to help them. Spotting one individual, a young man with long, tangled hair and patchy beard, he sidled over to him and crouched down to meet him.

"Hello, my name is Marin. I want to help you."

At first the young man was apprehensive but introduced himself as Yiannis. Slowly the council leader elicited further information from him. He spoke of his life before Hectin was slain, that he'd worked in his uncle's bakery making sweet, rolled pastries with nuts in. His eyes welled up remembering said uncle, as he had been unable to flee with the rest of them. Marin was expecting Yiannis to open up about life in the slums, but his first port of call was to recall his time before things changed. He couldn't blame the youngster for wanting to reminisce about the past when life was better for him, and then there was the notion of this person portraying themselves as they felt they really were, not what these circumstances made them. Nobody wanted to be seen as a poor refugee that was nothing more than a burden. In Yiannis's mind he was still the young man who carefully crafted masterful pastry delicacies. Eventually the conversation took a turn towards his current situation. His demeanour and voice radiated defeat, but still Marin had to continue his probing. He owed it to all of them.

"Tell me about life here. What do you need? What can we do?"

Some other people had begun to gather around and listen to this exchange. They were partly intrigued but mostly dismissive and prone to rolling their eyes. It was evident that they had little expectation that what Yiannis was saying would make any difference. Yiannis himself was a touch more optimistic – presumably the virtue of youth and a lack of experience in regard to bureaucracy, thought the onlookers.

The answers were surprising. Marin had expected him to ask for a better place to live, or more to eat, but that was not the case. The one thing he was most adamant about was the need for opportunities. He wasn't looking for things to be handed to him; he just wanted the means to earn them for himself. This suggestion stirred vocal agreement from the ever-growing throng of people now encircling them.

"We don't want to be taken care of, we want the opportunity to take care of ourselves," Yiannis explained, echoed by cautious cheers.

It shouldn't have been a revelation and the fact that it almost was to Marin was in itself another revelation. Refugees were just like everyone else. They had come to Caspir so that they could live and that meant everything from

CHAPTER FORTY-FIVE

working for a living, to falling in love and finding somewhere to call home. They weren't an issue to be dealt with; they were a fantastic resource of new citizens to grow the city for the better. The humbled council leader understood that he'd been going about this all wrong. It wasn't a case of giving them the resources to live, it was about allowing them to build their own lives. Several ideas formed in his mind; one in particular was quite radical but made perfect sense. For hundreds of years the walls of Caspir were a fixed structure purely because of Chase and his inability to leave those walls. Generations had passed and overcrowded the area within those original walls, all to support the ego of their council leader who wanted to keep Caspir within his field of influence. Now though, things were different. The walls were an arbitrary fixture; maybe it was time to change that. The farms and ranches that surrounded the walls left plenty of room for further building and the wide trading routes could have the city extend outwards along those paths, thus giving the ability to house more people and ease the overcrowding. Even on the outskirts of the agricultural land it was perfectly feasible to construct some satellite villages to give people a chance to forge their own lives whilst still being part of the city as a whole. It got Marin thinking about the skills and expertise that must be in the room, so he asked them.

"Tell me, what did you do before you left Illorne?"

There was silence briefly before someone shouted out "Potter". Then followed "Stonemason", followed by an avalanche of different professions being called out. Everything from doctor to poet. An entire community of people sat here, going to waste. If Marin could unlock their potential it wouldn't just help *them*, but Caspir as a whole. Between them and some help from other citizens of Caspir they could easily begin building new homes by knocking down parts of the wall and extending the limits of the city.

Feel-good moments were rare, yet Marin was sure he'd found one. He stood up triumphant in himself and told the warehouse full of refugees that he had a plan. A few of them almost dared to believe him, although further disappointment dissuaded most. The council leader tried to shake a few hands and convince as many as he could that things were about to change with some actual success. After a while he'd done all he could and felt happy with how things had gone. The warehouse was always supposed to be a temporary measure and now he knew what must come next. Walking back through the crowds, he no longer saw them as a problem that needed to be handled; instead they were an opportunity that had to be grasped.

Marin and Bemus left the warehouse and began walking away, only to be confronted by yet another problem.

It was Alyssa. She and a considerable group of her followers stood in their path.

"We understand you haven't charged the man who confessed to murdering one of our congregation yet. Explain yourself."

Direct and abrasive as usual, Marin wasn't going to let her get to him.

"That man to whom you refer has a name. Farid. And we now have evidence that he is in fact *not* responsible for murdering Rhodes."

Her face looked as if she'd just tasted something extraordinarily bitter.

"And what exactly is this evidence? How exactly does it trump a confession?" she spat.

"We can't discuss an ongoing investigation with you. Also, if you beat someone badly enough, they'll confess to anything, as I'm are obviously aware. Farid has now recanted his confession and we have no intention of charging him."

Marin was getting carried away and belligerent because of his revelation over the refugee situation.

"He's still in your cells, isn't he? That doesn't sound like an innocent man. The Children of Shiara demand justice," Alyssa howled, playing to her crowd.

"And that's exactly what you'll get! We're on our way now to follow up a very promising lead that will bring the real murderer to justice."

Bemus shot Marin an uneasy glance. He was overplaying his hand. Yes, they had a lead but they couldn't possibly claim to be close to solving Rhodes's murder.

"In fact," Marin continued, "we're so sure that we're going to release Farid. Right now."

CHAPTER FORTY-FIVE

He called over a guard from the end of the street, then shouted for him to release Farid immediately. The guard nodded and scuttled off down the thoroughfare.

"There. Now excuse us, we have a *real* murderer to catch."

Alyssa acted as if stunned; however, as they passed her that same wry smile she had shown before appeared. Marin's confidence had got the better of him and he'd had enough of people getting at him.

Bemus leaned in as they walked away. "Ya fink dat wer a good idea?"

The council leader knew it wasn't; sadly Alyssa had an uncanny ability to always get under his skin. He'd tried playing nice to get around her and failed; at this point he'd given up and desperately wanted a win.

"Bemus, when it comes to her, I'm not sure I've ever had a good idea."

CHAPTER FORTY-SIX

Tonight was the night. Since the reprisals there had been a huge surge in support for the revolution; it was all Koralia and her friends could manage to keep some citizens from starting the unrest at the wrong time. Not a day went by where they weren't having to restrain action to save it up for the right time. That time could wait no longer. The harvest was about a week away and keeping the newly acquired bloodlust of fellow revolutionaries at bay was becoming difficult. Since Nasos's death Koralia had stepped up as a more visual leader. Everyone knew it was her they had to thank for this path to freedom; after the fiasco of the attack on the guardhouse an authoritative hand was required. The plan would only work if everyone was on the same page and this could only be achieved by exerting some influence and order over the rebels. They still had no idea who was behind the slaughtering of the sleeping wardens; perhaps they were victims of the reprisals, but nobody was willing to admit involvement and people were falling into line.

The final day of field work as subservient citizens had finished. They paid special attention to where they left their tools for ease of access once it all kicked off. Lumis had produced as many weapons as he could without suspicion; they were now being distributed to the first wave of revolutionaries. These would be the ones to break through the gates and retrieve the farming tools to be repurposed as weapons. Some would no doubt perish whilst jumping the guards, but it was unlikely that more than a handful would be killed before the wardens were overpowered. The sentries sitting atop the wall would prove more challenging. The revolutionaries

CHAPTER FORTY-SIX

would have to rely on unhinged doors along with pots and pans to stave off as many crossbow bolts as they could. The guards had the benefit of more weaponry, but the number of people was where the real battle would be fought and the rebels had plenty. It was a physical impossibility for them to wade through the sheer volume of citizens in the uprising; many would fall but their weapons would be picked up by those behind them. The onslaught for freedom would not be quelled. The only sticking point was Takis himself. The library would hopefully provide enough of a distraction to keep him out of the fray, for he would not be overpowered by numbers. There was no overwhelming an immortal warrior of unrivalled strength. He had the might to turn groups of people into bloody messes with a single stroke. If he was not distracted by the library for long enough, countless people would lose their lives and it might even risk the revolution's failure. He was unstoppable. Or at least that was what people once thought. The part of the plan to smash his thrumming pillar was kept quiet. Only her close comrades knew, for if they failed to stop Takis, that would be it for them. It was all up to Koralia; the wardens would be drawn into the conflict and she'd sneak to the pillar. There it would all end. Once Takis was gone there would be nothing for the guards to fight for; they'd see their time was up. It was just a question of how many people would have to die before she could end him. And how long would the wardens keep fighting for? There was one other, major, concern before any of that could happen. Was Harun still alive, and if so, was he still on board? Koralia had chalked the wash-room just like they had arranged; only when she showed up after dusk would she know for sure. So much hinged on it; would she be able to find her own way in without him? Almost certainly not. Stefania had suggested setting fire to a nearby building instead; it would still give off the same signal from a distance and perhaps the fire would spread. It would be enough to start the insurrection but unlikely to draw Takis's attention. He'd no doubt be knee deep in the entrails of their comrades in no time at all. Harun had to come through; it would be the difference between hundreds, if not thousands, of people living or dying.

She packed her bag, being careful not to damage the containers of lamp oil. The last thing she needed was to go up in flames with the library. She looked at her friends, who were gathered together for what might be the last time.

"This is it," she said.

The whole crew were there, aside from Nasos, and they each had their parts to play.

"Do you think Harun will come?" asked Minos.

"He has to, and if he doesn't, I'm still going to set fire to something. You just worry about your own role; you all set?" Koralia replied.

Minos and Neela nodded and pointed to a bag of heavy tools. These would be used to break the thrumming pillar.

"Just make sure you two are there to meet me at the courtyard after the fire is set. Try not to get caught, especially considering that big nose of yours Minos," joked Koralia.

The group all laughed together. Humour had proven the best coping mechanism for just about everything they had been through up to now.

"The rest of you, ready?" Koralia asked.

"Yes yes, we've got it. We've been over it enough times," responded Stefania. She'd taken Nasos's death worse than the others; her usual spark of wit had felt a little shorter since then. Her role was also important; she was no fighter, but her words could make the difference in rallying the people. It was her job to stoke the uprising and inspire as many people to take up arms as possible. Lumis's best fighting days were also in the past, but his stocky build was formidable. His task was to get people equipped for battle and help distribute arms as they secured first the farming implements, then later the guardhouses and their troves of weapons. As a metalworker he was one of the few citizens who could be relied upon to use one of the warden's crossbows should they get their hands on some. The last two comrades were the ones Koralia was worried about most. She embraced them to say good luck, and also goodbye. Orestis and Castor would be wading into the fight and leading the charge. Castor was an impressive physical specimen who one could imagine might be able to survive such an encounter, yet Orestis… was not. He was by no means unfit, just average. And average people would

CHAPTER FORTY-SIX

be no match for a well-armed warden. Nevertheless, it was essential for the uprising. The inner circle of rebels had to be seen fighting alongside everyone else, and they'd been happy to do it. Well, not so much happy, but willing, which was enough. Koralia fought back a tear as she gave her cousin what may well be a final hug.

"Make sure you look out for Orestis," she said.

He nodded. Their reservoirs of words were dried up by the enormity of what was coming.

A final look and farewell to her companions who had all come so far with her, then she slipped out into the night.

It was probably all in her mind, but the air itself felt heavy and cloying. Almost as if every part of the city was tensed in anticipation. The wardens had been on high alert since the attack on their sleeping quarters, which meant slower progress in finding a route through the streets to the wash-room. Fortunately, the clanking armour of the guards gave some advance warning of their presence, making slinking into the shadows much easier. Given recent events, the guards were not going to leave themselves exposed and opted for the most robust armour they could find. Yes, this would make it harder to kill them once the uprising began, but right now Koralia was grateful for it.

Arriving at the wash-house, she was sure she hadn't been spotted along the way and saw nobody hanging around. This was both a good and a bad sign; whilst she didn't want wardens getting in the way, Harun was also nowhere to be seen. She hoped he was secreted inside. Their previous encounter and how that had made her feel like she was walking into a trap tickled the back of her mind. She swallowed down the apprehension and tiptoed into the tiled wash-room. Her eyes were slow to adjust; nothing. No movement. No shapes in the darkness. Just an empty wash-room. A windmill of thoughts began circulating in her mind, pondering every possibility and what that meant. Fortunately, for her sanity at least, this was cut short by a hand grabbing her shoulder from behind. Panic set in.

Uncontrollably inhaling as a substitute for speech, she managed to slowly turn like somebody cautiously peering at a wound as they peel back a bandage. Relief came when she saw Harun's face; her racing heart would take longer to get the message.

"Not a good time to sneak up on me," Koralia said.

"I could hardly call out, could I?" Harun answered back.

She had to admit to herself he was right, yet the excessive thumping of blood in her ears and chest was something she could have done without.

"I'm glad you came; I was worried."

Harun looked cross at her concern.

"You should've told me about that massacre. There were good people who didn't need to die," he replied in an aggravated tone.

"I didn't know," she pleaded apologetically. "They did it off their own backs and we still have no idea who it was."

Harun shrugged. He seemed to believe her explanation, but that didn't mean he was happy about it.

"It's done now. And they won't be the last of the good people who die because of this crusade. I hope your plan is worth it. Have you got the oil?"

Koralia nodded.

"Let's go then," Harun said as he led her out into the dark night once again.

She had never been this close to the library before. It was a remarkable building, ancient yet somehow pristine as if it were brand new. Smooth round stone pillars made up its four corners. They were at the far east corner, safely far away from the entrance.

"Can you climb?" Harun asked.

"Don't worry about me," Koralia responded.

Harun pulled himself up onto the ledge of a neighbouring building and clambered his way up its wall. Koralia followed with little difficulty, clearly finding it much easier than him, although she didn't want to make it obvious. A few minutes of ascension later, the entry point became clear. What was once a slit window to circulate air had become a small person-sized opening. It would be a tight fit, more so for him than her, but it would most certainly do. Harun pointed.

CHAPTER FORTY-SIX

"D'you think you can make the jump?" he asked.

Clearly Harun had not noticed how easily she had scaled the building upon which they were now perched. She smiled back at him knowingly.

He leapt first; despite claims that he had done this before he lacked the elegance of experience, although nerves could do that to anybody. Koralia followed suit, making it look a little simpler, yet without the finesse she would have liked. She looked down at the drop she had just jumped across, wondering if it would be more difficult to descend later with a fire lapping up the building. That problem was a fair few problems down the list right now and she'd deal with it when she got there. She disappeared from the street and into the library. She had breached Takis's sanctum.

CHAPTER FORTY-SEVEN

The paving stones were cracked and broken and the buildings in a state of disrepair, but it wasn't from the carnage of Latan's past. Thick trunks of trees uprooted what was once a thoroughfare. Sinewy green vines wove between the structures like emerald bunting at a parade. The reason the door had proven so troublesome to open was due to the shaggy stem of a large plant with pointed leaves jutting out in fan-like patterns. Neither of them had seen anything like it before. The closest Fredo could think of were the small palms that nobles liked to keep, although that still felt like a stretch.

"So much for that magic sinkhole putting off the plants," Fredo said, directing it to the enchanted blade with the snap of true one-upmanship.

"It is indeed strange," replied the sword.

Pushing back a large glossy jade leaf, Shiara peered down each street as far as she could see, which turned out to not be that far given the abundance of undergrowth.

"Do you think this means that Wasif is dead? More than just being a ghost, that is?" she asked.

"I suspect not. The plants outside the walls still seem deterred and I can feel the drawing in of magic from the city's thrumming pillar," answered the weapon.

Shiara clocked the word "feel", which she found odd coming from a piece of metal. However, it was a sentient weapon, so could she really say what was weird when it came to such topics?

CHAPTER FORTY-SEVEN

"And let's face it, who in their right mind would try to come and slay the mad ghost of Latan?!" remarked Fredo before catching himself and adding "present company excluded".

A flutter of Kerri bird wings erupted from nearby foliage atop a house as Shiara, Fredo and Scaley navigated their way through the former street. Clearly these birds were much less familiar with people than those in other cities. Kerri birds would usually peck at the crumbs by your feet, or even on your clothing at times, so seeing them this skittish demonstrated how far from Fredo's comfort zone this place really was.

"I've never seen plants quite like this before. What do you think they are?" Shiara queried.

"Well, I'd say that much like the cultivated crops of the cities and the noble's gardens, these plants have been bred over time to be like this." The enchanted blade was clearly guessing; it just did so in an authoritative manner.

"And who are you proposing did all this? Wasif?!" exclaimed Fredo.

"As you so shrewdly pointed out, it's not as if anyone else would come here," the sword rebutted.

"So you're saying that 'the mad ghost of Latan' butchered an entire city just to have a garden?"

Fredo was getting irate, which was sadly becoming a regular state when conversing with the magic sword.

"What else is there to do when you're alone for hundreds of years?" it quipped.

The street they were traversing was made up of smaller buildings that were likely once houses. Now they still teemed with life, just of a different kind. Even though the atrocity in Latan was long ago, Shiara and Fredo were expecting to see more signs of the violence and distress. As it was, it looked as if everybody had just left and nature had taken over the abandoned metropolis. At street level it was darker because of the canopy of branches and leaves stretching above them, effectively forming loose tunnel-like structures as flora grew first up the walls then between them. Each step had to be carefully placed to dodge the roots and other vegetation. Among all this wonder there remained an underlying fear that clawed at them. It may have seemed like a peaceful and tranquil slice of greenery, but it was still the site of the greatest massacre in history. And the one responsible for it was still here.

Every time a Kerri bird rustled in a tree they paused and held their breaths. Shiara may have slain three ghosts, but those were in duels. A surprise attack could yield a very different outcome and nobody knew much about the mad ghost, except his deeds. Shiara understood that there was nothing more terrifying than an unpredictable opponent who may well have no sense of self-preservation. If someone wanted to kill you at the expense of their own life it was exceedingly hard to stop them, regardless of one's skill.

Scaley seemed far less apprehensive and was even enjoying himself. Pushing his face through the leaves and examining what lay beneath them, he was looking for something juicy to devour. Every so often they'd hear him crunching what was presumably some sort of insect from the sound it made. Whilst Latan was still sparse in terms of larger animals aside from Kerri birds, there seemed to be a fair abundance of invertebrates. Chunky yellow caterpillars with green faces and black spines chowed down on the more succulent leaves. Bright blue segmented insects flitted between flowers. Stout purple beetles marched through the undergrowth; these seemed to be Scaley's favourite. The noise of chewing through their carapaces was not conducive to their attempts at stealth; neither was the swishing of the foliage as he poked his head through.

The further they penetrated into the city, the more different it became. The temperature and humidity increased as the dense thickets retained their heat and moisture. Odour-wise, the damp scent of mulching leaves and wet greenery continued to grow in strength. Such an environment was very far from their personal experiences. The entire region was generally on the dry side, hence why the cities were all built close to rivers. Their agriculture relied on crops that weren't especially high in their water requirements; water-rich produce like juicy tamatims tended to be produced in smaller quantities and were reserved for the wealthy. The only exception was Caspir's threadwurm trade; they depended on having a moist environment

CHAPTER FORTY-SEVEN

and Caspir in turn depended on their threads for commerce. Despite that, those soggy ranches felt nothing like this. The air itself was cloying and wet, and it even looked different. It was as if a very faint mist hung in the atmosphere, the sort only seen occasionally by rivers at first light. Somehow Wasif had turned the city into a place that was unlike any other. Shiara found herself thinking quite fondly of it.

"It's beautiful, isn't it?"

"I suppose, if you like this sort of thing." Fredo was somewhat less impressed.

"A far cry from what you'd expect from someone dubbed 'the mad ghost', wouldn't you agree?" added the magical blade.

"I'm not sure how an uncivilized and overgrown mess could justifiably be called sane." The silver-tongue understood the world of people and culture; given his recent experiences with owls one couldn't blame him for being a bit sceptical of more wild environments. Shiara disagreed.

"How is it any more crazy than a city full of rich people chasing after the newest fashion trend whilst others starve?"

She was right of course, not that Fredo wanted to admit it, even to himself.

The vegetation before them started to give way to a wider open clearing, which silenced their conversation. What was once one of Latan's many squares was now an unusual break from the almost jungle-like conditions surrounding it. Plants still snaked around the area but had clearly been pruned back and kept from invading the courtyard too much. It soon became apparent why. Upon each of the walls was splashed a different artistic offering. Two of them bore landscapes, an in-depth study of a river-bend and an immaculately depicted brush-land. Each brushstroke was majestic on its own, yet blended into the rest of the piece perfectly. The variety of hues put even the finest of garments from Caspir to shame. Another wall featured an exquisite portrayal of a brown, grey and white dappled Kerri bird with flecks of turquoise and just a hint of amethyst on the tips of its wings and around its head. The likeness was uncanny; every feather appeared to have been painted into place with inhuman precision. The final brick canvas was a very different story. Far from a scene of tranquillity or beauty, it bore a nightmarish vision that snapped them right back to Latan's terrible history. A scene of carnage and suffering played out in minute detail. A person cradling their entrails with a look of confusion on their face. Others fleeing with panic etched into their features. Splurges of reds and browns streaked across the street in the picture. And above it all, looming over them in the sky, a pair of disembodied eyes: gazing down without emotion at the slaughter from a swirling pink and grey firmament. The juxtaposition with the other paintings compounded its odiousness. Why create this scene? What did it mean? They all assumed the eyes were that of Wasif; did that mean he saw the atrocity not as they did but instead merely as an artistic spectacle? Was he trying to relive it through his art? Or could it have been a grim reminder or penance? It was impossible to say, and the excellence of the brushwork only prompted further questions. This was not the work of a manic and crazed mind; this was talented and precise. Calculated. That sort of a mind being the architect behind a genocide was far more disturbing than a deranged mind simply losing control.

Eventually one of them managed to find some words.

"Why...?" Fredo managed.

"I don't understand, why would anyone paint such a thing, let alone next to these other works of art?" Shiara said. "Such detail for something so horrid."

"Is that not the point of art?" The enchanted weapon's voice did not hold the same disgust as Shiara's and Fredo's.

"Excuse me?" said the indignant silver-tongue.

"Surely as someone who moved within the upper circles, you can appreciate art," it replied.

"Art? This is... repulsive."

"That guttural surge of emotion, is this not what art is supposed to do? Make the viewer *feel* something? An instinctive reaction that makes you question."

"Not like this," answered Fredo. "This is just gratuitous and unpleasant."

"Why is an unpleasant message any less poignant or relevant than a pleasant one? You cannot deny that this piece has moved you. Are your

CHAPTER FORTY-SEVEN

feelings of disgust not the exact point of such a thing?"

"Why would anyone want to look at this?" Fredo's voice was becoming louder and more irate.

"Yet you are unable to take your eyes off it."

Fredo understood the blade's point, and in other circumstances could have even agreed with it, but not now. Not with a depiction of mayhem by a mass murderer. Especially not whilst said murderer could be around any corner.

"What do *you* know? You haven't even got eyes. You're just a shiny bit of metal." It was a cheap shot from Fredo, but could a magical weapon truly feel offended? Did it have feelings other than smugness?

"I see what you are both saying, I just don't understand why someone with such talent would choose to use in such a way," said Shiara, cutting through the tension between her companions. "Why add this to the world when there is already so much horror; why not create something beautiful instead?"

"It's precisely because the world contains such horror, that art should reflect it," replied the sword.

They stood for a while contemplating the piece, finding ever greater details with each glance. There was silence, aside from the rustling and crunching of a hungry Scaley.

"It's the eyes I don't like. I never seem to get people's eyes right," came a wistful voice from behind them. Instant gut punches of fear emptied their lungs as they could only turn slowly to see what was behind them: a towering figure cut in the familiar form of ghostly translucency, stood with hands on hips. In any other context his appearance would have been far from threatening; if anything he seemed melancholy. A sort of longing and emptiness was etched behind his eyes, yet his clothing was the pristine regalia of a warrior, perfectly preserved by the same magic that sustained him. Somehow, he was a much less impressive image than the other ghosts, wide-eyed, with a smaller nose and unremarkable features. Tightly curled jet-black hair gave him far less presence than someone like Mara. He almost seemed... harmless.

He spoke up again.

"I've been waiting for you, well... anybody really, for a very long time."

CHAPTER FORTY-EIGHT

The district in which Marin and Rhodes were canvassing for information about someone known only as "Starshine" had strangely become a little less crowded since the refugees from Illorne had arrived. One would have thought the influx of people would have had the opposite effect, but a lot of this was down to the Church of Shiara. The growth of their congregation had proven successful, which meant lots of people had moved to live together in the same area; this freed up a little bit of space in districts like this one. Marin wondered if he could use this to his advantage to help the refugees from Illorne and those who would no doubt start arriving from Fimego before long. He would have to remember this for later. At present he was gaining a unique insight into human reactions, the kind that could only be gleaned by asking strangers if they knew someone who went by "Starshine". He and Bemus had knocked on enough doors to make their knuckles sore and still came up empty. Trying to ask if they knew Rhodes hadn't helped much either; as soon as they mentioned he was in the Church of Shiara people lost interest. "How am I supposed to remember a specific one of them when they all dress the same?" was the usual reply. Marin thought this was rather unfair, considering how handsome Rhodes clearly had been.

Caspir's obsession with fashion was certainly a hindrance for this investigation. Ask any of them to describe what someone was wearing, and they'd accurately convey every last thread and probably tell you the needleworker responsible for the design; getting them to recall a person based solely on a drawing of their face was pointless. Despite this, they continued. Like the "mortal gambit" in Bahlea, this was Marin's last-ditch effort. There were no other moves to make; they needed to find *someone, anyone* who could give them something to work with. Alyssa and the Church would not wait for long to capitalize on his lack of progress. He was positive that she was the person responsible for Andros's new-found vigour at council meetings and would surely push him to the next phase of whatever her plan may be. It wouldn't surprise him if she had also got to others, and was just waiting to make a move and take control of Caspir's government. He had to tell himself that every door knocked upon was edging a step closer to finding this "Starshine" person.

After a while they knew they were getting somewhere, as several people they called upon knew of Rhodes. Making sure to take down their details just in case, none of them, however, seemed to fit with what they were looking for. None of them came across as jilted lovers or partners; they were all rather mournful regarding Rhodes's passing and quite vocal about his horizontal prowess. These women and men were proud to have spent time with Rhodes – definitely not the sort who would have snuck around to enjoy his company on the sly. Some were even a little too proud, offering far too much detail in regard to his dimensions and techniques. Marin was far from a prude but could feel himself getting flustered, which was impressive given he'd read Rhodes's accounts of many a salacious rendezvous.

"I is startin' to fink dat de only people 'oo knew Rhodes wer ones wot wanted to sleep wiv 'im, not kill 'im," mused Bemus.

His council leader friend nodded in agreement; it certainly seemed that way so far. It was time to knock on yet another door; the pair had begun to play a game with one another where they guessed whether the person who answered the door either didn't know Rhodes or had slept with him.

They knocked. Movement came from within, but the door did not open. They turned to each other, then back to the door and knocked louder. No movement this time.

"Look, we know you're in there, we heard you moving about. We've come to ask you some questions..." Marin's words still didn't elicit a response. "It's about a murder. We're hoping you can help us."

CHAPTER FORTY-EIGHT

There were sounds from within of someone approaching the door, which was slowly opened. Keeping the door open only about a foot, the nervous-looking face of a man about thirty years old peered around it. He was slightly on the heavier side with eyes that spoke to a lack of sleep.

"Y... yes?" he asked tentatively, looking increasingly anxious with every second.

"It's about the murder of a member of the Church of Shiara. A man named Rhodes."

The man froze. Blood drained from his umber-coloured face. Then the corner of his mouth and one hand twitched as he fumbled for a reply. All of a sudden, he clasped his face and broke into tears.

"I'm sorry. It was all an accident." Other words followed but were indecipherable through the blubbing. Marin glanced at Bemus, both of them somewhat confused. Was *this* the person who had mutilated a body and hung it up? A man bawling his eyes out and breaking down at the first opportunity given? Hardly the angry or crazed killer that one would expect. The pair pushed the door open and stepped inside, closing it behind themselves. They thought it better to conduct this interview in private.

The man's house was nothing unusual. It looked as if it could have belonged to anyone, a noticeable absence of anything that screamed "murderer" or suchlike. Which, Marin thought, was exactly the point. They were working on the assumption that the murder was a crime of passion; only afterwards was the body mutilated in an attempt to divert suspicion. Bemus had previously discussed that murderers, for the most part, were not crazed killers but emotional people just like everyone else. It wasn't some hidden evil characteristic that made people kill; rather it was a combination of circumstances, impulse control, opportunity and a whole host of other factors. When it came down to it, people didn't sit around thinking about killing someone; it was a spur of the moment thing. Marin confessed to himself that the notion that the difference between a murderer and himself was so small was indeed troubling, despite he himself having known perfectly reasonable traders to fly into a rage over irrelevancies.

The man was still sobbing, but his breathing had slowed to the point where he could actually get out perceptible words, so Marin began.

"My name is Marin, and this is Bemus."

"I... I'm Amit."

"Tell us what happened," said the council leader, helping the weeping man to a chair and trying to make him as comfortable as possible in a bid to elicit as much information as he could.

Wiping a tear from his face and steadying the quiver of his lower lip, he began recounting his tale.

"I... thought... we were happy, y'know?"

"We?" prompted Marin.

"Me and Dara, I thought we were in love."

Everything clicked into place. All their speculations had been justified in an instant. Just like they had posited, this wasn't about the Church; it was something far more familiar and mundane: emotions. The fact that Dara had the same name as the East Star tied it all together – the nickname of "Starshine" made perfect sense.

As expected, the events as described by Amit aligned pretty closely with what they suspected. What really struck Marin was the emotional journey the man described. The bliss of obliviousness, disregarding Dara's increasing time spent with unknown "friends"; the distancing of their intimacy through various excuses and the ever-diminishing closeness. None of these occurred to him as meaningful until he overheard her conversation with one of her friends. Much like the jigsaw of their murder investigation, the pieces suddenly clicked together for Amit, allowing paranoia and emotion to take over. He told them how he followed Dara and watched her falling into the arms of Rhodes time and time again. He could never mention it to her. He said, "I didn't want to talk to her about it, because as soon as I did, I knew she'd leave me forever."

Both Marin and Bemus disliked this suggestion. Dara was not a possession; she did not belong to Amit and it was quite clear from the story that things were already over. It reassured the councillor though; far from a normal person snapping and becoming a murderer, there was an underlying perspective in Amit's mind that regarded other people as somehow lesser,

CHAPTER FORTY-EIGHT

or owing him something. Whilst people could snap into a rage, these sorts of unpleasant underlying worldviews could represent a warning sign and predispose people to such acts. There was no denying that Amit's tale was an emotional one, but it was hard to feel sorry for him given what he'd done.

"Tell us about what happened with you and Rhodes." As fascinating as this exploration of Amit's mind was, there was a pressing need to get to the point.

"I had to talk to him. He needed to know what he was doing to me. But I only went to talk; I never meant for anything else to happen."

"Did yer bring a knife wiv ya?" interjected Bemus.

Amit nodded.

"If yer didn't mean t' 'arm 'im, why d'ya bring a knife?"

"I... wanted it for protection."

Bemus was clearly not buying it and it was obvious that somewhere in Amit's mind, the intent to kill was there all along.

"Go on," said Marin.

He tried to place some of the blame on the victim, stating that he got into some kind of a struggle and Rhodes got stabbed. The council leader was sceptical; he'd come to understand Rhodes from reading his diary and talking to people whilst canvassing today. The idea of him putting his energies into anything that wasn't carnal pleasure didn't quite track. Amit's narrative had all the hallmarks of someone lying to justify things after the fact and the expression on Bemus's face showed he thought exactly the same.

"And what about the things you did to his body?" Marin already knew the answer and was just being thorough. As expected, Amit described carving up Rhodes to make it look like something other than what it was. He explained to Amit the consequences of what he'd done and how the Church had beaten a man named Farid. Amit pleaded that he was sorry, but neither Bemus nor Marin were convinced.

"Before we take you in, we have another question for you. Where is Dara now?"

Marin was right to be curious. Amit raised a hand and pointed to a room towards the back of the building. The councillor followed his directions and opened the door Amit had gestured to. Immediately his nose was hit by a smell that was sadly familiar to him now. It was the stench of death. Black specks of flies led like a trail to a cupboard. As he neared it, the odour worsened and red smears became visible along the bottom of the doors and the handle. He knew what he was about to find and even though every fibre of his being didn't want him to open the cupboard, his duty pushed him to. The door was stiff and required a forceful tug to open, billowing out the stink in a wave that caused his eyes to squint and nose to wrinkle. Within lay something that was not the body of a woman but rather the constituent parts, broken and twisted nearly beyond recognition. Unable to spend too long in the presence of this ghastly spectacle, Marin left the room and closed the door behind him. Walking over, he looked into Amit's face without saying a word; the man's reaction was clear.

"She... got angry when I told her. I had to do it."

For all the horror Marin had just witnessed, there were two positives. The first was that there was finally an end to the investigation; justice could be served and he'd be able to look Alyssa in the eye and have the upper hand, for once. The second thing was that he had learnt that the wedge between himself and a murderer was indeed far thicker than he had considered earlier.

CHAPTER FORTY-NINE

Having entered through the widened slit, the section of the library they found themselves in was dark. It was a walkway rather than an area lined with bookshelves, and something instantly came to Koralia's attention: the smell. Books were not that common in Maluani outside of Takis's library and this many under one roof was not something that was easily comprehensible. As such, the collection of parchments and papers together created a scent she was unfamiliar with. A little bit musty and woody, there was a pleasant and comforting quality to it. She wondered if Takis could even smell them, since he didn't need to eat either. The flickers of lamplight in the distance gave them just about enough illumination to see by. Koralia held her breath in a combination of fear and caution. Harun was somewhat more relaxed, having been within the library numerous times before by his own account. He led her along the darkened walkway with purpose; clearly he'd put some thought into where best to set the fire. Once started, the fire should spread of its own accord; the tricky part would be not getting caught by either Takis or the advancing flames. In the recent past Koralia would have found this entire situation far more worrying and would be entertaining paranoid thoughts of whether or not Harun was just leading her to Takis in some kind of trap. Experiences, both pleasant and incredibly vile, had taught her better. She had made peace with the risks she needed to take, knowing that worrying about something she had committed to do was of no benefit. Seeing Nasos's face in that pile of bodies really cleared her thinking. Koralia was just a single person, like everyone, like Nasos. Leading the revolution did not make her more important; if anything it made her fears disappear into irrelevance. Her concerns had moved on from thoughts about her own life; only the movement mattered. That image of Nasos burned into her brain laid it all out: the personal loss was enormous, but it was just one body in a pile of countless others. Whatever personal pain was being felt was dwarfed by what was happening to the people of Maluani as a whole.

Harun paused and raised his arm to signal Koralia to do the same. Slowly, he edged forward; she followed. The wall of the walkway ended, opening up to a much larger room of staircases and bookshelves lit by the orangey-yellow of oil lamps. Neatly lined up in wall-to-wall wooden frames were countless manuscripts. She knew this place would be full of them, yet actually seeing them was a sight to behold. It brought back those feelings of apprehension over destroying such an incredible trove of knowledge and literature. Thinking not about herself, but the wider context, the crime of destroying all these books was not a small decision. It was only a distraction to keep Takis occupied; was it even worth it? She would never even come close to imagining the things contained within these pages and here she was, willing to destroy them?

Harun led Koralia down the stairs as quietly as possible to the level below. The books were now in reach. She ran her hands along their spines and silently read their titles. "Cara owls: training and practices", "Law in the age of magic", "War and the artistry of battle", "Palaeontology: an artist's rendition of extinct megafauna". "The history of Maluani" spanned an entire shelf of volumes. Koralia carefully retrieved the book on palaeontology that drew her interest and flicked through a few of its pages. Spectacular illustrations of towering beasts and fantastic creatures were laid out with brief descriptions. An upright lizard of titanic proportions with a long, thin snout full of teeth; a large horned mammal with long curved ears; a colossal featherless bird, its head and back decorated with thin black filaments. Could these animals really have been real? What other revelations could be lost forever in the fire they planned? Harun looked disapprovingly at Koralia as her attention was held by the book rather than the mission.

"What are you doing?" he whispered.

CHAPTER FORTY-NINE

"Do you not think we should at least know what we are burning down before we do it?" she replied in a hushed voice.

He shrugged and shook his head. "We've got more important things to worry about right now."

Koralia was not going to be deterred. "I've got a bag full of lamp oil I'm about to empty; the least I can do is save a few of these books."

Harun rolled his eyes; this was neither the time nor the place for an argument. He pointed down another small flight of stairs, signalling the best place to set the fire. As of yet there was no sign of anyone. Takis was likely somewhere in the building, though thankfully not in this section of it. Harun went first down the steps, trying his best to keep the sound of his footfalls to a minimum on the hard stone stairs. Carefully, the pair eased their bags off their backs and began to lay out the oil in front of them. They had six jars between them, each of them about the size of an infant's head. Removing the stopper, Harun began to drizzle the thick liquid along the bottom of the nearest bookcase, not too thickly as only a small amount would be required to start it off.

"Pour the oil on the bottom; the flames will rise up the shelves on their own," he said softly.

Koralia was somewhat peeved by his comment; of course she knew to do it like this. She was unsure if his patronizing was down to the fact she was just a fieldworker or a woman; regardless, it was not the time to call him out on it. Having placed the palaeontology book in her bag, she tiptoed in the opposite direction from Harun with a flask of oil, leaving a flammable trail at the foot of the bookshelves as she went. She tried to eye up the books as she walked past them in the hope that she'd find some obvious ones to save; however, they all seemed to be contenders and who was she to choose which knowledge was most important?

She came to a whole shelf populated with books by the same author, Adanya Imani. Not a name she had ever heard before, but if this woman was indeed as prolific as she appeared to be, it would be remiss of Koralia not to save one of her works, but which one? "Scaled Heart"? "The Fable of the Clawed Man", "Tree of Tears?" In the end she settled for "A Tale of Sand

and Salt". Why exactly this was her choice she couldn't say; it was as good as any and found its way into her bag.

Having emptied the contents of one container, she began on the next, working back to cover as much of the room as they could. The smell of the oil forced its way up their noses until they could just about taste it. At this point, Koralia really hoped that Takis couldn't smell, for it wouldn't take long for the scent to waft its way through more of the building. Their dainty steps became more forceful in an attempt to speed them to completion. She found herself splashing a bookcase when she noticed something of concern. A gap in the manuscripts. "Encyclopaedia Magickus: Soul Bonding, part one" and "part three" sat with a space between them. Due to the dispersion of dust, it was obvious that this tome had been taken to read in the very recent past. In Koralia's mind this meant that it wouldn't be long before Takis would return for the third part. How long did it take him to read something? He could move inhumanly fast; if he could study text at a similar rate there would be every reason to expect him back imminently. She crammed the two volumes into her bag on the basis that if Takis was reading them, then they must be important. Splashing the last dregs of her container of oil, she met Harun back where they had started pouring it out.

"There's a book missing from that shelf," she said, pointing.

"So?" replied Harun.

"It means it's only a matter of time before he comes to put it back."

He grimaced at her words; she was right.

"We're nearly done here; help me rig these last two jars."

He laid the last of the oil jars on the edge of the walkway in a pool of oil. The plan was that once the oil lit up, the glass would break and send flaming liquid to the level below to ignite the books down there. Once this was carefully positioned, he produced a small flask of liquid from his bag and removed the stopper. Jamming some thread and parchment into the bottle for a wick, he had an ignition tool.

"With this, we can start the fire from a distance. Should give us more time to get clear," he said. "Although not *that* much more time."

They would have to be quick. Harun went to sling his bag onto his

CHAPTER FORTY-NINE

shoulders but Koralia stopped him. With one hand firmly on his bag, the other grabbed a handful of nearby books without even looking at them and made sure he didn't leave empty handed. A couple more filled out her own pack and they were ready to depart. Creeping back the way they had come, making sure to avoid treading in oil for their own safety, they managed to get back on the upper walkway. Harun looked at the wall-mounted lamp next to him, then to his bottle, then back again. He glanced up at Koralia.

"So this is it," he whispered.

"No, it's not," she said whilst grabbing the bottle out of his hand. "This is just the beginning."

She pulled back the cover of the lamp and lit the fuse on the small flask. Her eyes took in one last panorama of the library and its trove of literature and knowledge. Lungs filled with a deep breath, her arm let the bottle loose. Careening through the air, it crashed exactly where intended. A deep sound accompanied by something that sounded like rushing wind was let out as the flames spread in an instant, dancing across the walls and books, eating them like some ravenous spirit of orange and yellow. The pair darted down the once-dark walkway now illuminated by the growing flames. They heard the sound of glass shattering followed by a roar of new flame being brought to life. Scurrying through the slit they had gained access through, the pair leapt to the building adjacent and scampered down it. Grazes and scratches from the stonework marked their limbs and faces as panic hastened their descent. Jumping down the final storey, their adrenaline kept the pain at bay. They ran across the street to a more dimly lit avenue and looked back. Smoke was beginning to wind its way out of the windows, the flicker of the blaze within becoming noticeable. Within minutes it would be engulfed by the inferno; the signal to start the uprising had been set.

The arsonists stared at each other.

"Now what?" queried Harun.

"You let me worry that; you just get to safety and try to convince as many of the guards as possible to not stand against the people."

"What about these books? I can't be seen with them, and *I* didn't want them in the first place!" he said shrilly.

Koralia sighed. She by no means had to do everything, although sometimes it certainly felt a bit like that.

"Give me the bag." She threw the bag's strap around her shoulder and straightened it up. "Goodbye, Harun. Thank you for this. I hope we'll get to see each other again one day."

"Where are you going now?" he asked.

"Well someone has to kill Takis, and I'm that someone."

She departed into the night, leaving Harun with his mouth agape. He was unsure what startled him more – her matter-of-fact attitude, or the fact that he suspected she might just succeed.

CHAPTER FIFTY

Shiara's hand slowly slid to the hilt of her blade whilst keeping eye contact with the ephemeral being in front of her.

"No need for any of that," said the ghost casually. "I mean you no harm."

The words did not reassure them, but it halted any progress towards her weapon. Wasif shrugged with open arms in a display that was indeed very unthreatening. With this relaxed and laid back gesture, their caution gradually began to subside, eventually allowing moisture back into their dry throats to bring forth a reply.

"Forgive us for being concerned, but you do have a history of being... less than safe to be around," said Fredo, pointing at the painting of carnage they had previously been looking at.

"Don't worry about all that," replied Wasif dismissively. "That was a long time ago, and let's face it, the pair of you are not exactly a deeply entrenched system of inequality, are you? Anyway, I've got other plans for you."

Those last few words sat uneasily with Fredo and Shiara. What sort of plan did he have in mind? It was hard to see Wasif as sinister based on how he spoke and acted, yet his history was always hanging over everything.

"Plans?" queried Shiara.

"You can let go of that sword of yours, which I must say is quite lovely; they'll be plenty of time for you to use it shortly, so best not to waste the energy. Please, walk with me."

One thing was becoming apparent from Wasif's words; the image of a crazed ghost didn't seem accurate at all. It wasn't a surprise that stories generations removed from the events themselves had been embellished or changed. This was not a person one could picture as "the mad ghost", and the sword's previous speculation about the genocide of Latan being about an opposition to the system rather than insane bloodlust was becoming far more convincing. Disturbingly, that placed Wasif in a much closer circle to Shiara than she cared to imagine. The scenes from Fimego replayed in her head again.

Wasif began walking through the overgrown streets in the direction they were already heading, so they decided to walk with him. It was, at the very least, safer to keep him in sight.

"What do you think of my garden?" asked the immortal.

"It's... very green." This was about the best Shiara could manage, with most of her mind pondering other things.

"Do you think it's a bit too much?" asked Wasif.

"There is an awful lot of it," replied Shiara, "but honestly, I quite like it."

She'd spent much of her life surrounded by plants rather than people, and she had to admit a certain pleasure from seeing a city succumb to flora, even if it was of a cultivated non-natural variety.

"Your scaly friend certainly seems to like it. Does he have a name?"

Wasif's face expressed genuine childlike joy at watching Scaley rummaging around in the undergrowth. He had an air of contentment and happiness that neither Fredo nor Shiara had seen from a ghost before.

"Yes... He's called, err... Scaley." The slayer of ghosts couldn't help herself feeling somewhat embarrassed at saying it aloud.

Wasif let out a rapturous laugh. "Brilliant. You can't deny it suits him! And he's such an inquisitive little fellow too."

He reached out a spectral hand to give Scaley a good scratch. The lizard cocked its head and seemed to rather enjoy it for a few moments, before resuming his mission of putting his face through every piece of foliage in search of crunchy beetles.

"I'm so glad you brought him with you; he really livens up the place," commented Wasif.

"If you don't mind me asking, is this what you've been doing for the last

CHAPTER FIFTY

however many years?" inquired Shiara.

"Among other things. I had to find something to keep myself busy and stop myself from going crazy in here on my own."

Fredo and Shiara looked at each other with dumbfounded expressions.

"Cultivating the plants was very important to me; this big old empty city needed some life in it to brighten up the whole place."

Eyebrows were raised involuntarily upon hearing this. Fredo felt he had to say something.

"A bit of life to the place? Do you know what people in other cities call you?"

The ghost shrugged. "I'm surprised they've even heard of me. I've been here on my own for so long."

"The mad ghost. They call you the mad ghost, because you *killed everyone* in Latan. Now here you are talking about bringing life to the place?!" Fredo's indignation had got the better of his survival instincts. Here was the genocidal terror of children's bedtime stories and he was talking to it in a very disrespectful fashion.

"Really?" said Wasif. "After all this time? And mad?" he laughed. "Is it *mad* to put an end to an oppressive regime? Is it *mad* to fight against tyranny?"

"If you are doing so by committing genocide, then YES! It is mad," bawled an exasperated Fredo, the composure of his silver-tongue years washed away by his bewilderment at the situation.

"It's certainly less mad than all those people dying in wars or in poverty so others can drink the fanciest wines. And let's face it, nobody can deny how peaceful Latan has been for all these years," said Wasif nonchalantly, unfazed by Fredo's frustrations.

"Peaceful? Of course it's peaceful, there's no people here!" the silver-tongue shrieked.

Wasif leant down to him, putting his face right next to Fredo's before replying in a very calm and reasoned tone, "Perhaps that says it all... Mr... ummm..." He snapped back upright and returned to his louder and more exuberant tone: "You two never did tell me your names!"

THE SIX CITIES

Shiara saw that Wasif's last point about people and peace had left her companion stunned, so she answered for the pair of them.

"I'm Shiara, and this is Fredo."

"A pleasure to meet you both. So what brings you and your adorable sandback companion to Latan?" asked Wasif.

Shiara pondered whether or not she should tell the truth; despite Wasif's past atrocities, he did not give her the impression of being much of a danger. A bit disturbing in how he discussed his past, but for the most part he was quite amiable.

"As it turns out, I'm here to challenge you."

"Oh..." said Wasif. "That certainly makes things a little easier."

"What things?" Shiara asked nervously, instinctively moving her hand towards her blade.

"Asking you to kill me... Now come along, I've got plenty of things to show you on the way."

The pair of travellers were perplexed. They'd never even considered the possibility that an immortal would want to give that up. Wasif was continuing to prove himself to be very far from their expectations.

Wasif toured them through the winding streets of Latan, going into great detail about how he had selectively bred specific plants for generations in order to create the specimens that now filled the city. Each one he had named, and it seemed as if he were acquainted with every single leaf. He led them into a glass house that filled an entire square, asking that they leave Scaley outside. Inside the heat was intense, much more so than outside. The glasshouse was filled with spectacular, colourful flowers in extraordinary shapes. Some hung down from the ceiling with crescent shaped petals of purest orange. Others sat atop delicate stems with spiralled petals of purple and yellow; blues, reds, greens and just about every conceivable hue was present. Even some of the leaves displayed exquisite colours of their own; maroons and even cerulean patterns played out within the greens of the leaves.

"These are what I've been working on lately," he told them.

CHAPTER FIFTY

Just like the cultivation of the threadwurms, Wasif had managed to selectively grow the perfect selection of iridescent colours; as he explained his process the parallels became clearer. There was a consistency and symmetry to nature that Fredo especially had never taken the time to think about yet was illustrated here perfectly. Shiara, on the other hand, was far more in-tune with the natural world. The beauty of what the supposed "mad ghost" had created was staggering. Considering her dislike for metropolises she thought this place was virtually a utopia, almost forgetting how this situation had been brought about through bloodshed. Fredo was more distracted by the insect life buzzing around in his face. Wasif explained the balance of the symbiotic relationship between insects and plants: the plants needed enough insects for pollination, but too many would overwhelm and destroy the plants with their grubs. It was a delicate balance that had to be struck, which was why Scaley had to merely watch from outside as a buffet of delicious winged invertebrates went about their business on the other side of the glass. Wasif drew particular attention to a group of fleshy looking flowers because of their odour and prompted his guests to smell them.

"Unfortunately, my sense of smell isn't what it was when I was alive," he explained.

Each one of the flowers had a unique scent; one was incredibly sweet and almost syrupy, another had a delicate woody note like ground qarfa that was used to season spiced dishes. Shiara's favourite had a slight savoury odour with a clear, fresh, green character and just a touch of sweetness. Wasif was very interested in having his guests describe them as precisely as possible so he could jot down what they said in a book he kept on the workbench in the glasshouse. Genuine glee lit his face up as he vigorously nodded and smiled at the revelations being delivered thanks to the sensitivity of noses belonging to the living. When asked about the book, Wasif informed them that he had hundreds of volumes cataloguing his work and listing the varieties he'd developed over time. Most of them were kept in a small library that he said he'd be sure to point out when they passed it. They spent a considerable stretch of time assisting him with his notes, all of which felt slightly odd given that Wasif apparently wished to give up his life. All that really mattered to him at this moment was sharing his passion with someone else, and Fredo was struck by the innocent elation the ghost found in such things. Fredo had seen ghosts laugh and enjoy themselves but never before had he seen one so wrapped up in caring about something quite like this. He imagined trying to tell people at court about this encounter and how, despite his ability to persuade, none of them would believe it. Then he remembered that the job of silver-tongues visiting courts would probably remain a thing of the past. They stayed sniffing the plants for quite some time, until Wasif was content with his notes.

Having left the glasshouse behind, they continued their journey towards the centre of Latan. The frequency of art adorning the walls increased and Wasif was only too pleased to point them out and explain how his technique had progressed over the years. They were impressive, even if the ghost didn't think so himself; for an immortal being he was certainly modest. Conspicuously absent from all his paintings; mirroring the city itself, were people. Landscapes, animals, cityscapes and plants, but no people – even in the pictures that naturally would have had them, like farmland or marketplaces. The work they had been looking at earlier, depicting the atrocity, was very much the odd one out. Shiara now felt comfortable enough to ask about it.

"Why is it that of all these paintings, only one of them showed the killings that happened here? There aren't even people in any of the other ones."

"To be honest with you, I never really got the hang of painting people and it's not as if I've had any subjects to draw from for quite some time," Wasif replied.

He went on to describe that he did try to capture those events numerous times in the past but was displeased with the results. His lack of remorse over the subject matter was still moderately disturbing, yet at least he was consistent in his reasoning that he did it for the greater good, regardless of how horrific that sounded. Far from mad, was Shiara beginning to... like him? First Mara and now Wasif? Life was far less black and white than when she started out to fulfil the prophecy. It was becoming clear that "good"

CHAPTER FIFTY

people were capable of doing "bad" things and vice versa; without knowing, you'd be hard pressed to convince anyone of Wasif's past actions. As these thoughts rattled around her head, the "mad ghost of Latan" suggested they take a slight detour to see some of the art they had asked about. Apparently, he had been intentionally avoiding it due to disappointment with his own artistic rendering of people. Sure enough, they found themselves in a square covered in detailed scenes of violence. Overly critical of his proportions and skin tones, there was no remorse or issue with reliving the events through his artistry.

"Hands were never something I could get to look right either," he reflected, nonchalantly glossing over the fact that the painting to which he was referring featured only severed limbs.

"Birds are much better than people; wings are more elegant, and their little feet are a joy to paint," he continued.

"Do you not feel bad for the suffering that these paintings are based on?" inquired Shiara.

"It was a long time ago, and these sorts of things have to happen to bring about change. Do we feel bad for the old plants we dig up to allow new life to flourish? It's just the way of things. They'd all have been long dead by now anyway."

Wasif's reply felt somewhat dismissive; he was far more concerned with what is than what was. He could spend several minutes pondering a single brushstroke whilst not giving much thought to the forgotten dead. He was the only one who could remember them, and he didn't want to; was it a burden or an irrelevance? Shiara could not work out which and had no desire to think too much on the subject, given the similarities between herself and Wasif that she had come to identify. Wasif's guests were eager to move on from these pieces; if anything, the stories didn't do justice to the horrors, assuming these paintings were an accurate account. Resuming their previous path, they eventually neared the centre of Latan. Wasif pointed out his library, which was a rather humble building surrounded by far more impressive ones. It seemed odd that he should choose this as the place he'd spend his time in, with far more luxurious options only a stone's throw away. He then directed their attention towards the thrumming pillar. Unlike in other cities, it wasn't locked behind big gates or in an arena, but was instead easily accessible. The stone structure around it remained but any semblance of gates had long been removed, even detecting where hinges would have once been proved impossible. As with everything in Latan, trails of thick green plant-life snaked their way in. If they hadn't known what the pillar was it would have seemed just another irrelevant part of the surrounding architecture.

"This is what you came for, isn't it?"

The joviality slipped into something a little more sombre.

"It is, but I have to ask, why do you want to die?" Shiara inquired.

He smiled and nodded in acknowledgement of the question.

"I've been around for a very long time. I've turned this prison of stone into a paradise of green. And now I'm tired. I've been tired for many years and lonely too. But most importantly, I believe in what you're doing and the prophecy. I recognize the magic of that blade you carry and know what needs to happen."

The blade to which he referred had been suspiciously quiet since they got here. Although she thought it was probably due to the sinkhole effect that had kept it silent before, it did seem a little odd that it went from chatty to entirely quiet without warning. Magic remained a mysterious thing outside of her understanding and she imagined it would always be that way.

"I see," she said.

"I may have brought an end to inequality in Latan but whilst I'm still around I can't do anything to change what happens beyond the walls. I can't kill myself either – not for lack of trying – so I need you to help me rest."

For a person dealing with their imminent demise, Wasif was incredibly calm and relaxed. Fredo was fascinated by this; whilst the other ghosts would sacrifice everything to keep themselves safe, as Chase had tried to do, here was one wanting to end it all. What's more, he was willing to do so for a greater cause.

"What do you know of the prophecy?" Shiara asked.

"Not a great deal, just that ending the era of ghosts would bring about a

CHAPTER FIFTY

better world and I couldn't agree more."

"And what of your garden?" she said.

"It'll be fine on its own for a while. Perhaps someone will find it one day and tend to it; I've certainly written enough of it down to help them. The plants in the glasshouse will die but I've stored their seeds away so they can be planted. What I've come to learn after all these years is that life, even that of a ghost, derives its worth from being finite. A stone can stand forever but a life has to end, and that's where it draws its beauty from. I've enjoyed countless lifetimes, yet for it to mean anything it has to end. Every book needs a final chapter."

There wasn't much more to say. Wasif had squared away his entire existence ready for this moment. Shiara had come here looking for a duel against a crazed fiend fuelled by bloodlust, only to meet a compassionate gardener offering his life. Expectations rarely proved accurate and this was a fine example.

"I... understand." Shiara felt saddened; she had come here to slay a monster and now she only wished to talk to it for a little longer. The parts of her she saw within him made her want to find all that was good within Wasif for her own sake. Later, he would utter his final "Thank you", smoke would billow and stone would crumble; the legend of "the mad ghost" would end. For now, she just wanted to sit with him for a while longer.

CHAPTER FIFTY-ONE

The sky was lit in orange. Swirls of smoke spun into the air. Koralia had done it. Castor and Orestis were now leading the charge as they rushed the gate to the fields, a swarm of people surging out of the darkness towards the handful of guards protecting it. A couple of wardens were poised on the wall and despite being taken by surprise managed to unload a few bolts from their crossbows into the crowd before those on street level were rushed. Three of the four guards managed to draw their weapons, the other wasn't quick enough and felt nothing but the piercing of his throat and the taste of metal. In a fountain of red, he fell to the floor to be trampled underfoot. Those with weapons didn't last much longer. The frenzy of the mob had no concerns for the safety of individuals and simply swamped them. A few people fell to the ends of their blades, but this was no situation for swordsmanship or even slashing; the best they could do was hold out their weapons and allow some of the horde to impale themselves. In less than a minute they had all been reduced to disfigured smears of crimson. The odd projectile from above ripped through someone, making no discernible dent in the mob or its fervour. Removing the wooden beam that barred the gate, the weight of people crashed through the doors and into the fields in which they had spent so much of their lives. Some headed for the stairs to take on the sentries atop the wall; the rest stuck to the plan and began to empty the tool-shed. Castor distributed the scythes, mattocks and other implements in what was a controlled line of citizens ready to inflict carnage on their oppressors. Tooled up and ready for blood, the horde marched back into the city. By now

CHAPTER FIFTY-ONE

the other wardens were aware something was up and had taken to the streets fully equipped. The pace of the crowd slowed as the line of armoured guard stretched across the thoroughfare in front of them. This wouldn't be like rushing them in a surprise assault at the gate; this was going to be an actual battle. A wave of apprehension built among the people; nobody wanted to be the first to charge, their rage briefly tempered by self-preservation. Castor and Orestis knew what they had to do. Letting out booming shouts and raising their weapons they advanced on their oppressors. Those behind them followed, riled up and rallied by the cry. As they approached they could see the wide eyes of the wardens: it was the look of fear. For the first time, the people of Maluani could see fear in the eyes of the wardens. In all of their eyes, except for one: The Owl. Far from terror, his face was lit up with glee as if all his carnal desires were being seen to at once. This man was a talisman for everything cruel and tonight he would be unleashed.

Castor was the first to strike a blow, his impressive muscularity making him a force to be reckoned with. His blade was parried, but his offhand held a club-like hunk of metal that could not be stopped so easily. The strike crumpled the armour of an unfortunate warden, no doubt causing similar damage to the bones beneath. A whole line of citizens were now engaged in the fray, the yellows and oranges of fire in the sky reflecting off steel and giving the whole affair a peculiar sort of beauty among the chaos. Screams and roars from the wounded and those fuelled by anger and bloodlust produced a cacophony, a symphony of carnage. Swinging weapons was impossible in the crowded space. Short sharp stabs and pressing blades into people's flesh was about all most could manage. The Owl was prepared for this; eschewing swords, he had small, sharp, serrated knives. Unrestricted by the claustrophobic conditions by his choice of weapons he was carving through person after person. The effort it took him to slash a throat or rip through an eye was minimal in comparison to wielding a bulky sword or club. Orestis found himself confronted by this maniacal sadist. They caught each other's gaze. Orestis could see the murderous intent in The Owl's eyes and how much pleasure it was bringing him. The Owl's wide smile, painted with sprays of blood, widened further as he found himself next to one of those who started the charge. Orestis tried to place his sword in the way, but he was too slow. The Owl's knife slipped through the flesh of his arm and he felt the vibrations as the serrations momentarily chipped and sawed into bone. Orestis lost the grip of his blade and could do nothing but raise his other arm to stop the next attack from piercing his body or neck. A geyser of blood erupted from his forearm. The knife had found the artery between bones. Orestis's face was now soaked in his own gore. He could only see out of one eye, and all he could see was The Owl brandishing his blades, surgically trying to take him apart with ruthless elation. Castor could see these events unfolding and pushed his way towards this live vivisection. He was only in time to watch as a steel point disappeared into Orestis's eye socket and The Owl's fingers pressed into the mangled jelly that was once an eye. Castor's friend convulsed and twitched, falling back into the throng and vanishing beneath the next wave of angry revolutionaries bounding forward to claim their flesh from the guards. There was no time for mourning. Castor struggled to keep his balance on the stones that were now slick with slippery innards. He was a few feet too far from The Owl to exact the vengeance he felt he needed; instead he had to focus on those directly in front. Nicks and gouges adorned his impressive physique, but this did nothing to slow him down. Strong enough to use the limp frame of a warden to stave off attacks from one angle, he was able to thrust his blade with more freedom, sometimes striking off of metal, most of the time finding soft flesh. The fight was being won, but slowly and with heavy losses. From the other end of the street behind the guards there was a rumble of people. Reinforcements had arrived. Castor feared the uprising would not be able to survive another wave, but it wasn't more wardens that had joined the fight – it was a large gang of fellow citizens, not armed with cumbersome swords or clubs, but spears they had fashioned by shaving the tips of tools and sticks into points. They were the perfect weapons to inflict maximum damage with minimal losses. For once, The Owl knew terror.

Lumis wound back the string of the crossbow with his powerful arms and loaded a bolt. The recoil from the weapon as he fired it jarred his elbow,

CHAPTER FIFTY-ONE

but it did far worse to the warden on the receiving end. Thirty feet away was not far enough for the light armour to avoid being breached. The guard skidded backwards in a mess of flailing limbs. Back slid the string, then out fired another bolt. This one missed the target; the wardens in this street were now in full retreat. The revolutionaries had managed to take a guard house along with the bounty of weapons within. Combined with their superior numbers they had become a force to be reckoned with. Just as planned, Lumis had become the makeshift master of arms, sizing up each revolutionary and telling them which weapon to grab. He sat by the cache of weapons they had retrieved and placed out on the street, the idea being it might encourage a few more to take up arms and would be easier than countless people shuffling into one building. Bodies from both sides lay strewn across the street, definitely more people than guards, but the ratio was certainly not too bad. For a bunch of overworked field-hands and simple tradespeople, they had put up an impressive fight so far. Each warden that fell made the numbers far more favourable; they would run out of men long before the resistance. Stefania stood behind Lumis cheering on those who passed and delivering the odd short speech to convince the reluctant to grab a blade and join their comrades.

"Kill two of them for every family member they've taken from you, then kill two more!" she bawled. Stefania's body coursed with righteous fury. Her friend and potentially half-brother had been ripped from her and she wanted them to suffer for it. Every blow that landed on a warden produced an ovation from her. Each guard lying lifeless in the street was a trophy. They weren't just fighting back; they were winning.

The mob slowly and methodically moved down, street by street. The same picture played out throughout the district and they hoped throughout the whole city. Leaving the weapons stash behind, they needed to keep advancing. They couldn't allow the guards to regroup, or worse still, get aid from Takis. Thankfully it seemed like the fire in the library was occupying him just as they had hoped it would.

Twisting and yanking out the bolts from the corpses they passed, Lumis was making sure he had plenty of ammunition. He'd been waiting a long time for a night like this, so he was going to make the most of it. It had been years since his wife took her own life rather than live under Takis and for the first time in forever it felt like he was truly honouring her memory. He never considered himself violent – none of them did really – yet in this crucible of carnage they felt reborn. A lifetime of pent-up hopelessness and misery was unleashed in a primal rage. It felt good.

"Don't, please!" cried out a heavily wounded young guard slumped against a wall, crossbow bolt protruding from his leg. Lumis and Stefania loomed over him.

"I've never mistreated any of you. I've never even drawn my weapon. I'm not like the others," he whimpered.

"Is that so?" asked Lumis.

"Yes. Yes. I've never supported the way some of them treat you out in those fields. I only became a guard to have a comfortable life. Please. I'm not like them," he begged.

"Well... What have *you* ever done to stop them?" inquired Stefania.

"Sorry?" said the warden.

"If you don't support the way we've been treated, what have *you* done about it?" she answered back.

"I... I... I don't know. I'm just one person. I couldn't have made a difference." Tears were now flowing freely down his cheeks.

"We are *all* just one person, yet here you are, bleeding away while we stand in judgment over you. Truth is, you don't know if you would have made a difference, because *you didn't try*." Stefania's words were clear in their tone.

"But... I never... joined in with how they treated you..."

"I'm afraid that's not good enough. *Doing nothing isn't good enough.* If you aren't opposing oppression, you are part of it." Stefania's eyes narrowed with the last sentence. She turned her head away from the man in disgust and began to walk off. Lumis wrapped his hand around the bolt in the man's leg and retrieved it with a crunching twist. Blood gushed from the wound. An artery had been fatally opened, but it wouldn't be quick. Lumis's face was mere inches from the man's yet he felt only the mildest of sympathetic twinges. Maybe this youngster wasn't so bad, but that wasn't the point.

CHAPTER FIFTY-ONE

This was a revolution, and *everything* had to be torn down. He wore the uniform; this was on him. Lumis placed a small dagger in the man's lap, then stood up to follow Stefania.

"Fast or slow. The choice is yours."

Even though the violence was far away, the sounds of conflict stretched right to the centre of the city where Koralia found herself. Peering around every corner, she was constantly on the lookout for wardens who would no doubt cut her down without a moment's hesitation. The fire made the sticky night air much hotter and illuminated everything, removing any shadows in which she could have hidden. A light dusting of ash and soot was beginning to pepper everything near the library. She wondered how Takis was dealing with the situation; did fire represent any physical challenge to him? Koralia suspected not. He was most likely rummaging through the fire to save as many books as possible; at least that was the plan.

At the end of this street lay the very centre of Maluani – Takis's thrumming pillar. It appeared that any guards who may have once been there had been called away to fight the uprising. As she neared the gates to the courtyard that contained the pillar, she saw a couple of familiar figures, one of them easily recognizable from his distinctive nose. Minos and Neela were cautiously looking around but saw no signs of impending danger. They raised their hands and ushered Koralia over, nodding that the area was clear.

"What took you so long?" asked Minos mischievously.

She didn't feel much like joking right now, given both the enormity of the situation as well as the fact she'd just torched an irreplaceable collection of literature and knowledge. She didn't begrudge Minos his jest though; humour was his way of coping with things, even though he wasn't actually very funny.

"Take this," Koralia said as she handed over her bags, swapping them for the sack of tools Minos held.

"What's in it?" he queried.

"Books," she replied.

"I thought you were going to *burn* them, not *steal* them?" teased Minos.

Koralia just looked at him and sighed.

"I couldn't just burn all of that history and art without at least trying to save some of it."

It wasn't a thing Minos had thought about much, but hearing it out loud, it made sense to him.

"Let's not stand around talking," interjected Neela. "We've got a tyrant to kill."

The first challenge was the chain on the gate. Lumis had assured them the long-handled metal cutters would do the job and he was right. It was startling quite how easily the blades sliced through the robust chain. The gate itself was heavy and took all three of them and quite some effort to open. It had been so long since the door had been used that the hinge had oxidized and become incredibly stiff. Working together, the trio managed to pull it free and get inside. The courtyard was surprisingly clean, with barely even a coating of dust. It seemed unusual that somewhere left alone for so long could look this way. Was it the architecture that helped? Or the magic? Did Takis clean it himself sometimes? Who could say, although right now the three of them didn't much care about speculating.

There in front of them, just as imposing as Takis himself, was the thrumming pillar. It let out a low-level hum that was almost imperceptible. Its edges were immaculate; its lines perfect. Not a crack or blemish could be seen on the pristine stonework. There was almost a polished quality that reflected the shimmering colours of the fiery night sky. Koralia stretched out her hand to touch its surface. Rather than a cold slab of stone there was a faint warmth to it. Understanding this magic that was so far removed from their lives was impossible; perhaps at a later date she could read the books she had salvaged and start to unpack it all. She pulled out the large chisel that Lumis had provided for them. He told them that if anything could break a magical stone pillar, it would be this. Neela held the large chisel in place, its point resting on the thrumming pillar's perfect face. Large metal hammer in hand, Koralia looked at her comrades. This was it. This is what they'd been working towards. This was the end of Takis.

"Are you ready?" she asked. A question that had so many facets. Being

CHAPTER FIFTY-ONE

ready to kill Takis was just the beginning; what about the challenges that would come next? Were they ready for the change? Was anybody?

Her partners nodded. They all held their breath as Koralia swung back then let loose an almighty blow. The connection with the chisel was perfect. The ding of metal and stone reverberated loudly in their ears, yet nothing. Not a dent or scratch.

Again she swung. Increased ferocity made the clang louder; once again, nothing.

A third strike that pulled at all her muscles, using every shred of her strength, connected with the chisel.

All their planning and machinations had led them here. The revolution and that last swing of the hammer both amounted to the same.

Nothing.

ACT FIVE

CHAPTER FIFTY-TWO

There was something about Caspir that seemed a little different today, a little brighter perhaps. Marin finally felt like he was getting on top of things and was on his way to formally inform Alyssa that Rhodes's *actual* murderer had been apprehended. Finally he had one up on the woman who had become his rival, who had always seemed to be a few steps ahead until now. The last time he walked down these streets and into what was now known as the "Church District", he felt like an outsider that they had no reason to trust. Today was a new beginning. He had promised them he would deliver justice, staking his entire position on it, and he had actually delivered. Marin was as surprised as everyone else, but now he wasn't just successful, he was energized. His experiences with Bemus filled his head with ideas of reform and rejuvenation. If their methodical approach had delivered justice in this instance, why should it not become the normal way of things? It could make Caspir a better place to live for everyone, which is all he ever really wanted.

Instead of looking away from members of the Church as he passed them, he made an effort to smile and wave, even offering pleasantries to some. They were still not that receptive, but Marin couldn't detect any hostility this time and he was more than happy to take that as a win. The cooing of the Kerri birds was even a little more musical to his ears. In weeks past he would have been looking for the next impending disaster to poke a hole in his successes and preparing for the worst, yet today he truly felt like Caspir was finally on track. That's not to say there weren't problems; a few refugees had begun arriving from Fimego and they seemed as if their very souls had been removed, tormented husks of people who had seen and endured more than anyone should; nevertheless Marin had found somewhere to keep them comfortable. He suspected they would never be whole again; there was only so much a full belly and a roof over one's head could achieve. Despite this, he was confident he was doing right by them. All of his successes of recent days brought him joy, yet he knew that what was really making him beam with glee was that he was about to get one over on Alyssa. For all the altruistic pleasure he could muster there was no denying the superior enjoyment derived from besting one's adversary.

The smell of cooking meats once again filled his nostrils, a scent he had often caught himself thinking about in less guarded moments. Whatever and however they were preparing it, it was delectable. He made a mental note to return at a later date to sample their inviting cuisine.

The building that was the central place of worship for the Church of Shiara had come a long way since he last saw it. The outside had been painted with very flattering murals of Shiara and new statues had been erected flanked by perfectly trimmed trees in pots that would not have looked out of place in the gardens of the wealthiest of nobles. The street had been cleaned to a pristine standard and fresh petals of orange had been scattered across the stones. Browns and greys were generally the preferred colour scheme for the Church of Shiara, but he had noticed a penchant for orange becoming more frequent. It made the place a little brighter and more approachable, which he welcomed. Apparently, some of the land outside the wall had been purchased by the Church and was being cultivated to grow these flowers – not only for petals, but drying and crushing parts of the flower produced a fine spice that was said to be delicious. Perhaps that was what made their cooking so aromatically tempting, Marin mused.

Stepping inside, the warehouse now resembled an impressive hall: well-lit and spacious. Huge windows that flooded the space with light had been installed into the sides of the building, illuminating every corner. More statues and murals had transformed the former food store into something dramatic, reverent and even holy. It felt like the place of worship it was meant to be and it was still a way off from being finished. People were

CHAPTER FIFTY-TWO

working on wooden structures that looked like tiered benches and platforms. The unmistakable early draft of what would become a kitchen sat in one of the corners. Far from being the cult he had worried about at times, it was a fully fledged church; whether or not that was better or worse would be a topic for later deliberation.

What exactly they believed in was a bit of a grey area for Marin. He thought it odd they revered a living person, especially one he knew personally. She may have been an incredible person, but she was still just a person. As far as he understood it, there was a holy text currently being written by the senior members of the religion – mainly Alyssa – about all the things one would expect: how to live your life, the nature of right and wrong, its own take on existence itself. The standard stuff, really. So far there wasn't much to go on outside of a collectivist approach that came across as deeply opposed to class division. In a lot of ways, it had more in common with a political movement; Marin supposed that was probably the norm for religions in their infancy. Under different circumstances he could have seen himself partial to such a movement, but he was the council leader and Alyssa still scared him.

Members of the congregation were milling around in the hall despite no official services or ceremonies being on; a few "Blessings of the Slayer unto you" left their lips, lacking the distrust he had perceived from them on his last visit. Again, he made his way to the end of the hall and into the office at the back, knocking as he entered. The room had changed from what he remembered. Bookcases in the process of being filled now stood against the walls, a large window had been put in and yet more potted plants like those outside, but smaller, were strewn around. Upon the desk were reams of paper, drafts and plans, presumably for the holy text they were writing. Behind the desk sat Alyssa, flanked by a couple of followers with papers in their hands.

"I hope I'm not interrupting," Marin said, "but I wanted to come and tell you the good news in person."

The woman known as the First Child of Shiara – a very strange moniker given her relative age to Shiara – put down the papers in her hand and looked up, somewhat unimpressed. Fighting the urge to say "Your resignation?" she instead replied with a knowing look.

"I'd like to say that the rumours surrounding the capture of Rhodes's killer are indeed true. We have found the *actual* murderer and he is to face justice."

Standing up to match eye level with Marin, Alyssa adjusted her cloak to maintain her carefully managed appearance and image of respectability.

"That is of course welcome news, even if it did take this long." Her choice of words indicated she was still trying to find ways to establish dominance, which must have been a useful trait as the head of a religion, although now Marin had all the cards to play and was in no position to lose the high ground.

"Yes, it is a shame that we had to waste so much time on the false accusation and confession you managed to coerce from Farid. I'm sure we can both sleep well in the knowledge that an innocent man isn't being falsely punished. He was kind enough to not seek charges against you, either."

"Indeed."

What Marin would never find out was that Farid had been missing since the day he was released, and Alyssa's associates had made sure that his body would never be found. She thought she was doing the right thing at the time and did actually feel bad about it upon reflection, if only briefly. Nevertheless, she wouldn't lose any sleep over it.

"Is there anything else you came down here for?" she continued.

"Actually, there is," he replied.

"Go on."

"I was hoping that you could help me; well not just me – rather the whole of Caspir."

Alyssa looked confused, trying to work out and understand what angle he was trying to work and stay ahead of the game. This approach was irrelevant, as Marin was being genuine.

"Be aware, the Church of Shiara does not work for your government," said Alyssa.

"Of course not. You see, when we first met, I was sceptical of you, and we

CHAPTER FIFTY-TWO

both know we've had our differences..."

"Agreed," she interrupted.

"But, having seen what you've done for some of the poor and especially some of the refugees from Illorne, I've honestly been impressed."

"You have?" asked Alyssa suspiciously.

"Very much so. Your Church helped them set up new lives and I'll be perfectly honest with you, we need more of that."

"Is that so?" She was struggling to work out where this scheme of his led. Was he trying to set her up to fail by giving her too much responsibility? That didn't make sense, as this sounded like the sort of gift of influence she needed.

"Fimego has fallen and from what we're seeing it's even worse than Illorne. We've started seeing refugees and there are more coming every day. Caspir could really use some help from the Church to get these people settled."

She frowned distrustfully.

"Is that not the job of the mighty council of Caspir?"

Marin began to nod.

"Yes it is, but I don't think it's something that we can easily achieve without help from the people of the city, and even then it will be difficult."

"So what is it you want us to do?"

"I'm glad you asked. Firstly, I'd like you to keep on doing what you're doing already with your current members. Secondly, I'd like the Church to officially help greet new arrivals. Let them know that they can find a new sense of community here and see if any want to join you."

"Anything else?" she inquired in a disgruntled yet amiable fashion.

"As I'm sure you're aware, we've begun building a new settlement outside of the wall. Anyone in your congregation that is willing to help with that would be appreciated. You're greater in number than any of the guilds and we could do with any assistance your congregation can offer."

"Your solution is to build a shanty town outside to keep them separate? How is that any different from the slums you oversee?" Alyssa said.

Marin recognized the words he had already heard from Andros's lips;

it was the exact same turn of phrase that he had only heard before in the council chamber.

"Quite the opposite. We plan to dismantle a stretch of the wall to extend the city's outer edge, giving them enough space to be comfortable, whilst still being a part of the city."

That was his plan, at least; getting the council to sign off on it was a very different prospect, but one battle at a time was the only way he had found to cope with leadership.

"I see." Alyssa nodded reluctantly. "The Church of Shiara is of course interested in improving people's lives. We shall see what we can do."

"Oh, and one more thing."

"Yes?"

"Could I try some of that delicious cooking I keep smelling?"

CHAPTER FIFTY-THREE

Leaving Latan gave both Shiara and Fredo a sombre feeling, but in a very different way not only to what they were expecting, but to what they had experienced in Fimego. In Fimego Shiara thought she would be ending a tyrannical religious rule and giving people their freedom; in reality it unleashed an incomprehensible wave of horror. In Latan she thought she would be killing an insane mass murderer responsible for atrocities; once again her perceptions were off. Instead of some kind of victory, she had left feeling like she'd been involved in a sad mercy killing, which in many ways was exactly what had happened. She empathized with the Wasif that she had met, a tender artist and gardener, unable to square that with the monster people spoke about in hushed tones. What started out as a righteous quest to end the rule of ghosts for the freedom of all people had so far proven to be far more complicated than she had envisioned. Shiara had always supposed the duels themselves would be the most problematic part, yet that was far from being the case. People clung to their way of life and those who ruled over them, making it impossible to end the age of ghosts without consequences. Shiara had begun toying with the thought of whether or not she would have acted the same way in hindsight. The notion of placing the fallout of slaying the ghosts firmly on her shoulders was not something she could abide; she stopped her brain from wandering down these avenues by focusing on the prophecy. She was only doing what was destined and that destiny would bring freedom, once completed. It was far easier to think of herself as an instrument of fate rather than a person making free choices and taking responsibility for the results.

The next leg of her journey was free from ambiguity and moral pondering. The other cities may have been new to her and hard to understand the dynamics of, but Omdurtur was different. This was her birthplace; the place that had consumed her childhood, where she had watched friends and family choke on the smog from the stacks – the towering monuments to inequality that devoured countless lives in pursuit of profits for the wealthy. The wealthiest of them was Kadar, the city's ghost. Whilst other cities saw their ghosts as political or even spiritual leaders, Kadar was different. He straddled the line between wealthy businessman and political influencer, turning Omdurtur into a production line that used people as if they were a resource like any other. He understood something that most did not – true power wasn't wielded by political institutes; it was money that exerted absolute control. Councillors came and went; money was the eternal dictator. Shiara recalled her time growing up listening to those around her parroting the mantra that money and work would bring them prosperity and freedom. One day they too could become part of the wealthy elite; even as the soot slowly lined their children's lungs, they still believed. Her parents were no different; only with the death of her brother did her father realize the sham they were living in, although all that achieved was a new and stupid way for him to die. Her thoughts of him always strayed to anger before she repressed them and focused her mind elsewhere. Kadar. That was whom she should focus on. This ghost eschewed an official capacity in government in favour of an advisory role. Far easier to shape the city from the sidelines in an unaccountable and hidden position. Of course, *everybody* knew who he was; that was just part of how things worked. Why wouldn't the council look to an immortal being with hundreds of years of experience? It was all so easy for people to justify, yet the cost of doing so was paid for by those with nothing. Every other city was part of this too; Kadar relied on trading with other cities to extend his wealth; they were all complicit, which was why Shiara knew she was doing the right thing. The whole system needed to be felled, not just parts of it, and she was getting closer.

With all this whizzing around her brain, she took one last look back at

CHAPTER FIFTY-THREE

Latan as it began to shrink into the distance; in many ways it was her idea of paradise: no-one taking advantage of other people, stone giving way to greenery, true freedom. She could tell Fredo felt differently. For him it was a waste of a perfectly good city that could be filled with the hustle and bustle of metropolitan life; maybe one day it would return to this again. They had filled their packs with fresh produce from Wasif's extensive garden in preparation for the journey and now trundled along atop their scaled companion. Scaley was not burdened by the moral pontifications his riders were; he was, however, rather disappointed to be leaving a city literally crawling with bugs that gave him such joy to crunch through.

Fredo's mind journeyed elsewhere. He'd spent a lifetime working to get ahead within the system and now found himself riding alongside someone intent on destroying it. He knew that there was nothing he could do to stop her even if he wanted to – which he didn't – besting her in any form of combat was beyond a joke. It wasn't so much what was happening that bugged him; it was the fact he was merely a passenger. Haggling away and trying to prise information about a harvest or batch of wine saw him carving out every last advantage he could for himself, but now? At best he was a guide. It was quite surreal to him that he was no longer the main character in his own life's story. Perhaps Omdurtur would provide him more agency. Contemplating his own inadequacy, he decided to direct it outwards to distract himself.

"You've been awfully quiet lately. I didn't hear you say a single word in Latan."

Shiara swivelled her head and offered a confused look.

"No, not you, that sword of yours."

"Oh," piped up the blade, "were you missing me?"

Fredo instantly regretted his choice to engage the blade in conversation.

"You two aren't going to start up again, are you?" Shiara asked, like a disappointed teacher or parent.

"I certainly won't start things," said the sword. "I just finish them."

Shiara wasn't sure why the enchanted weapon and Fredo didn't get along but she could speculate. She wondered if it was because as a silver-tongue,

Fredo represented the excesses of city life under the ghosts; the blade had been forged and taught by the Great Wizard Ezekiel, who despised such things.

"I was just wondering why you hadn't said anything for so long. Especially given your previous empathy for Wasif, it seemed strange to me that you didn't want to at least offer a few words."

Fredo was right; it did seem a little odd that the sword, which had been ever so chatty and vocal in its support of "the mad ghost", had remained silent.

"As I previously explained, the thrumming pillars act like magic sinkholes. It was more of a case of couldn't rather than didn't."

"Yet we left Latan some time ago and saw Wasif slain even longer back," interrogated Fredo.

There was a pause. If the weapon could have made a facial expression, Fredo was sure it would have looked stumped. For some reason he didn't trust the magical blade and thought he'd found a way to tease out some morsel of information he could hold aloft and say, "Look, I knew it couldn't be trusted!" Alas, that was not to be.

"Truth be told," – a phrase that in Fredo's experience was only used by those about to conjure up dishonesty – "I've spent such long periods of time unable to speak, that I'm used to it and even forget that I can."

The sword had an answer for everything, but that wasn't going to stop Fredo trying.

"Well now that you've remembered, is there anything you'd like to say about Wasif being slain?" the silver-tongue asked.

"No," replied the blade.

"Not even about his asking to be killed?"

"No. It seemed like a perfectly reasonable request to me."

This conversation was going nowhere; he'd have to try something else. He still wasn't sure why he was so intent on trying to get one over on a talking sword, he just knew he was. Looking back seemed fruitless; the topic of conversation steered towards the future instead: Omdurtur. Shiara was scathing in her comments about the city and the sword agreed. Fredo was

CHAPTER FIFTY-THREE

in a minority in their travelling party, as he had taken many trips there and enjoyed the theatres and food immensely. When he thought of Omdurtur it wasn't smokestacks and poverty that came to mind; it was people striving for greatness; it was dinner parties and concerts. It wasn't that either of them was wrong; it was that both of these realities were true. Omdurtur was divided in a way unlike any other city. Caspir had its Brown Quarter yet that was nothing compared to the inequality of Omdurtur. People drank ancient wine from crystal glasses and sat on chairs plated in gold whilst others were stuck in backbreaking jobs to put insubstantial meals on their plates. There was a phrase often bandied about in the city, that "anyone could make it big". Anyone could work hard and go from nothing to joining the wealthy elite; people earned their lot in life. That had always been how Fredo had seen it; he himself had become a silver-tongue from impoverished beginnings. Omdurtur encapsulated that process in his mind.

"I understand what you're saying, but there are people from all walks of life who have succeeded, so there are opportunities for everyone," said Fredo defensively.

"Not all opportunities are equal." Shiara was trying to keep her temper; however, this was the fuel that powered her entire cause. This was why she was challenging the ghosts; she had seen first-hand the inequality they created.

"Hard work has to be rewarded though," he replied.

"Do you honestly think hard work is all that it takes to succeed in a place like Omdurtur? Can you genuinely say that a wealthy merchant works harder than a slogger in the stacks working twelve-hour days of body-wrecking labour?"

"Sure, not everyone is born into the same circumstances; however shouldn't parents who've worked hard be able to give their children a head-start in life? Some parents work hard to make sure their children don't have to. I don't see what's wrong with that," replied Fredo.

"I knew dozens of people who worked hard in the stacks; do you know what their parents did?"

Fredo shrugged, although he suspected he knew what the answer was.

"They worked in the stacks," continued Shiara. "And you know what their children went on to do? They worked in the stacks too."

"That isn't everyone's story though. Some people do get out of the stacks. Some get other jobs; some become successful. The city needs the stacks; its economy depends on them; without them more would go hungry," retorted Fredo.

Shiara shook her head.

"The stacks kill people. If your society is built on killing people, it's not worth having."

"How many would die without a source of income to put food on their tables? I'm not disagreeing that there are problems; improvements do need to be made," said Fredo.

"Improvements? Do you know how many times improvements have been promised? A new council member is elected, one of us, promising to help the workers. A few token improvements are made, but never enough. Meanwhile people keep on dying," Shiara fired back.

"The very fact that someone from the stacks can rise up and become a council member should tell you something. Trust me, I've known enough council members over the years to know that the problems are due to individual greed, not necessarily the system as a whole."

The slayer of ghosts was becoming frustrated with the conversation, but before she could formulate another response, her sword joined the fray.

"Have you ever considered the possibility that these recurring problems of individualistic greed are themselves a product of the system?"

The silver-tongue was dumbfounded. It certainly made some degree of sense that promoting the values of individual success would create such an environment. People were a product of the society they grew up in, so perhaps the problems were deeper than he originally wanted to acknowledge. It was time for a verbal retreat and regrouping by Fredo.

"All I'm saying is that *I* came from basically nothing and worked my way up to becoming a silver-tongue. My hard work *has* to mean something?"

Shiara nodded, taking on board the personal dimension in regard to someone she now called her friend.

CHAPTER FIFTY-THREE

"Of course it means something. *You* succeeded against the odds, but that's precisely the point. These odds existed and *were* against you, just like for the people of Omdurtur. Your success doesn't mean the struggles of the people are somehow invalid. You may think you worked hard, and I'm sure you did, but you were also lucky. Lots of people work hard, harder than either of us, yet they don't get lucky."

For all the verbal tricks and teasing things out of people Fredo had spent his life perfecting, there was no substitute for the raw passion and fire that Shiara showed. He wondered how many just like her there were in the cities, those who wanted desperately for things to change yet remained powerless in the face of everything. Then here Shiara was. Not only with the mindset, but with the ability and opportunity to act upon it. Fredo had always known the way things were wasn't right, yet the clarity and conviction of how she laid it all out was still disarming.

"I see where you are coming from. Working hard is no guarantee of success, but not everywhere is quite like Omdurtur. I think it's important to note that."

"It doesn't matter where you are; luck plays more of part in most people's lives than effort ever does," said Shiara.

It was a bold statement, and it rang painfully true. If even the woman who had pulled herself up from the stacks to become the slayer of ghosts was willing to downplay her efforts in the face of fate, then who was he to argue? However, he was certainly not beyond highlighting the irony of the situation for a laugh.

"That's easy to say when you're the one whose destiny has been prophesised."

CHAPTER FIFTY-FOUR

The wardens had been pushed back in ever smaller circles. The end of this was coming, but not in the way the revolutionaries thought. By now they assumed Koralia was taking down the thrumming pillar and victory was just around the corner. They were oblivious to their comrade's failure, yet it was about to become clear in the most brutal of fashions.

The guards were boxed into just one square and its side streets, the angry mob bearing down on them and picking off any who were not quick enough with their retreat. Firing off bolts and jabbing spears whittled their numbers down with each advancing pace. Then it came; the most foreboding of spectacles. A milky-white swirl of mist that heralded only misery. The distraction of his library in flames no longer held his attention. Behind the baying crowd now stood the mighty form of Takis. Usually, emotions beyond apathy and derision were not seen on his face; now his visage wore an expression of towering rage. Having cornered the wardens, many of the revolutionaries were now trapped themselves. A crack of what sounded like thunder alerted those at the front of the crowd who had not seen their tyrant appear. The noise was followed by a shower of blood with chunks of meat and bone, finely dispersed as a single gruesome wave. The rebellious cheers of triumph turned to abject horror. Some of them tried to flee, trampling and crushing one another; others foolishly tried to fight. Koralia had spoken to them about the "Slayer of Ghosts" being able to defeat these immortal beings as just one person, and that the might of all of them combined would surely be enough. Very few, if any, believed it, but given their situation

CHAPTER FIFTY-FOUR

they had little choice in the matter other than to give it a shot. A man even more muscular than Castor swung at Takis and found himself unable to make contact. The ghost sidestepped with such speed that a trail of ethereal smoke lingered in the air. Again the man swiped and found nothing. Takis wasn't going to entertain his attempts any further. Before he could let fly his third blow, the man found himself off the ground with a blade through his belly. Suspended feet above the ground, the man heard the sound of his own innards slopping onto the stone street below, drowning out the bustle of the crowd around him. A flick of Takis's wrist rendered him asunder like a ripe, juicy fruit being popped. Others tried and fared just as poorly. Steel blades were no defence against the ghostly edge of the immortal's blade. It cleaved through flesh and metal alike, each sweep snapping like a whip as the air itself was pushed aside at lightning speed.

Those furthest away from the carnage found the ground beneath their feet becoming slick and slippery, awash with red. A tide of crimson seeped its way through the rebels, who were now in full panic mode.

Stefania and Lumis were far enough from the ghost to be safe, for now, but they could see the writing on the wall. Koralia, Minos and Neela must have failed. With each passing moment it became clearer that salvation wasn't coming. The throng of people no longer pulsed with fervour and righteousness but with defeat and terror. A desperate struggle to escape had begun as Takis made his way through the people, cutting them down like so many of the fallen had done with crops in years past. It wasn't a battle or a fight; they were being culled. Stefania and Lumis held hands to try to keep close to one another, battered and pushed around by the crowd as they ebbed and flowed in search of a way out. One had been found through the door and windows of a building, but this only agitated the people more. All that spirit of camaraderie and solidarity was thrown aside in a desperate struggle for survival. Buffeted by the horde, the strain on Stefania's arm was too great and she lost her grip of Lumis's hand. She was being swept away by the mob. Lumis did not fare as well; shoved in the back, he dropped to his knees then was pushed onto the floor completely. Stefania caught a brief glimpse of his face looking up as he disappeared beneath a stampede of feet. His expression seemed to say, "Get out if you can." The image of his face trodden into the ground would leave a lasting impression if she could live to see another day. If the crushing weight of those above didn't get him, the deepening pools of blood would surely fill his lungs. She knew this would be the last she ever saw of him; for pragmatism's sake her attention had to focus on getting out alive. How quickly the tide of victory could turn. She went with the crowd and let it carry her like a strong current, trying her best to stay on her feet so as to not suffer the same fate as Lumis. If their revolution had indeed failed, perhaps he was the lucky one as he would not have to bear witness to the aftermath.

Stefania was bundled through a window by the tide of fleeing revolutionaries; fortunately she managed to keep on her feet, but others were not so lucky. The uneven fleshy surface under foot was hard to maintain balance on and she tried her best to not think about the poor souls trampled beneath; there was nothing she could do about it anyway. The door to this building had been ripped from its hinges; panicked rebels spilled out into the street and scattered in all directions. Nobody cared where they were going as long as it was away from the ever-living ruler currently tearing through their fellow citizens. Over the roar and shouts of the people the bone-splitting sound from each swing of Takis's blade filled their ears. Every few seconds a rhythmic, wet, thudding, cracking noise edged closer. There was no telling how many people had been cut down and looking back was not an option. The trickles of blood had made their way around the corner and into the next street that Stefania now found herself in. There was now more room to move as the mob dispersed as quickly as possible down every side street and alley, leaving behind them a trail of maroon footprints as if the pavements were some macabre canvas.

She took pause and considered her situation. The plan had obviously failed; what did this mean? How severe would the recriminations be? With this many guards killed, would Takis police them all on his own? Surely not. Likewise, he wouldn't be able to simply kill all of them as that would disrupt the running of the city and the trade that Takis was keenly committed to. Without the growing of crops to trade to other cities, he would be cut off from

CHAPTER FIFTY-FOUR

the outside world. Left alone with no way of building, or rather rebuilding, his library. There was no predicting what would happen next, just that it would be bad. For now, she had to work out where she was going to run to. It was at this moment she noticed the largest contingent of rebels were beginning to head in the same direction. At first she wondered why, yet quickly realized that was the way to the nearest city gate. They were fleeing Maluani altogether and Stefania couldn't think of a better option, so went with them. The revolution within the walls was defeated; perhaps someone could get out and find this "Slayer of Ghosts" to bring them salvation? She convinced herself this was her plan, although deep down it may well have just been good old-fashioned self-preservation.

Stefania's legs were tired; still she jogged on. The sound of slaughter had disappeared behind her some time ago. The city gate had been flung open, with several people working on the outer gate. Most people were congregating on the farmland between the walls, making sure they were beyond the original outer wall that marked the perimeter of Takis's influence. The crops they had spent months cultivating were squashed underfoot. People tried to gather what they could and fill bags and pockets with anything edible to keep them going in case they managed to leave the city. There was no real idea of where any of them might go; anywhere but Maluani was very much the mindset. The thick chains on the gate were proving troublesome but progress was being made, albeit slowly. It was not the freedom any of them had hoped for and certainly not the vengeance Stefania craved; this was the sad reality of their failed uprising. She was roused from her contemplation by an eerie silence that washed over those around her; looking up she began to see why. Once again, the swirl of white smoke that heralded doom appeared. In the gateway, still within the boundaries of the original wall, stood their tyrant. Even though they knew he could not pass beyond it, terror set in.

"People of Maluani. Tonight has been a bleak chapter in the city's history but there is still time for you to salvage it." His voice boomed with confidence and lacked the anger one would have expected from him.

Ruthless pragmatism was one of his defining traits, so it served his purposes best to remain unemotional. The sound of marching wardens loomed out of the dark as they began to line up behind their immortal ruler. Many of them had fallen but there were still enough to execute the people now cornered between the walls, especially since most of them had dropped their weapons when they fled. Those working on the gate chain increased their efforts to a more furious pace.

"Now, we all know that I can't kill everyone in the city; Maluani needs to function. So you *can* keep quiet and your little revolution's leader will probably be spared, but some of you will die for it. I just want to know the person behind it all. Tell me, and not only will you be spared, but those who come forward will be rewarded with positions as wardens. A better life awaits for those who cooperate."

Takis's words instantly sent a chill down her spine. For all the vigour and passion they had to fight for an active cause, ordinary people were very unlikely to be willing to die for a defeated one. Chatter resumed among the people; Stefania was unsure if they were discussing whether they should turn someone in, or if they actually knew who to turn in. She worked her way towards the gate; there was no doubt that some of them knew her involvement so it was essential that she was one of the first to slip out, provided they could open the gate at all.

"My patience does not share the same longevity as my existence. If none of you are willing to do the right thing, we can put you down and find another group of people who are more receptive. Why die, when you can live as privileged guards?"

There was no way this bargain would be resisted. Finally they managed to file through one of the chain links and crack the door open a couple of feet. It wasn't much, yet it allowed some to slip through. Others were too fixated on the prospect of earning the privileges of the wardens that had oppressed them for years. There was something very desirable about becoming the powerful thing you feared and hated. It was certainly an easier existence to imagine than struggling beyond the walls.

"Koralia!" shouted one person. Then another. Then a whole slew of them.

CHAPTER FIFTY-FOUR

It had been surprisingly easy to build the rebellion but even easier for Takis to get those people to sell it out.

Takis smiled. He knew he had won. Unexpectedly, he took a step towards the crowd, crossing the threshold of the wall. Astonished looks spread around the onlookers. Had he somehow broken the rules that kept him bound to Maluani? The truth was far simpler: the outer wall had always been the original structure; the inner wall was constructed later but over time he had convinced people differently. Not a difficult feat for a centuries-old being. This provided him with the opportunity to instil fear and wonder within the populace in a situation just like this. If they considered his power boundless, any thought of fleeing became pointless. The display had the intended impact. No longer were there people scrabbling to leave; to them it now seemed futile. In their minds Takis really was the omnipotent master they had come to know. Fortunately for Stefania, this provided an opportunity for her to slip out just as the former revolutionaries were walking towards their dictator to pledge allegiance.

Outside of the wall Stefania was taken aback by what she saw. In the large tracts of open land dotted with scores of trees, people scrabbled like animals, some even crawling on all fours, spewing forth in all directions fuelled only by primal survival instincts. How far they had come from the proud revolutionaries! Stefania herself had only ever known the city and the walled farmland. Whatever came next for her would be new. Those who didn't scamper off like beasts were wandering around almost as if in a daze. She didn't have this luxury; as one of the few true revolutionaries still around Stefania felt compelled to do... something. Before her stretched out a couple of barren brown scars on the land: trade routes. Each of these led to other cities. One to Illorne, the other to Omdurtur. She knew there was nothing for her in Illorne, since Hectin was already slain; however, in Omdurtur there may be a chance for her to find this "Slayer of Ghosts". She had no idea how long it would take to get there or what travelling along the route would be like; all she knew was her moral imperative and the tiny scrap of hope to which she desperately clung.

CHAPTER FIFTY-FIVE

The river flowed blackened with red smudges: Omdurtur must not be far away. Soot and the run-off from smelting tarnished the water that had once flown clear. With this pollution, the buzzing activities of wildlife had been banished to much further downstream where the water eventually ran cleaner. It was hard to square this rusty-coloured flow with the vibrant scenes they had passed on the way to Fimego; Fredo missed the bustling birds and insects. The scene before them was not one of life. Even the few plants that were there looked stunted and sickly; this effect spilled out beyond the river itself, which was no longer lined with grass or other foliage, but was a barren-looking scrubland. Only about a hundred feet from the water did the normality of nature return, leaving something akin to a gaping wound in the landscape inflicted by industry.

It wasn't just how the river appeared either; it was how it smelled. An overpowering odour of metal filled their nostrils until they could taste it like blood in their mouths. Fredo had not seen this before; ordinarily he travelled by the main trade routes, which were far away from this scene. He'd seen the outflows from the city and was aware of the pollution – he just hadn't expected it to have stretched this far downstream. The grubby consequences of Omdurtur's industry were of course known to all; it was just much easier to ignore it when it wasn't in plain sight. Nobody travelled between Omdurtur and Latan, so it didn't seem to matter. The city's farmland had to be concentrated on the other side of Omdurtur where the land was more fertile and not poisoned.

CHAPTER FIFTY-FIVE

"Disgusting, isn't it?" said the gleaming blade.

They both had to agree, before Fredo found himself wondering something. "So, you can see this then?"

"Of course," replied the sword.

"How exactly does that work then? It's not as if you have any eyes."

"Well," said the weapon authoritatively, "this may have somehow escaped your attention, but I am a magical sword. I don't have lips either, yet for quite some time you have been conversing with me without pondering on that one."

Fredo wasn't trying to be snarky; he was genuinely curious. "I was just trying to understand, how *do* you see?"

"You know how magic works? Oh that's right, you don't do you? At this point it would be like explaining Bahlea to a Kerri bird."

"For someone that's hundreds of years old, you manage to be very childish," interrupted Shiara, like a mother irritated with her bickering children. The weapon did not reply; neither did Fredo, although he secretly counted it as a win.

"I haven't been back to Omdurtur in a long time," said Shiara sadly. Fredo wasn't sure what about the situation was getting her down; was it the fact she found herself coming back and reliving those unpleasant memories? Or did she have regret for those she may have left behind? Either way, he wanted to find out. He told himself it might provide some pertinent information that could aid their mission, but it was far more about sating his own curiosity.

"You don't talk much about your time in Omdurtur. Is there anything I should know?"

Shiara looked to her silver-tongue companion with an expression of bitterness and determination.

"There is plenty you *should* know. You *should* know that the price for every banquet you attended was paid for by the backbreaking work of the poor. You *should* know that the people of Omdurtur are nothing but numbers on a business ledger to the wealthy. You *should* know that watching your younger brother choking to death in your own home isn't some kind of one-off accident; it's a day-to-day 'acceptable cost' for maintaining the luxury for a few."

The slayer of ghosts was physically worked up as she spat the last few words out, her breathing harsher and more pointed as if every exhalation was a jabbing accusatory finger towards those she despised. The specific example was easily picked up by Fredo.

"I'm... sorry. About your brother," he said.

"This isn't about my brother. Do you think this is all some personal vendetta for me?"

"I... don't know," mumbled the wrong-footed silver-tongue.

"You're right, you don't know. This isn't about revenge. I'm not doing this because of my family; I'm doing it because it needs to be done."

"I see," said Fredo, trying to placate her.

"*Do you?* I don't think you do. Personal tragedy has nothing to do with it. Anyone who's been paying attention to the way people are treated in the cities can see that it needs to stop. My family have nothing to do with it. You want to know about my family?"

"I'm not rea..."

"I'll tell you about my family. My brother got soot in his lungs and died, but rather than mourning and thinking about the rest of his family, my father decided to challenge Kadar, throwing his own life away and making things worse for his wife and daughter. Capping off years of being a mediocre parent with being a stupid and terrible one. Honestly, I couldn't care less about my family. Yes, he was put in a horrible situation but that's no excuse for making an awful decision that harms others. Regardless of how much mother claimed it was an honourable thing to do, it wasn't. It doesn't matter what the situation is; people will make stupid decisions and they should own them. Poverty doesn't excuse someone from being a shitty parent. All I'm concerned about now is removing the system that puts people into horrible situations. It won't stop shitty parents, but it'll help everything else."

It was a lot to process. He merely wanted to pry a little and instead found a gushing geyser of information. He himself had come from poverty and known hard times, yet the cold and resentful description of her childhood

CHAPTER FIFTY-FIVE

caught him off guard. After their last conversation about Omdurtur Fredo was reluctant to dive back in again; even though Shiara had made some salient points he was convinced there ought to be some middle ground between the way things were currently and destroying everything entirely.

"The fires of childhood forge the blade of adulthood," said Fredo.

"Sorry?" replied Shiara.

"It's just something someone told me a long time ago."

"A poet?" she queried.

"No," laughed the silver-tongue, "a drunk. A particularly nasty drunk for that matter."

"Who were they?"

"My father."

Shiara often forgot that Fredo himself had come from a more than patchy background, although it was easy to do given his role as a silver-tongue.

"I didn't know," she said.

"Don't worry about it; if you rummage around in anyone's cupboards long enough you're bound to find a skeleton or two. I should know – rummaging in people's cupboards was pretty much my job before all of this," he chuckled. Shiara just rolled her eyes.

"I suppose you and I aren't so different when you think about it," Fredo continued.

"How do you figure that one?" questioned the slayer of ghosts, who was clearly irked by such a suggestion.

"We both left unpleasant situations to make it on our own, the only difference being I took to the streets whilst you went beyond the walls."

"I don't think that's the *only* difference," said Shiara.

"Picking berries and eating leaves isn't too far away from scavenging for scraps, really."

"Isn't it?"

"And whilst you chose a sword as your weapon for survival, I instead honed my wits. It's more or less the same process, wouldn't you say?" surmised Fredo.

Shiara was sceptical.

"If that's the case, how come you ended up as a part of the system whereas I am the one breaking it?"

"You say that, but I'm here now, aren't I?" quipped the silver-tongue. His charm finally found purchase and produced a smile from Shiara, albeit a small one. The rest of the journey would go a lot more smoothly.

Omdurtur, the city overshadowed by the dark clouds of industry. They had arrived. In the distance the mountains could be seen; misshapen and distorted from blast powder and mining, they were rich in ore that was the main source of wealth in Omdurtur. The other cities had metal shops but nothing on the scale of Omdurtur. Entire mountains had been torn down to fuel the insatiable march of industry. The river was now an even darker colour, with visible lumps of detritus carried in its flow. The water entered the city's north side and flowed through the smelting district, where metals and equipment were cooled directly in the running water, then it snaked its way out the east side where Shiara and Fredo now stood. This kept the industry contained to the north-eastern quarter of the city and away from the affluent south-western quarter. It also had the added effect of keeping visitors away from these less pleasant scenes, as the trade routes generally coalesced in the south-western section given the irrelevance of Latan to the south east.

The most unnatural thing about the river was how warm it was. As they approached where it left the city, they could feel the heat emanating from it. The water was almost boiling, which meant they could not simply try to swim upstream. They would have to cling to the brickwork and climb through the outflow, avoiding dropping into the water for fear of burns or poisoning. Fredo was right about this place being the most secretive entrance to the city; it was almost ridiculous to even call this a way in.

Once again it was time to leave Scaley behind; whilst some lizard species were adept at clinging to walls, Scaley was not. Sandbacks were far too big. Shiara tied him to a rather scraggly looking tree and left him most of the remaining fruit and vegetables they had picked from Latan. They weren't intending to be in Omdurtur for long; no doubt people would go to

CHAPTER FIFTY-FIVE

extraordinary lengths to stop her from upsetting the status quo that had been so profitable for the powerful. Stroking his dewlaps, she bid Scaley goodbye.

Shiara was far fitter and more physically able, so she offered to take Fredo's bag for him. He declined, explaining, "This isn't my first time sneaking in. Just you watch."

With that, he ducked down and gripped the brickwork. The outflow was essentially a brick arch over the water and whilst there was a small ledge, it was not sufficient to be any more than a tiny foothold. He pressed his hands palm side up against the underside of the arch and dug his fingers into the uneven surface for grip. Slowly he shimmied along, step by step.

"It's important to make sure you are secure with your other hands and feet before moving one of them. Take it slow and concentrate," he advised.

Shiara was impressed at how easily he managed it, even if his comments seemed rather patronising to her. Shiara stooped and tried to arch her back at several different angles before deciding on one. The brickwork was rough to the touch and slightly damp from the water below, which did not fill her with confidence. She may have been far more athletic, but this was her first time doing this, whereas Fredo had the experience. The ledge she was expecting to be slippery was surprisingly good for grip; the heat and chemical-laden atmosphere had prevented anything slippery from growing on it. Her second hand found purchase, so she shifted her whole body until it was under the arch of the outflow. Fredo had told her to go slowly, yet she wanted to make a spectacle of how easy it was by rushing to get it over with. Scrabbling away, she felt the brick dig into her fingers and split the skin. Making sure not to betray any signs of discomfort, she finished making her way across. Fredo offered an outstretched hand to help her complete the final few feet; Shiara stubbornly declined. It was a surprisingly challenging physical feat; the fact that the silver-tongue had handled it with apparent ease was remarkable given his stomach must still have been a way off being fully mended after his encounter with the Cara owls.

Once through the outflow, they found themselves in a district that was obviously a poor industrial one. Plumes of steam puffed out from behind buildings, accompanied by the unmistakable hisses of hot metal dipped into water. Houses were nestled between larger buildings that looked like warehouses and some even larger buildings that looked like slums in tower form. A layer of black coated everything. Steps had been built down the riverside to allow easy access to the water. Various rigs and contraptions for lowering smelted products into the flow consisting of chains and metal beams punctuated the waterside. Manning them were numerous muscular individuals slick with sweat that had mixed with ash and soot into a shiny dark grey colour. Amid the muscles, peculiar lumps and bumps were visible on some of their arms. They were the work of Gall wasps, a four-inch-long insect common in the poorer areas of Omdurtur, where they fed off of the slag beetles. Slag beetles themselves were an insect only found around the stacks; they ate industrial by-products and because of this were poisonous to just about everything, except Gall wasps.

"So those lumps, I've always wondered, are they stings?"

"Not exactly," said Shiara, "the wasps inject their larvae into people, and this makes the flesh turn into small growths whilst the insect grows within."

Fredo was visibly disgusted.

"Actually, they're tumours," said the magical blade, "and they serve as protection for the larvae."

"That's even worse," said Fredo, having found an even more repulsed expression to wear.

"It wasn't always like this. They used to lay their offspring in a certain type of tree but the entire forest was cut down for lumber, so they adapted," informed the sword.

"Why don't they remove the tumours?" Fredo asked.

"You *can* do that, but you have to be very careful and it's not worth trying," answered Shiara.

"Why?"

"Because they eat so many slag beetles they're also poisonous. If you try to cut out the larvae and get it wrong, you risk poisoning yourself. Better to let them hatch out than risk it."

Fredo thought he knew about poor living conditions; however, he was

CHAPTER FIFTY-FIVE

clearly uninformed on how bad it could be in Omdurtur.

Shiara raised her arm to something in the distance: a tall building that Fredo knew well. It was the centre of the city, the home of Kadar's thrumming pillar. Unlike in the other cities, this one was built in an elevated position, so the courtyard looked down on the whole of Omdurtur. Other buildings had been constructed around it over time, but none as big. Kadar was the most renowned and wealthiest in the city so had to have pride of place.

A fitting representation of how the rich elite considered themselves above everyone else, thought Shiara.

CHAPTER FIFTY-SIX

Despite the sounds of hammering and digging of trenches, Marin still found it more peaceful outside of the wall. The refugees from Illorne had been making real progress digging out foundations for dozens of new buildings and shaping stones. The quarry was about an hour away by foot, making for slow progress, but it was progress nonetheless. Marin had negotiated with the stonemasons' guild to help things run smoothly, but until the council approved taking down a section of the wall there wasn't a vast amount they could do. The plan was to use the stones from the dismantled wall and repurpose them to build new structures and whilst this made perfect sense to Marin, convincing the council would be no small task. What really concerned the council leader at this moment in time were the refugees from Fimego that were mounting up. Some were sat with vacant looks, dotted around the outer wall as if they had stopped the moment they found civilization. Many of them looked famished; all of them looked dull behind the eyes. Marin was fully aware of the privileged life he had led yet he suspected even the most impoverished of Caspir's people would also be unable to imagine the horrors these people had survived. A lot of them still bore cuts and bruises, with reddish-brown stains soaked into their clothes. Some residents had taken to calling them "The Wandering Dead"; the hostility many once had for those from Illorne had been powered up and moved onto them instead. Reports of beatings and muggings to take the few possessions they had managed to salvage before leaving were common, as was the odd one being found dead from starvation.

CHAPTER FIFTY-SIX

Bemus had come along with Marin to check up on how things were going; the pair had fostered a kind of a friendship and Bemus had advised him to not go alone. The absence of guards around the building sites was conspicuous, not least because Marin had specifically given orders for guards to be posted here. Unfortunately, Bemus had an answer for this that Marin did not want to hear.

"Ya see, we been told dat der aint 'nuff coin to pay us 'n' we 'ave to wait fer it. Sum weren't 'avin dat so dey didn't show up fer work. Aint you s'posed to know 'bout dis stuff?"

Bemus was right; he *was* supposed to know about this.

"So some of the guards just haven't shown up to work today?"

"Today? Dis been goin' on all week. 'N' it's not jus' some of 'em, is at least 'alf of 'em."

That was the last thing that Marin needed; just when things were getting back on track another crisis loomed. At least there was some kind of normality attached to lurching from one problem to the next; in a peculiar way there was something unsettling about things actually going his way, even if only briefly. He would have to add this to the long list of things he needed to cover in the next council meeting.

"It would have been nice if someone had told me about this sooner."

Bemus shrugged; it was just as bewildering to him that the man in charge was having to learn about the vital running of the city from him.

Focusing on the task at hand, the council leader and his companion examined the progress that was being made; it was slow and hard work. Marin always held a great respect for those with skilled hands; the various guilds of Caspir were what kept it running and for all his prowess with words and numbers he envied those who could actually make something. Chatting to the workers there was a mutual air of respect, albeit a fragile one. The refugees from Illorne were naturally distrustful, as one would expect given their situation, yet they had to acknowledge that despite the bumps along the way Marin was indeed trying to help them. There were of course two major concerns that repeatedly came up as he spoke with them. When the wall was going to come down, and what they were expected to do about "The Wandering Dead", who were increasingly gathering around their settlement-to-be. The council leader was confident this section of the wall would be dismantled soon, allowing them both the materials needed and the sense of belonging to the city as a whole. His inability to provide an exact date proved irksome for most, but the last thing he wanted to do was falsely commit when the council had yet to agree, especially given his earlier grand idea becoming a slum. The second issue was a much more difficult one to gauge. The troubling realization was that those from Fimego didn't just need a place to call home and go about their business; they were also deeply broken people. They required far more care and support, something that Marin was wholly unprepared for. If they were struggling to pay guards how could they even hope to provide this level of assistance? This was what he was hoping Alyssa and the Church of Shiara were going to help with. The familiar sights of their dull cloaks had indeed extended into this settlement beyond the wall. A few were among those doing the digging and laying foundations; most were circulating around "The Wandering Dead" and the people from Illorne not involved in the construction. These Illornians had already refused the Church's offer in the past and were equally unreceptive this time around. As for the broken people of Fimego, there was little getting through to them. Trying to converse with them was a chore at best; they barely seemed to acknowledge other people and when they did their sentences usually trailed off. For the most part, conversation was not the goal. The Children of Shiara were doing their best to deal with the physical side of things: feeding them, giving them water to drink and providing them with new clothes or blankets to keep them warm at night and erase their recent bloody past as best they could. It was genuinely quite heart-warming for Marin to see this and he even began to think he'd misjudged Alyssa, but only briefly. It wasn't stone or cloth that was the greatest resource, it was people, and he was certain Alyssa knew this just as well as he did. It may have been cynical that he could see the long game playing out in his mind, but he couldn't help it. These were vulnerable people who'd just lost their god; all that devotion would need a new home and she was happy to oblige. It could take months or even years to get these

CHAPTER FIFTY-SIX

people back to some normality and for her to put them to use, yet there was no doubt in his mind that this was the overarching plan. Control enough of the people and you control the city. Nevertheless, that was an issue for another day. Right now, these people needed help and the Church were the ones in the best position to do that. Given his recent success in getting justice for Rhodes he'd bought himself some favour among many in the Church, even if Alyssa and himself were still adversarial at best.

Alyssa herself was not absent from the Church's efforts here and having spied Marin and Bemus, she decided to make her way over.

"Council leader. Nice of you to finally come along." If there was any doubt as to who had the moral high ground to grandstand on, Alyssa was sure to remove it. After all, she was the one doing him and Caspir a service here.

"Greetings Alyssa," he said, making sure not to use her self-ordained title. "I'm surprised to see you here, rather than just your followers."

"Surprised? You and I both know I am very much a 'hands-on' leader. And *you* did ask *me* for help personally. So here I am."

"Either way, myself and Caspir thank you for your efforts," he replied graciously, with a solid veneer of respect.

"The Church is glad to help those in need. And I have no doubt yourself and Caspir will happily return the favour when required."

With Alyssa it felt like there was no such thing as a good deed, just another angle for a grander plan.

"I'm sure the pleasure of supporting others is reward in and of itself," Marin smiled.

"Quite," said an outmanoeuvred Alyssa.

"Just as finding Rhodes's *real* killer and getting him the justice he deserved was also reward enough."

"As you say; now I must return to my work," finished Alyssa through gritted teeth. "Blessings of the Slayer unto you."

"And to you," Marin replied dismissively.

Despite his wrangling, he knew that the aforementioned favour would most certainly be called upon in good time and whether or not he could refuse would be a problem for future Marin. As of right now he was thinking that perhaps his prowess with words wasn't quite as mediocre a skill as he had previously considered. Soon he'd need to use all his expertise if he had any hope of convincing the council to implement the changes he had planned. A healthy dose of luck wouldn't go amiss either.

CHAPTER FIFTY-SEVEN

The heat emanating from the river and molten metal running alongside it was stifling. Although as the northernmost of the six cities Omdurtur should have been a bit more temperate, the machinations of industry had other ideas. The air itself was thick with pollution and water vapour. Fredo had been to Omdurtur more times than he could remember but had rarely visited the stacks. Towering round furnaces that dwarfed the surrounding structures pumped out acrid black plumes skywards, dispersing fine particles through the air to then settle on everything in a thin black film. The silver-tongue didn't want to think much about what this must be doing to his lungs.

The faces of those working along the river did not strike him as sad or unhappy; they were too busy to contemplate such things and a resigned apathy had gripped them. Shiara explained that these people had been told they could work hard and succeed. They'd been convinced that they were making contributions based on their ability and received the corresponding success. She said they were unaware of their exploitation; they thought they were simply doing a job and working for a wage. In their eyes this wasn't servitude; it was working hard for their families. Fredo more or less felt the same. The slayer of ghosts, on the other hand, described this simply as slavery, albeit with additional bells and whistles.

"Slaves who didn't know they were slaves were the most profitable resource imaginable," added the sword. When Fredo first joined Shiara on her journey he couldn't really understand what her point was outside of fulfilling some prophecy; now though, having listened to the ideas that drove her, there were definitely some shifts in his own views. He'd long toiled with the idea that there were problems with society when walking through the Brown Quarter, but the concept of a different way being possible eluded him. Was her dramatic plan for change too severe? Who was he to say? At least she had a plan and a prophecy behind her. The silver-tongue had always thought of these workers as willing participants; the notion of them being unknowingly exploited was fascinating and had some merit, but he was not convinced it was quite that black and white.

"It's not as if there isn't enough money; there's plenty of that. The issue is that the money is unfairly distributed. There's no reason why those who own the stacks can't have a few less gold trinkets so that everyone else can have a bit more food and comfort," she explained.

Fredo's whole life had been about courting the "wealth creators", the rich people in charge of huge swathes of industry. There was this accepted notion that they were the ones doing their workers a favour, providing them with jobs and purpose. Yet the more he saw, and the more Shiara elaborated, the more clearly he could see that whole narrative was inaccurate. He concluded that it was the workers who did the hard labour, the bosses who provided tools and means, and only together were they real creators of wealth. They should have been equal partners instead of glorified slaves. Everyone just bought into this narrative of the wealthy being the charitable hard workers because everyone was attracted to their success. Nobody liked to think they were being exploited so it just rumbled on for so long that it became an accepted fact. In Omdurtur everyone was obsessed with their own "value"; people didn't want to be seen as poor or struggling because there was this insane concept that people got what they deserved and that they earned their lot in life.

"How is someone born to a family working in these stacks supposed to compete with those born into families of wealth and privilege?" Shiara said.

Not a single person wanted to be seen as a failure; they'd deny their poverty and justify their meagre lot in life before admitting the difficulty of their situation.

CHAPTER FIFTY-SEVEN

Their path diverged from the river as it bent north. Heading towards the centre of the city would soon take them into more pleasant surroundings; the further from the river and stacks they got, the more affluent the neighbourhood. Shiara stopped briefly at the end of a street and looked down it. Fredo would never know this, but this street was the place of her childhood home: in the shadow of the stacks and well within the soot-fall. She wasn't one for sentimentality, yet she felt a brief moment of reverence and remembrance for where she came from was required. Then she was back on the move.

"Let's go, Fredo," she whispered, "there's somebody following us."

He was wise enough to not look around and invite further suspicion; if there was one thing he was a master of it was choosing how he presented himself to onlookers.

"Who do you think they are?" he asked in a hushed voice.

"Could be anyone – a beggar, a thief or a private agent for the council or Kadar. At this stage it's not a surprise we were coming. If anything, I'm surprised it was so easy for us to get into the city without any drama."

"You're welcome," replied Fredo.

Fredo had known Kadar for a long time and he wasn't the one for a big spectacle. He operated behind the scenes to exert his influence, so a few lookouts to trail them was exactly his modus operandi.

"I'll try and take a look," said Fredo as they turned a corner, giving him the opportunity to glance back. He only caught a glimpse but instantly recognized who it was – a man named Panos, with whom he was very familiar. He was one of the council's agents, with whom he'd he shared many drinks at numerous meetings, a pleasant yet unremarkable fellow being groomed to become a silver-tongue in the future, although he required a lot more training.

"It's OK, I know him. He's all right."

Fredo told Shiara they should just wait around the corner and it wouldn't be long before Panos tried to follow and walked right into them. Within a couple of minutes he was proven right, as Panos turned into the street only to find the people he was meant to be shadowing were looking right at him. His extremely thick eyebrows jumped in surprise like a pair of startled threadwurms.

"Hello, Panos. Glad you finally came over to introduce yourself," smirked Fredo.

Panos knew he'd been rumbled so had no other choice than nodding and looking sheepish.

"You *were* following us because you wanted to meet Shiara, weren't you?" Fredo said patronizingly.

"I think we both know why I was following you," Panos replied candidly.

"In that case, allow me to introduce you to Shiara, the slayer of ghosts," Fredo said.

"Hello Panos," said Shiara, "lovely that you could join us on our way to see Kadar."

The colour could be seen draining from Panos's face, even underneath the fine layer of soot it had collected.

"So you're *really* doing this? And *you're* helping her?" asked Panos.

"I've seen her kill three ghosts already, so even if I wanted to stop her – which I don't – it's not like I could," answered the silver-tongue.

Shiara beamed with a little bit of pride – not because Fredo had acknowledged her prowess in combat, but because he was on board with her fulfilling the prophecy.

"Panos," she said sternly, "do *you* want to stop me? And are *you* going to try?"

His mouth went dry. He was being directly confronted by someone who looked inconspicuous enough, but he knew full well that she could end him with ease.

"I... I'm just doing my job," he croaked.

"And what precisely is that?"

"I was told to keep an eye out for you and if I spotted the pair of you, to observe and report back," Panos said.

"Oh, in that case, what would you like to know?" Shiara smiled. "I'm here to walk right up to Kadar's thrumming pillar, challenge him, then kill him. If you can call slaying an immortal ghost 'killing', that is."

CHAPTER FIFTY-SEVEN

Panos took some time to work out what he was supposed to do with this information. He was not too sure what he was meant to find out, really; he just knew that people with far more power and money told him to do it and that was the way things worked in Omdurtur.

"Fredo, do you really think I can go and tell Kadar that?" asked an exasperated Panos.

"It's the truth, so you don't seem to have much choice, really. Don't worry, once this is all over we can grab a drink." Fredo's words were all very matter-of-fact and comforting.

"So you think she'll beat Kadar?" said Panos.

"Excuse me, but *she* is right here, and has a name," snipped Shiara.

"Apologies, Shiara."

"Panos, we've known each other a long time. I watched Shiara best Mara and we both know Kadar isn't half the fighter she was. You've got to face facts; things are changing."

The silver-tongue was frank but not condescending; it was clear he had a semblance of a friendship with Panos and wanted to tell him everything was going to be all right. Hearing that the very underpinning of your life was about to be dismantled was not easy to hear for the Omdurturian.

"Tell Kadar we're coming for him," interjected a malice-filled, disembodied voice that took Panos by surprise.

"Who... said that?" he asked.

"Oh, don't worry about that. It's just Shiara's sword. I don't think it likes Kadar very much," replied Fredo.

"A... talking sword? That's... unusual," said the man with the impressive eyebrows that had miraculously reached even higher levels of astonishment.

"You think that's unusual; wait until you hear its thoughts on 'the mad ghost of Latan'," quipped the silver-tongue.

"So... what do we do now?" Panos said.

"If I were you, I'd run along to tell Kadar that I'm coming and there's nothing he can do about it. Or you could join us, so we arrive together; however, I've got a feeling he'll like that even less," said a grinning Shiara. Panos glanced at his old friend Fredo as if waiting for confirmation.

"Don't look at me!" exclaimed Fredo. "You heard the lady!"

With that Panos spun round and took off up the street in a half-jog. Fredo shook his head a little; Panos was a *very* long way off from being the silver-tongue he was aiming for. Nevertheless, he was a decent guy; perhaps that was the problem.

"He's a nervous one, isn't he?" remarked Shiara.

"It's not his fault really; I'd be nervous in *his* shoes too."

The pair resumed their walk, leaving the stacks behind them.

The streets were becoming noticeably more affluent, and rather than heading down the big thoroughfares where numerous eyes were undoubtedly watching, Fredo took them down side streets. Panos may have only been following them to collect information; others may not be so passive. He had no doubt Shiara could deal with them, or even deter them completely from trying anything, but avoiding them was just easier. From everything he'd learnt about her, he thought she'd prefer to avoid drawing her blade against anyone who wasn't a ghost. The scent of the stacks no longer filled their nostrils and the great tower was drawing closer. Today was the day Shiara had dreamed of for years; she positively glowed with the prospect of it. Her sword had waited far longer and pulsed with even greater anticipation.

CHAPTER FIFTY-EIGHT

The streets were not a safe place for Koralia. Her revolution had failed; the people were angry and scared. She knew it was going to be bad but seeing the streets full of blood and bodies was worse than even her most horrific expectations. She felt responsible, a sentiment that many of the residents of Maluani agreed with. A few of those still sympathetic to her cause had warned her about the manhunt that was now underway: those who had taken up arms to join her had now sold her out. The blame for all this carnage was now placed squarely at her feet by just about everyone. She didn't fault them for it; it was much easier to focus one's frustrations and anger on an enemy who *could* be defeated, unlike Takis. The failed rebellion was easier to blame than the system that had crushed them to the point of rebelling. It didn't matter that everyone wanted the change; now it wasn't coming everyone wanted to distance themselves from it and make the best of a bad situation: it was human nature. Unfortunately for Koralia, that meant every warden and Takis himself were scouring the city looking for her. She had told Neela to go her own way and take the books with her; perhaps they could come in useful one day and there was no point in Neela throwing her life away too. She had that spirit and fire within her that any future attempts at insurrection would so desperately need. Minos, on the other hand, was proving more difficult to get rid of. There was no need for him to get caught with her, yet he refused to leave her alone. They had taken up shelter in a disused storehouse. It had been many seasons since crops had been kept here and it was easy to see why. It was damp and had black mould creeping across most of the surfaces; long abandoned buckets of brown water and broken tools were the only reminders of what this place used to be. Koralia's plan was to try and escape the city; however, when dawn came they had no choice but to hide out until the following night. Moments of sleep were snatched here and there but were wholly insufficient, the growling of their empty bellies the only distraction from tiredness. Each patter of footsteps outside gave a jolt to their systems that were now running solely on fear, adrenaline and basic survival instincts.

"You really should go home," she said.

"It doesn't matter how many times you say that; it isn't going to happen," replied Minos, managing a brief smile.

"If they catch me while you're here, they'll kill you too. There's no reason for us both to throw our lives away."

"Personally, I was planning on neither of us not getting caught in the first place," he joked.

Koralia shook her head; this was serious, literal life and death stuff, yet here was Minos trying to make light of the situation and risking his life needlessly.

"The streets are filled with people looking for me. It's probably not a matter of *if*, but *when* they find me."

"We've been friends since before either of us can remember. I simply *can't* leave you alone. Besides, we face a much better chance of getting you out if we work together. And who knows, maybe they're looking for me too?" Minos posited.

"Well, if they *are* looking for you then we're in real trouble. Anyone could spot that nose of yours from a mile off."

Their half-hearted laughter was cut short by footsteps outside, their breath held as the group of people going by paused near the entrance to the building. They couldn't quite make out any words but there was an angry tone that set them on edge. One of the people shouted something and they all bolted away from the storehouse. Every moment felt like borrowed time to Koralia. This had been a lucky escape, but what about next time? By the time night fell, guards would have covered every way out of the city. Even

CHAPTER FIFTY-EIGHT

with her climbing prowess, the odds of getting out unseen were slim. It was best not to think about it right now.

"Minos, you saw the bodies, or what was left of them at least. How do you suppose an ordinary person could have bested a ghost in combat? I just can't get my head around it."

Her friend shrugged. It was indeed a hard thing to wrap one's head around.

"I suppose not all the ghosts are equally terrifying. Perhaps we just got unlucky by being stuck with this bastard?" suggested Minos.

"Maybe you're right. I saw all the books he had in that library of his, about magic and all sorts. I doubt any of the others take the time to make themselves more powerful. After all, why would you, when you're already an immortal being?"

"For some people, there's no such thing as enough power," he said, a surprisingly profound comment for someone most considered a clown.

"I just hope that *something* in those books Neela has will give us something we can use. The fight doesn't have to end. It may have gone badly, but..."

"Badly? You know I care about you, but this isn't the time for you to be thinking about this. Who knows how many people died last night? We *tried*. We *failed*. We have to accept that. Survival is what matters now," Minos interrupted.

"I know. I'm just saying..."

"Don't. Please."

"But the books... they might have the answer we are looking for," Koralia protested.

"You may well be right, and I hope you are; however, this isn't your fight anymore. I know you're looking for something to cling to and I'm usually the last one to be a cynic, but I'm scared, Koralia."

"All the more reason why you should go home," she said.

"I'm not scared for myself; I'm scared for you. Let's face it, I can crack all the jokes I want to, yet every time someone even walks near the door of this place, our hearts feel like they are nearly bursting. Best-case scenario, we get out – then what? Wander the wilderness? Could we even make it to another city if we wanted to? And the worst-case..." Minos shook his head. The worst-case scenario wasn't just the most terrifying, it was also the most likely. Koralia let the words hang in the air for a bit before offering her reply.

"I see that. I really do. *I'm* probably never going to see a free Maluani. This whole thing, though, was *never about me*. I didn't want to free us from Takis for my own sake; to be honest I went into this not expecting to survive. And you know what? That's okay. I came to terms with that a long time ago; what I won't let you do is take away hope. It's the only thing we've ever had and look how far we came with it! As for the best-case scenario, it doesn't include me either way. The books may be a long shot, but they are still something. Perhaps in hindsight, the real best-case scenario is the one we should have held out for in the first place."

Tears were filling Minos's eyes. It felt like she was giving her own eulogy.

"And... what is that?" he asked.

"The slayer of ghosts is *still out there*, Minos. She might still come and do what we couldn't."

It pained Koralia to admit she had made a mistake. She had wanted to be the one to save Maluani and bring down Takis; she had thought the people could do it. She was wrong. As it turned out, their best option was to do nothing and wait for someone else to be their salvation. Through all the death and misery, that option was still just as likely as it ever was. This was what kept her strong.

KNOCK KNOCK KNOCK!

The banging on the door destroyed the moment. They both leapt to their feet. Audible shouts rang out, telling them to "open up", followed by "We know you are in there!" Whether or not they did, or it was just a bluff on the off chance they were in there and it could make them come along more peacefully, was irrelevant. No doubt they would be armed and the pair of revolutionaries would be without a hope of fighting back. Koralia only saw one option.

"Minos," she turned to look him right in the eyes, "I will miss you. And I'm sorry."

"Sorry?" he asked, but before he could ponder on the subject more,

CHAPTER FIFTY-EIGHT

Koralia's right fist hurtled into his cheekbone and laid him out flat. The doors burst open and a group of six people funnelled in.

"Oh, so you've come for me too? Reckon you can do better than the last person who tried it?" She made a very clear point of gesturing towards Minos as if the posse should be scared of her, when in fact it was all just an act to keep her best friend safe and dismiss any notion of him being a co-conspirator. The people who had come for her were not the wardens she had spent her life in fear of; they were ordinary people. Just like her. They may well have been those who stood alongside the other rebels to face down their oppressors; now they were in league with those they once rallied against. The desire to be on the "winning side" was strong – not merely for survival, but due to an ingrained sense of wanting to be on that "winning side" after a lifetime of being an ignored member of the "losing side". All they had ever known was being on the wrong end of the stick, yet with the failed revolution they finally had an opportunity to see themselves in a different light. Obviously for Koralia this was a terrible situation, even though she could understand the human nature behind it.

Steel was pointed at her; she had no choice. Resist and die, or go quietly with them. Either way would likely be fatal, but making the choice to give up one's life there and then was not easy. For all her bravery, she wasn't going to do it. She told herself it was about hanging on in case the slayer of ghosts arrived in time rather than the truth of just wanting to live a little longer; basic survival instinct and fear of death had been a common motivating factor for everyone in the city and she was no different.

Raising her hands in compliance, she let them take her. A firm set of arms restrained each of hers, comrades turned captors. Her uprising had been roundly defeated in both body and mind. Now she would face the consequences. Now she would finally face Takis.

CHAPTER FIFTY-NINE

Red splashed across Marin's tongue and down his throat. This was far from his ideal beverage; it was instead the current trendy wine in Caspir, and he was not a fan. It was made from a grape he ordinarily enjoyed a great deal after it had at least five years to mature into being smooth, rich and fruity. For some reason unbeknownst to him, a trend had developed where people drank it after it had been only a year or two in the barrel. The result was supposed to be lively, tangy and spicy on the palate; to the council leader it was a sour, vinegar-like waste of good grapes. His friend Edwin was also not a fan, just nowhere near as vocally opposed or irate about it.

"It's not just that they've made something awful; it's that they've wasted perfectly lovely grapes to do so," Marin declared.

"If you really don't like it, you could always try *not* drinking any wine this evening?" suggested Edwin.

"Alternatively, the quicker we help them get through this barrel, the quicker we can get them to open up something good instead," chuckled the man whose beard was back to its immaculate state of being after many stressful weeks.

The pair raised their beakers to one another and gulped back a mouthful with grins that became winces due to the beverage's high acidity and astringency. In many ways it felt like old times again, sitting in the Moth & Scale playing Bahlea, with the main problem facing them being tomorrow's council meeting. Marin was trying to pitch some radical ideas to a group of people mostly stuck in their ways – not only knocking down part of their

CHAPTER FIFTY-NINE

centuries-old city wall but also reforming how they approached criminals and the justice system completely. And of course, the biggest issue, the one that always reared its head: how to pay for such things.

Edwin was of a mindset that them talking about it now wasn't going to make tomorrow any easier; nevertheless, he wasn't going to stop Marin if he wanted to, provided the wine and games of Bahlea kept flowing. As of right now, the Bahlea was flowing in his direction, putting him two games up over Marin and he was moving a piece to corner his prince yet again.

"Don't think you can get me that easily," said Marin as he moved his piece to safety.

"Not *that* easily; it will take me three more turns by my calculations."

The council leader took a moment, working out the moves with his fingers and pointing to the pieces so he could position them in his mind to work out what Edwin was talking about. It took him a couple of increasingly laboured minutes to puzzle it through. Frowning with mild disappointment, he searched for a solution. He finally found a small triumph, sort of.

"Actually, if I move this piece... here, it'll take you four turns!" Marin rejoiced a little at finding what even the most generous of people wouldn't call a victory. The pair laughed together and began resetting the board. Their drinks were also ready for a refresh, so they beckoned over the bar lady. The Moth & Scale was rather empty today, so they'd have to do a lot of the work themselves if they wanted to get onto the next barrel. The reason for the lack of patrons was in itself a grim reason for the councillors to drink. It was no secret that trade had been drying up – an unfortunate consequence of Shiara's success in other cities. The people of Fimego would not be looking to buy fine silks anytime soon, which meant less money for everyone, which in turn meant fewer people spending their coin in the Moth & Scale. The same story played out across all the taverns in Caspir; once hives of activity, they were now muted places propped up by wealthier customers and those who felt the compulsion to drink. The patrons that *were* in the tavern were certainly loud enough to keep the place feeling more packed than it actually was.

"So Edwin, do you think they'll go for it?"

"I'm afraid you'll have to be a bit more specific; which of your outlandish ideas are you referring to?" quipped his older friend.

"Good point," said Marin begrudgingly. "I suppose… any of them?"

Edwin laughed.

"How very optimistic of you. Honestly, I don't know. Aside from those who will vote against you no matter what, it depends on how you sell your plans."

"And how do you think I can convince them?" asked the council leader.

"Simple. The same way you convince any of these people to do anything. Pure self-interest."

"And you joked about *my* lack of optimism?! Where's your faith in your fellow man?" Marin joked.

Edwin lowered his head and looked up to give an expression that exclaimed "Really?!", then raised his beaker and took a long sip of wine without breaking eye contact, before placing his drink back down and sighing.

"I've been on the council for more years than either of us can count, and in all that time I've never seen anyone care about anything except themselves. Present company excluded, of course. You have to understand that everything the council does is driven by self-interest. Paying people more only matters when it can increase profits. The homeless are only an issue when they get in the way. Guards are only seen as something to protect themselves, not other people. If you want to get them on board, you have to appeal to that."

Marin was stunned at the depressing picture his companion painted and was determined to find fault with it.

"The council isn't what it used to be. Things have changed since Chase died. We have ordinary people in the chamber now," he reasoned.

"Ordinary people? Just because someone isn't a noble doesn't mean they don't see themselves in the same way. A guild leader might have less wealth than a noble, but you can be certain that they see themselves as important and influential, a long way above the people in their factories."

"Sure. But what about the farmers we have on the council?" said Marin.

Edwin shook his head and wagged his finger.

CHAPTER FIFTY-NINE

"They're not field-hands; they own the tracts of land. There's also the fact that just by *being* on the council they have an over-inflated ego. For hundreds of years the city has held up the council as some kind of paragon of superiority, so the moment someone joins it they automatically think they are somehow more deserving."

"So power altogether is pointless then? After all it will just taint all who obtain it, by your reasoning?" accused the council leader.

"No, not necessarily. It's not so much the power or influence that is the issue; it's the culture surrounding it. Take you, for example. Power isn't a badge of honour for you, nor is it a tool to serve your interests. *You* see it as a means to a grander vision. *You* haven't bought into the same frame of mind as everyone else. They see power as something they deserve that validates them, whereas you see it as a necessary route to bring about positive change."

Marin nodded. "I'm flattered you think so highly of me."

"I didn't say you were right; as far as you know I could be calling you a delusional idealist," smirked Edwin.

"Actually... I think you've described me with those exact words before."

The pair snickered and swilled some more wine into their bellies.

"What about you then? Where do you fit into this theory of power for validation?" Marin probed.

"You know me; I was born into this and never once had to question my own worth. I'm wise enough to know better than most, but old enough to remain stuck in my ways. Change is a young man's game; I'll support you all I can, but don't expect me to lead the charge. It's your future, not mine. I'd sooner spend my days beating delusional idealists at Bahlea than attend another council meeting... Which reminds me, it's your move."

Marin's hand hovered over a piece, then another, then another, constantly surveying not only his own thoughts but his opponent's face in hopes of finding some kind of tell to make sure he didn't play right into his plan.

"Thanks for calling me a young man; however, you won't be beating *this* delusional idealist anytime soon," said Marin as he moved his piece across the board.

"I wouldn't be so sure about that... You just exposed your prince."

A disappointed sigh left Marin's lips.

"Or... is that all part of my plan?" bragged the council leader in a failed attempt to justify his error.

"If that's the case, my advice to you would be to make better plans in future. Preferably not ones that involve you losing your prince in... six moves."

"Why do we even call them princes anyway? It was hundreds of years before even the ghosts were made that we last had anything resembling royals," said an irritated Marin.

"Would you like to rename all the pieces of this thousands-of-years-old game just because you're losing? What would you prefer to prince? Ghost? Or perhaps you'd like it to be council leader?"

"How about 'tawdry old man called Edwin'?"

The pair erupted into laughter at such a volume as to attract looks from other tables.

"So what do you reckon things were like back when there was royalty? Never-ending struggles to kill the heir to the throne like in Bahlea?" wondered Marin.

"I highly doubt it. To be quite frank I suspect it was much the same as things are now," replied Edwin.

"How so?"

"Lots of self-interested people vying for power, playing little games to one-up each other in day-to-day petty trivialities. The names of things may have changed from court to council; tithes to taxes..."

"Kings to immortal deity-like ghost protectors?" interrupted Marin in an ambitious yet mildly successful attempt to inject some more humour. The wine was no doubt greasing the wheels of comedy somewhat generously.

"Indeed. Regardless of how much things change, some things stay the same. You can mark your calendar by the greed and arrogance of small-minded men trying to pander to their own egos. So no, I don't think the days of royalty resembled a complex game of perfect strategy; it was probably a lot more like a bunch of conceited drunks boasting about who has the biggest penis. Albeit with a bit more stabbing and gaudy gold jewellery."

CHAPTER FIFTY-NINE

"Quite the picture you paint there, Edwin. If someone didn't know better, they'd think you held a dim view of those in power!" said a smiling Marin, his voice dripping with sarcasm.

"Decades of sitting in that council chamber having to be polite and respectful to the various sycophantic dregs that pass for councillors will certainly give you a perspective that's less than... wholesome."

"Sycophantic dregs? 'Delusional idealist' doesn't sound quite so bad anymore."

Warm smiles reserved for only the best of friends spread across both of their faces. Tomorrow would be a challenging day of snide debates and battling for every inch of reform, but knowing that Edwin would be by his side made the task a little more palatable for Marin. Like his wise companion had said, some things may change a lot, but many stay the same; he was thankful that Edwin's friendship was one of them.

CHAPTER SIXTY

The thrumming pillar of Omdurtur sat atop a large building within a semi-enclosed rooftop courtyard. More like Fimego than Caspir or Illorne, it formed the centrepiece of the city instead of being left alone and ignored. The tower-like building itself predated the ghosts; the thrumming pillar had been constructed upon it at a much later date. Unlike the other ghosts, Kadar saw this place as his home. This opulent structure that towered over others was the perfect residence for the person who wielded the most power in Omdurtur. He may not have been on the council but through his money and connections he more or less decided who was. Large glass panes covered one of the sides to the building, with precise designs carefully etched into the stonework on the others. An exterior staircase encircled the building; an ornate pattern of shimmering metal embellished the banister, glinting gold, bronze and silver in the late afternoon sun. At the bottom of the steps was a quartet of armed men; these were not city guards but private blades for hire. There were very few city guards left in Omdurtur; most of them had been replaced by what were in effect mercenaries. Originally posited as a means to save the council money by letting the wealthy pay for their own law enforcement, the reality was turning access to protections under law into a right that only the rich could afford. As such there was no end to the armed resources Kadar could muster.

The foot of this tower now lay in Shiara's view; the only memories of it she had were fleeting ones of looking up the staircase as her father ascended it with her dead brother in his arms. Fredo, on the other hand, knew it very

CHAPTER SIXTY

well. He had spent many an evening sharing drinks with businessmen and politicians in the rooftop courtyard, all in the company of Kadar. Omdurtur's ghost had the sort of arrogance only made possible by gratuitous wealth; for all the discussions and meetings Fredo had been a part of, never once had he seen Kadar give even an inch to anyone else. He was always right and had the power to make sure of it.

Nearing the end of the walkway, the pair were interrupted by a group of armed men who fanned out to block their path. The group of six only shared a handful of teeth between them; the lighter etchings of scars on their faces hinted at the past violence that was the cause. Their mismatched armour formed a stark contrast with the city guards of Caspir; these were not a force for law and order – they were glorified bandits.

"Stop right there," barked the largest and roughest of the men.

Shiara was most certainly not in the mood. Fredo had never seen her fight with a mere mortal before and didn't much fancy seeing such a slaughter take place, even if the victims were to be such unpleasant characters. He gestured to Shiara to give him a chance to talk to them first.

"Gentlemen. I don't think this is necessary," said the silver-tongue smoothly.

"Considerin' we wanna get paid, I think you'll find it is," replied their leader.

"What I mean to say is that it's not necessary to throw your lives away like this," clarified Fredo.

"There's only two of you, and six of us," snarled the mercenary.

"And how many ghosts have you slain between you?" quipped Fredo.

The men looked at each other then back to Shiara. They were beginning to become unsettled.

"You're tellin' me that she's supposed to be the one what's going around killing ghosts?"

Fredo nodded.

"I don't believe ya." With that, the sword for hire drew his blade and took a few steps towards Shiara, the weapon pointed at her face.

"Please don't do this," begged Fredo, although it was difficult to discern whether it was directed at Shiara or the man bearing down on her. Shiara sighed. She had no intention of killing these men, regardless of how unsavoury they may be. Through her logic, they were yet another product of the system they lived in and were not to blame, not completely anyway. Fredo figured he knew better; everywhere he'd been he'd met people without scruples. Shiara waited until the man's sword was only a foot away from her nose before unsheathing her own weapon and swinging it through the air in one swift motion. A ripple of colour hung in the air for a moment, and the man's blade fell to the floor severed in two. His trembling hand clutched what was left of his weapon as his mind caught up with what he'd just seen.

"As my friend Fredo said, it's not worth losing your lives over this," reiterated Shiara quietly.

The five men slunk off rather sheepishly; their leader would require more time before he could bring himself to move again. The pair walked past him and left the street behind them.

As Fredo and Shiara approached the tower, the men sat on the steps of the tower could be seen readying themselves and turning their bodies to face the oncomers they had been warned of. The familiar face of Panos was among them. Stopping about ten feet away, the slayer of ghosts looked them up and down and adopted a very relaxed position, throwing a telling look Fredo's way, as if to say, "It's my turn."

"Good to see you again, Panos. I assume you've told these men who I am, right?" she asked confidently.

Panos nodded; the men around him did not seem happy with the situation.

"And they're still here?" Shiara queried.

"We all have to make a living," answered Panos, his thick eyebrows quivering.

"I think we all know that I'm walking up those stairs. I understand you've got a job to do but what exactly is it you plan to do here?"

Her point was a salient one. There wasn't much call for them to ever employ their swords in actual combat, so they were far from well-practiced. Rather than the group Shiara had just dealt with, these were nothing more than deterrents whose usual activities were simply guarding property. The

CHAPTER SIXTY

prospect of jumping into action against someone who had killed immortals was as terrifying to them as it was pointless. She took a step forward, raised her shoulders and hand, then cocked her head as if to say, "Are we really doing this?" It took a minute, but the four of them looked at one another questioningly before taking a few paces to the side and opening their palms in front of them to show they weren't going to be grabbing their weapons anytime soon.

"Good decision there, guys," said Fredo.

"Being honest with you, we aren't paid enough to get involved with this," replied one of the guards to enthusiastic nods from the others.

"Don't worry Panos, we'll still grab that drink later when this is all over."

Fredo's words didn't do much to quell the shaking of Panos's eyebrows; nevertheless, the thought of a stiff drink about now was indeed welcome.

Shiara and Fredo left them behind and made their way up the steps. As they got higher the view opened up, revealing a spectacular panorama of the city. Streets buzzed with a flurry of activity that, by the time they reached the top floor, seemed more like insects working away below. Other structures reached for the sky in tribute to this central tower, each one with its own intricate architecture and splendour. One had coloured glass in vibrant hues, another was strewn with countless brilliant mosaic tiles emulating a glorious sunrise. However, distant plumes of black smoke marred the horizon to the south-west and acted as a constant reminder of the cost of all this lavishness. Along the way they passed doors to each level, some of them open, revealing the luxury inside: expertly crafted wooden furniture from Illorne upholstered in the finest of silks from Caspir. It was the perfect antithesis of how most people here lived. How Shiara had once lived.

Reaching the top of the stairs, the space opened out onto the roof as a walled courtyard. A thin roof that looked newer than the rest of the structure covered most of the courtyard. At first Shiara considered it to be there to provide shade; its real purpose was to block out any ash-fall. At this height flecks of soot from the stacks still hung in the air. The thrumming pillar stood in the centre, and the size of the courtyard meant that tables and chairs could occupy a corner to offer their occupants an unparalleled view of Omdurtur – occupants that consisted of several decadently dressed men and one muscular figure of milky-white luminosity: Kadar. The other men looked to the pair of intruders then back to their ghost protector to see how he reacted. He just sat there, calm and collected.

"Shiara, isn't it?" Kadar said in a commanding and confident tone that could only have been cultivated by centuries of superiority and privilege.

"Yes, it is. And you know why I'm here," she fired back.

He rose to his feet and paced over, wearing a smile. The slayer of ghosts was instantly suspicious of his demeanour. Her heart began beating like it had never done before. This wasn't just putting an end to a ghost but putting an end to *the* ghost that had started her down this path. Was he trying to catch her off guard? Was he buying time for some kind of a trick? What was his plan?

"Something about fulfilling prophecies and making everything better, right? And how has that been working out for you so far? Illorne is a lawless mess of gangs and violence, and as for Fimego.... Do you really think you are helping anyone?" His words stung because for all their venom, they contained the truth.

"I'll tell you one thing I know for sure. *You* aren't helping anyone but yourself," retorted Shiara.

"Oh, aren't I? I provide jobs for people so that they can feed their families. I provide schools to teach people important crafts for their future employment. I give people a chance to better themselves and strive to achieve!" Kadar's words came across with one clear and distinct trait that Shiara was not expecting: honesty. He genuinely believed the things he was saying.

"These people aren't your employees; they are your slaves," she spat.

"Slaves?!" he cried. "You would look upon these people making an honest living as slaves? Do we not pay them? Do they not willingly choose to work for me or others?"

"Choice? What choice do they have? It's either working for the bare minimum or having nothing. That's barely living, let alone making an honest one. How much money do you make from them whilst they can only

CHAPTER SIXTY

scrape by?"

"Do I not deserve recompense? They work with *my* materials, with *my* tools, at *my* factories. Without *me*, there would be no money for any of them." Kadar was becoming visibly irritated by the conversation.

"Without *them*, *you* would be the one who had nothing." Shiara spoke with a burning clarity she had stoked all of her life for this very moment. Kadar just shook his head in defiance.

"Oh, I understand what this is all about. What it's *always* been about with your type. Envy. You resent those of us who have succeeded and want to drag everyone down, is that it? Fredo, I thought you of all people would have been able to talk some sense into her by now," said Kadar.

"Envy? You think I'm envious? I don't want to be like you. The whole point is that I don't want *anyone* to be like you!" raged Shiara.

"So it's the very notion of success you despise? Omdurtur is the most profitable and thriving of cities," boasted the ghost.

"Success? You call people living in slums and toiling all day a success? Money is not a measure of success."

Kadar responded with a belly laugh.

"Money is not a measure of success? What other *possible* means of measuring success do you suggest? *Money is everything.* It's the clothes on your back, the shoes on your feet, the meals in your belly. There is nothing else."

Fredo could feel the rage radiating off his companion. He had come here to see a fight of weapons but was being treated to an even fiercer one waged with words.

"Therein lies the problem. All you can see or care about is money. It's been so long since you were human that you can't even understand basic humanity anymore," Shiara said scornfully.

"You weren't even human before you were made into a ghost," added the enchanted blade, now pulsating with light, mirroring Shiara's anger.

The talking sword caught Kadar off guard even though Panos had told him about it, but he would not be deterred from his argument.

"Do you think all these houses and amenities would have been built without money? My money?" Kadar went on.

"Building things to maintain your exploitation isn't some noble pursuit. It's like a slaver investing in new chains."

"Exploiting them, am I? Do you think these people would build houses and metalwork shops with this money? No, they'd squander it and fritter it away. They need someone like me to direct them and spend the money wisely. I am a guiding hand for these people, and you want to take all of that away? Take your friend Fredo for example; where would you be if Chase hadn't had faith in you and shown you what you could become?" Kadar asked the silver-tongue.

Fredo was reluctant to answer, yet the power and sway of the ghosts was something he had spent his entire life not being able to deny; even after all he had been through it was no different.

"On the streets." Fredo's words were inflected almost as if he were framing it as a question.

"Exactly my point. I've seen it over hundreds of years. People need others like me to help them become who they can be," said Kadar.

"People shouldn't become who you want them to be. They should be free," replied Shiara.

"Free? You mean like the animals beyond the walls? Every single citizen in Omdurtur has the freedom to walk out those gates and live in the wilderness if they want to. You know why they don't? Because freedom, true freedom, is nothing but suffering. People *need* order. They need structure to their lives. We give them that; now you want to take that away from them?"

"No," Shiara said with conviction, "I'm not taking anything away from the people; I'm giving something back to them. The only one I'm taking anything away from is you, and I'm taking everything." Shiara's hand now clenched the hilt of her blade.

"Money it is then. Take it. Take the money I've *earned*. How much do you want? We need not bother with trivialities like fighting; I can give you enough wealth so you can be like the rest of us successes." Kadar gestured towards the onlookers, who seemed incredibly uncomfortable with being brought into the heated exchange. Everything she had said about Kadar

CHAPTER SIXTY

also applied to them, and they knew it. The ghost's plan now came into view. Like with everything he had experienced over hundreds of years, he expected to be able to buy his way out of it.

"I *don't* want your money," she said, drawing her blade, "and you can't stop me from taking what I *do* want."

CHAPTER SIXTY-ONE

Four walls and a heavy door of wood and metal were Koralia's comrades now. A few small holes in the ceiling let in tiny streams of light that just about illuminated her surroundings now her eyes had adjusted. The worst part, for now at least, was the smell. A foetid combination of human bodily products had built up over what she assumed must have been decades. The unmistakable metallic tinge of blood was also clearly present. There was no way of telling how many people had spent their final days in this cell; keeping prisoners wasn't something Takis favoured – he usually preferred swift executions. Koralia knew that she was no ordinary prisoner; she was the one responsible for burning his library and stoking the fires of rebellion. Considering all the horror he had exacted on others for lesser crimes, the prospect of what she would face was harrowing beyond contemplation. She had only been locked up here for a few days, or at least that was her best guess given the number of meals she had received, if one could call the bowls of sludge meals. The people who had turned her over to the wardens cheered in triumph as she was taken into custody; how quickly one's perspective changed – Koralia was sure that she'd seen one or two of them at a meeting arranging their failed uprising. It had been surprisingly easy to inflame the spirit of revolution yet extinguishing that flame proved even easier. She thought she had started a movement, built up something that would outlast her and organize in new ways to fight for their freedom; the truth was painful. At best she had created a one-off event, at worst she had destroyed any faith in rebellions for generations to come. Wanting to make a difference

CHAPTER SIXTY-ONE

apparently was not enough. Scrunched up in the corner of her cell on soiled straw, her self-criticism and failure put her actions on trial in her mind.

"I was too arrogant and naive," she cursed to herself. "How could I have thought that any of us, especially me, could have changed things for the better?" Every doubt and apprehension she had pushed to one side revisited her now. She had been so concerned with being the one to do something that she hadn't thought about things objectively. It should have been obvious that a bunch of field-hands wouldn't stand up to the might of an immortal ghost. The plan to smash the thrumming pillar seemed inspired at the time yet it should have been obvious that putting all their eggs into one basket of blind hope was stupid. How could she have gambled with everyone's lives on basically faith alone? Beating herself up about it now achieved nothing, yet she found herself unable to stop.

She felt responsible.

She *was* responsible.

Not for the failed rebellion so much as the peddling of false hope, based on her own hubristic belief she would be the one to end Takis's reign. Doing nothing would have been the better option. The slayer of ghosts actually succeeding in killing an immortal shouldn't have been a sign for Maluani to take on Takis.

"It should have been a clear call for us to all bide our time and wait in real hope for someone who could actually slay Takis to arrive." She had begun vocalising her thoughts in animated whispers to herself.

"But no. *I* had to be the one to do something. *I* couldn't just wait. This life isn't shaped by normal people doing things; for all our passion and will, us ordinary people don't matter. It was stupid to think we could make any difference. In the real world it's only a handful of people who can shape such things. Special people. Exceptional people... lucky people. For all my efforts I was never going to amount to anything. I'm just another one of the small people who dared to dream above my place in the world. Why didn't I just wait? Let this "Slayer of Ghosts" come and do their thing. Leave it to the people who matter."

A lifetime of insecurities and self-doubt had finally surfaced. She'd always tried to be practical and forceful, telling herself it was in service to a greater good, that these things needed to happen. Perhaps this was true but the notion that it was on *her* to make such things happen had been thoroughly dismantled. There were a hundred different ways she could blame herself and find fault with what she had done, and she was determined to dwell on each of them.

An hour or two passed, which saw Koralia's mind find a way out of her maze of negative thoughts. The conclusion she settled on for now was that in the end, she didn't matter. Either way, she and everyone else were likely to end up the same way. Better to die fighting than to be ground down. Believing in miracles of someone coming to rescue you was nice but that was no way to live one's life. It was not the most comforting of realizations, yet it would suffice for now. Koralia wondered how long she would be kept in this place and ultimately what her fate would be, and as if in answer to her pondering a milky swirl began to form before her. Should she face him on her feet? Better to not give him the satisfaction, she supposed, choosing to remain propped up in the corner of the cell instead.

There he now was. Koralia had never been this close to him before. An impressive figure with immaculate features, magnificent in stature. The thought that immediately occupied her head was "How could someone who has everything use it to deprive others of so much?" She had long suspected that this power and privilege was in itself part of the problem. If someone was considered "special" by every metric for as long as they could remember, it would seem natural to assume others were inferior. For an immortal being like Takis, that would be magnified inconceivably.

"Hello," said the ever-living figure, not in the tone of a cruel dictator exacting vengeance but in a voice more akin to a learned scholar. "Koralia, isn't it?"

She nodded.

"I was expecting someone a little more... volatile. You have caused me a great deal of trouble." Still his words were calm and precise, not the whirlwind of rage she envisioned. Was it intended to put her guard down?

CHAPTER SIXTY-ONE

At this point it seemed irrelevant; whatever she said made no difference to her fate, so why not take the opportunity to stand up to authority once more?

"It was more than trouble I wanted to cause you," she spat, chin held high.

Rather than annoying Takis, it seemed to please him to see a bit of fight left in her.

"Destroying my life's work, or rather death's work I suppose, would certainly fit as 'more than trouble'. Do you have any idea how many irreplaceable works of art and knowledge you destroyed?"

"What use were they if only *you* could read them? And how many irreplaceable people have you destroyed?"

"People?" he laughed. "People are *the most* replaceable of things. So few of them step outside the circle of mediocrity; most of you are just interchangeable nobodies doing the same as one another until you cease to be, only to be replaced by more of the same."

"You have no idea of the good people you've ruined," Koralia said boldly.

"Good people? You think there is such a thing? Good and evil are just things we call our preferences to assert our views. One person's 'good' is another's 'evil'. Things just *are*; moral aggrandizing is merely self-indulgence."

"What about the self-indulgence of a ghost protector turning a city into slaves just to further his pet library project?" Koralia was sure that Stefania could have come up with a more cutting way to skewer Takis on his own hypocrisy; nevertheless, she was pleased with herself.

"Self-indulgence? Preserving the very best of humanity is about as selfless as one can be."

"Selfless?! You're not the one paying the price; you make that burden fall on others."

"Only a timeless being can curate a timeless collection. No mortal has the means or the ways to accomplish such a task. And remember, I've seen countless people come and go, dying with nothing to show for it. If anything, I *am* giving them a greater purpose." Takis didn't speak like a riled-up dictator; he seemed to passionately and genuinely state his case.

"So art and knowledge is the greater purpose for you?"

He nodded.

"Why does it have to be done under pain of suffering?" she asked.

"Pain and suffering are just fleeting moments, like the lives of all humans. The truth is, nobody matters. Nobody is important. People are just like animals, no better, no worse. The only difference is that people can produce that which is timeless. The flesh and blood are irrelevant but what they leave behind can matter."

"How many potential artists and scholars have you condemned to a life in the fields? Robbing them of an opportunity to contribute to what you think 'matters'?"

Koralia had found it. The chink in Takis's armour of reason. His face showed as much; for the first time in a long time his world view had been challenged with some modicum of success – mainly because nobody had dared to for so long. What if she could actually get through to him? What if words could succeed where actions had failed? What if this was the real basis for change?

"True talent cannot be suppressed. The steel of brilliance is forged in the heat of adversity. Did your people not resort to painting murals and symbols in response to the very conditions you are complaining about? Only when things were perceived to be too bad did any of you pick up a brush. If anything, it supports my position precisely."

It was perverse reasoning that barely hid the outright hypocrisy. His learned language did nothing to temper the depravity of his views in Koralia's mind.

"And what of knowledge? How can anyone learn from and build upon anything when they are forced to work all day and are forbidden from seeing your collection?"

"Only I have the time to learn from all that has been written."

Koralia shook her head.

"All of this... justification. It's nonsense. It's all in service to yourself; claims about higher purpose and the preservation of knowledge are just

CHAPTER SIXTY-ONE

denial. Everybody in this city knows it and you must know it too; all you care about is your own power and excuses to wield it in the most disgusting of fashions."

"You have made the mistake of assuming that my power and this 'higher purpose' are mutually exclusive. I *am* that higher purpose; I am the only one who can become the sum of knowledge."

Koralia rolled her eyes. "So it's not denial, but delusion?"

"There is nothing deluded about the reality that I am the only one who can read this all. This isn't my desire as an immortal; it's my duty. Do you honestly think anyone will remember you in fifty years' time? What about a hundred years' time? Two hundred? Don't you see? None of this here and now matters."

Her own reflections about how ordinary people didn't matter were being reflected back at her through the darkest of prisms. She had been distressed at having to burn the books and had only done so out of what she considered a necessity, saving as many as she could to atone, and for the exact same sort of ideal Takis was now espousing. It was hard to argue with an immortal about the fleeting nature of human life, or anything else for that matter.

"What now? Your library is ash, its contents just as short-lived as any of us," she said.

"It's true, I was not able to salvage as many as I would have hoped. Now the memory of many of those tomes only lives within me. If anything, you've strengthened my resolve. For all that was lost, I am what remains."

That was it. There was no way of getting through to him. He'd spent centuries justifying his own actions to himself; for all the protestations about the 'greater good', Takis was what Koralia had always thought he was: a cruel dictator.

"As for 'what now'," he said, "you must face the consequences of your crimes. Although I must thank you for giving me an opportunity to talk candidly with someone. Only those who know they are about to die are *this* honest with me."

"Is that it, then? You're just going to kill me here like an animal?"

"Of course not. *I* won't be killing you at all. The people will. You are to be publicly executed at the hands of other mortals in a few days. It sends a much stronger message," he replied calmly.

"Then everything goes back to normal?"

"More or less, albeit with a lot fewer mouths to feed and the notion of rebellion thoroughly crushed," Takis said matter-of-factly.

"Until the slayer of ghosts gets here." Koralia's last hope was also the final way she could see to try and get one over on Takis. Of everything that had gone before, this was the thing to enrage him. He rushed at Koralia and placed his shimmering, ethereal face right in front of hers, then spoke with the venom that she had expected from the start.

"Nobody is coming to save you. Nobody is going to slay me. Whilst the other ghosts grew lazy, I honed myself into the sum of knowledge. Pushed the boundaries of what is possible. I'm not just immortal, I'm eternal. Nothing can slay me."

This was the one time the mask of arrogance slipped, and she knew the underlying reason for it, a reason she was overly familiar with herself: fear. He disappeared from the cell just as quickly as he had appeared earlier. If there was even a shred of doubt in Takis's mind, enough to instil fear within him, then there was hope. If he feared death that meant he knew he could be bested, and for now, that was enough. That was the only victory the leader of the rebellion could cling on to. Hope. Not just for the salvation of Maluani but for her own. There were only a few days until her execution; if the slayer of ghosts was indeed coming to kill Takis, Koralia needed it to be soon.

CHAPTER SIXTY-TWO

The shimmering hues of Shiara's enchanted blade shifted like a river of luminosity. Dazzling, but deadly. Kadar leapt backwards leaving a faint swirl of fine white mist trailing behind him. A coalescing of fog spread out from his palm until the form of a blade took shape, just in time to parry a darting strike from the rainbow sword. Fredo edged his way to the corner of the courtyard to avoid any personal danger, not wanting to sit with the others, even though he knew them. He had become part of Shiara's quest; despite sharing numerous drinks and banquets with the businessmen and councillors here he no longer felt a part of their world. A big question that played on his mind was "What happens if she loses?" There was no way this silver-tongue would be able to rub shoulders with the elite like he used to and who knew what Caspir was even like now. Fortunately, it didn't seem the most pressing of concerns as Shiara had Kadar on the back foot already.

Her cutlass darted at the ghost from numerous angles; he was surprised by her speed. Each time, he managed to deflect the blade, but the purpose of these attacks was not to wound – they were testing the water, breaking down how Kadar moved to expose any weaknesses or flaws in his abilities. Kadar realized what was happening; there was a need for him to go on the offensive as it would only be a matter of time before her prodding and probing were successful. He twisted and wound his arm back to create space for a swing; Shiara too changed her approach as soon as she noticed this. She had seen enough of his defence; it was time to observe his offence.

The ghost's arm struck in big sweeping arcs that split the air with a faint rumble. Each one came close to Shiara, but none of them landed. Her movement was fluid and swirling like a breath of wind. Elegant. Precise. Beautiful. Against Mara she had looked poised but had clearly adapted her style to combatting Mara's glaive; now she could enter fully into the dance of swords, pivoting and shifting through the air on nimble feet. In other circumstances this could have been a spectacle of artistic talent. To look at them, they appeared incredibly mismatched yet Shiara made Kadar's size and power seem immaterial.

There was no denying that Kadar had the greater range with his powerful arms and longer blade; nevertheless, the disparity appeared irrelevant as Shiara twirled through the air. Much like when she had fought Mara, Fredo noticed she had become less focused on attacking and more concerned with dodging and observing his movements. This made a lot of sense given that the ferocity of one swing from the ghost could cleave her in two. The ghosts could not tire, but Kadar was becoming noticeably frustrated. Like the other ghosts she had fought, he was now contemplating what had previously seemed impossible: defeat.

The onlookers had no idea how the situation was really playing out. They were men of business and politics; to them it looked as if Kadar was mounting one powerful attack after the next, only missing by the slightest of margins each time. Surely it would only be a matter of time before he landed one? They were wrong. With each failed blow, the ghost knew his victory was less likely.

Shiara had spent enough time examining her foe; it was time to strike. She noted that his footwork was far more rigid than it should be; he relied on his raw strength instead. Surely he must have fought differently as a human to become the ghost protector? Perhaps the centuries had made him lazy or his immortality had made him arrogant. Either way, the opening was there.

A jet of black smoke erupted from Kadar's thigh and cascaded upwards like steam, dissipating as it hit the roof. Shiara's blow was far from fatal but it hammered home the reality of the situation. This was not a duel or matching of wits in combat; this was a vivisection. A follow-up strike could

CHAPTER SIXTY-TWO

have easily been deadly; instead the slayer of ghosts issued another plume of smoke, this time from Kadar's upper left arm. His anger and frustration were fruitless. The onlookers could see it on the ghost protector's face: centuries of arrogance and superiority undone in moments. Another stream of black spewed from the back of his right knee, forcing him down onto the other knee. His swipes were no longer attacks; this was defensive flailing like a creature resigned to its fate but not yet willing to give up, as if some miraculous intervention could still save them. But there would be no intervention.

Shiara's blade coursed with light. Each nick and cut into Kadar fed its brightness. The blade dug into the ghost's sword arm from just above the elbow, then tore through to his fingertips. His weapon fell and dissolved into smoke as it hit the floor. His arm became like two estuaries of midnight-black water flowing into the atmosphere. His shoulders slouched. The resignation of defeat was there. There was neither will nor ability left to fight; the most powerful being in all of Omdurtur was rendered helpless.

"So... this is... it," remarked the ghost, sputtering ebony vapours as he spat out his words.

She nodded.

"It's been a long time coming," said Shiara.

The tip of her blade twisted into his open shoulder wound. Black smudges covered the weapon but were burned off by its brightness in moments.

"Do you even feel pain?" she asked.

His expression did the talking for him. A grimace answered, even though he tried his best to hide it.

"Just... finish it already," crackled his once commanding voice.

"You had all this power. The ability to shape things over centuries, and *this* is how you chose to use it?"

His weary neck craned up to look her in the eye, inky blackness billowing out from a neck wound as he did so. Fredo had never seen this side of Shiara before; the calculated necessity of battle had given way to something else: enjoyment. She was revelling in Kadar's anguish and even though the silver-tongue understood why, it was still troubling to see his friend this way.

"Maybe having all that power... was the problem," were Kadar's final, stuttering words.

The glowing edge of her blade split him in two from the belly up in a fountain of onyx. His words troubled her. Power wasn't the issue; it was evil and selfish men using it. In the right hands a government could shape society for the better. Power was no excuse for cruelty. Without the ghosts, everything would be better.

The thrumming pillar began to crumble as the vapours of Kadar dispersed. Once again, her blade grew brighter and began to hum. Then brighter still. And louder. And brighter again.

The sound grew deafening. The light blinding. The air itself crackled and fizzed.

This was not like before.

This was something different.

CHAPTER SIXTY-THREE

The council chamber had slowly been filling with members. However, its leader had been at the ready in his chair at the head of the table well before the doors swung open for the others. In Marin's mind this was the real test of his leadership and vision; up until now he had been putting out fires and trying to salvage things, lurching from one crisis to the next. Today though, he would have to paint not only a picture of what the future of Caspir looked like but also the path upon which they would tread to get there. Many of those needing to be convinced were already his most scornful critics; to describe the task as difficult would be a most colossal of understatements.

The chamber was just about full and it was time for him to call the meeting to order, though order was the last thing he was expecting. He ran through the usual introductions and formalities that he'd ideally like to get rid of, although that would be a pointless war against tradition just to save a few minutes of words. Edwin gave him a nod of reassurance as the formalities came to a close; a deep gulp of air later, he began.

"Esteemed council members, I have two significant issues I wish to table and deal with in this session. The first one is what to do with the growing numbers of citizens in the form of refugees. As I'm sure you are all aware, we need to get out in front of it and I have a solution. By knocking down a section of the outer wall, we can..."

The jeers and grumbling rose to a crescendo in an instant, cutting him off from even finishing the proposal. Banging on the table, he bellowed, "Let me finish!" which had the desired effect, albeit taking a few moments whilst councillors made sure their grumbles were added to the chorus.

"As I was saying, we can repurpose the materials from a section of the wall to expand the city outwards and construct new buildings to house those that need it, thus extending the limits of our great city. We already have the people and skills in place to make this happen and the stonemasons' guild has agreed to it. All that is required is the approval of the council."

Expecting a cacophony of bawled responses, Marin was shocked when greeted with silence instead. Whether or not this was a better or worse situation remained to be seen. The councillors were looking at each other, waiting for someone else to go first. To the surprise of nobody, Andros was the one to kick it off.

"Knock down our wall? A wall that has protected Caspir for centuries?" he said snidely.

"There hasn't been an attack in hundreds of years! What is it you want protecting from, a particularly strong gust of wind?" Edwin piped up, partly in defence of the idea but mainly for the opportunity to mock Andros. The laughter from other members confirmed his success.

"Go ahead, laugh all you want!" yelled Andros. "We may not have been attacked in hundreds of years, but you know what else we haven't been for hundreds of years? Without our ghost protector."

Again the room fell silent, cutting off the remaining sniggers in their tracks.

"And what's more," continued Andros, "every one of us has heard the stories of Illorne being controlled by gangs of bandits, or Fimego descending into chaos. Weakening our protective wall invites these troubles into our homes and no doubt even worse things, which we can't even imagine. Never before has a time seen such great upheaval; we should be reinforcing our defences, not dismantling them."

Chatter went around the table, most of it receptive to what they'd just heard. Marin needed to regain control of the situation and play Andros at his own game.

"What about those people who've come to Caspir to make a life for themselves? What would you have us do with them?" the council leader

CHAPTER SIXTY-THREE

asked.

"We need to look after ourselves, not waste resources on these other people," Andros replied predictably, sadly procuring some approving looks and nods of heads.

"So you would choose to make an enemy of these people? This wouldn't be improving our defences; this would be actively creating an enemy at our very doorstep! Not only this, but these people are not some useless drain on resources – they're carpenters, chefs, labourers, farmers, and everything else you can imagine."

Marin punctuated each key syllable with pointed gestures, deploying his whole body behind his words. Each phrase was a perfectly delivered masterpiece as if from a thespian of great renown. He continued.

"They don't want to come here to make things worse; they actively want to be a part of our great city and make it better. It's easy to sit inside your luxurious house and talk about our way of life, yet answer me this: What better specimen of humanity could you ask for than someone who fought for their family's lives and made a journey to leave behind everything in search of a better life? Who better to join our city?"

And now for the final framing of his argument to throw back Andros's own argument in his face.

"Lastly, who better to defend it? Remember, they aren't asking us to look after them; they just want us to let them be a part of Caspir and help make it more prosperous for us all."

The speech took hold of his audience; expressions of approval grew as the words and their meanings sunk deeper into their minds. Appealing to self-interest was the steely tip of his argument's spear, pushing through the noise and penetrating right to the heart of what mattered to these people. He could have spent all day expressing the finer points of diversity, humanitarianism and empathy and not got anywhere. As Edwin had so eloquently described the night before, people in power were all too often petty and individualistic. Showing how something benefited them personally would always triumph over any moral reasoning or overarching pragmatism. Marin looked at Andros, just waiting for another retort to come his way, but he had been silenced by the immaculately bearded man's trap. If he disagreed he would be directly supporting the creation of literal enemies at their gates, and agreeing was not something he was about to do as it went against his principles; he instead settled upon a dissatisfied sneer. There was still the point that knocking down a wall *would* make it slightly easier for people to get into the city, but the last time they had locked the gates was when Chase had tried to stop Shiara getting in and they all knew how that had worked out. Nevertheless, the notion of increased prosperity was enough to sway some people. No doubt they were envisioning a new workforce they could exploit, but Marin had plans to stop that from happening and make sure people were getting fair pay. However, there was no harm in letting them think that if it got them on board for now. Fighting all your battles at once was not a smart idea.

"Any questions, or can we move to a vote?" asked Marin.

A voice spoke up. It was one of the younger council members, Vastor, who represented a poorer district near the section of the wall in question. He had the ideal face of a bureaucrat, bland and forgettable. Disappointingly, his voice was more memorable, with its unflattering monotone and nasal nature.

"Precisely how much of the wall are you proposing we dismantle?"

"A hundred feet," replied Marin, knowing full well that half that amount would be sufficient.

"Hmmm" replied the nasal man, "That does seem like quite a lot. I will have to think about how this will impact the people of my district."

The council leader smiled; he was already prepared for such an objection.

"The sooner we get the work started the sooner we'll all be able to reap the rewards. How about to begin with, we dismantle a smaller stretch of the wall then revisit the topic later as and when required?"

"I believe that would be acceptable. Shall we say fifty feet?"

"Let's meet in the middle at seventy-five?" bargained Marin.

The councillor thought for a moment as if pondering the differences being discussed like some kind of engineering genius. The truth, as Marin knew it, was that this individual was just like any other busy body bureaucrat and merely wanted to be involved to claim some kind of influence to bolster his ego and reputation.

"Seventy-five it is," he finally concluded.

"Let's put it to a vote. All those in favour of allowing this seventy-five-foot section of the wall to be repurposed, raise your hands."

The vote was closer than he had hoped; when asking for those opposed there were not many, but a significant number of abstentions narrowed the margin. Because of the scale of the project, some didn't want to be associated with it one way or the other for fear of the later questioning of their judgment if things went well or poorly and they were caught on the wrong side.

A bang on the table signified it had been carried; the first of the hurdles had been crossed with far less friction than he had been expecting. He thought that the next item on the agenda could possibly go with similar ease.

He thought wrong.

At first the council were somewhat receptive. Coming off a high from his previous success, Marin attempted to keep them interested, but as soon as he mentioned that they could learn from Bemus, the goodwill evaporated.

"Learn from him? The man can barely string together a sentence let alone a system of law and order!" came the cry from a sickly-looking man named Tomys, and many others followed with responses in a similar vein. His biggest detractor, Andros, was yet to weigh in, so no doubt things would only get worse, yet as one mocking criticism of Bemus ran into the next, his adversary remained silent. Then it clicked. Of course! He wasn't going to disparage the man who got justice for the murder of one of the churchgoers. Alyssa *was* the one pulling his strings, so joining in with the narrative of Bemus's incompetence would diminish the justice that had been delivered as well as painting the Church's own attempts at justice in an even worse light. Marin saw this as an opportunity; he'd suspected a number of council members were secretly backed by Alyssa and this provided a sly moment to test that out. Sure enough, several councillors were conspicuously quiet as the others laid into his less than well-spoken friend. He made a mental note for later; if nothing else came of this debate he would at least have a better idea where potential political knives might come from in the future. Eventually he managed to get them to be quiet enough for him to defend himself.

"All right, here's something we can all agree upon: nobody wants to be the victim of crime. Right?" His audience obviously approved, albeit reluctantly.

"What better way of dissuading people from committing crimes than making it much more likely they'll get caught?" explained Marin.

"We could always just build a wall to keep the poor people away from us!" blurted out one of the nobles, who was every bit as unpleasant as his words suggested. Annoyingly it produced laughter and cheers from some of the others. "We could use the stone from the wall to do it instead of giving it to those refugees." The man's second comment created an even more hysterical reaction from the chamber. There was nothing quite like a bunch of privileged egotists making light of other people's misfortunes to erode one's faith in humanity. Marin reflected that at least it was better than when the entire council was composed of just himself and nobles; that being said, none of those sat around the table were anything other than well off.

"Very funny I'm sure, but let's remember the topic at hand. Without the sort of investigation Bemus and I conducted, Rhodes would never have been delivered justice. Surely some of you can agree with that?" The council leader was careful to let his gaze linger on those whom he now suspected were being supported by the Church, knowing they would be inclined to agree.

Andros sat up in his chair and sighed before making his first comment on the topic.

"Yes. I suppose that is true. However, what *precisely* are you suggesting?"

"As it currently stands, whenever there's a serious crime nobody looks into it beyond the obvious, leaving most of them unsolved. I propose a new contingent of guards designated with the specific task of investigating crimes to find perpetrators who would have otherwise evaded capture. By compiling procedural guidelines and offering training, I think we can bring more criminals to justice, which means less people committing crimes

CHAPTER SIXTY-THREE

against all of us." Marin tried not to let his passion colour his words too much and keep things objective, whilst appealing to their self-interest at the same time.

"And who will oversee this project?" asked Andros.

"Myself and Bemus," Marin replied.

"Bemus?! He should run a bath, not a project!" came the predictable joke from Tomys.

"Excuse me," interrupted Andros, using his sway as one of the wealthiest nobles, "but we are all aware of the good work Bemus and... Marin did." The praise stuck in his throat on its way out. "And we can all certainly agree that strong law and order is the backbone of a civilized society. My reservation on this matter is twofold. Firstly, if you are busy with such a project, will your duties as council leader not be neglected?"

Marin could instantly see what Andros was angling at – undermining his position as leader to make way for a new council leader that presumably would be him. He had probably already canvassed for support should the situation arise. Fortunately, Marin had come prepared with an answer to shut this avenue down.

"I'm glad you brought this up. I agree that such a project could result in my attention being split. As we know, Shiara as the *rightful ruler* of Caspir appointed me to be council leader and until she returns and says otherwise; that won't be changing. However, to cope with increased demands on my time I will be appointing a vice-leader to act on my behalf when required. Shiara placed her faith in me; now I place my faith in Edwin."

This was as much of a surprise to Edwin as it was to Andros. He didn't really want the role, but the grimace on Andros's face was enough to convince him.

"Thank you, council leader; you can depend on me," said Edwin.

The disgust emanating from Andros was almost tangible, yet he could not go against Marin's invoking of the Church for fear of alienating himself from Alyssa and her influence. It was certainly easier for others to agree with Edwin's appointment given his long-serving tenure on the council and his reputation for wisdom.

"Andros, you mentioned your objections were twofold?" the council leader reminded his adversary. It took Andros a few moments to compose himself after such a comprehensive defeat and reply.

"Yes. There is one significant issue you seem to have overlooked. Coin. Or rather, the lack of it."

Telling mumbles echoed around the walls. It was no secret that the financial capability of the council had been in trouble for some time and things had only been getting worse.

"Very true. There's no denying that trade has plummeted as other ghosts have been slain. Illorne and Fimego routes have dried up completely. No trade means no taxes," said Vastor in his usual irritating tone.

"Half of the guards we already have aren't turning up to work because we can't pay them, and you want to employ more?" added Tomys, with a rather aggressive jabbing motion of his index finger.

"And I remember not too long ago that our esteemed council leader argued for a reduction in guard patrols in the gilded quarter to save money. Now you're asking for more guards?" Andros chipped in.

It was true. Things had changed. He tried to explain this to the council with varying degrees of success, but the debate raged on. There *was* an issue with money; it *did* need to come from somewhere, and there *weren't* any easy answers they would like. People, especially those who were well off, would have to contribute a little more. This was the opposite of the appeal to self-interest he had won his previous victory with and it didn't look like being resolved anytime soon. He could get them to agree that things had changed and that other things needed to follow suit to keep Caspir running, but convincing someone of their privilege and responsibility was a difficult and thankless task. After a couple of hours of debate, if one could call it that, Marin found his mind wandering back to the day they heard the news about Hectin's death. How Fredo had burst into the council chamber and turned everything upside down. Yet somehow, after all that upheaval and disarray, after a centuries-old way of doing things had been torn apart, some things still remained exactly the same.

CHAPTER SIXTY-FOUR

The blade surged with energy in Shiara's hand; it was like holding it into the flow of a coursing river. The air itself blurred, colours bleeding into one another. The shaking of the weapon became too much for her and she let go, yet the weapon did not fall: it remained suspended in the air, held by the invisible strings of magic. She looked over to Fredo who was equally confused. He shrugged and said something that was inaudible over the whirring sounds filling the air. Kadar's guests, already stunned by witnessing their ghost protector slain, had now found a new level of astonished horror. The unknown was terrifying to them and that fear would turn out to be well placed. Like an eggshell, cracks spread along the sword that were just about visible in the dazzling show of light. Abruptly, the sound ceased. The pulsating light stopped cycling. The cracks widened until the blade shattered, not into shards of metal but into puffs of smoky dust – just like that of the thrumming pillar and the ghosts. It was at that moment that Shiara understood what was happening. So many things found new context in her memory. Fredo's realization was not far behind but the other onlookers were none the wiser. They were too busy screaming.

Tearing her eyes away from the light she began to see why. Hunks of flesh were being torn from their faces and ripped from their bodies through their clothes by unseen workings. The chunks hurtled towards the light and remained hovering in the air as further pieces followed, trailed by droplets of blood that floated in the air rather than dripping down.

A thunderous cracking could be heard over these sounds. This was not the sound of thunder; it was breaking bones. Slick wet bones pursued the slabs of meat. A parade of organs danced through the air in a grisly ballet of viscera. At this stage any fight had long left the men, most of whom were dead; only one clung onto the last vestiges of life for a few moments more. The ethereal culling had created a mass of human parts encircling the light. They undulated and spun round, slowly shaping and taking form: the form of a man. Transfixed by the abhorrent spectacle, Shiara was unsure if it had taken hours or minutes, but before her now stood a man of flesh, woven together before her eyes like an exquisite garment. Skin spontaneously broke out and grew over the open red flesh like flame being set to a trail of oil. Now there was no great light, no pulsing sound, just a naked man that showed no evidence of the macabre display that had birthed him. Shiara's breathing raced uncontrollably; Fredo had passed out at some point during the man's construction – or rather reconstruction, she thought. Steadying her nerves and lungs, she spoke to confirm what she suspected.

"Ezekiel?"

The figure nodded whilst stretching out his arms as if he had just risen from a night's sleep.

"How... is this possible?" she asked.

"I think you already know the answer to that," replied the familiar voice that had once been attached to her blade. It seemed slightly deeper and resonated more, which was hardly a surprise given it was now coming from a man rather than a lump of metal. He was right; Shiara knew what she had witnessed and why the Cara owls had attacked them before. The sword was just the same as the thrumming pillars of the ghosts, just a little more sophisticated. It now made sense why the sword had only begun talking when several of the magical "sinkholes" had been removed; it was trying to tap into that exact same power. She now understood it all, but seeing magic – *real* magic – was wholly different and it had felt like the reverence of asking "how" was the only natural response. She put that behind her now, for there were bigger questions still to pose.

"But... the prophecy? Takis of Maluani still stands. It's incomplete; yet here you are?"

CHAPTER SIXTY-FOUR

Ezekiel sniggered.

"Oh, that old thing? Don't worry about the prophecy. I just needed you to slay enough of the ghosts so I could access enough magic to rebuild myself. Apparently five was all that was required."

"That wasn't the prophecy; all of them needed to be slain," she replied.

The Great Wizard shook his head.

"The prophecy wasn't real. You didn't think you were *special*, did you? You're hardly the first to try and fulfil it; you were just the first one skilled and lucky enough to actually succeed. No fate or destiny about it, just the inevitability of numbers and time."

Her stomach churned. Her life and everything she believed in was a deception.

"So it was all a lie?"

"Was it? It *has* happened, hasn't it?" He laughed. "Look, I saw what the city leaders were doing with the ghost protectors and despite my best warnings they went ahead with it anyway. I wasn't going to live in a world with them sucking up most of the magic so I did the only sensible thing a great wizard could do. I wrote a prophecy then bound my immortal soul into a sword for future use."

"Sensible?!" cried Shiara.

"I thought so. The cities were changing for the worse and I could see it would take a long time for it to change for the better. Writing the prophecy was the easy part. If you turn people into immortal gods, of course they are going to ruin people's lives over time. And with the concentrations of power in the cities, plenty of people would be pissed off enough to want a way out. Scribbling down that someone poor and downtrodden would slay them was always going to be an easy sell. After all, the nobles who prosper from the system are the last ones to want change. It was only a matter of time before some impoverished person had had enough and found the blade to give it a go. A few dozen attempts later and here we are."

"And the promise of a better life for people – that was all just another lie to trick someone into doing what you wanted?" spat the slayer of ghosts.

"Oh no, on the contrary, that is entirely true. A world without these *ghost protectors* and the systems they inhabited will surely be better."

Her actions had weighed heavy on her since she had slain Mara and seen the consequences; Ezekiel's attitude did not offer the justification she desired.

"Tell that to the people of Fimego," she retorted.

"The people of Fimego have been oppressed for generations. We have given them a fresh start: a break from the past. Short-term carnage to destroy the old is a small price to pay for ending centuries of suffering and exploitation. I thought you of all people understood that."

No wonder the blade had defended the actions of the "mad ghost" Wasif; they were cut from the same cloth. All this time she thought she'd been working towards salvation, not destruction.

"Destroy? I never wanted to destroy things; I wanted to improve them. Ending the ghosts was supposed to give the people a chance to change things for the better," said Shiara.

"Change? Change?! You can't tweak a broken system and fix it. There is no *changing* that which can never work. It *all* has to be torn down. Let it all crumble to dust and then from that dust, something new can emerge." His words came across as almost poetic, like he was pontificating on an abstract thought experiment, but he was not. He was talking about people's lives, and their deaths.

"What about Caspir? They didn't descend into chaos like Fimego and *are* improving things."

"Are they? I'm sure people still go hungry. Making improvements to something awful doesn't save anyone; it just prolongs their suffering with false hope. Can you honestly say much has changed?" His words were condescending, or like a parent correcting a child.

"I believe that Marin cares about the people. He will make things better."

"Better just *isn't enough*. He may well care about others, but none of that matters. Structures of centralized power like councils and governments will *always* see people suffer," said Ezekiel.

"So just like Kadar said, you think power inevitably corrupts people?"

"It's not that power corrupts people; it's that when you create a platform

CHAPTER SIXTY-FOUR

for power, corrupt people are incentivized to obtain it. This isn't something new; this is just the way things are."

"So according to you, there's no point trying to help people?" spat Shiara.

"Not at all. The problem is that it's impossible for people to truly help each other in a world of sprawling cities and governments. Ask yourself: of all the places you've been to and all the people you've seen, which group had the best lives overall? Who were the happiest?"

Her mind instantly homed in on the answer. It wasn't anyone living within the walls of a city; it was those living in their own small communities far from the walls. The people who had helped Fredo after he'd been attacked by Cara owls were often in her thoughts. That simpler life with fewer complications and no ambitions for power had always appealed. She could see what Ezekiel was getting at, and that annoyed her.

"Life away from the walls is all well and good, but not everyone wants to live like that. Who are *we* to decide how people should live?"

"You're a fine one to talk! Did you not just slay Kadar because you didn't want *anyone* to live the way that some people in Omdurtur live?" Ezekiel said.

"That's... different." She was *sure* it was different; she just couldn't explain why.

"You know as well as I do that people in this city willingly sign up to be exploited. Putting their faith in electing councillors and striving to obtain a quality of life they can never have."

"They don't know they're being exploited! They are victims of the system..."

"Exactly!" pronounced Ezekiel triumphantly. "*You know better. You know they shouldn't live like that, even if they think they want to.*"

"We can't just force people to live a certain way," she protested.

"Can't we? Isn't that *precisely* what you've done to the people of the cities you've visited? Wasn't that the whole point?"

"Stopping people from living a certain way – in exploitation – is not the same as making them live in a specific way," argued Shiara, making a good point that Ezekiel didn't have an immediate reply for.

"Hmmm, what do you think happens if we don't? Take this city for example; if we just left now, what would become of Omdurtur?"

"I... I'm not sure," she replied.

"I am. There's a never-ending line of people just like Kadar waiting to take his place. Rich and influential men with a lust for power and control. Of all the cities, deep down you *know* that this is the worst."

"Worse than Maluani?" queried Shiara.

"Who do you think keeps Maluani propped up? Who's buying all the cheap produce and trading with them? Omdurtur calls itself a hub for trade and business; in reality it merely preys on exploitation, not just within its walls but across the other cities, especially Maluani. Takis couldn't rule like he does without the businessmen of this city."

Again, he was right, which was just as sickening as the revelation itself.

"So what are you proposing?" she asked reluctantly.

"The city has to be broken."

"Broken?"

"Yes. The stacks cannot continue to function, the walls must come down and the monuments to decadence must be levelled," proclaimed the Great Wizard, gesturing to the affluent buildings they could see from the rooftop.

All her life she'd dreamed of seeing the stacks fall silent, no longer filling the air with columns of black. But like this?

"And you can just do that?"

"Yes; with a click of my fingers I can raze this grotesque place and everything it stands for to the ground." Ezekiel discussed inconceivable destruction as if it were nothing. What untapped power could the Great Wizard wield and what else would he use it for?

"If your magic is so powerful, why must you break things? Surely you could fix things?"

"How can I fix greed or the lust for power? You don't get it. This way of life is *unfixable*."

"So you intend to just smash it all up and hope for the best?" said the disgruntled slayer of ghosts.

"*You've* already done quite a good job of that. If you really want to end the

CHAPTER SIXTY-FOUR

suffering, I could kill *everyone*; that would do it, but I doubt it's what either of us want."

Kill everyone? Was he joking? Was it even something he was capable of?

"If you hate people so much, why *don't* you just kill everyone?" she snapped.

"On the contrary, I don't hate people; people are wonderful, they have limitless ability to create art and beauty. *People* were never the problem. The issue is, and always will be, when *too many* people pool their resources and power and give bad people the opportunities they've been waiting for."

He was consistent, she had to give him that.

"So what will you do after you 'snap your fingers' here?"

"Once I leave Omdurtur I'll do the only thing I've ever wanted to do. Write my books, enjoy nature returning to the way it should be, and just generally live my life on my own terms away from these prisons of stone," he replied.

That was it? That was his big master plan? Meddle immeasurably in the lives of everyone then simply leave them to it?

"What about the other cities?" Shiara asked.

"You've already done enough to them. It's only a matter of time before they see the folly of their ways now."

"And Maluani?" Her voice was full of indignant concern.

"Well, Maluani... will serve as a powerful reminder of everything wrong with the ghost protectors."

"You're just going to leave those people to suffer?" she shouted.

"With the fall of Omdurtur things will change for them. Anyway, if you're so concerned, why not go and fulfil the prophecy by yourself?" Ezekiel said mockingly.

The thought had crossed her mind, but without the magic sword she'd relied on would it even be possible? Especially given the stories of Takis's might being beyond fearsome, even by ghost protector standards. Maybe she should at least try? Did she owe it to them? There was too much to dwell on right now to get fixated on what she should or shouldn't do in the future.

This "Great Wizard Ezekiel" had exposed everything she had fought for and believed in to be a lie. She had thought she was the vessel of positive change, yet she had unwittingly been the instrument of destruction. She kicked herself; should she have known? There had always been doubts, especially after Fimego. Should she have stopped? It all meant nothing now. A man with more power than all of the ghost protectors put together had decided and there was nothing she could do to stop him. Perhaps, deep down, Shiara thought that Ezekiel was right. It was clear that she had no time for leadership or power; she couldn't get away from Marin and the council of Caspir fast enough. Maybe that sort of power and influence *wasn't* something any person should be able to wield? Was tearing it all down the correct thing to do? She didn't know. Nevertheless, there was one thing she *was* certain of; for all she had done, she was now much less sure of everything than when she set out.

Ezekiel walked over to the edge of the rooftop and looked out. His dark, bald head glinted in the few shafts of sunlight that pierced the smog overhead. Raising up his left hand placing his fingers ready to click, he took one last look at the scene before him.

"How many?" interrupted Shiara.

"Sorry?"

"How many people are going to die when you level half the city?" she demanded.

"Honestly Shiara, I have no idea."

SNAP!

CHAPTER SIXTY-FIVE

The emptiness in Koralia's belly had become a constant over the last few days; the indescribable slurry she received twice daily in her bowl was not enough to sustain her. The aim was to keep her alive long enough so she could walk to her own execution. Takis wanted people to see the proud leader of the rebellion put to death, not some sickly or beaten husk of who they formerly were, and today was the day.

It hadn't been difficult for her to mentally prepare. She'd expected to die somewhere along the way and was ready; the waiting was the surprisingly difficult part. Given all that time alone with one's thoughts, knowing what was going to happen, did not make for an enjoyable experience. Koralia suspected that if she had been given more to eat, she might well have thrown it up from anxiety. Hopefully her body would catch up to her brain and settle down, but she doubted it.

The stench of the cell was no longer noticeable to her; some of her own waste mingled with the older filth to make it more familiar and somehow bearable. Those she would be leaving behind weighed heavily on her mind. She had no way of telling if her ploy to take suspicion away from Minos had worked or which of her comrades had survived the failed uprising, if any. Neither Takis nor the wardens had made any effort to get information from her about her co-conspirators, which did not bode well. Koralia hoped that was purely down to Takis viewing them all as inconsequential rather than having already found them. The one bit of good news she could pull from the wreckage of her movement was that nobody had asked her about the books she had stolen from the library, which could only mean one thing: Takis didn't know they had them and thought they had burned. It was a bit of a long shot, but one of those pages might provide an end to this tyranny. Not for herself, of course – it was far too late for that – yet one day down the road it could yield something for the others. Even if there *was* something useful, who could say how long it would take for them to be able to use it and, in the meantime, what would become of the people of Maluani? This was far less of a mystery, in Koralia's opinion. For hundreds of years the people of Maluani had accepted their fate and servitude; they would fall back into that pattern – it was inevitable. People wanted change, just without making the sacrifices required. Takis could not do without them all and she was positive that most of the people knew this too; the issue was that nobody wanted to be the ones killed to prove such a point. Self-preservation was a stronger force than the greater good. A life of hard labour was still a life.

It was easier for her to blame the unwillingness of others to sacrifice for change than it was for her to deal with the realization of her own faults. Her plan all along was a bit of a gamble at best. She had freely admitted that smashing the thrumming pillar was a stab in the dark; nevertheless, she had sold the idea as if it was a real solution, betting with other people's lives. Only once it had failed did she pivot to thinking about how Takis needed a certain amount of people to keep the city running, again speculating on how to spend other people's lives for her own cause. Koralia had fallen into the same trap of every revolutionary: thinking that everyone should be invested in the cause just as much as they themselves are. Obviously people want freedom from tyranny, but not everyone experiences that oppression in the same way and they certainly aren't all willing to pay the same price to try to fight it. For Koralia no price was too great to pay – not just for freedom but even for a likely-to-fail attempt at winning said freedom. Being on the side of the greater good is often enough for revolutionaries, even if they are destined to fail and make things worse. In some untouched corner of her brain this introspection had been tucked away to never again see the light of day. At a certain point along the way, full commitment had taken root. She no longer saw herself as an individual; she was solely one

CHAPTER SIXTY-FIVE

with the cause, rendering reflection and criticism obsolete. Now with it all having fallen down around her, what was she left with? Herself. No longer as the spearhead of a cause, but just an ordinary person who had failed. Her arrogance dressed up as righteousness and determination had real consequences for people. Consequences she would not have to live with for long.

The key turned in the lock. The sound of metal on metal snapped Koralia out of her thoughts. Two large men clad in black entered the cell and lifted her to her feet. A third man lingered just outside with a blade drawn, waiting for an excuse to run her through. She would not give him the satisfaction. She needed to face the people she had let down and show them that she was always willing to pay the price that many of their loved ones had. Then there was that other reason. That tantalizing thread of hope. The slayer of ghosts was still out there, and what if...

She was pulled roughly through the door and down the corridor, her feet barely touching the floor and occasionally scraping along the hard uneven stone in the torchlit passageway. Light crept around the door at the far end, along with a rumble of voices. The third man led the way into daylight; her eyes took a moment to adjust, as did her ears. A cacophony of noise buzzed as people lined the streets, cursing and shouting at her. This was what she expected: she knew it would be far easier for them to blame her for the tragedy than themselves or even Takis. This way of thinking let her consider herself a martyr rather than acknowledging the part her own hubris had played in the misery. Several onlookers tried to spit at her; fierce glares from the guards dragging her along soon put paid to that. As she was marched down the thoroughfare, it seemed to her as if most of the city had turned out, regardless of whether they wanted to or not. Takis was keen to make sure everybody saw what happened to those who defied the status quo; by focusing on her and not trying to seek out other rebels it made it easier to reframe the narrative of "us" and "them", where Koralia was the outcast set against all the people, who were now one. It was simple; the most effective things usually were.

The crowd swelled as they approached the largest square in the city; in its centre a platform had been erected from wood and steel. Atop the platform sat a wooden block with the distinctive curve on which to place someone's neck, and with stocks built into it to keep one's arms and therefore body in place. Beside the block stood a selection of people, mostly guards, but there were a couple of citizens in plain clothing. Takis, however, was sitting on a rooftop terrace overlooking the square. The script and visuals for this execution had been carefully constructed; for his purposes it was essential that this was seen as an act of citizens punishing a traitor rather than him exerting his own will. Koralia wondered how much it really mattered given his insurmountable power, but the victory over minds was a far more potent one.

Then she saw it. Towards the back of the platform stood her executioner. With a large axe in hand and ceremonial black cloak, that wasn't what shocked Koralia – it was his face, a face she knew: Harun. The man who had led her to the library and helped kick off the whole insurrection was to be her killer. One of the assets she had hoped would be a part of future uprisings was now to be the one ending her and the cause. She speculated that perhaps Takis knew he had helped her, and this was his punishment. Even though it would have been bad form to kill one of the wardens at a time like this, she was sure he would have torn through Harun in a second if he had discovered he was responsible for his beloved library being set ablaze. The truth, she told herself, was far more mundane and disheartening: that inevitable instinct for self-preservation. Harun had escaped the violence on the streets and was no doubt paranoid that someone might notice. Volunteering to execute the head of the rebellion would no doubt seal his loyalty. In reality, he had just been the unlucky winner of the lottery among wardens to see who would get the "honour". At this stage, Koralia was observing wheels within wheels that weren't there; her brain was racing to pull theories and narratives from thin air as if trying to get in as much use as possible whilst it was still attached to the rest of her body.

They lugged her up the steps and positioned her upright at the front of the platform for all to see. She dared not look back towards Harun, to spare him from any perceived connection to her. The throng of people before her

CHAPTER SIXTY-FIVE

stretched beyond the limits of the square – most of them angry, all of them unhappy, the stones beneath their feet still stained with the crimson of their fallen comrades. Her eyes scanned the mob trying to find those she knew, hoping they had been spared. "Surely Minos's big nose can't be that hard to spot," she told herself, desperately clinging to a running joke as a way of distancing herself from what must happen. In the end, it wasn't his nose that she spotted but the large purple and blue bruise that adorned his face. She must have hit him harder than she thought. Next to him stood Neela, and both them looked up at her with sombre expressions. There was nobody else. None of those she had first plotted with all those nights ago stood beside them. Rumours that some people had escaped the city were of no comfort; given her friends had needed to lead from the front, she suspected the worst.

One of those in plain clothes on the stage waved to the people for silence as he began to read out the proclamation of her crimes and execution.

"Her crimes were not just against the city and our protector Takis; they were against each and every one of us. Streets ran red with blood from all of us, due to *her* actions. She was not a person but a plague on us all, infecting those around her with dangerous ideas. Those who were misled by her treasonous words are victims just as much as those we have burned in recent days. No more shall her insidious lies be spread; like with any blighted flesh it must be cut out for the good of the body, for the good of us all."

People cheered every sentence. The uprising had shown already that they could be worked up into a frenzy of bloodlust; all that rage now focused solely on her in the form of sadistic glee. A forceful kick knocked her to her knees. Firm hands locked her in the stocks, head positioned on the block. Craning her eyes up as much as possible, she continued to survey the masses for any sign of hope, for that miracle she had once refused to wait around for but now craved with all her being. Footsteps on the wooden boards beside her drew hushed breaths from those assembled. Harun was next to her; in moments the axe would be in the air. Still her eyes flitted from face to face in desperation; then she paused. Her eyes came to rest on an unfamiliar woman in tattered clothes whose expression differed from the rest. Was this her salvation? Had the slayer of ghosts finally arrived? Was believing in that miracle actually rational?

No.

The axe fell.

THE END

EPILOGUE

CRUNCH!

The hard carapace of yet another beetle found its way between the lizard's teeth as it continued its relentless foraging among the foliage, staring intently between the leaves to size up its next meal before being distracted by the sounds of larger insects going about their business in the undergrowth. The sandback had uncovered quite the feast in the form of four beetles, each about the size of a fist, with intricate horn-like structures protruding from the front of their heads. Their exoskeletons were black yet shimmered with hues from across the spectrum as the light caught them. The purest of blue stripes rimmed their wing cases and a distinctive red splotch sat on the back of their heads. An unassailable armoured champion of the undergrowth. None of that mattered to the hungry reptile.

CRUNCH!

Nearby a glasshouse glittered in the midday sun. Within it, the sounds of someone toiling away could be heard: the clattering of tools and pots. A woman wrapped in dull brown clothes was scooping soil into a pot, placing it carefully around the delicate roots of a plant nestled within. She delicately drizzled water from a jug onto the base of the plant in its new home, being careful not to damage the fragile stem. All the while she was continuously referencing back and forth between what she was doing and a chunky handwritten book. The tome bore little smears of all shades of green and brown, not only on its hardback exterior but in the corners of the pages, pages which were no stranger to the ravages of time and had clearly been thumbed through countless times. She continued to pot up seedlings before moving onto sowing ungerminated seeds. Opening a chunky wooden box filled with compartments, each containing different seeds, she carefully plucked one out and placed it next to a drawing in the book for comparison. Presumably unhappy with the choice, she selected another and again placed it side-by-side with the picture. Confident she had chosen the correct one this time, her finger slowly pressed it into a small pot of soil she had prepared earlier. Unsure of how far beneath the surface to bury it, the index finger and thumb of her other hand tried to measure the depth against the side of the pot. A wrinkle of frustration and some obvious mild irritation resulting from doing something that she was unfamiliar with mired her face. Eventually she either got it just right or couldn't be bothered to adjust it any further – a sprinkling of water and a bit more soil and she was done. Looking at the rest of the pots lined up on the workbench, she sighed.

A short while later she left the warmth of the glasshouse and began walking the streets of the overgrown and abandoned city, her sandback following behind with the odd detour to chomp on a mouthful of bugs. Stone had been reclaimed by vines and trunks; among these walked the brown-clad woman, the wind whistling through the empty streets that still hinted at the metropolis of the past. Her raised hand brushed through the leaves as she passed and the rustling caught the attention of her scaled companion, distracting it from its open-air buffet, but not for long.

The sides of buildings that weren't obscured by plants were adorned with fantastic murals and powerful images. She stopped at one in particular and stood there staring up at it. It was an unfinished piece, the top edges swirled with blues, whites and bronzes depicting a fantastical skyline. Grey clouds edged with violet stood out from the blue in a foreboding fashion, as if emotions like frustration and angst had been given visual form. Beneath this, the distinctive image of a city skyline was portrayed: a thick wall with rigid rectangles emerging above it, all painted in black silhouette. In the foreground the structures had more colour – pale yellows, browns and greys were dappled to add texture to the surfaces of the stones. The foreground,

EPILOGUE

however, was incomplete. A number of people had been started off, their basic forms outlined, yet different elements of each of them remained unfinished – legs, arms, and most disturbingly, faces. The featureless flesh-coloured ovals had a haunting appearance that the woman could not avert her eyes from. Surrounding these human forms, the streets beneath their feet and the buildings themselves melted away into the unpainted stone of the wall. She cocked her head at different angles to try and make sense of the artwork and what it meant or represented. The clouds were clearly casting the cityscape into darkness, and even without faces the body language of the people seemed troubled and fearful of what was above. Having finished with her examination, she set off down the street with purpose.

After some considerable time, she returned with a wooden box spattered with flecks of paint in one hand and yet another book in the other. Setting down the box and flipping it open, a whole host of jars filled with different colours were wedged in alongside brushes of various sizes and qualities. Standing before the half-painted wall she opened the book, flicking from page to page in search of something specific. Holding up the book in front of the mural, she glanced between them, the corners of her mouth turning down with apprehension. The sandback still hovered around her, sniffing at the paints and glancing up at the woman in bewilderment. Despite the creature's tiny brain, it looked as if it were making a detailed assessment of the whole situation. Whatever was really going on in its mind, it seemed none the wiser.

"What do you reckon?" asked the woman of the lizard.

This only added to the reptile's confusion. Pointing between the wall, the wooden box and herself, the woman tried to explain, without any iota of success. One thing was clear about her: she had not been around other people for quite some time. Eventually she gave up with a deflated huff.

"Well, you're no help, are you?" The sandback may not have understood the word, but withdrew its head disappointedly as if it could decipher something from the tone. The woman picked up a paintbrush, cautiously contemplating her next move before thinking better of it and returning it to the box.

"Not today, Scaley. Not today."

Printed in Great Britain
by Amazon